Praise for *T*

"Gripping account of three conflicting personalities on an epic life-and-beyond journey. Accurately researched, beautifully written."
    —**DONN TAYLOR**, author of *Lightning on a Quiet Night* and *Rhapsody in Red*

"Three people from totally different walks of life—a crook, a widow with faith, a child with a deadly disease—unexpectedly join forces on a wild cross-country trip on old Route 66. A trip that changes the lives of all of them, and a story that will surely affect the life of anyone who reads it."
    —**LORENA MCCOURTNEY**, author of the Ivy Malone and Andi McConnell mysteries

"*The Road to Terminus* is a fast-paced, breath-robbing, cross country trek with the most unlikely trio racing toward an unexpected and multi-faceted conclusion. Catherine has created three unforgettable characters and a story to match. Well done!"
    —**SHARON K. SOUZA**, author of *The Color of Sorrow Isn't Blue* and *Lying on Sunday*

The Road to Terminus

THE ROAD TO
TERMINUS

Catherine Leggitt

To Ocaletta —
Many blessings on your
road to eternity. May you find
rest and joy in God.
Catherine Leggitt

Mountainview Books, LLC

To Deborah,
my sweet, funny child, with love and great admiration.
In grace and dignity you traverse paths I never imagined for you.
Your wisdom amazes; your strength inspires.

Acknowledgments

I've traveled a long road to publication of this book. The greatest blessing is that I didn't journey alone. Other pilgrims joined my odyssey—some for the duration, others coming and going for specific purposes. Once again, God supplied everything and everyone I needed.

First my dear husband, Bob—without his generous gift of time I would never write. I've lost count of how many times he did the laundry and got his own breakfast and lunch while I wrote this book. In addition, reading and commenting as I limped along, he caught a good many errors. I had forgotten about the little wing windows on cars of that era and those funny little bumper jacks we used to change tires. Thankfully, Bob remembered. What fun to bounce ideas off his creative brain.

My children—awesome human beings, all—supported and encouraged my writing in ways I truly appreciate. Thanks and much love to Jule Wright, Deborah Anderson, and Jason Leggitt, who are each on difficult journeys of their own. I admire their tenacity and applaud their wise choices. How often I thank God for preserving their marriages and providing for their families. In addition to being my biggest fan, Jule supplied Stryker's legal name—Grace, God's unmerited favor—the perfect name for the child.

Thanks to my best cheerleaders, Pill and Gene Rogers, Mom and Pop, for keeping the encouragement coming once again. Since I so often second guess my ability to write, this is one of the best gifts I could receive. Thanks to my beautiful sisters, Florenza Krnich, Toni Deaville, and Patty Little and my awesome brothers, Bobby Walker, Danny Walker, and David Jaggers for blessing my life in ways too numerous to mention.

Early on (in the planning phase back in 2012) I asked Facebook friends for ideas about character names. Thanks to Billie Ford for coming up with the name Stryker. I loved it the first time I said it out loud. Deborah Walton suggested Lily. That also stuck with me. Hence Stryker's legal name, Lily Grace. Also thanks to Tanya Roberts, Ginger Dunn, Renee Brumburgh, Rita Coleman, Beth Reno, Jeris Hamm, Pam Dion, Marcia Lahti, and Dina Schlie Preuss for great contributions.

Sherri Horn Myers suggested the name Kendrick, which I used for George's middle name—George Kendrick Stanton. Also thanks to Nancee Marchinowski for the name Vincent, which became George's cover name. Jule Wright, Pam Dion, Tanya Roberts, Nancy Anderson, Gary Wright, and Kathleen Wright had other wonderful ideas for George. Many thanks.

Mike and Ginger Dunn suggested a hot car for George to drive, but when my clever former student Joseph Hisquierdo suggested a black 1955 Lincoln Continental, I knew he nailed it. Absolutely the perfect car for George Stanton. Thanks, Joseph.

Special thanks to the incredible women of the Stockton Bible Study Fellowship class. Years ago, I asked God for Christian girlfriends, and He continues to answer that prayer with such bounty. Your prayers and encouragement are greatly appreciated. Thanks for your sustained interest in my work. Especially, I thank our fearless leader, Pam Regan. God blessed me greatly when he introduced me to you.

Back in my early BSF days, I was part of Janet Arnold's leaders group in Vista, CA. Each year she told us to write down prayer requests. I always asked for creativity. Thank you, Janet, for praying, and thank you, God, for supplying. Often when I write, I am aware God is giving me the words. Oh Creator, whose imagination knows no limit, thank you for continuing to share a little creativity with me.

This book would not be half the book it is but for the incredible contributions of my ACFW online critique group, Scribes 212. Many thanks to Valerie Massey Goree, Marcia Lahti, Loretta Boyett, Marcy Dyer, and Linda Machett for patching up the holes and pulling out the fluff. I love you ladies. You're the best.

Thanks to my cousin, Dr. Darrell Woodruff, for consulting about Stryker's diagnosis. Although your specialty included neither pediatrics nor oncology, I hope you approve of my literary license in the use of your name as the pediatric oncologist in the story. Thanks also to Dr. D.P. Lyle for suggestions regarding the proper diagnosis of the symptoms I described.

To my editors and publishers at Mountainview Books, there would be no book without you. Your contribution was more than vital. It was encouraging and enlightening. Thank you seems not enough to say. But I'll say it anyway. Thank you, C. J. Darlington, for this awesome opportunity.

So now we come to the end of the road, Terminus. What a long and arduous journey. I could never have completed this odyssey of discovery without my Lord and Savior, Jesus Christ. Most thanks to you, oh awesome Living Word. May You alone receive honor and glory from my feeble attempts to praise your holy name in story.

Catherine Leggitt
Lodi, CA
2015

ter-min-us:
noun, a final point in space or time; the end of the road

"The wolf also shall dwell with the lamb, and the leopard
shall lie down with the kid; and the calf and the young lion
and the fatling together; and a little child shall lead them."
Isaiah 11:6

1

MABEL
St. Louis, 1955

Seated on the aisle seat of the padded family pew, Mabel Elizabeth Crowley roused herself from drowsiness. With a quick sideways glance, she checked to see if anyone had noticed, but everyone seated near her still stared ahead. She heaved a ponderous sigh, shrugging off the burdensome futility which had become her constant companion. Then she forced her attention back to the pulpit, shifting position and refolding her gloved hands. What was Reverend Harry Stapleton speaking about this morning?

The heavily-carved red oak doors of Trinity Church groaned open a few inches. The creaking echoed off the thick, stone walls. Mabel turned to appraise the irreverent disturbance.

Through the gaping door, a trail of sunlight expanded down the polished marble tile like a pathway to a secret playground. A zigzag line of misfit children paraded in as if dancing to inaudible music. Some chased dust motes filtered through historic stained-glass panels along the sides of the sanctuary. The pack dispersed around the room, whispering and twittering like garden finches.

Giggles ricocheted through the hallowed space. Mabel pursed her lips. How dare these noisy children intrude on Sunday morning worship.

Her gaze darted to the front platform. The commotion had interrupted a scholarly point. The Reverend's sentence hung incomplete in the sacred air. Sparks from his flinty gaze scattered over the congregation. His brow furrowed. If Mabel set his expression to words he might be saying, "Unruly children are an abomination."

Several people stood, monitoring the unwanted guests. A murmur swelled through the pews. Ladies' gloved hands fluttered to well-clothed chests or to gaping lips. All around her, words scattered like bats exposed by a searchlight.

"Filthy rascals!"

"Who are those urchins?"

No ordinary children had invaded Trinity Church. The *St. Louis Post Dispatch* had reported about such a gang of orphans. The bane of city councilmen and the mayor alike, these ragamuffins haunted the streets of the city. Ordinances could not control them. Rumored to be more animal than human, they'd been known to swoop down on small grocery stores or restaurants to forage for food in trash bins. Wild packs slept in parks and alleys, violating neighborhood boundaries or huddled in abandoned buildings during storms. Every winter one or two unfortunates died of exposure.

Dressed in dirt-crusted clothing, some barefooted, some with mismatched boots minus socks, the vagabond troupe continued largely unmolested down the center aisle. The team of ushers bustled to life, scurrying after the larger waifs, tugging them by collars or forearms and in some cases lugging smaller children like potato sacks back down the aisle the way they had come.

A boy no bigger than a twig dragged a filthy stuffed animal down the aisle where he stopped to gape at Mabel. She stared back, cocking her head. A film of pain overlaid his pale blue eyes. Without a smile, she wiggled her fingers at him in a dismissive gesture.

He didn't move.

"Go on," Mabel whispered. "You don't belong here."

From the pew in front of Mabel, Esther Calkins turned to glare.

But the child continued his stare, drawing his filthy stuffed toy to his chest. Such wistful regard pierced her heart, awakening long dormant motherly concern. Memory of her long dead son tortured Mabel with such sorrow she could hardly bear it. Would the wound never heal? A decent mourning period ended long ago. No one spoke his name anymore. Not even Mabel.

She must help this child. How she hoped someone would have rescued Richard in a similar circumstance. Pushing to a tortured stand, she grabbed her overcoat and pocketbook. Gathering the boy with an arm around one shoulder, she hobbled him and his toy toward the thick arched doors. Heedless of neighbors and friends who whispered and pointed, she tottered down the aisle.

With one hand she straightened her Sunday hat, pushing it back until the rim hit her tight gray chignon. An old woman could be forgiven for assisting a needy child. It was her Christian duty.

Once outside, Mabel steered the boy across the formal landing. Most of the gang had fled by then, but a few stragglers tripped down the stone steps, dodging cars across Bellevue Avenue. Children's voices lingered in the air before spiraling upward with the wind like whispered petitions.

The sanctuary doors closed behind them with a heavy, somber clap.

Mabel pointed the boy's face toward the street and gave his back a gentle shove. "Go now. Catch up with your friends."

Instead of running after the others, he turned to blink up into her face. "Thank you, miss."

His reedy voice was pitched higher than she would have supposed, even wheezed out of so thin a boy.

She bent toward him. "What are you thanking me for?"

He produced a wan smile that melted a chunk of her frozen heart. In that instant, she wanted this child to stay. Ridiculous. Whatever would an old woman do with a runaway boy? "What's your name, child?"

He lowered his eyes. "Stryker."

Mabel lifted his chin with one hand. "An odd name. How old are you, Stryker?"

He blinked. "Fifteen."

Mabel pinched her lips together, holding back a chuckle. "You sure? You don't look a day over eight." She nodded at the motley animal. "Most fifteen-year-olds don't play with toys."

His blue eyes snapped. "I'm twelve. Well, nearly twelve. That's the truth. As for the monkey, I don't play with it, but I promised to keep it with me always."

Mabel allowed a chuckle to surface with her words. "Much better. Tell me, Stryker my friend, what are you doing with those rough kids?"

Stryker's gaze raked across the street where the children had disappeared. Brow furrowed, he tugged his arm free, tossed the stuffed animal over one shoulder, and started for the stairs.

A couple of long strides had Mabel panting, but she managed to catch the boy. "Hold on there." She couldn't allow him to live on the streets. Not for another minute. "Where do you think you're going?"

The boy squirmed in her grip. "They're my family."

"Your family?" Mabel straightened, heart still pounding from the exertion of catching up to him, one hand clamped firmly to the child's shoulder. "They're hooligans, that's what they are. Disrupting a holy church service is disgraceful. No respect for the sanctity of worship. Where's your mother?"

The scrawny shoulder under her hand lifted in a weary shrug.

Mabel appraised him over the top of her glasses. "See here. I'm trying to help you. That's no way to answer. When asked a question, you are to speak. Don't be disrespectful." Her fingers gave the boy a slight shake. "Let's try again. Where is your mother?" Such a reprehensible woman must be found at once and held accountable for her cruel abandonment of this frail child.

Stryker lifted stormy eyes. Tears collected on puffy lower lids. A drop broke loose to carve a wavy line through the dirt on his cheek. His lips quivered while Mabel waited, stifling a desire to tap her foot.

"Don't know."

"What do you mean you don't know?"

"She . . ." He swallowed hard. "She gone."

"Gone where?"

Another shrug. He averted his eyes. "Don't know."

Mabel bent to stare into his face. "When did you see her last?"

"She ain't coming back."

Her hearing worsened with each passing year. Surely she misheard. He didn't mean to say he'd been intentionally abandoned, did he? This beautiful, fragile child? The words of Isaiah came to mind: *Can a woman forget her sucking child, that she should not have compassion on the son of her womb?* What sort of woman left this child to fend for himself on the street with nothing but a stuffed monkey? Mabel pursed her lips, fighting the urge to shake her fist at God. What kind of sovereign being took away her own wonderful son and gave such a despicable woman a child she refused to care for?

A sudden torrent of tears flowed from the boy's eyes, and he didn't bother wiping them away. He made no sound but lowered his chin and let fat droplets fall to the ground like a sudden Midwest thunderstorm.

"There, there." Mabel patted, wishing she'd been blessed with the gift of compassion. "Crying won't help, will it?"

He swiped his nose with his dirty shirtsleeve, then shook his head so hard he knocked off his gray tweed beret. The boy's small head, shiny and smooth, possessed not a single follicle of hair.

"Merciful heaven. What happened to your hair?"

Downcast eyes. No answer.

She emphasized each word, hoping to add a tone of authority. "I said. What happened. To your. Hair?"

Words breathed out on a hiccup. "Mostly fell out. Before Mama left."

The bleak possibilities compounded. What decent woman would abandon a sick child? "Hair doesn't fall out for no reason."

"Mama said it was the curse."

That she surely didn't hear correctly. "The what?"

"The curse," he whispered, letting the "s" slink away on the wind like a hissing snake.

Should she laugh or run? "Don't speak foolishness, child. There's no such thing as a curse."

Stryker's eyes widened. His dark pupils expanded outward until the colored part filled with black. The stare he fixed on Mabel sent a shock wave down her spine.

Maybe curses *did* exist.

Mabel tilted his chin upward to study his pitiful face. Strange blue-green lumps spread across his hollow cheeks imparting a disturbed quality to the face, like a demented old geezer trapped in the body of a child. What torments had this child survived in his short years? Clearly he had not led the life a boy his age should. Not the life she'd been careful to provide for Richard. And so thin too. Must not be eating properly. A curious pallor plagued his face, a contrast with the tiny red spots that speckled his skin. Mabel tsked. Starving *and* in need of medical treatment.

Beneath the obvious physical problems, she sensed excruciating loneliness, hopelessness, and deep despair. Unlike any child she'd encountered in the years since Richard's death, his plight reopened the wound in her heart. New tenderness struggled to root where love had died when her only son had been killed on the beach in Normandy. A sense of duty followed closely behind, birthing emotional fortitude deep within her bosom. Somehow she must help this child, whatever the cost.

She slipped her hand down to his elbow. "What you need is a safe place to get your strength back. May I introduce myself? I am Mabel Crowley. My husband and son are gone to Heaven and these days I live all alone. Come home with me tonight—you and your monkey friend. I have plenty of room. You'll feel better after we get you cleaned up and fed."

Without waiting for an answer, she squeezed his arm and led the child down the steps toward the parking lot around the side of the stately brick church. "And tomorrow . . . well, tomorrow we'll figure out how to help you. Don't worry. I would never let a nice boy like you—"

Until then, Stryker had yielded to the pressure on his arm. At her words, he wrenched free, skidding as he dug in his feet. "I'm *not* a boy!"

Stepping back, Mabel considered the child from his torn overalls and sloppy men's shirt clear down to his nearly black-with-dirt feet. She crossed her arms across her bosom. "What do you mean, not a boy? What are you then, a man?"

"No!" Stryker fairly shouted. "I'm a girl!"

2

GEORGE
Chicago, 1955

George Stanton sniffed the night air and smiled. The cease-less Uptown wind mixed layers of pollution into a near-stupefying odor. Such a stench would serve him well. Brain numbing, that's what it was—mental anesthetic. Too much thinking might send him running back to the train.

Not that he was afraid. The pursuit of drugs stimulated his warrior instinct, intensified his determination to triumph. Shoulders back, he braced for the coming transaction. He would be victorious. Fine practice for success in business.

He shivered as he stepped off the L platform gripping his black fedora. With one hand he pressed the hat on his head. With the other, he clutched his second-best overcoat tightly around his chest. Horns honking amid the roar of passing traffic contended for his attention, but he ignored them and tensed for another freezing walk through the slums. Collar raised and head lowered, he hurried from streetlight to street-light, avoiding eye contact.

Must avoid personal interactions. Get in, complete the deal, and get out. That's how he stayed on top.

His Italian leather shoes slapped a steady rhythm on the sidewalk. Two blocks, three blocks, four. At five, he spied the street sign he sought. He passed the boarded-up theater and hesitated in the alley entrance while his pupils adjusted to the darkness.

Visibility faded after a few steps. Whether the alley ended in a wall of bricks or continued through to another street was a mystery. He narrowed his eyes. The darkness appeared to crawl with evil adventure. From his inner pocket, George tugged out a Lucky Strike pack. Turning his back to the wind, he cupped his hands and lit a cigarette using his engraved silver lighter. When the tip glowed, he snapped the Zippo shut and sucked in a long draw.

A click drew his attention back to the passage. An answering beacon appeared. The flickering yellow flame of another cigarette. The shadowy smoker hacked a coarse cough, a black widow spider lurking in a giant unseen web.

"Whattcha waiting for, an invitation?"

Instinct whispered, "Stay away!" but the promise of chemical courage lured George forward, and the thrill of conquest pumped strength into muscles limp with unease. Pitching the cigarette to the sidewalk, he mashed out the smoldering end. "Didn't see you."

He squared his shoulders and marched into the sentient darkness.

Even up close, George could barely make out a person. By mutual consent, he never contacted his supplier outside this alley. Hadn't asked for a name. Better that way. If questioned, they could never identify each other.

"Got the bread?"

Thick smoke blasted across George's face and he stepped back. "Don't snap your cap, pal." He jammed his hand into his overcoat pocket and retrieved a large envelope, which was immediately snatched away. Seconds later, a sustained rustling indicated the fanning of five-dollar bills.

"It's all there." No point in cheating the dealer.

"Price changed today."

"We made a deal. You quoted—"

"Want the stuff or not?"

George mentally sorted his options. He had the usual wad of money, but the deal had already been agreed upon. Why must they always haggle over the price? "Look. Either give me the pills or I'm outta here."

"Costs an extra C-note today."

"That's double." George hurled a curse. "Believe me, you don't want trouble—"

"Fork it over or hit the road, son."

His eye twitched in that annoying way it always did when someone pushed him against a wall. "You've been paid."

"Down boy." A throaty laugh sliced the darkness. "Just rattling your chain."

"Yeah." Few things George tolerated less than being laughed at. He opened his clenched hand. "Well, if you've had your fun."

A small package slapped George's palm.

Nerves humming like hot electric wires, George closed his fingers over the bundle. What started last year with a legal pre-scription for muscle relaxants had become a weekly quest from illegal sources. Chicago might be modern in 1955, but not everyone was hip to the benefits of drugs. The doctor warned about physical and psychological dependence after taking the pills for more than two months, then cut George off when he requested a third refill.

No one could call George Stanton an addict. Lowlifes and scumbags got hooked on drugs. He used drugs recreationally. Take 'em or leave 'em. Sure, he looked forward to the jolt of power the drugs infused in his muscles, but he didn't use every day. The worthless doctor gave him no other alternative than to procure street drugs.

Anticipation filled George's body with longing. He wanted to tear open the package and pop a few pills before taking another step. Not here.

He started walking, slow deliberate steps at first. Desire welled in his throat, threatening to overcome him. He stopped under the streetlight at the first corner to swallow a couple of pills—enough to quash the threatening nausea.

Light footsteps tapped a pattern behind.

Was he being followed? Over one tense shoulder, George visually retraced his path.

No one there.

He squeezed the package tighter and broke into a jog.

Behind him, running feet peppered the sidewalk. The sound echoed in the alleyways and throbbed in his head.

Heart pumping at breakneck pace, he sprinted.

The chasing feet kept up with his long strides.

Paranoia squeezed his throat. Breathing became shallow. Who was following him? Couldn't stop to check. Had to make the L before his would-be attacker outran him.

Why didn't he pack his gun?

Ragged gasps replaced measured breathing. A river of sweat drained down his spine. Pain pounded his brain. A bizarre tightness gripped his chest.

Still he ran. One streetlight, two. Fatigue retarded his progress, but he dared not pause to look back.

At the next light he slowed to catch his breath. Bent double from fatigue, with his hands on his thighs, he panted as he glanced behind.

No one followed.

He straightened to a stand, gaze flicking right and left.

Hunched by the Chicago cold, scattered pedestrians hastened along the sidewalks without a sideways glance. A green-and-yellow Checker cab rambled past, closely followed by a boxy white delivery truck. Shadows danced here and there, tossed like leaves by the wind. Traffic ebbed and flowed in the late-night Uptown pattern, same as always.

He cursed his overactive imagination as he straightened his overcoat, tugging it closer around his chest. Jaw grinding, he set his face toward the few remaining blocks to the L and ramped up his speed.

A tall figure draped in dark clothing stepped directly into his path.

Head down, George smacked into the man at full bore. The impact sent him staggering backwards, stunned.

A second hooded assailant grabbed George's arm.

Kerchief masks concealed their identities, but heartless eyes drilled him with evil intent. Something sharp pressed George's chest. Under the streetlight a large hunting knife glinted.

"Hand it over," a husky voice whispered.

George's voice squeaked like a teenager. "Hand what over?"

"Your money, big city man." He drove the blade closer. A second before a fist smashed into George Stanton's chin, he caught a glimpse of a black glove. No time to duck. The wallop drove him backward in quick steps, crashing into the side of a brick building. His fedora went flying, and one of his flailing hands slapped the bricks.

The first wave of euphoria from the happy pills rushed through his veins, empowering him and elevating his perceived potential strength, but it was useless to fight. One thug towered over him, padded with at least fifty extra pounds of avarice. His colleague, though shorter, displayed less mercy.

"Stop."

Foul air pummeled George's skin in sync with the blows.

"Stop." Squeezing his lids shut, he held his breath.

"Somebody. Help!" George crossed his arms over his face.

Each punch sent thoughts scattering wildly through his brain. Should have gone into the army with his friends and learned to fight. Would someone rescue him? "Help me." His words hissed out. Not enough air to speak.

Nobody heard him anyway.

Unauthorized fingers ripped one side of his overcoat from his shoulder and dug into his pockets. In seconds, they stripped away everything of value—his package of drugs, his gold engraved money clip, his Swiss watch, and his thick wad of cash.

Even his silk handkerchief.

Without another word, the two slithered into a nearby alley.

George collapsed against the building. For a few fleeting moments, spurts of relief infused his chest. His life had been spared. Then reality—he'd lost the drugs. His stomach flip-flopped. How would he quench this gnawing anxiety?

One consolation. He hadn't been wearing his most prized

possessions: the heirloom, three-carat diamond ring his father handed down when George married Gloria, the blue diamond his great-grandfather brought back from a trip to India in the mid-1800s. George never risked losing it in this part of town. The flawless gem was worth a small fortune. He also left his gold Rolex at home, choosing a slightly less expensive watch to wear into Uptown.

His heart hammered. How dare these worthless cretins attack him! If not for a killer headache, the incredulity would have been laughable. He snatched his fedora out of the gutter. Sweat as thick as blood dripped from his forehead, but he had no handkerchief to soak it up.

The disrespect galled him most. George straightened to a wobbly stand. Obviously, these thugs did not know who George was. No one acquainted with the Stanton name would have such audacity. George Kendrick Stanton—heir of the Wall Street Stantons, toasted son of Margarita Kendrick, the supreme hostess of Manhattan—had been robbed of dignity. Not to mention his valuables.

He mashed his hat on his throbbing head and winced.

Echoes of his father's mocking voice taunted him. He shrugged away childhood memories of cruel ridicule. A shiver vibrated through his body, so intense it nearly knocked him over.

The miserable thieves left him no money to buy more pills tonight. His need spread like scandal through his brain. He cut loose a string of curses and willed himself to stop trembling. He brushed off his overcoat and shrugged back into his confident posture.

Easy enough to find another supplier. Plenty of other alleys in the city. He need never return to Uptown.

George brushed moisture from his lip. Blood. He ground his jaw. No handkerchief to wipe it off.

Two-to-one, not a fair fight. He squeezed his fist tight and made himself a solemn vow. No one would ever humiliate George Stanton like this again.

3

STRYKER

Stryker had never seen such a big house. Must be a mansion where rich people live, like the ones Mama talked about when she had too much to drink. She peeked around the doorway. Did servants in starched uniforms hide behind closed doors waiting to attend to her every desire?

Curious though. The lady from church didn't drive a fancy car. Her dark brown 1948 Studebaker Champion four-door sedan was plain and already seven years old. The stale smell gave away its age.

Stryker knew a lot about cars. The last guy she and Mama lived with taught her all about them. She could identify make, model, and year of any car on the road, whether she saw the front or the back and sometimes just the outline.

Who would guess a woman driving such an ancient car lived in a house like this? With her bare toes digging into the soft rug in the parlor, Stryker turned slowly to admire her surroundings—a brick fireplace, matching chairs that looked truly comfortable, a couch with colorful pillows, a see through vase with real flowers. Clean and tidy like a magazine picture. Food cooking somewhere else in the house made her mouth water.

She pinched her arm, glad to feel pain. Definitely not dreaming.

Mrs. Crowley shrugged out of her overcoat and hung it on the hall tree in the entry. "What's the matter, child?" One wrinkled hand covered Stryker's forehead. "Are you ill?"

She lowered her gaze and waggled her head.

"Well, for pity's sake. Don't stand there dawdling. We've things to do." Mrs. Crowley tucked her arms over her full chest. "Should we bathe you or feed you first?" She tilted her head. "You must be starving and the chuck roast will be done soon. How lovely to have Sunday company for a change. Come along to the kitchen and we'll get something to eat." Without a backward glance, Mrs. Crowley hurried through a swinging door at the far side of the room.

The familiar pangs of hunger growled in Stryker's stomach. She blinked, hoping to stop the gathering tears. With halting steps, she followed Mrs. Crowley through the door. In the kitchen, the old woman tied an apron around her wide middle and began throwing together a meal. While she worked, she sang. "Leaning, leaning, safe and secure from all alarms . . ."

Soon enough food to stock a neighborhood grocery store covered the counter. Was she expecting other people?

While she sang, Mrs. Crowley peeled potatoes. Warmth and happiness crowded the room like guests at a party. The aroma of cooking meat swirled the air with abundant goodness. Stryker remembered this aroma from the neighborhood lunch counter. Sometimes Mama left her there while she conducted business. The scent of a roast nearly sent Stryker straight to Heaven every time. Bet it tasted every bit as good.

Peelings flew left and right, some landing on the floor as Mrs. Crowley's fingers labored over the bowl of potatoes. A kind smile gave the woman the appearance of a plump fairy godmother. "As soon as these potatoes are cooked and mashed we'll be ready to eat. Put your monkey down and set the table, won't you?"

Stryker didn't move. She had never eaten at a table before. How would she know the right way to set one?

Mrs. Crowley took Stryker's hands into her own, examining them over the top of her wire-rimmed glasses. She tsk-tsked. "Look at the dirt under those ragged fingernails. Better wash up first." Mrs. Crowley nodded toward the sink. "There's a brush with the soap. Scrub those nails good now. That's a dear."

After arranging her stuffed monkey in a chair, Stryker approached the sink, pushing up her sleeves. She stood on tiptoes to crank the faucet open. Clear water gushed out. Incredible. No rust. For a moment she simply stared. The water was so beautiful. Pure. Not like what they got out of garden hoses on the streets.

Hand trembling, she reached a finger toward the silver ribbon and giggled. She wanted to jump into the sink and let the water flow over her whole body. What would it feel like to dangle her feet in it? Gulp it down her throat? She cupped her palms and splashed a handful on her face. Cool refreshing water dripped off her chin.

"For heaven's sake, child. Don't play in the water. Get those hands clean." Mrs. Crowley gave the water a quick test with one finger, then reached toward the spigot and turned the handle the opposite direction. The water became warmer. "That's better. Use the soap now."

Stryker examined the white bar, sniffing and tracing the slippery surface with one finger. She did her best to concentrate on washing but couldn't quit staring at the clear, fresh water.

Mrs. Crowley turned toward her. "That's enough playing for now. Dry your hands. The Sunday china is in the cabinet beside the table. Take out two plates. The silver is in the long drawer." She nodded toward a cabinet.

The plates looked like something fragile a princess might use. Must handle with care. Mrs. Crowley continued issuing directions. After several wrong choices, Stryker finally managed to set the table in the room Mrs. Crowley called the dining room. When the potatoes were deposited in a bowl, Stryker eased into one of six matched chairs with the monkey pressed to her chest.

Across the table, the old woman placed her napkin in her lap and bowed her head. Arched eyebrows and a nod must mean Stryker should follow suit.

"Dear Lord, thank you for the bounty you have set before us."

Stryker squinted through one eye until she could see Mrs. Crowley whose eyelids were squeezed tightly, palms together, fingers pointed upward. Stryker imitated.

"And thank you for my young guest. Reveal your will concerning this child. Lead us to the mother."

Stryker's eyes popped open. Did this lady intend to find Mama? No one could find Mama. Not where she'd gone this time. Stryker hung her head.

"Keep us from temptation and deliver us from evil. Make us available to those less fortunate. In the blessed name of Jesus. Amen."

Stryker dropped her head again and waited, but the prayer seemed to be ended. When she opened her eyes this time, she found Mrs. Crowley busy scooping mounds of peas and mashed potatoes onto two plates. Next she reached for the platter of roast. Forking two huge pieces of beef on each plate, she set one in front of Stryker.

Stryker stared at the steam rising from the food. Such a big pile—enough for several of her friends. How would she eat it all? She squirmed in her chair.

"Put that filthy monkey down." Mrs. Crowley pointed to a chair with her spoon, chewing a mouthful of roast along with globs of potatoes and gravy. When she had swallowed, she asked, "Does your friend have a name?"

"Sophia." Stryker positioned the brown monkey on the seat next to her. Not knowing what to do next, she laced her fingers together.

"What's wrong, child? Don't like my cooking?"

Stryker swallowed over the lump in her throat. "It smells real good."

"Well, get to eating." Mrs. Crowley lifted her fork to her lips and chomped a chunk of chuck roast before sawing off another bite with her knife.

Stryker inspected the room. "Where's yer help?"

"Help?" Mrs. Crowley's fork stopped moving toward her mouth. "Do you mean servants? Good gracious, I don't have servants. Whatever makes you ask such a question, child?"

"The house. It's big."

Mrs. Crowley chuckled. "Not so big. Well, maybe it seems big for one person. When we moved here there were three of us, but I'm the only one left. No help. Whatever would I do with help?" She covered her mouth with one hand and smiled with her eyes.

Stryker stared at the shiny knives, forks, and spoons. She didn't know what they were all used for. She watched Mrs. Crowley poke the fork into the roast with one hand and slice off a piece of meat using the knife in the other hand. It looked like a lot of extra work.

She grabbed a handful of mashed potatoes and stuffed them into her mouth. Buttery goodness soothed her anxiety. Potatoes melted on her tongue. No need to chew. Such deliciousness brought tears to her eyes. Stryker blinked hard and gulped, reaching for a second handful.

Face beaming, Mrs. Crowley held up one palm. "Slow down, child. We'll chat while we eat. That's what people do in polite society—have dinner conversation."

Stryker strained to return the smile. "Thank you." Mama would be proud of her good manners. She bit off a piece of meat and stuffed several handfuls of food into her mouth.

"Try using the knife and fork."

Mrs. Crowley used her fork to gather potatoes and peas, but Stryker kept eating with her hands. Eyebrows raised, Mrs. Crowley sawed off a chunk of meat. They ate in silence for a few minutes. "Tell me. What's your mother's name?"

Shoulders slumped automatically as Stryker lowered her gaze. Peering through her eyelashes, she stared at Mrs. Crowley. Questions about Mama must not be answered.

"Here, here, child." Mrs. Crowley dabbed her lips with her napkin. Her voice sounded friendly. "I must know her name if I'm to find where she's gone."

Stryker swallowed, not knowing what to say.

"I don't understand why you won't tell me."

Pain began to throb in Stryker's head. She pressed her temple with one hand. The lump in her throat had grown to a boulder.

"Is Stryker your given name?" Mrs. Crowley scooped up more food. "Do you have a last name?" She popped the spoon into her mouth and it came out empty.

Stryker jiggled her head back and forth. Shaking made her head hurt more.

"Tell me something about your mother." Mrs. Crowley's tone had become tense. "Where did you live when you were together? When did you see her last?"

Mustn't cry. Stryker flapped her eyelids rapidly. She couldn't tell about Mama. No matter how nice this lady seemed. She promised. Stryker's hands went clammy, and her tight shoulders trembled. Tears flooded out all at once, but she had no power to stop them. She'd kept this sorrow inside for all the long months since Mama went away. It wouldn't stay put any longer.

Unable to sit another second, Stryker snatched up Sophia. Jumping from the table, she ran out of the room. She didn't know where to go, so she tugged open the first door she found. The door led into a tiny room with coats hanging on hooks. She fell in a heap in one corner and tucked her knees tight to her chest. Then she let the crying loose. Sobs escalated into wails.

Her brow a mass of wrinkles, Mrs. Crowley appeared at the door. All the color had drained from her face. "Did I scare you, child? You mustn't be frightened. Come on out."

The pounding in Stryker's head paralyzed her. Even small movement made the pain worse. She hugged her knees closer and dropped her forehead between them.

"Oh, dear," Mrs. Crowley said, her hand covering her cheek. "Please don't cry so hard. You're getting pale. Your food will get cold. Come on now. I'm far too old to bend into the closet. Please come out, Stryker. I won't ask any more questions tonight. I promise."

When Stryker wouldn't come out, Mrs. Crowley brought

a dining chair and settled outside the doorway. For a few minutes, she alternated between coaxing and praying. Then she fell silent, hands folded in her lap.

No matter how long she waited, Stryker wouldn't come out. Couldn't.

The tall clock in the hall bonged several times. Shadows drifted across the wide planks on the floor. Hours must have passed before all the tears dried leaving behind an occasional hiccup. Stryker's body relaxed and she released her stiff knees. The monkey landed on the floor with a plop. Weary almost to the point of collapse, she lifted her eyes.

A wrinkled hand extended into the closet. "Come out now, Stryker dear. You must be exhausted. Let's run a bath and get you off to bed."

Bed sounded wonderful, but her legs wobbled when she stood. Unsteady, she fell into Mrs. Crowley's strong embrace, feeling both safe and uncomfortable at the same time.

Upstairs, Mrs. Crowley busied over a big tub where the same delicious clear water poured onto a shiny white surface. Mrs. Crowley shook something out of a purple box into the water. Steam rose, lightly scented with a fresh, flowery perfume.

"Give me that monkey." Mrs. Crowley reached, fingers wiggling in a gimme gesture.

"N-n-o!"

"I need to wash it."

"Mama said I mustn't let her out of my sight."

"For pity's sake. Set her down here then. You can't take a bath with a toy and all your clothes on. Come on, sweetheart." Mrs. Crowley tugged the toy from Stryker and placed it on the floor near the tub. "Let's get these clothes off you. Tomorrow we'll get you new clothes, something proper for a girl." Mrs. Crowley loosened the overalls at the shoulders and tugged the big shirt off. "Mercy, these things aren't suitable for a living soul. Have to throw them in the incinerator." Pinching a small bit of grimy fabric between her thumb and first finger, she dropped the shirt on the floor.

Under the loose shirt, Stryker's ragged undershirt clung

to her chest like a second skin. She hadn't taken it off for a long time.

All of a sudden, the bathroom air felt cold and hostile.

Mrs. Crowley tsk-tsked. "Oh, my dear. You are quite thin, and this undershirt is much too small for you. I hope we can get it off. Might have to use the scissors." She tugged on the undershirt, but the cloth ripped to shreds as she yanked it over Stryker's bald head.

A loud gasp tumbled from Mrs. Crowley's lips. "Is that dirt?"

Mama said no one should see you without your clothes. Stryker folded her arms close to her body and tucked up her knees.

Mrs. Crowley paid no attention. She was busy rubbing Stryker's back with a wet cloth. "Child, this isn't dirt. You're covered with bruises." Her expression tight, she scrunched her mouth. "Who did this to you?"

"Nobody." Stryker jerked from the tight grasp. "Leave me alone!" She grabbed Sophia. Unwanted tears flowed and she pushed her fist into one eye. Crying showed weakness. Pulling back, she pushed Mrs. Crowley's hand away. "I can take care of myself."

4

GEORGE

Another fight was coming. George prepared as best he could with feet apart, stabilizing his body against the wall.

The three thugs advanced.

He lifted his fists. How did these punks get all the way to the tenth floor of his office building, past the night watchman? Did his drug supplier send these idiots? Couldn't be. He had never given his name or any form of identification. Besides, he was square with the dealer.

What happened to the orderly world George had methodically created? In a mere two days, his life had crumbled. He wasn't safe on the street or in his own office either. The audacity of these hooligans to come after him in the penthouse suite within the sturdy, granite sanctuary of the largest law firm in Chicago.

Across the desk, the biggest goon leaned toward George. "Maybe we don't gotta rough you up."

They hovered like vultures about to dine on rotting flesh. Up lit by a thin stream of light from his brass desk lamp, the faces looked ghoulish.

Smack. Smack. One leather-gloved fist pummeled the other.

Those fists could mess up a guy. Fear descended like smothering smoke; George smelled it, tasted it. "What do you fellows want?"

"You know what we want. The scratch."

George's heart raced. The scratch? That answered who these wise guys represented. His gambling debt must be over $10,000. He'd planned to repay it with his next win. That's what he always did. Only he hadn't been to a high-stakes poker game in weeks. Had to assemble the right group of suckers.

He could pay them off right now with money hidden in the office, but he didn't want to cut into his nest egg. To buy more time, he raised one palm. "No need for muscle. I always make good on my losses."

"Yeah, well, the boss don't keep tabs forever. He wants you should pay up today."

How could he get rid of these creeps before they ruined his perfect plan? George squeezed out a nonchalant laugh. "You fellas . . . surprised me is all."

A modicum of dignity edged into George's chest. Unwise to show they had intimidated him. George settled back into his chair. "Give me a minute, okay? I am not accustomed to being bullied."

They cackled like a flock of hens.

Would the watchman do rounds soon?

"Shoulda thought before you milked the boss, buddy." A pointer finger prodded George's chest, keeping time with his words. "He don't like that. See?"

Another of the wiseguys leered. "Ain't tidy. The boss likes tidy."

The third added another sharp laugh. "Yeah. Tidy."

"Well, the . . . uh, boss should know businessmen don't keep cash around the office. Wouldn't be smart."

"Not smart?"

Mocking. Very unwise.

A big face inches from George's nose. "Okay. Where *do* you keep cash?"

Where the sun don't shine, moron. "Look, give me a few days. A week. He'll get paid, but I need a week."

All three froze, expressions confounded like the Three Stooges with a problem. Did they have trouble understanding English? Then another *smack*—a black-fisted glove walloping the other hand.

George flinched.

"The boss ain't gonna like to wait. Whatcha want we should tell him when he says suppose you skip town before you pay up?"

George didn't need an answer.

A quick *rap-tap* sounded at his door and a voice called, "Mr. Stanton?"

No one moved.

With any luck it would be the watchman.

The door blasted open, rattling the windows. In the doorway, a broad-shouldered stiff in a serious black suit scanned the office. Behind him a second fellow lurked in the shadows, hooded eyes partially hidden under a gray felt hat with a distinctive U-shaped rut in the crown.

The leather-clad gangsters recoiled as one, whispering.

What now?

The suited stranger pushed thick, black-rimmed glasses onto his nose before asking, "What's going on here?"

Why were the lights out in the hall? Pain pulsing through his injured jaw, George feigned composure, elbows and forearms firmly on the desk. "It's after hours. If you gentlemen come back tomorrow, I'm sure someone can help you."

In two long strides, the large man reached the desk. From inside his suit, he dragged out a badge holder and flipped it open. "Agent Frank Pinasco, FBI."

George tried to focus but caught little more than a blurry glint of gold in the dim light.

Hawkish eyes swept the now-motionless group. "Which one of you is George Stanton?"

"Lookin' for George Stanton, are you? Then you don't want us." The thug backhanded his nearest cohort and jerked his head toward the exit.

Slinking off, the big guy rubbernecked to toss back a threat. "You ain't seen the last of us, buddy-boy."

The sharp bang of the door jump-started George's heart. "What do you gentlemen want with George Stanton?"

"Answers." Pinasco swung his leg into a chair. "We got plenty of questions. You George Stanton then?"

No use denying it. "Yes."

The gent in the gray hat closed the office door, shrugged out of his overcoat, and dragged over another chair.

"Looked like you needed a little help with those creeps." Pinasco indicated the closed door with a tilt of his head.

George rubbed his chin. "Thanks."

Arching his eyebrows, Pinasco produced a single nod before glancing at his comrade. "At this particular time, we have no interest in them. Meet Matthew Alton." He nodded toward the man in the gray hat. "Mr. Alton here is a detective."

Alton removed the hat and carefully placed it upside down in his lap before meeting George's gaze. "Do you know why we're here, Mr. Stanton?" His deep voice had a slow drawl. Slipping his slick leather gloves off finger by finger, he deposited them in the silk lining of the hat.

George fumbled through his pocket for his Zippo and Lucky Strike pack. "Hope you don't mind. It's been a rough day." He bumped out a cigarette but couldn't control his trembling fingers. With luck they wouldn't notice, although good fortune had evaded George of late. "Fellows?"

Pinasco declined George's offer of a smoke.

"No thanks," said Alton.

George pointed to Alton's hat with his cigarette. "That's a doozy. Mind me asking who made it?" Maybe small talk would relax him. George sucked in a long drag.

"It's a Stetson." Alton crossed his hands at the wrist. "Open Road."

"Mr. Alton hails from Texas," Pinasco interjected. "Real popular hat down there."

"Really?" Stalling, of course, but would they notice? Right now he needed the happy pills. His last belt of whiskey had long since worn off.

Why would a detective from Texas be working with a G-man?

Smoke briefly camouflaged George in a dense haze, giving him the illusion of being slightly insulated. "Okay. Why are you fellows here?"

Pinasco extracted a notebook and paged through, stopping to consult a few dark scribbles before speaking. "We traced a series of large deposits to this office." He paused. "Which seem to have disappeared."

George broke eye contact, lowering his stare to his desk.

Pinasco didn't wait for George to comment. "We figure you got something to tell us."

Tapping ashes in the overloaded ashtray, George sucked another puff. "Large deposits, you say?" He swiveled his head to one side to blow smoke out the corner of his mouth. "Could you be more specific?"

Pinasco leaned an elbow on the desk. "Best take this seriously, Mr. Stanton. We are. In fact, the United States government instructs you to turn over your books for a complete audit."

Alton reached into his overcoat and withdrew a folded sheet of paper. "Here's the subpoena." He slapped it on the desk.

"What's this nonsense?" George steadied his cigarette in the ashtray and picked up the paper as if it might contain a viper. He unfolded the document with exaggerated care and skimmed the legalese all the way to the official judicial seal. He couldn't quite focus on the words, but the subpoena appeared to be legit.

George's hands went slimy with sweat. His mouth, on the other hand, became dry as a good martini. He gave the door a sideways glance, gauging the distance. Too far for an escape. Under the desk, his knees bounced nervously.

Who squealed? Bits of office conversation ping-ponged through his brain—Francine questioning one of the ledger entries he submitted yesterday. His secretary had never acted in such a manner before, not once in the ten years he'd worked as an accountant for McBride, Reynolds, and O'Neill. That reminded him of an odd conversation between Burns and Gleason last week. Why would the junior partners discuss one of his clients in the cafeteria? Several other times, people whispered his name when they didn't think he heard. Why else would Old Man Reynolds and that weasel O'Neill quit talking so abruptly whenever he walked into the conference room?

Someone had discovered his creative accounting.

But how? He'd been meticulous, confiding in no one. Well, they weren't going to catch him. No, sir. George Stanton wouldn't go down, not for missing money the company owed him anyway after all the extra work he'd done and being overlooked for promotion twice. Another employee would get caught holding the empty deposit bag.

He'd see to it.

His eye twitched as he slowly refolded the paper. Muscles in his forearm quivered when he pressed the subpoena into the desk surface. He drew his index finger along the crease with calculated precision. Must throw these bozos off his trail. "I'm afraid you fellows have made a big mistake. Pity to waste your valuable time slugging through my files. What you want is the big fish, right?"

Pinasco and Alton communicated something through a veiled glance between them.

"You suggesting a deal?" Pinasco bent closer. "Let's hear what you got."

George hesitated, his body flushed with anxiety. He struggled to control his tone. "You may find a few irregularities in my books and you may not, but the crime you're interested in happened higher up the food chain." He pushed the subpoena back across the desk. "I suggest you have this rewritten. You fellows are snooping in the wrong files."

Alton steepled his well-manicured hands. "You'll guarantee us access to the correct files?"

"Can't guarantee, but I'll do my best." George leveled a conspiratorial look on the interlopers. "But you gotta help me first."

"Not saying we can, but whatta you want?"

"Immunity and protection."

The wall clock ticked and tocked. George mashed the now-consumed cigarette butt out in his ashtray, crushing the tiny glow.

Alton turned toward George with a shrug. "Whattya got in mind?"

George eyed them. The hopelessness of his situation breached the wall around his heart. His drug source compromised, thugs demanding money, betrayal within the office, now these G-men. The timing must be significant. Couldn't be coincidental. He felt the noose tightening around his throat. Surely a sign the time for his exit had arrived.

With a sudden rush of power, survival instinct kicked in gear.

He would not be caught and prosecuted. Not George Stanton. He knew exactly what to do. Had been planning it for a couple years. His life in Chicago may have come to a screeching halt, and he would bow out a winner.

"Here's the plan . . ."

5

MABEL

Next morning Mabel discovered the girl sleeping on the guest room floor among a tangle of bedclothes. At some point during the night she must've dragged all the covers off the bed.

So small for an eleven-year-old, yet her bald head made her appear older than her years. "Poor little chickadee." Mabel clucked. "Didn't so much as drag a pillow down with her. Must be uncomfortable."

The tranquil scene awakened sweet memories. Mabel never tired of watching Richard sleep when he was a boy. She let out a heavy sigh. Busying herself at the window, she tied back the thick drapes. Sunlight flushed away the morning gloom.

After the child finally went to sleep, Mabel had pried the filthy monkey from her arms and laundered it. Hanging it overnight near the heater had almost dried it. Now she tucked the slightly damp but clean monkey into Stryker's arms.

Mabel spoke in a soft, gentle voice so she wouldn't frighten the child. "I hate to wake you. I imagine you could sleep a hundred years and still not get enough rest."

Stryker moved her elbow to shield her closed eyelids.

Mabel bent closer. "I've been up since dawn. After I dressed and finished my devotion time, I called my friend Bessie."

Locating the child's mother topped Mabel's to-do-now list. She'd stressed this with Bessie using the strongest words in her vocabulary. "Bessie will ask her policeman son to help us. You'll like him. He's a good chap. She promised to do her best but said not to get our hopes up."

The sleeping girl didn't budge while Mabel babbled, so she kept right on talking.

"Then I made an appointment with Dr. Marston. You need a thorough checkup." As a long-time patient as well as a friend, Mrs. Crowley received special consideration. The receptionist would squeeze Stryker in at one o'clock, leaving plenty of time for a hearty breakfast before and a much-needed clothes shopping trip later.

Stryker stirred, mumbled, and rolled on her side facing the wall.

Mabel spoke louder. "Then I got the best idea. Last week, Trinity Church concluded a clothing drive for the missionaries. So I called my friend Libby—she was on the committee with me—and asked if we could borrow some of the girls' clothes in the barrel we packed. Guess what? Right away Libby brought over a little dress and some shoes. We'll return them after we buy proper clothes for you. I can't wait to see if they fit."

The hour hand on the bedside clock clicked nearer to eleven.

"I don't think you should sleep any longer." Mabel leaned as low as she was able. "Stryker? Ready to wake up, dear?"

Stryker stretched one arm high over her head, fist clenched. Her sparse lashes swept up and her round azure eyes blinked a few times. As if awareness of her unfamiliar surroundings dawned all at once, the petite body bolted upright. Stiff-backed, she scanned the bedroom. Her fingers closed around Sophia. Wide eyes sparking with fear shifted to Mabel.

Extending her hand, Mabel produced a smile she hoped would be reassuring. "You stayed at my house last night.

Remember? We ate dinner and took a quick bath. You were ever so tired. I put you to bed. Don't know how long you might have slept if I hadn't come to wake you."

Stryker's glance ricocheted off her monkey to Mabel.

"I washed your toy. Doesn't she look better now?"

The child clutched a fistful of blankets in her thin fingers, tugging them to her chin.

"You're wearing one of my pajama tops. It's far too large, but I didn't have anything in your size to choose from. Today we'll buy suitable clothes." Mabel refreshed her smile, but the panic reflected in Stryker's face didn't subside.

"Wait until you see these clothes." Mabel bustled from the room and returned with the dress, shoes, and underwear from the missionary barrel. "You're tall but slim. These may fit, if a bit baggy. They won't be perfect, but they'll do until we buy clothes that do fit right."

Stryker only stared.

Mabel dropped her shoulders. "I'll leave them here. Put on the clothes and bring your clean friend downstairs when you're dressed. Breakfast is waiting, and we have places to go."

Stryker hadn't moved a muscle.

Not the reaction she hoped for. "Don't dawdle, now."

Lips pursed in a thin line, Mabel flounced out the door and stomped downstairs, hoping to convince Stryker she had no plans to lurk upstairs and supervise the dressing process.

"What if she won't put the clothes on?" Mabel muttered to herself as she opened the refrigerator and hauled out the milk container. She closed the door with her hip, poured frothy white liquid in a glass, and set it on the kitchen table. "She must, that's all. I'm not strong enough to dress her, make her eat, and haul her to the car." She lifted her gaze heavenward. "Dear Lord, please get the child moving."

She kept up a steady stream of words while she fussed over breakfast. Eggs sizzled in the skillet. Grits bubbled in a pot. Mabel hadn't cooked a breakfast like this since Paul died.

Just as Mabel set steaming biscuits on the table, a sound made her turn.

Framed in the kitchen doorway, Stryker posed in the

borrowed dress and shoes, holding the monkey tight to her side. She appeared far girlier than Mabel thought possible for someone with a bald head.

Mabel clapped her hands over her mouth, chuckling with delight. "Why, you're positively beautiful. I never had a girl to dress before. Oh, we're going to have such fun." She pushed Stryker's shoulder to make her twirl. A hat to cover her shiny head should be their first purchase. "Wonderful. The dress fits perfectly. How are the shoes?"

Stryker stared down. "They squeeze my feet."

"But you got them on anyway. That's good. We'll buy the proper size soon enough." She gestured toward the table laden with food. "Here's breakfast. You need to build up your strength." Taking Stryker gently by the arm, she led her to a chair.

Stryker carefully place Sophia in the chair next to her. "I'm too old to play with a stuffed animal."

"Of course."

"But Mama said to keep her close to me."

"Oh." Mabel smiled. "Why did you name her Sophia?"

Ignoring the question, Stryker scanned the table before settling next to the stuffed animal. "Who's eating with us?"

"No one, dear." Mabel surveyed the bountiful food on the table—sausage patties, fried eggs, steaming grits, fluffy biscuits with sausage gravy, and three kinds of homemade preserves. "I wanted to be sure I made enough." She drew up a chair. "Let's thank the Lord and then you can get busy eating before the food cools."

Mabel bowed her head and thanked God for providing health, sleep, and nourishing food. "Amen." Her gaze swept over the table. "Where do you want to start?"

Conflicting emotions danced across Stryker's face.

"You are hungry, aren't you?"

Stryker dipped her head in a single nod, but her expression remained uncertain.

"Here. I'll help you."

Stryker didn't move, so Mabel spooned eggs onto her plate. She tore a biscuit apart and slathered butter on both sides. "I canned these preserves last summer to sell at the church bazaar. They turned out wonderfully—grape, apricot, and cherry. Which will it be?"

The girl gingerly picked up a spoon. In an attempt to gather a bite of eggs, she chased them around her plate. Lips twisted to one side, she pushed a pile on the spoon with her fingers and popped the contents in her mouth.

"What's this stuff?" The mouthful of food muffled her words.

Mabel understood well enough. "Fried eggs. Like them?"

Eyes gleaming, the girl nodded and picked up a sausage patty. She examined both sides before stuffing it in her bird-like mouth and turned questioning eyes to Mabel.

"Sausage. Good, isn't it?"

Another nod. Stryker picked up half a biscuit. Butter trickled down her fingers. She crammed the half into her mouth and licked butter off her hand. Her cheeks puffed out like a squirrel with a cache of nuts in its cheeks. She blinked at Mabel.

"That was a biscuit. Would you rather put gravy on it?"

The jangle of the kitchen wall phone startled them. Mabel plucked the receiver off its cradle. "Hello."

"It's Bessie. I'm afraid I don't have good news."

Mabel sighed. "Let's hear it anyway."

"My son says you have insufficient information to hunt for a mother who abandoned her child in St. Louis. Too big an area. You need to know names. He checked hospitals downtown and in all the outlying areas with no success. There isn't one single missing persons report on a woman in that age range."

"Oh, dear." Hard to believe a city as large as this wouldn't have one missing woman of childbearing age on record. "What should I do?"

"The police can take her into custody, try to find a home for her. What about foster care? Can't do much more than that. My son says these street children usually run away again as soon as they get a chance."

Mabel shifted her gaze to the child stuffing her mouth at the kitchen table. "She's a baby." Cupping her hand between the phone speaker and her lips, she turned her back to Stryker and whispered into the phone. "Maybe I'll keep her."

"Now Mabel. We're not talking about a puppy. Think about this. You're in your sixties and not in the best of health. You have Paul's pension to live on, nothing more. Why, there's hardly enough for *you*. You can't—"

"Thanks, Bessie. I appreciate your help." Downcast but not discouraged, Mabel hung up the receiver and returned to breakfast.

Later at the doctor's office, Mabel gave Stryker a quick check after she had re-dressed. Dr. Marston's examination must have felt like abuse, given Stryker's reluctance to be touched. It took both the nurse and Mabel working together to keep Stryker's flailing arms and legs from injuring someone while the doctor drew blood and inspected the bruises. Worst of all had been the undressing. Apparently, Stryker had an aversion to anyone seeing her unclothed, doctors included.

Suppose she never had medical care before?

"Sit up on the table, dear. Dr. Marston will be coming back."

A look of terror crossed Stryker's face.

Mabel smiled. "Don't be scared. He wants to talk. Nothing more. He's finished his examination."

The doctor strolled into the cubicle reading Stryker's chart. Stryker stiffened. Her gaze raked the room resting on the door as if given the chance she might bolt.

Dr. Marston appeared oblivious. "This one's a puzzler. There's definitely something going on with this young lady, but I can't tell exactly what. The bruises are symptomatic. Several possible diagnoses come to mind, all serious. Best plan would be to order a series of tests to rule out everything possible. Is that what you want to do?" He glanced up at Mabel.

"Someone must help her. Anyone can see she's sick and needs treatment."

"You'll be required to pay for her tests. Some are quite expensive."

Mabel turned to look at Stryker.

Her slumped shoulders proclaimed her vulnerable state.

In the harsh office lighting, her bruises stood out garishly against her pale complexion. A definite yellow tone mottled her delicate skin, but the bald head plucked at Mabel's heartstrings. This child needed her. Didn't Proverbs 31:9 say "Open thy mouth, judge righteously, and plead the cause of the poor and needy"? How could a Christian woman ignore this little one's desperate situation and send her away to live in foster care or on the streets for even one more night?

Without considering a moment longer, Mabel nodded. She'd been saving for home repairs, but the leak in the roof wasn't so bad. Rainy season was nearly over. Likely a delay wouldn't cause real problems. The money would be far better spent helping this unfortunate child.

"Tell me where to take her."

6

GEORGE

George chain-smoked while he tossed bank statements, memos, and client files into a crate. He left his expensive desk set. Didn't need it. Half-opened drawers in the filing cabinet had been rifled through earlier. He scattered reference books across his desk to look as though someone had gone through each one, knocking over his desk lamp in the process. The ransacked appearance would keep them guessing for a few days. Besides, this gave him a chance to inventory all the items in his office. Must not leave anything incriminating behind.

One long gulp drained the last drop of whiskey from his silver flask. With the back of his hand he swiped moisture off his lips. He'd stop by the liquor store on the way out of town.

The happy pills would've helped a lot, but he hadn't found another drug dealer. No matter. A light alcohol-induced buzz numbed the worst of his anxiety.

He drew a final drag on his cigarette and stubbed it out. A dusting of ashes drifted from his chrome ashtray onto his desk while he surveyed his handiwork. Reaching into his pocket for his white-and-red Lucky Strike pack, he extracted the lone survivor, balled the empty pack, and tossed the wad in the direction of the waste can. He'd buy cigarettes at the liquor store too.

No regrets. He'd be glad to be out of this place. His stay in this office had been productive—until someone had screwed up his plan. He lit the last cigarette and clicked his Zippo shut.

The G-men bought his improvised scheme to examine documents from the company's CEO. At least his suggestions satisfied them enough to keep them from leaving the subpoena. George's promise must have held a note of sincerity. He had mimicked the puppy-eyed expression his bratty children always adopted to get their way. The corner of his mouth twitched. He wouldn't miss *them*, of that he was certain. Snot-nosed and whiny—always sniveling about something. Not his fault. He wasn't the one who insisted on children. Never liked the little vermin, his or anyone else's. Too needy.

Memories of his children connected to thoughts of Gloria. Should he leave her a note? What would he say? "Sorry for leaving. Have a good life."

A lie. He wasn't sorry. She'd become a real drag, a nag like Mother. Gloria never understood him. Not from the beginning. She had the looks he sought but she didn't make him happy, and apparently he never did anything to suit her either. All she did was complain. No matter that he gave her all he wanted—his prestigious family name, children, the big house with the right address, a jewelry box full of expensive gems, a housekeeper and snooty cook plus the fancy car. All that stuff should count for something. Well, good riddance. She was welcome to all of it, including the debt.

Only one more thing needed—cash. With a grunt, George tugged the Jackson Pollock painting from the wall behind the desk and ripped off the stuffed manila envelope taped to the back. His stash—nearly three hundred fifty thousand unreported dollars—should go a long way toward a fresh start in Mexico. He'd hoped to stay at his desk long enough to accumulate a million. But this would have to do. Not a fortune, but enough for now.

George tossed the cash bundle in the box.

Pollock originals were selling well these days. Should he take the painting? He loved the frenetic dripping and swirling. So like life, no sense to it whatsoever. This particular work might be worth a lot of money but was too large to transport.

What if he ripped the canvas off the frame and rolled the picture up? He examined the back and shook his head. Too risky. Wouldn't be worth much with a tear.

He shrugged and hung it back on the wall for Gloria to sell.

Satisfied he'd cleared out everything he might need, George donned his overcoat and collected his best brown fedora from the hat rack. He picked up the box and pulled his office door in a slow, fluid motion until he heard it click shut. Didn't want to draw attention to his exit. Must dodge the night guard. Wouldn't want to get caught carrying away this box of papers and cash.

In the hall, George passed doors with gold lettering identifying the partners' offices. As soon as they discovered him missing, the conference room would buzz with gossip. He suppressed a chuckle. Too bad he couldn't be here to listen. If he sent a ransom note from somewhere on his trip they might suppose he'd been kidnapped. One side of his mouth curved into a smile. Wouldn't Reynolds and O'Neill be surprised when the FBI came calling with their subpoena? Months might pass before those numbskulls figured out what happened to the "missing" deposits.

Over the past few days, George had meticulously planted misleading documents in key files, leaving enough evidence for the authorities to wonder if one of the partners might have bumped off poor George Stanton to divert suspicion from his own creative bookkeeping. Oh, the fun those halfwits would have following George's crumb trail. By the time the FBI pieced together all the clues, George would be basking in a villa on the warm coast of Mexico, toasting his new life.

At 12:47 by his watch, he pushed open the door to the stairs. With any luck, the night watchman might still be enjoying his habitually-extended dinner break.

He trudged down the back stairs to decrease the chance

of being spotted. This plan seemed like a good idea on the top floor, but ten flights of stairs toting a loaded crate proved more exercise than George had bargained for. More than once, he stopped on a landing between floors to rest. Huffing and coughing from deep in his chest, he finally made his way to the lobby.

No one manned the front desk.

A gleeful burst of energy propelled him through the double doors. Perfect. George Stanton signed in but didn't sign out, another curious detail ripe for breakroom speculation.

Outside the office building he lingered a moment, gaze sweeping the imposing edifice bottom to top. Ten long years chained to a desk in that reformatory. "So long, chumps!" He'd salute if he had a free hand. The exhilaration of freedom surged through his body like a massive drug infusion. What an incredible natural high. Should've run away years ago.

Bent over his crate, overcoat trailing in the ceaseless Chicago wind, George hurried along the darkened streets to his parked car. First glimpse of his new 1955 black Lincoln Continental Mark II made his heart sing. What a beauty. Truly a rolling work of art as the ads promised. No flashy chrome, nothing but understated elegance.

Didn't have time to stop for admiration. Mentally he patted the straight, shiny fender on his way to the trunk.

After wedging the heavy box in the trunk with his packed suitcase, he slammed the signature Lincoln trunk lid—complete with its hidden spare tire—and removed his overcoat before sliding onto the fresh-smelling leather seat behind his custom steering wheel. With a grin, he tossed his overcoat in the back seat.

Key in the ignition, George allowed a moment to savor the sweetness of escape and to congratulate himself on a brilliant plan executed with skill. He couldn't keep the smirk off his face. No one would suspect George Stanton. He'd played the part of dutiful employee perfectly.

Never had he felt so fully alive and invigorated—and without his happy pills too. Chin high, he cranked the engine to a roar.

Leaving the metropolitan area, now and again he peered in the rearview mirror, watching the dramatic Chicago skyline fade away. So long, windy city. He wouldn't miss Chicago. Not for one second.

Excitement mounting, he veered onto the road out of town.

George pounded the calfskin-wrapped steering wheel with one fist. Nothing was out of his control. He had covered every contingency. Freedom would give him the chance to start over in Puerto Vallarta.

This time those numbskulls had gotten in his way. But so what? He set up a near-perfect moneymaking scheme once and he could do it again. Over the years he skimmed enough to provide well for his next venture. In the process he also learned many important things. He would figure out how he got caught and be sure not to make the same mistakes again.

The whole world waited. His nest egg would provide a fine start in Mexico where the economy hadn't caught up to the United States. Out of the country he could be anyone he wanted.

Anyone.

He blew out a stream of smoke and watched it swirl through the car.

With a toss of his head, George focused on the path lit by his powerful headlights. Ahead lay adventure and conquest—stimulating, exciting, limitless. He welcomed the challenge with an open heart. Victory belonged to George Stanton.

No one could stop him now.

7

MABEL

Mabel's fingers gripped the metal office chair until they went numb. Leaning forward, she concentrated on Doctor Marston's moving lips, trying to make sense of his words.

While the doctor turned the pages of a stack of test results in Stryker's chart, he spewed a litany of technical data liberally sprinkled with medical terms.

What was he talking about? Might as well be speaking a foreign language. Whatever he said, it didn't sound good. Mabel blinked back tears and dug in her pocketbook for her lace handkerchief.

Doctor Marston fanned through the chart with a long sigh. "All the tests are completed. The child presents a wide variety of maladies. The most significant results came from the blood analysis. The WBC count is abnormal—her bone marrow overproduces white blood cells. At the same time anemia is present—unusually low red blood cell and platelet count."

Both his tone and his words emphasized the seriousness

of Stryker's condition, but Mabel didn't understand. How did this little girl get so sick? Mabel tried to pay closer attention.

Doctor Marston's words dribbled into her brain like torturous drops from a leaky faucet. "That would account for the bruising."

With her handkerchief, Mabel dabbed moisture off her cheeks.

"Blasts. Abnormal blood cells." Their gazes connected as he glanced up from the chart and removed his glasses. He delivered his diagnosis with the finality of a guillotine. "Stryker has acute myelogenous leukemia."

Stomach rumbling, Mabel felt dizzy. Leukemia? She pressed her lips shut, unwilling to acknowledge more than a casual familiarity with the word. Always associated with . . .

Was he saying Stryker would die?

Questions bombarded her brain but wouldn't form in her mouth.

Doctor Marston continued. "Leukemia is cancer in the blood. In ninety percent of cases the disease is fatal."

In her white fist, she clutched her hanky tightly. Her trembling hand covered her lips. Thank goodness Stryker was in the waiting room and didn't have to hear this devastating news.

"I'm sorry to say current remedies generally do not produce a successful outcome. Treatment is complicated. Abnormal cells cannot fight disease like normal cells, leaving the patient susceptible to pneumonia or urinary tract infection. Simple ailments become life-threatening. She'll need constant monitoring."

Sensibility drained from Mabel's body. Constant monitoring. Woodenly, she nodded once as if she understood.

"You must also limit her physical activity. She'll be easily fatigued with shortness of breath after the slightest exercise. The red pinpoint dots on her legs or arms may get worse. She'll bruise easily, as you have seen, and tend toward nosebleeds. You might see more bleeding than usual when she brushes her teeth."

Confusion louder than a freight train rumbled through Mabel's ears. We should buy a toothbrush today. Mustn't forget to write that on the shopping list.

"Do you have any questions?"

His query yanked Mabel from her fog. She struggled to organize a sentence. "You said something about . . . is there . . . treatment?"

"A few options are available." Doctor Marston folded his hands over Stryker's chart. "Traditional treatment includes radiation, arsenic, or aminopterin, a folic acid inhibitor." He stroked his chin. "Aminopterin users report a one in ten success rate. A few clinics find chemotherapy successful to poison the abnormal cells in certain patients."

Mabel shook her head, internally repeating the inventory of treatment. Did he say arsenic? Rat poison? Radiation? "What would be best for Stryker?"

Doctor Marston cleared his throat. "In Stryker's case, the prognosis is not hopeful. She's already a sick child. The cost of any of these treatments is prohibitive. You're not a young woman and Stryker is not related to you. You aren't even her legal guardian. I'm speaking to you as your long-time friend as well as your doctor. Why put yourself through such a thing, Mabel?" He placed his hand on her shoulder. "Perhaps the kindest thing would be to leave her in county care. Their facilities are not as . . . modern as ours, but they offer excellent service for terminal patients."

Terminal. The word stung like a slap in the face. Dr. Marston expected Stryker to die.

Mabel shuddered back a gasp. *Dear Lord, this can't be true. You didn't bring someone who needs me only to take her away with this horrible disease.* Mabel refused to accept this prognosis. "Doctor Marston, she's a child."

The good doctor's shoulders slumped. "I'm sorry, Mabel." He met her teary gaze. "If it's any consolation, county nurses have a fine reputation for competence."

Leave Stryker to die alone in a sterile place surrounded by strangers? A girl who could barely endure being touched? The child would be terrified. That would amount to another abandonment. She'd be no better than the girl's mother. "Surely I can do something for her." Hand pressing her chest, she leaned forward. "Please, Doctor. Tell me what to do."

Doctor Marston pushed his glasses back on his nose and thumbed through Stryker's chart giving Mabel the distinct impression he aimed to avoid her plea. After a prolonged silence, he punched a button on his intercom and waited. "Nurse Wright. Get me UCLA Medical Center. I want to speak to Darrell Woodruff in Pediatric Oncology." The button snapped off.

"Went to med school with a fine chap. Works out in California now. I believe he's had some success treating myelogenous leukemia. His work is experimental in nature, but UCLA is a teaching hospital, which means financial aid might be available."

Gratitude surged over Mabel. "Thank you, Doctor. Thank you."

Doctor Marston held up one flat palm. "Too early for thanks. Let me speak with him first, send the test results out there. Then, *if* he agrees to treat Stryker, get her to UCLA as quickly as possible. She has no time to waste." Over the top of his glasses, his gaze telegraphed concern. "It's a long way to California. Are you prepared for that?"

She mumbled an affirmative answer, and Doctor Marston promised to contact her after he heard from the doctor in California. He kept talking for several minutes, but Mabel was lost in her thoughts.

Might as well be talking about walking to India. She'd never been to California before and had no idea what might be involved. *God help me.* With the whispered prayer, a certainty settled over Mabel. God would help her get the child to a place where treatment might lead to cure.

Commercial airlines would be far too expensive. Besides, Mabel had never flown on an airplane before. If God meant her to fly, he would have provided wings. Air travel was out of the question.

What about a train or a bus? All those long miles with sneezing strangers carrying who-knows-what contagious diseases made any kind of public transportation sound dangerous. Stryker was extra sensitive to infectious germs. She must be protected from sick people.

That left one option: drive to California. Alone. Mabel had never done such a bold thing before. The mere idea terrified her. So many things to plan—packing and gasoline, where to eat and stay overnight along the way. Goodness, she hadn't yet bought clothing or toiletries for the child.

Did Mabel even own a highway map that showed the way to California?

How would she locate the best route? Surely such a trip would take several days. Would the old Studebaker make such a long journey? She had put off having the oil changed. Must get that done right away.

One overriding thought prevailed. This child had no one else. All obstacles could be—must be—overcome. A strong sense of purpose infused Mabel's heart for the first time in many years. Certainly God appointed her to this task. Although she didn't know how, she must find enough life in her old bones to get the two of them to the west coast.

As they exited the doctor's office, Stryker clung to Mabel with one hand, clutching the little brown monkey in the other. Backing out of the parking space and heading toward the street, Mabel continued her silent prayer. She brushed away a tear, thanking God for the kind nurse who stayed with Stryker while the doctor spoke to Mabel in private. How would she explain all this to the child? *Dear Father, give me the right words.*

Mabel's gaze caressed Stryker, sitting stiff-backed on the passenger side with eyelids lowered. After a few minutes she relaxed a bit. Her bald head dropped onto Mabel's arm and her breathing regulated.

What a sweet girl. She must be exhausted by such a fuss. "Lord," Mabel whispered, "I know you brought us together. Give me strength to complete this task. Please, heal Stryker of this awful disease." Ever so gently, she laid one hand on Stryker's prickly head. "Use this precious child to bring glory to your name."

Flooded with peace, Mabel committed her heart completely— she would get Stryker to California. God had always provided everything Mabel needed in the past. She would trust Him to provide for this trip.

Suitcases she hadn't used in years must be collected from the basement. She'd get Stryker to help her drag them out. The library might have a map, and maybe someone could recommend a route. What kind of weather might they encounter? She needed to start a list of clothing Stryker would require.

What about funds? The answer came in a flash. Shortly before his death, Paul had placed municipal bonds in a shoebox on the shelf in the bedroom closet. In all this time, Mabel had never touched the box. Some of the bonds—if not all—must have matured. What more appropriate way to use the money? By God's grace, she might be able to gather enough cash to drive to California.

Please Lord, get us there in time.

8

GEORGE

One final stop remained before George left the city. On the way through Cicero, he located an all-night liquor store and stocked up on Johnnie Walker Gold Label and Lucky Strikes. Filling his silver pocket flask with expensive eighteen-year-old scotch made him feel invincible, veins surging with raw energy even before he'd taken a drink.

Supplied with cartons of cigarettes and a crate of liquor, he swung behind the steering wheel of the Lincoln Continental. He twisted off his gold-and-diamond wedding ring and tossed it in the glove box. Raising his flask, he toasted his reflection in the rearview mirror. "To freedom." Liquid gold trickled down his throat. So smooth.

George revved the engine and zoomed away. When he got on Route 66, he could hardly contain his glee. His finger traced the four-pointed star emblem on the wheel. "Let's find out what this baby is capable of."

Heart pumping, George depressed the gas pedal. The Lincoln Continental catapulted into breathtaking speed, embracing the curves and racing along straightaways with the stamina of a two-year-old stallion newly loose in the pasture. Under his breath, George swore with delight. This powerhouse satisfied every craving for muscle he'd ever dreamed of, worth every penny of the ten grand he'd forked over. If this car was good enough for Frank Sinatra, it'd be the perfect car for George Stanton. No compromise in quality here.

With a peek in the rearview mirror, George tilted his fedora at a jaunty angle and laughed, relishing oneness with the superlative car. He planned to take Route 66 for a while and then veer south to Mexico. Once in Mexico, he'd head west to Puerto Vallarta on the coast. If he drove seventy miles per hour on the open road as the salesman promised he could, he'd easily make St. Louis by midmorning.

Lighted truck stops and home-style diners blurred as he sped toward Springfield, Missouri. Miles and hours ticked by. He smoked a couple packs of Lucky Strikes until the ashtray overflowed and the Lincoln's interior filled with smoke too thick to see through. Then he opened the wing window and let the smoke drift out. The distinct odor of farm animals and alfalfa cleansed the air, but the outdoorsy smell soon overwhelmed him. Quite unsophisticated for his cosmopolitan nostrils. Before long, he flipped the window shut.

Route 66 from Chicago to East St. Louis was the first fully paved highway in Illinois. For once, he approved this public expenditure. About time he benefited from his yearly state contributions.

He had to slow down as he passed through each of the many towns dotting the highway. He never spied a police car, but he couldn't chance being stopped for speeding. Practically no one was on the road in the middle of the night in these rural areas. Keeping a watchful eye, he ran the speedometer needle up at every opportunity.

About four in the morning, drowsiness threatened. The happy pills might have kept him awake and empowered for a couple of days. Too bad he didn't have any. He swilled more whiskey. Maybe he could find the pills in Mexico—probably easier to procure there. Might be cheaper too.

At four thirty, George turned on the radio. No matter

what direction he twisted the dial he picked up nothing but static. Figures, in these backwater areas. Slowing to enter Litchfield as eastern light appeared, he spotted a flickering neon sign advertising Varner's Café and Standard Station.

OPEN 24 HOURS.

George desperately needed a pit stop and to stretch his limbs. The gas gauge indicator had been dipping for the last hour. The Lincoln's impressive 368-cubic-inch V-8 engine had plenty of power, but it guzzled fuel like a wino fresh out of the holding tank.

He climbed out of the car and covered his suit with his overcoat. He tipped his fedora forward to shade his eyes, cursing under his breath. His suitcase was full of suits and dress shirts he'd been sneaking out of the house over the last week. Didn't want to create suspicion by taking out too many clothes. Why didn't he pack anything casual? He'd thought of everything else. His regular work suit and overcoat lent anonymity in the big city, but these small-town hicks didn't dress formally. This getup would mark him as an outsider like a giant red arrow pointing at his head.

The next-door café was also open twenty-four hours. While the freshly-uniformed attendant pumped gas, washed the Lincoln's windshield, and emptied the ashtray, George considered breakfast. He wandered over to peek in a window right below the painted words *Air Conditioning.*

The small restaurant displayed none of the high-dollar charm which suited his taste—old and maintenance-neglected despite the modern refrigeration. Probably infested with roaches. The mental image of a filthy men's room made him shiver. He checked his Rolex. 7:54. Best head on. St. Louis was nearby and he would find something more suitable there.

Back on the road, he floored the accelerator to blast by the turn-off sign for Staunton. Wide-open farmlands extended the horizon on either side. Flying through Edwardsville the scenery changed. More and more houses popped onto the scene, then neighborhoods, and finally the imposing MacArthur Bridge across the majestic Mississippi River. From a previous business trip, he recalled a treacherous bend on the St. Louis side.

Even after the reminder, George underestimated the curve. Too fast on the approach, he pounded the brakes and gripped the steering wheel to maintain control. The Continental's nearly-new tires screeched and left a strip of rubber behind but held to the road. He wiped beads of sweat from his brow. With no one driving toward him on the bridge, he used the whole road to maneuver the powerful car. He couldn't keep the grin off his face. Operating this baby was like driving a racecar.

Speeding through St. Louis, a series of signs touted the New Wagon Wheel Restaurant in Cuba as Missouri's newest and most delightful dining spot. The restaurant claimed gourmet food and attentive service.

"Now we're talking."

Steak, eggs, a pot of black coffee. His mouth salivated and his stomach rumbled reminding him he'd skipped dinner.

As he sped into the Ozark Mountains, he passed a series of auto courts and cottage-style motels. Instead of stopping for a few hours' sleep, he swigged from his flask and searched for directions to the Wagon Wheel.

At ten fifteen by the dash clock, stomach woozy with hunger, he turned into the restaurant parking lot. Before leaving the car, he refilled his empty flask with Johnnie Walker. He tipped out a cigarette, and stuffed the Lucky Strike pack in his pocket. Then he slid the cigarette behind one ear. Ready to light up.

The Wagon Wheel appeared tidy and recently decorated with burgundy leather booths that looked comfortable enough. The smell of sizzling bacon activated his salivary glands and made him swallow. Stomach gurgling, George requested a corner booth and then followed a skinny waitress to a seat where he had full view of anyone entering the restaurant—in case someone followed, which no one would.

All the way to the booth, the waitress babbled. He didn't listen, checking out the other diners as he walked. The waitress favored him with a full-toothed grin before handing him a menu. To shut her up, George removed his overcoat and slung it in the booth. Without a glance at her, he plunked onto the seat and lit his cigarette. Opening the folder, he stuck his nose inside.

Puffing until a cloud of smoke swirled overhead, George skimmed past the Duncan Hines travel guide endorsement and perused the breakfast items.

The waitress pranced off, returning a minute later with a pot of coffee.

No time for small talk. Without making eye contact he ordered a hearty plate of eggs and steak. "And keep the coffee coming."

While he waited for his food, George sipped his hot beverage, smoked another cigarette, and cased the restaurant. Very few tables and booths held customers. Not one person dressed in a suit, overcoat, and fedora. He must find a men's store.

Breakfast fulfilled every expectation. He had to remind himself to slow down. Gobbling food would give him indigestion and make additional stops necessary.

Couldn't afford that.

When he finished, George stared at his reflection in the men's room mirror. Stubble grew on his chin, more than a shadow. He'd never considered growing a beard, but this might be the perfect time. A disguise without any effort. Might also give him a certain rugged appeal.

Back on the road, George's full stomach begged for a nap. Innumerable cabins, tourist courts, motels, and resorts with signs promising TVs, quiet restful nights, and modern accommodations taunted him. He stifled a yawn. No time to stop now.

Sun warmed the windshield and interior of the Lincoln as the morning wore on. George twisted the radio dial searching for news—anything to stay awake—but found only annoying country music or static.

The rolling Ozark hills supplied a vista as eye pleasing as a postcard if you liked endless expanses of green. As pleasant as the view was, before long George yawned in boredom. Never understood why some folks preferred the country. To amuse himself, he concentrated on the delights of maneuvering his powerful car, turning all the knobs and trying different combinations with the heating and air conditioning levers on the dash. Didn't need cold air on a day like this or heat either, but the mere luxury filled George with delight.

The Lincoln whizzed into Rolla, Missouri at about twelve forty-five, past another row of motels and travel courts interspersed with restaurants and filling stations.

Mesmerized by a prominent billboard advertising The Bypass Motel & Café, George drifted into the wrong lane. The driver of a farm truck loaded with produce swerved to the right to avoid hitting the Lincoln. A crate of produce tipped off the truck, crash-landing on the pavement. The farmer laid on his horn and glared as he passed, mouthing words George didn't try to comprehend.

The honking jolted George back into his lane. "Idiot," George said, as if the farmer could hear him.

A nagging inner voice urged George to pull in at the next motel for sleep. Instead, he drained his flask. Even with his digesting breakfast, he imbibed enough to supply a buzz. A long yawn magnified his desire to sleep. The verdant scenery went fuzzy. He blinked hard to restore clarity, then depressed the accelerator and flew out of Rolla's tempting clutches.

The speedometer needle ascended like a jet airplane at takeoff. George rubbed his grit-filled eyes. Then he gripped the wheel with both hands to pass both a gray Chevy pickup and a brown Hudson in one long burst of speed. Outside the city limits with no other cars in sight, he floored the gas pedal, thrilled as his speed approached one hundred miles per hour.

A "Sharp Curve Ahead" warning sign registered in his vision as he flew by, but the meaning didn't penetrate his brain until the forty-five-degree turn appeared. Too late, George mashed the brake with all his might, screeching into the curve on two wheels. He wrenched his foot from the pedal. A horrible sinking sensation dropped into his gut.

Too late.

The Lincoln careened out of control.

The steel frame shuddered as George fought to reign in the powerful beast. The car flopped back onto all four tires, rocking the interior like a rowboat in a tropical storm. One chrome hubcap flew over the hood. Spinning with wild abandon, the disk crashed seconds later in a shower of sparks. The mighty Lincoln fishtailed wildly, veering off the gravel shoulder in a blinding cloud of dust. Pebbles spun onto the side of the car like shotgun pellets.

George barely made out a blurry outcropping of sandstone lining the hillside. The left rear fender slammed against it and banged away like a bumper car, grazing a telephone pole on the opposite side of the highway.

The engine roared at deafening intensity. The car pitched left, then right. Had the brakes locked? To test this, George slid his foot off the brake pedal.

The wild ride continued unabated.

Bumping over rocky terrain, the mighty Lincoln raced ahead as if it had acquired a mind of its own. Unrestrained, the car crashed through a barbed wire fence, dragging out several buried fence posts. Wood bashed the sides of the car. Sweat poured from his brow as his white-knuckled hands seized the steering wheel trying to regain control.

With the car jiggling up and down over the rough field, George could not focus. Thick dust limited visibility to a few feet. Out of the dirt cloud a deep ravine appeared too suddenly to swerve. The front end lurched downward with a bone-c runching jolt. The impact hurled him forward into the windshield.

Darkness closed in, punctuated by a final glass-shattering scream.

His own.

9

MABEL

A few miles outside Rolla on Highway 66, Mabel spotted a "Sharp Curve Ahead" sign. Always a conscientious driver, she mashed the Studebaker's brake until her foot cramped. When she could no longer hold the pedal down, she released it and then managed a few more quick pumps. By the time she rounded the bend, the heavy vehicle had decelerated from thirty-five miles an hour to nineteen. The car crept around the curve allowing her to take in an awful accident scene spread across the rural landscape like a gaping wound.

"Dear me." She cupped her cheek with her hand. "The poor driver must've lost control. Maybe he missed that big sign." She clicked her tongue and focused on Stryker. "That's why we must always keep our eyes on the road and obey speed laws."

In the passenger seat, Sophia fell to the floorboard when Stryker pushed to a stand, craning her neck. "Looks like a Lincoln Continental Mark II."

Mabel read a strange hunger in the girl's expressive blue eyes.

"Never seen such a flashy car up close. Can we stop?"

Mabel truly didn't care what kind of car lay strewn across the field in pieces, but an accident of this severity meant someone needed help. People might be seriously injured in the twisted wreckage. Someone might be . . . *Dear Lord, help these unfortunate people. Send aid for them.*

"Please," Stryker wailed. "Stop the car."

"These people could be badly hurt, dear. I'm not a doctor. There's probably nothing we can do. We'll drive on and find someone to help them. Every minute is precious if they're injured."

"No. We should stop."

A small voice in Mabel's head whispered a verse, Philippians 2:4. *Look not every man on his own things, but every man also on the things of others.*

She heaved a mighty sigh. Sometimes she wished she hadn't learned so many Bible verses. At the least, she should investigate.

Mabel steered the cumbersome Studebaker onto the pasture, following the path of smashed weeds where the black car had apparently dragged out the fence. A safe distance off the highway, she braked and turned to Stryker. "I suppose it's my Christian duty to see if I can assist." She shoved her door open. "You stay here. I'll be—"

Stryker didn't wait for the end of Mabel's sentence. Flinging her door ajar, the girl jumped to the lumpy ground and raced toward the wreck, leaving her little monkey behind. Mabel hobbled along with as much speed as she possessed, holding on to her hat with one hand and waving her lace hanky with the other.

"Stryker, wait for me. Slow down, dear."

The thick heels of her driving shoes sank into the loose earth and filled her shoes with dirt. She stopped to pat perspiration off her forehead and catch her breath. "Oh, my goodness. Who knows what we might find in such a bad accident?" *Lord, please don't let the child discover a dead body.* She didn't need to see such a terrible sight. "Stryker . . ."

The pompom atop Stryker's new blue knit hat bobbed up

and down as she ran. Did the child realize she'd left her toy in the car? The toy she said she was supposed to keep with her always. Why wouldn't she stop?

By the time Mabel arrived on the scene, Stryker had already jumped in the ditch. Tiny body bent nearly double, she gawked inside the smashed interior. With the vehicle pitched at an uneven angle, the driver's-side door dangled on its hinges. Shards of jagged glass littered the ground beneath the shattered window.

Mabel's trembling hand covered her racing heart as she peered slowly inside.

The front seat was empty. A flood of sweet relief gushed over her.

But where had the driver gone?

Mabel scanned the wreckage. Steam hissed upward from the boxy front grille, now firmly lodged in the ground. The long hood was bent and twisted. Whitewall tires still spun but appeared to be winding down. A few feet away, a man in a rumpled suit crouched in the dirt, holding his head in his hands. Beside him lay a collapsed hat, tipped on its crown and smudged with blood and filth.

An ugly gash zigzagged across his forehead. Blood dripped from the wound, a rivulet running through his dark hair and down his neck, where it soaked into his clothing.

Nausea rumbled Mabel's stomach. Apprehensive as she was about getting involved in a stranger's mess, she must consider her Christian duty. She exhaled the breath she'd been holding and pressed her lips into a thin line. His laceration would surely require stitches. Why didn't she bring medical supplies along? Doctor Marston had warned about Stryker having nosebleeds.

With so much blood, Mabel conceded the urgency of the situation. Might as well get it over with. She placed one hand on the man's shoulder not covered in blood, wishing again she'd been blessed with the gift of compassion. "You had a nasty accident, mister. Are you okay?"

The man didn't respond.

She bent closer and applied tentative pressure to his shoulder. "Sir? Was anyone in the car with you?"

He didn't answer.

Where had Stryker gone?

When Mabel straightened, she found the girl circling the crash, hands stuck firmly on her thin hips. Captivated by an automobile? Mabel shook her head. What a strange child.

First things first. She squeezed his shoulder. "Can you hear me, sir? Speak." She shook him gently, leaning toward his face. "Were you alone?"

Sluggishly, he raised his head. Bloodshot brown eyes fixed on Mabel without any sign of comprehension. "I'm . . . fine."

Mabel detected the strong odor of alcohol. Had he been drinking when he spun out of control on the curve? Questions for another time perhaps.

She stepped away, pulling off one shoe to dump out dirt. "I'm not a nurse, young man, but I'm certain you need a doctor."

"No." His breath hitched when he shook his head. He brought up one hand and pressed it against his temple. His expression exuded pain. "I'm okay. Nothing to . . . worry about. Be on your way—"

"You're bleeding, sir." She pointed to his head with the second shoe she emptied.

He turned his head to one side and back. "Where?"

Perhaps the man had a brain injury. For sure he needed prompt medical attention. The bleeding might not stop on its own.

Mabel slid her shoe back on her foot and scanned the horizon in all directions. No sign of civilization. No barns, no houses. No other vehicles on this stretch of highway. The next town was miles away. Rescue apparently fell to her.

Heaving a long sigh, Mabel spoke slowly. "Can you stand, sir?" She held her hand out, ready to assist. "If you are able to walk to my car, I'll drive you to a doctor to make sure you're fine."

The stranger opened and closed his eyes a couple of times. "I told you . . . I don't need help."

"Very well, then. Stand up." Mabel wiggled her fingers to indicate her availability should he topple. She adjusted her stance for greater stability. "Come on. Up you go."

After a few seconds, he reached for her hand. His arm shook and his legs wobbled.

Mabel wasn't strong enough to lift him, and he lacked enough strength to pull toward her. "Stryker," she called. "Can you help us?"

Stryker came at once, and Mabel immediately wished she hadn't asked. Such a frail child. Not much stronger than Mabel.

After a few false starts, they worked the stranger to an unsteady stand. His knees quivered, threatening to buckle at any second. Mabel looped her arm around his middle to hold him upright.

When she urged him to walk, he objected. "Wait. Everything . . . I own is . . . Can't . . . leave the—"

"Oh, come now. You're not leaving your stuff forever. I don't think we can get the car out of that ditch right now, and even if we did you wouldn't be able to drive it. You mashed it up pretty good, mister." She hoped her smile would reassure him. "Once the doctor mends you, there will be plenty of time to collect your belongings."

Mabel ignored his steady barrage of objections, concentrating on staying on her feet long enough to propel him to her car. Along with that, she worried about Stryker. The child was sick. She shouldn't be overtaxed no matter what the emergency.

After stopping several times to remind him to cooperate, they resorted to dragging him. Panting, Mabel asked, "Is he too much for you, dear?"

Stryker shook her head, but huffed and puffed as if she couldn't speak, which worried Mabel.

At last they reached the fender of her car and leaned the man against it.

Mabel pressed Stryker's hand on his chest. "Hold him there for a minute or two."

Breath raspy, Stryker nodded, spreading her feet wide apart in the dirt.

"He's losing a lot of blood. Got to bandage his head." Mabel said between pants. She opened the trunk and rifled through the luggage and bedding. "Here's a pillow. That'll do."

She tugged off the pillowcase and folded it into a pad to press on the wound. "Hold this." Then she groped in her suitcase until she found a belt to secure the makeshift dressing. "At least it'll keep him from dripping blood all over the seat."

Mabel opened the back door. With a grunt, she shoved him onto the seat. After more effort, they swung his legs inside and closed the door. She'd have to find some place to wash all this blood out of their clothes and the pillowcase before it set.

Sliding behind the steering wheel, Mabel's heart beat rapidly. "My blood pressure must be sky high," she muttered as Stryker climbed in and slammed the door. "You shouldn't be doing all this heavy work either. We make a fine pair, don't we?"

"Wait," the man said, louder than before.

Mabel and Stryker swiveled their necks to stare at him.

"I . . . need my things . . . my overcoat and hat, my bag, cigarettes . . . especially the box." With his stained sleeve, he wiped a dribble of blood from his brow. "In the trunk. Can't leave them." His hands trembled worse as he became more agitated. "You must . . . important papers . . . can't leave." Apparently, the energy required to communicate this string of words wore him out, because as soon as he finished he dropped his head against the seat and closed his eyes. "Please. I beg you. Get the box," he whispered.

"Surely your things will be fine for a day or so. How about if we stop at the local garage? We'll get someone from town to tow your automobile."

Leaving his belongings simply would not do. No matter how she reasoned, he insisted, becoming increasingly distressed the more she objected.

When it became clear no amount of reason would appease him, Mabel and Stryker tramped back through the plowed field to what was left of the Lincoln. Stryker gathered the overcoat and fedora. To get into the trunk required more muscle than either possessed, but the resourceful child crawled through the once plush interior to a small gap where the back seat had been dislodged. Diligently pushing and pulling the heavy items back and forth by the corners, together they tugged out the box of papers and one suitcase. That would have to do for now. No one needed cigarettes, least of all an injured person.

Mabel spied a partially-empty Johnnie Walker bottle on the seat. A little whiskey might dull his pain. She stuffed the bottle in the box.

The heavy crate tipped over as they trudged back to the Studebaker, distributing file folders and a fat manila envelope on the weedy ground. The wind took some papers flying. Stryker chased down everything she could catch. Nothing could be done about the rest.

Barely able to bend low enough to put her own stockings on, Mabel did not chase papers. Stryker collected most of the spilled contents, stuffing the large envelope into one side of the box where it wouldn't easily fall out again.

Together they hauled the items back to Mabel's trunk. Rearranging the contents took more precious time. By then, the stranger lay slumped across the back seat, eyes closed and body limp. Mabel checked for breathing. Air blowing against her hand confirmed he still lived. She threw his overcoat over him.

"I expect he's sleeping," she said to Stryker as she brushed dust from her skirt. Once behind the steering wheel, she slipped on her driving gloves. "Poor thing. He surely needs to rest." She backed the Studebaker out to the highway.

Face streaked with mud from dirt and perspiration, Stryker appeared much as when Mabel had first seen her at church. "Not making much progress today, are we dear? We already need another bath." Mabel rubbed a spot of dirt off the child's face.

Stryker wrenched away. "Will he die?"

"I don't think so. Perhaps we should pray for him. When I'm afraid, praying always makes me feel better." Eyes on the road, Mabel asked for God's help and healing. After she said "Amen" she patted Stryker's thin knee. "Don't worry. We'll find someone to help him."

For a few miles they rumbled along the rural highway in silence. Then Stryker scrambled onto her knees. Chin resting on the seat back, she kept vigil. Did she think he might die if she took her eyes off him?

When Mabel glanced into the rearview mirror, she noticed a spot of blood growing larger on the outside of the pillowcase. She'd never get that pillowcase clean.

According to the map, Lebanon was the closest town. She hoped to high heavens it had a hospital. If not, they'd have to hurry on to Springfield as fast as possible. Perhaps she'd even have to drive over the legal speed limit.

"Ma'am?"

Mabel peered into wide blue eyes as turbulent as a stormy sea.

Stryker's voice trailed out thin and whispery. "He's dripping blood all over the seat."

10

STRYKER

Perched on her knees in the front seat, Stryker studied the stranger. Even caked with dried blood his face was still pretty. From under the pillowcase, thick, root-beer-colored hair curled. Mama would call him handsome. Dark eyes like she preferred. She'd say, "I likes 'em dark, like coffee."

A whisper of longing whooshed in and then out again almost as soon as it occurred. Most days she didn't care that Mama was gone, but every so often she remembered something special and a lonesome little hankering would skip through her heart. Not having Mama around, she didn't have to account for her comings and goings. Being on the streets gave you freedom. That's what all the kids said. No one to boss you around. No one to clean up after when they got sick. No one to hit you if you said something they didn't like.

She stole a guilty peek at Mrs. Crowley, watching how straight and proper she sat with her funny little green hat balanced sideways on her head. Mrs. Crowley wasn't like most grown-ups. Stryker frowned. Sure, she insisted everything be done proper-like, but she didn't yell and curse. She was different, softer.

Stryker rested her chin on the back of the seat. Who was he? Must be well-heeled. Lincolns cost a pile of money. Everyone said so. When she'd ogled the inside of his fancy car, she'd inhaled a delicious new leather smell mixed with the gasoline and burning oil. Stryker never saw a more wonderful machine.

The man groaned. Stryker stiffened, alert. Was he waking up?

He moved his head to the other side, dislodging the belt holding the blood-soaked pillowcase in place. The trickle from his head wound had slowed to an occasional drip. While she watched, a big red drop plopped onto the seat.

She turned to inform Mrs. Crowley. "He's still bleeding."

"Oh, dear. Blood stains will be hard to get out." The old woman gave the rearview mirror a quick glance. "But I'm going as fast as I legally can. I think we're almost to Lebanon."

A long time passed. Still no town in sight.

Mrs. Crowley straightened and craned her neck. "Look at the sign ahead. How many miles to Lebanon?"

Stryker looked where Mrs. Crowley directed, but the sign made no sense to her. She shrugged as it passed from view. "I can't read it."

Mrs. Crowley's brow furrowed. "What do you mean, sugar plum?"

Stryker hitched one shoulder.

"You mean you didn't see the sign or you don't know how to read?"

"Can't read."

"Mercy! We'll have to do something about that."

Stryker tilted her head. "Why?"

Another quick frown before Mrs. Crowley stared back at the highway. "There are so many wonderful books to read, dear. Reading takes you anyplace you want to go. You can explore the whole world in the pages of books. After you're grown . . ." She didn't finish her sentence, but her voice went wobbly as it dropped off. Did she have a tear in her eye?

Mrs. Crowley sniffed and fished another handkerchief

out of her jacket pocket. "Well, never mind. There'll be plenty of time for learning to read, I'm sure."

Stryker returned to her observation post, wondering about the everlasting supply of hankies in Mrs. Crowley's sleeves and pockets.

A few more miles rolled under the Studebaker's fat tires before the stranger groaned and blinked his eyes open. He struggled to sit but couldn't. "What . . . where . . ."

"He's waking up," Stryker reported without turning her head.

Mrs. Crowley spoke louder, her voice calm. "Sir. Please lie still. You had a bad accident. We're taking you to a hospital. I think we're almost to Lebanon."

"No. *No!*" He wailed. "Can't—"

"Now, now. You're going to be all right," Mrs. Crowley continued. "Don't get yourself worked up. You need rest. We got some of your things out of your trunk, so you needn't worry. We'll get you to a doctor as soon as we can."

He thrashed back and forth and then whimpered, gripping his pillowcased head with both hands. "What happened?"

"You crashed your Lincoln Mark II." Stryker interjected. "Didn't you notice the curve in the road?"

His voice hitched. "What curve?"

"You musta been sleeping, mister. That curve was a doozy." She shook her head. "Too bad about your Lincoln though. What a beauty! Are you rich?"

"For shame, child. That's not a polite question." The stern tone of Mrs. Crowley's voice made Stryker lower her eyes for a moment.

When she peered into the back seat again, the man was studying her with one eye opened a slit. "Why do you ask?"

"Your car. I never seen a new Lincoln Continental Mark II before. Heard of 'em, though. What a car. Bet it cost a fat bundle. Probably more than a Cadillac."

He shuddered as he dropped his eyelid.

Stryker had plenty more questions. "How fast can you go in that thing?"

"Let the poor fellow rest."

His eyes remained closed, but his voice gained energy. "Fast. Lots of power. Passed sixty-five in over a minute. Got the speedometer over a hundred on straightaways."

Stryker grinned. "Wish I could ride in it. Got to ride in a Cadillac before, but it weren't new like yours. I like your Lincoln better."

"Humph," he mumbled. "What do you know?"

"I know cars," she straightened her backbone, trying to appear taller. "Try me. Next one what comes along, I'll give you make and model."

"Sure thing." He turned his head to the opposite side. When he swung his gaze back, he peered through slits. "The box. Where—"

"In the trunk. One of your suitcases too."

Eyelids dropped like a curtain over his glazed brown eyes. Maybe he was sleeping.

Soon the highway became smoother and Stryker could see a town come into view.

"Lebanon at last," Mrs. Crowley breathed. "Now to find the hospital. Sometimes they have signs to point the way. Stryker, dear. Keep watch for a hospital sign."

Obediently Stryker scooted to the side window where she could see better. "What does one look like?"

"I forgot you can't read." Sigh. "Oh, well. There's a filling station ahead. Perhaps they can give us directions." Grasping the steering wheel with both hands, Mrs. Crowley turned the sedan off the highway into the station. An attendant in a clean uniform hurried to meet them and waved the Studebaker into a space next to the tall gas pumps.

Mrs. Crowley rolled down her window. "Thank you, young man. I don't need fuel right now. We happened upon an accident up the road, and the driver needs medical attention. We've got him in the back seat." She indicated with a head point. "Does Lebanon have a hospital?"

The attendant scratched his head, dislodging his creased cap. "Got ol' Doc Adams. He's out at the other end of town. After you pass the Munger Moss Motel. Has a real big sign. If you stay on the highway you can't miss it." He pushed back his sleeve to check his wristwatch. "It's nigh on one o'clock. Doc oughta be back from lunch by now."

"*Nooo*," the man whined from the back seat.

Where'd that come from? Stryker stared at the stranger.

He struggled to sit again but managed nothing more than raising himself on one elbow. "No doctor. I'm fine. Find someone to fix my car. Then I can get on the road."

Mrs. Crowley looked puzzled. To the attendant she said, "He's awfully concerned about the fancy vehicle he drove into a ditch a little while ago. Perhaps you'd be so good as to direct us to someone with a tow truck. If we take care of that matter quickly, maybe he'll let us take him to the doctor."

"Sure, ma'am. We got a tow truck out back." The attendant dug a small pad of paper and a chewed off pencil out of his hip pocket. "Where'd you leave the vehicle?"

Mrs. Crowley spoke so low Stryker had to strain to hear. "He missed the bad curve right after you leave Rolla even though a huge sign warns you—"

"Turner's Corner." The attendant shook his head. "Wish I had a nickel for every vehicle missed that sign." As he noted the location, he continued chattering. "They oughta make the sign bigger or put neon on it or something. 'Course you couldn't see neon in the daytime." He peered in the back seat. "What kinda car, mister?"

The man opened his mouth, but Stryker answered for him. "A Lincoln Continental Mark II, black and shiny new."

The attendant whistled. "Ain't never seen one of them around these parts. Saw one in a magazine once. Think President Eisenhower drives a Mark II. When he drives." The man bowed over his writing pad. "Name?"

Stryker couldn't answer that question. The stranger moved his lips then closed his mouth. Had he forgotten his own name? Maybe he hurt his brain like Mrs. Crowley said.

Seemed like forever before his eyelids fluttered a few times and opened. "Morelli." He said with no more hesitation. "Vince Morelli."

"Address?"

"Just say St. Louis. Can't be many Morellis around here with a Lincoln." Strain showing on his face, he groaned as he pushed himself to a sitting position. "I'll stay with it until you're done."

Eyebrows raised, the attendant straightened. "Sure, I guess that'll do."

Mrs. Crowley pursed her lips. "Let the doctor decide if you're able to stay, Mr. Manicotti. First things first. We need to wash this blood off our hands and clothes, but I suppose we can do that at the clinic. We should get going." She leaned her head out the window. "Do you need anything else, young man?"

The attendant slapped the pad shut. "Nope. We'll get the tow truck out right away." He grinned, adding a quick gesture to indicate the exit.

Mrs. Crowley rolled up the window and pulled the steering wheel left. The heavy auto lumbered back on the highway. "Now, Mr. Macaroni, let's get you patched up."

"The name is Morelli." His tone sounded prickly.

"Right."

Storefronts and businesses in downtown Lebanon rolled by as Mrs. Crowley introduced herself and Stryker. Over the next few minutes, she explained they were taking Stryker to California to a special doctor.

"California?" Mr. Morelli grunted. "Pretty far for a doctor. Why not find someone to treat her in St. Louis?" One hand pressed his forehead. "What's wrong with her?"

They were talking about her like she wasn't there. Stryker squeezed her lips together, mentally crossing her arms.

Mrs. Crowley paid no attention to Stryker's disapproval. Why was Mrs. Crowley taking so long to answer this question? Stryker wondered about the same thing. St. Louis had plenty of doctors and hospitals. Why go so far away to find a different one? She hugged Sophia closer. Not that she had the slightest idea how far California might be. She didn't know much about doctors or hospitals either. Other than Doctor Marston, she'd never met a real one before—nearby or far away. And she wasn't looking forward to meeting any new ones.

Mrs. Crowley swallowed before speaking. "She's a very sick girl. Few hospitals in this country treat the kind of sickness she has. My doctor in St. Louis arranged for her to be evaluated at a big teaching hospital in Los Angeles. We're going out there as quickly as we can." She patted Stryker's knee. "Then Stryker will get well and have lots of energy to play like a normal girl." Her shaky smile looked a bit crooked.

Stryker narrowed her eyes. So Mrs. Crowley didn't consider her normal? Why had she glanced away? Usually when people looked away, it was because they weren't telling the truth.

"What's wrong with me?"

Mrs. Crowley reached for the hanky tucked into her sleeve and dabbed at her eyes. "Doctor Marston gave your sickness a long name. You've probably never heard it before. The important thing to remember is his friend in Los Angeles knows exactly how to help you."

"What's the long word?"

For a while, Mrs. Crowley bit her lip and stared at the road. A tear formed in her eye. Finally she spoke. "Acute myelogenous leukemia." The words came out shaky like this was a very bad thing.

Mr. Morelli arched his eyebrows.

Blinking, Stryker tried to make sense of what Mrs. Crowley said. It was a big word. 'Normous, the kids would say. She tried it out in her head. Cute mylognus loo . . . Wasn't cute a word used for puppies?

Mrs. Crowley changed the subject. "So, Mr. Spaghetti. What brings you to Rolla today? Are you on a business trip?"

Stryker rolled her eyes. Why couldn't Mrs. Crowley remember his name? Stryker hunkered over the seat to catch his response.

Mr. Morelli's gaze darted out the window like he'd been caught with stolen goods. The next instant he swung his feet onto the floor and sat forward like a person who might run if he got the chance.

"Actually, I'm on vacation. Left St. Louis on the way to visit my . . . younger brother in . . . Texas. Houston. Haven't

THE ROAD TO TERMINUS

seen him for a long time. I'm anxious to get there." He gripped the door handle.

His glance bounced between the back of Mrs. Crowley's head and Stryker's stare. Those brown eyes flashed with something Stryker had seen many times before. She cocked her head, listening with care. She couldn't imagine why, but no doubt about it.

The stranger was lying.

88

11

GEORGE

In the passenger seat of the clunky Studebaker sedan, George fingered his bandaged head while Mrs. Crowley drove. Even tiny pressure from his touch ignited searing pain and set his head to throbbing. The country bumpkin who stitched his forehead had been quick, but not much else recommended him. Zero charm and personality. Probably not qualified to practice medicine in the big city. He'd seen dirt embedded in the clinic floor. An offensive odor like rotten antiseptic hadn't improved George's opinion.

Imagine a town so small they didn't have a taxi. Good thing the Crowley woman agreed to wait while the doc patched him up. Gave her time to wash up and change clothes, she said. The blood stains worried her. Crazy like. Schmoozing her with gratitude helped. She accepted his offer of cash for her time without much coaxing. Everyone had a price. He congratulated himself on pinpointing Mabel Crowley's. Now if only the old gal would remember his made-up name. She'd mispronounced it so many times he feared he might forget it himself.

The ancient Studebaker's cracked seats and splitting dash

weren't the only parts lacking modernity. The thing had no power. No modern gadgets at all. Didn't even have a radio. Plus the interior smelled like the old folks' home where he'd visited his grandfather for the final time. The tedious rhythm of tires slapping pavement would have lulled him to sleep but for the growing anticipation of reclaiming his Lincoln.

George checked the speedometer. Mrs. Crowley held the speed steady at thirty-five. His shoulders raised and lowered as he expelled a long sigh. "You can drive a little faster, you know."

"Speed limit says thirty-five. Maximum," she answered without glancing in his direction.

The kid in the back sat forward. "See the green pickup ahead of us? It's a 1951 Ford."

"Easy." George cocked his head. "Says Ford in big letters on the tailgate. But what says it's a '51?"

"Bigger window in the back. Has to be '51 or '52."

He grunted. "Good guess."

"Not a guess. I told you. I know cars. Pick one and try me."

A blue-and-white four-door sedan passed on the left as they rolled away from the next stop sign. "Okay. That one."

"1954 Chevrolet Bel Air." Stryker held her head high, pale eyes glittering.

"Not fair; you read the words off the side."

Mrs. Crowley threw a cold response over her glasses. "She can't read."

"How'd you know then?"

Stryker's smile widened. "Chevrolet changed the grille and headlights in 1954. Did you see the way it passed us? The newer model also has more power than the '53 did."

He arched an eyebrow. "Where'd you learn that stuff?"

All conversation ended when Mrs. Crowley veered into the filling station.

The mangled remains of the once-magnificent Lincoln had been dumped to the side of the station like a pile of scrap metal. The sight of what was left of the elegant car made a lump form in his throat. How would they ever put her back together? Such a miracle would take more time and money than he could afford. Plus, what mechanic would guarantee she'd drive the same after being rebuilt? Better to buy another vehicle. Save time too. Would this hole in the wall have a car dealership?

"Well, Mr. Rigatoni," Mrs. Crowley was saying. "Here you are."

George opened the passenger door, set one foot on the pavement and froze.

Three men stood near the Lincoln gesturing at the vehicle. One looked familiar. A chill shot up his backbone like a lightning bolt. The distinctive gray Stetson—Matthew Alton, the Texas detective who had invaded his office to serve the subpoena.

Impossible. How did Alton get way out here? The feds couldn't be on his trail yet. He only left town yesterday.

From this angle, George couldn't see more than their backs. Judging by the one-piece uniform, the man on the left must be the tow truck driver. Who were the other two? Why were they examining his car? George couldn't afford to stick around and ask questions.

He hauled his foot back inside the Studebaker and tugged the door closed. "Say, Mrs. Crowley. It appears that my Lincoln is beyond repair. How about if I ride with you two a little longer? You've got a long drive ahead. I can spell you with the driving so you can rest along the way. I'll chip in for fuel too. What do you think?"

The old woman blinked rapidly. "What about your car? You can't leave it here. That wouldn't be right."

"Hey. They'll sell the metal if I don't claim it. Save me the trouble of junking it. Nobody loses. See for yourself. The damage is beyond repair. How about if I pay for *all* the fuel for your trip?" He turned his overcoat collar up to shield his face and motioned for her to leave the station.

"I don't think—"

"Drive on, ma'am."

Her grim expression reproached him.

"Look, I don't have time to bother with this wreck right

now. Didn't say so before, but about my brother in, uh, Austin
. . . He needs to move pronto, and I gotta get there to help. Has
a bad back and can't do it alone. After that I must hurry back
to St. Louis. Several important deals are in the works. If you
don't want me along on your trip, I'll buy another car in Springfield and be on my way."

"You're in no shape to help anyone move furniture."

Stryker spoke up before he responded. "I thought you said
your brother lives in Houston."

George mashed his lips together. Figures he'd get mixed
up with a little brat who never forgot anything. "Did I say
Houston?" He managed a fake chuckle. "Not Houston. Must
have been the accident talking. My brother lives in Austin."

Mrs. Crowley's brow wrinkled. "Leaving the car without a
word of explanation is not right."

George half heard her complaint. Another obstacle had
occurred to him—the registration. Permanent license plates
hadn't arrived yet for his new Lincoln, but a temporary registration certificate was nestled in the glove box. George's
stomach went queasy. The feds would know he'd been here.

He must get out of Missouri fast. Letters and phone calls
going back and forth might take days, maybe weeks before all
the paperwork passed between here and Chicago. Plenty of
time to get to Mexico and disappear. Traveling with Crowley
and the kid was a great bit of luck. Who would guess George
Stanton left Lebanon in an old Studebaker?

The more he considered the idea of the feds trying to
figure how the Lincoln got mangled and abandoned in Lebanon, the more he appreciated the irony—another loose end
meant more headaches for Gloria and the partners. He'd have
smiled if not for the pain.

Body rigid, Mrs. Crowley stared out the windshield.

"Not to worry." He said, forcing a more benevolent tone.
"I'll make it right. On my way back through, I'll pay the garage
owner for his time and inconvenience. I promise. Right now, I
need to go to Texas." He leaned forward. "Get a move on."

Her gloved hands tapped the steering wheel a couple of
times before she shifted into gear and drove back onto the

highway in a wide arc. "Doesn't seem honest." The scowl on her face carried over to her posture. "Maybe you aren't thinking clearly, young man, even though the doctor said you show no signs of a concussion. Still, with—"

"I said I'd take care of it."

The infuriating woman didn't respond verbally, but her demeanor clearly communicated intense disapproval. Exactly what he needed, another conscience.

He knew she wasn't completely on board with this idea, but he managed to convince her to continue. The Studebaker lumbered out of Lebanon headed toward Springfield.

George's fingers trembled as he extracted his Zippo and Lucky Strikes from his inner pocket. He shook out a cigarette. Head bent to light up, he caught Mrs. Crowley's disgust in his peripheral vision.

"What do you think you're doing, young man?" Indignation oozed between her words.

He sucked in a soothing drag of smoke before answering. "What's it look like?"

"I don't allow smoking in my car."

George glowered. Was this abuse worth having her for a cover, even for a short distance? "You do now." Fleetingly, he considered bailing out of the infernal vehicle. Rather be almost anywhere else than stuck in this ancient excuse for an automobile with this irksome woman.

"At least open the window. Blow your smoke outside, if you must."

George obliged, rolling down the window a couple of inches. The ensuing gust of wind carried the smoke back inside. "Happy?"

Stryker coughed.

Mrs. Crowley's gaze jerked to the mirror. "How about you? Does it give you pleasure to make a sick child cough?"

After inhaling another long smoke, George made a dramatic show of tossing the barely-smoked cigarette out and rolling the window back up. He'd have to come up with a better way to get his mind off the aches and pains he suffered from being tossed about the cab of the Lincoln.

Not until that moment did he remember he'd left the crate of Johnnie Walker along with his cartons of Lucky Strikes. Sure could use a painkiller. Under his breath, he cursed the thugs who stole his happy pills.

Shifting to a more comfortable position, he winced. Every single muscle in his body hurt. His neck ached, his back too. Jolting in this old bucket of bolts didn't help either. The shock absorbers must be shot. However would he manage to ride for miles on end?

Mentally, he began planning a shopping expedition. So many things he needed—top of the list a new vehicle. Also casual clothes, whiskey, and cigarettes. Luckily, at the doctor's clinic he located the envelope with his stash and withdrew a couple thousand dollars, which he folded into a big wad and stuffed into the inner pocket of his suit.

Alton's presence at the garage niggled at the back of his mind. Didn't make a lick of sense. He'd left a tangled mess behind in Chicago. They couldn't have sorted through it already. He'd been planning this getaway for a long time. Reviewing his movements of the past few days, he commended himself for taking every possible precaution. How did they locate his Lincoln so quickly?

Must be a coincidence. Couldn't have been Matthew Alton. Other men wore Open Road Stetsons. The G-man said they were popular in Texas. Or perhaps George imagined seeing Alton. Might have a small concussion after all, enough to cause hallucinations.

George slowly turned his head to see the road behind them, but even his careful movement jabbed his neck and shoulders with excruciating pain. His hand reflexively braced his smarting neck. Why didn't auto manufacturers include mirrors on the right side as standard equipment so everyone could see behind without turning around?

Anyone suspicious following them? Should have taken note of the other vehicles at the filling station. Maybe the whiz kid would remember.

Stryker sat stiff as a corpse in the back seat, clutching her stuffed toy to her chest. Her inquisitive gaze bore into the back of his head.

"Hey." He tried to lighten his tone. "Let's play the car game, okay?" The twisting movement had made his neck ache.

The girl slid forward, her eager face waiting. "Sure."

"Picture the filling station in your mind."

She nodded, tilting her head.

"How many cars did you see, not counting the pile of junk that used to be mine? Bet you can't remember."

Stryker tilted her head the other way, staring at the ceiling liner. "Three others, I think." Her glance connected with his. "Right?"

"Pretty good, kid. Now the hard part. What were they? Make and year."

A broad grin replaced her questioning gaze. "Not hard at all. At the gas pump was a blue Mercury . . . '52. A 1950 mist-green Chevrolet pickup came in minutes after we got there. And, um, parked on the same side as your Lincoln was a '53 Buick Roadmaster. Black and shiny."

"By golly, you *do* know cars."

"I got it right then?"

George produced the A-OK sign with his fingers and flinched when he peered out the back window.

The Chevy directly behind was white.

A sparkly black sedan followed. From his vantage point, it had the same front grille as a Buick.

A bead of sweat trickled down his head and off his chin.

While he blinked in disbelief, the black sedan slowed and turned off the highway at the first street in Springfield. Relief flooded over George like soothing salve, but in that moment he acknowledged a simple fact—he had no choice but to continue the journey with Crowley and the sick girl. If someone followed him—and suddenly he realized such a preposterous assumption was possible given all the people who might be searching for him—he had a far greater chance of getting away if he traveled with an old woman and a child than if he made the trip alone.

12

MABEL

Through gritted teeth, Mabel endured the interminable drive. By concentrating on other things, she tolerated the stranger's tiresome grousing about his problems. She drove too slowly. He needed a cigarette, a drink. His head hurt. Endless reminiscing about his wonderful vehicle, comparing it to the run-down Studebaker. People took what they wanted, didn't keep their word, on and on and on. She tried to let her mind meander where it would.

During the first leg of the trip, the promise of his departure in Springfield kept her from wailing, but when they entered Springfield city limits, he ordered her to drive on through.

In her best no-nonsense tone, she questioned him about his plans, but all he would say was he wanted to stay with them all the way to Texas. He repeated his promise to buy another automobile as soon as they arrived in the Lone Star state. When he offered to pay, she gave in. Not because she relished the thought of traveling so far with such a disagreeable person, but because gas prices proved to be higher than she anticipated. She must make the money last all the way to California.

Springfield sprawled across many miles with multi-storied buildings dotting the downtown area. She'd never been here before. Too bad they couldn't do any sightseeing.

The Studebaker made good time, old car that it was, crossing the Kansas border well before dinner. They stopped to refill in Galena at Kan-O-Tex filling station and grabbed a bite to eat at the Main Street Deli. Then the tiresome fellow had the nerve to insist they get back on the road. Every muscle in Mabel's body ached from sitting so long. Her knees had stiffened and her back throbbed, but she climbed in the driver's seat and drove onto Route 66 for the short journey through Kansas into Oklahoma.

Over the Neosho River Bridge heading into Afton, they passed a sign for the Buffalo Ranch. Mabel didn't mention the tourist attraction to Stryker. The child would want to stop and gawk at the fifteen-hundred-pound creature advertised on the billboard.

Incessant hours of banter between What's-his-name and Stryker concerning every make and model car or truck running along the roads of America droned on until at last Stryker sprawled across the back seat and fell asleep.

A sign whizzed past showing Oklahoma City still over two hundred miles away. Mabel could keep silent no longer. "Is it your intention to drive through the night? Because I'm not certain I have strength to do that."

"Just a couple more hours." He glanced sideways at Mabel. "Even in this old bucket of bolts, we can make Tulsa with no trouble."

Insulting the Studebaker didn't endear him to Mabel, but she pressed on.

A few minutes after ten, they rolled into Tulsa. Darkness constrained them like a nun's habit as they searched for lodging. When Mabel spotted a vacancy sign in front of the Oasis Motel, she veered onto the asphalt driveway leading to the office.

Out the side window, he scanned the long, low string of connected rooms then glared at her as she prepared to turn off the engine. "Not this one." His voice approached a tyrannical tone.

Mabel quit groping for the key. "What?"

"Keep going." He motioned toward the highway.

"Why?" Mabel lowered her head to scrutinize the establishment. Floodlights illuminated the main office building. With her headlamps, she couldn't make out much beyond the front. "This seems perfectly fine, and the vacancy sign is on."

He shook his head, frowning. "Too old and run-down. Find something nicer."

"*Nicer* means more expensive, Mr. Macaroni."

"Morelli," he corrected. "I'm not staying in a dump. I'll pay for the rooms."

Mabel squeezed her lips tight lest an unchristian retort slip out. Proverbs 17:22 tapped across her mind like tickertape. *A merry heart doeth good like a medicine.* She exhaled an exasperated breath through her nose. "Fine."

She reversed and then jammed the shift into first, although she was far from success at working up cheerfulness. Grinding gears screeched protest. The heavy vehicle rumbled out to the highway. She couldn't imagine being too puffed up to stay in a perfectly fine motel. Prideful. She tsk-tsked. Who did he think he was?

A minute ticked by in vexing silence.

Then two. They passed the Tulsa Ranch-0-Tel, the Flamingo Motel, the Will Rogers Motor Court, but Mr. Uppity chose none of those perfectly appropriate establishments. In less than ten minutes, they had entered downtown Tulsa where churches that looked like castles, tall offices buildings, and banks surrounded them. Traffic was heavier and Mabel drove with careful deliberation.

"Perhaps we were too hasty, Mr. Macaroni." Mabel refused so much as a peek his way, afraid she might not be able to refrain from slinging darts. "Doesn't appear the downtown area has many—"

"There," he said all of a sudden. "Pull in at the front." He pointed to The Mayo, an imposing multi-storied stone building, surely the grandest hotel in Tulsa in size if not in style.

"Here?" Mabel sized the building up as she slowed the Studebaker. "This is a fancy hotel."

"Exactly."

Reluctantly, Mabel steered to the entrance where her passenger gave the doorman the once-over.

"Wait here." He jumped out and opened the trunk. Grabbing his overcoat, he hefted the luggage onto the sidewalk. A few bills changed hands before he hopped back in the car. "Now find a place to stow this clunker."

Stryker roused from sleep as Mabel fussed over locating a parking space. "Where are we?"

No one answered.

With the vehicle safely parked a block from the hotel, Mabel switched off the ignition and turned to Stryker. "Mr. Maletti wants to stay in an elegant hotel tonight. It is quite generous of him to pay for our room. Think of this as an adventure. Be a good girl now and gather your belongings."

Stryker tugged the knit cap over her bald head and scooped up Sophia while the stranger retrieved his box of papers from the trunk.

Inside the huge lobby, the doorman had neatly stacked their luggage to the side of the front door. Curious stares followed the trio as they entered the exquisitely-appointed reception area with its checkered marble floor. What a sight they must be. Single file, they trailed between round columns, up several steps to the polished cherry check-in counter. Stryker lingered, running her fingers over the ornate furnishings.

Such opulence overwhelmed Mabel. For once in her life she had no words. She listened as their benefactor requested two rooms for the night. When the clerk quoted the cost of each her jaw dropped and her chest clenched, but Mr. Morelli did not flinch. From an inner pocket, he withdrew a huge roll of bills and peeled off the required amount.

Woozy, Mabel sank into a nearby plush chair. One night's stay in this palace equaled a month of her meager stipend from her husband's pension.

He completed the transaction then turned to Mabel with a key nestled in the palm of his extended hand. "I requested adjacent rooms." Without another word, he turned toward the bank of elevators.

"Mr. Spaghetti." Mabel stood, hand on her chest. "You forgot your bags."

He kept walking, carrying his box close. "The bellman will bring them."

On the way up to the sixth floor in the elevator, Stryker's blue eyes grew wider and wider, but she kept a tight grip on Mabel's hand. Silence prevailed.

"Sixth floor," chimed the uniformed operator. The doors rolled open and the three stepped onto a landing with cushy carpeting and a hallway leading in either direction. Mr. Morelli charged ahead as if he owned the place.

Halfway down the corridor to the left, they located the rooms.

"Here we are." He shoved his key in the door lock. "I'll be ready to leave by eight."

"Eight," Mabel repeated.

"Meet you downstairs at the restaurant." He pushed the door open, hurried inside as fast as a person carrying a heavy box could, and slammed the door behind him.

The adjacent room radiated elegance from the oriental carpet to the sumptuous pillows and coverlets on the beds. Heavy floor-length curtains veiled the view, but Stryker pushed one aside to peek out. Forehead pressed against the window, she spoke without turning around. "There are miles of lights. The cars look like toys on the street. Come and see."

Mabel had already removed her shoe. Seated on one of the single beds, she massaged her swollen ankle. "Maybe tomorrow, dear. I'm so tired right now."

Stryker wandered back to her. "I never slept in a hotel before."

"As I said, think of this as an adventure. We're not likely to repeat this extravagance. I cannot believe how much money such a room costs." She surveyed the tasteful paintings and polished furniture. "Whatever possessed him to pick this hotel? He wasn't at all surprised by the price of the room. Do you suppose he truly *is* someone important?"

"Must be very rich. The car he crashed cost more than half a dozen of yours." Stryker wandered into the adjoining bathroom. "This room is bigger than your bedroom."

The sparkling-white tiled bathroom did not disappoint. Neither did a leisurely soak in the large porcelain tub, which relaxed Mabel's sore muscles. A half hour later when she crawled between crisp, smooth sheets, Stryker was already asleep in the other bed. Among the palatial surroundings her little face looked positively angelic. So endearing.

Mabel smiled. A bald angel.

Up and dressed by seven, Stryker thoroughly explored the hotel room, opening every drawer and closet. Riding down the elevator in the light of day with a well-rested child proved beyond taxing. Stryker seemed compelled to poke and prod every surface, peer out every window, examine every gadget from the room to the lobby. By the time they reached the dining room, Mabel longed for a nap.

Seated on an overstuffed banquette, Mabel examined the girl over the top of her glasses. "Really, Stryker. You must settle down. We'll order food and wait patiently. Our friend will be along shortly and he won't want us to dawdle."

Elegant people spoke in hushed tones while a string quartet played background music. Silver clinked daintily on china plates. Gentlemen and ladies dabbed their lips with linen napkins. A bevy of waiters in starched white coats stood ready to fulfill every whim.

A glittering chandelier dominated the dining hall ceiling. Large original paintings in ornate frames adorned the walls. Stryker could hardly sit still, but Mabel reminded her to be polite. This required further explanation, which Mabel provided. By the time the bacon, eggs, and toast arrived Stryker was pouting, but the sight and smell of the steaming plates revived her and she ate voraciously.

Mr. Morelli appeared at the dining room door at precisely eight, overcoat folded over one arm and lugging his box of important papers. He had dressed in another blue suit and looked quite businesslike, except that he had neglected to shave. Perhaps some injury from the crash precluded the cutting of facial hair, but Mabel couldn't imagine what that might be. If not for the bandage covering a large portion of his head, no one would guess he'd so recently been involved in a serious accident.

When he spied them, he hurried over and slid beside Mabel. "Good. You're already here." He snapped his fingers for a waiter. "Bring me a cup of coffee, toast, two poached eggs, and half a grapefruit."

With a tip of his head the waiter rushed off, returning soon with a china cup and saucer in one hand and a silver carafe in the other. They ate without much conversation. Stryker gawked at people, and Mabel frowned at Mr. Morelli who appeared oblivious.

After Mr. Morelli paid the bill, they returned to the parking place. Mabel and Stryker toted their luggage. A uniformed bellboy followed behind, pushing the remaining suitcase and box in a cart. After the young man loaded the trunk, Mr. Morelli gave him a tip. Mabel couldn't tell how much, but the bellboy appeared quite pleased. Must have been generous.

Closing the trunk, Mr. Morelli announced, "I'll drive today."

What an irritating chap. Mabel considered arguing about the wisdom of this decision, given he had recently suffered head trauma, but decided not to challenge him. The day before had been long for a woman her age. In spite of getting a good night's sleep, her back and legs ached. She did not relish driving another day.

A mile or so from the hotel, Mr. Morelli made a right turn at a stop light and parked the Studebaker in front of a posh menswear store. "The bellman told me about this place. I need a few items for the trip."

Before Mabel could manage a retort, he had rushed into the shop. "We'll wait right here then," she said without turning to Stryker in the back seat. "I'm sure he won't be long."

When he emerged, he had exchanged the suit for a blue plaid open-collar shirt and pleated casual pants. Across his shoulders he slung a dark blue-striped sweater. Very country club. He had changed shoes too. The effect was transforming—he now looked like a prince on vacation. His chestnut hair would have lent his face an attractive quality had it not been for the bandage and purplish puffed skin on his face. If he weren't so disagreeable, Mabel might have considered him handsome in a dark sort of way, despite his injuries.

She sniffed as he opened the trunk and deposited bags and boxes emblazoned with the haberdashery logo. Why did he need more clothes?

"Well, well," she said when he climbed into the driver's side. "You found a lot to buy in a short time. Why do you need all those?"

He grunted and started the ignition. Questioning him seemed pointless.

Out of Tulsa in a blistering flash, they sped over the 11th Street bridge across the Arkansas River headed to Oklahoma City. Speed signs blurred. The Studebaker had never been driven at such velocity. Never.

Stryker squealed. "Wheeeee!"

"Watch your speed, Mr. Manilla," Mabel protested. "You don't want a ticket."

He glowered and depressed the gas pedal. "The name's Morelli. Can't you remember that?"

"I declare," Mabel huffed and crossed her arms.

The faster he accelerated, the more the frame shimmied and rattled. The old Studebaker couldn't possibly continue at this breakneck speed.

Stryker rolled down her window and stuck her head out. "Yeeeeah."

Mabel's blood pressure elevated as she wondered about this stranger. They knew so little. Rich and reckless. He had enough money to buy another vehicle. Why did he insist on riding with them? She didn't believe the story about the brother in Houston. Or Austin. Where was he going in such a hurry? He acted as if he was running away from something or someone. Might explain his change of clothing. Mabel gripped the armrest. Unless he wrecked this car too, she'd have hours to consider possible explanations.

That's when she heard the siren.

Turning, she peered out the back window, trying to see around Stryker's bobbing head.

Red light blazing on top, a police car appeared behind them.

Mr. Morelli switched lanes to pass a white sedan.

Hand to her throat, Mabel's gaze flitted between Mr. Morelli and the approaching squad car. "I told you not to speed, but you—"

"Shut up." Mr. Morelli glowered into the rearview mirror. "He's not coming for me."

But he was.

13

STRYKER

At first Stryker thought Mr. Morelli might try to outrun the police car. A current of excitement electrified her whole body. Up on her knees, she blinked at the speedometer, watching the needle tick higher—fifty miles an hour, fifty-five, sixty. Did he think he was still driving the Lincoln? The engine shuddered and misfired. She looked out the back window to see a plume of black smoke shoot from the exhaust. Stryker rolled her eyes. This tired old Studebaker couldn't outrun a bicycle.

The police light flashed red and the siren wailed as Mr. Morelli finally pulled off the road. Dust billowed around them. Stryker strained to see out the window, hoping to get a glimpse of the policeman as he exited his black-and-white 1954 Ford. Bet it was equipped with the big Mercury engine for extra power. If only she could get a look under the hood.

Out of the dust cloud, a frozen-faced officer appeared on the driver's side, motioning Mr. Morelli to roll down the window. "You're driving pretty fast, fella. What's the hurry?"

"Look, officer . . ." A phony grin infused Mr. Morelli's voice. "Got a very sick child in the back. Must get her to Texas

THE ROAD TO TERMINUS

for treatment on the double. She's getting worse by the minute. Don't know whether we'll make it in time."

"That so?" The uniformed officer bent, staring at Stryker in the back seat. "You sick, little girl?"

Stryker touched her knit hat, pasted a stricken expression on her face, and nodded.

Mrs. Crowley looked like she might hit Mr. Morelli.

The officer's gaze snapped to Mr. Morelli. "That your kid?"

"Yes, sir."

In Stryker's heart, affection for Mr. Morelli swelled.

"You don't look so great yourself." The officer tapped his forehead. "Are you okay to be driving?"

Raising his hand to his bandage, Mr. Morelli gave a quick nod. "Just a little accident. Looks a lot worse than it is. Been cleared by the doctor."

"Uh-huh." Both hands on the window frame, the officer peered over his sunglasses at Mrs. Crowley. "Who might you be, the grandma?"

Blinking and frowning, Mrs. Crowley opened her mouth, but the officer had already straightened up and tugged out his ticket pad.

Mrs. Crowley tightened her lips into a thin line.

"Gotta say, that's a new one." The policeman scratched the back of his head with his pen, tipping his hat forward. "Men with pregnant wives always tell me they're hurrying to the hospital, but—"

"We would greatly appreciate if you would look the other way. We dare not waste another minute." Mr. Morelli's voice dripped with sincere concern. Could he be a Hollywood actor? Sure was good at acting like he cared.

"Perhaps this will help." Mr. Morelli unfolded a few bills from a large wad of money. He must have money hidden all over his body.

The officer raised his eyebrows and pushed his hat off his forehead. "Are you offering a bribe to an Oklahoma police officer? I oughta arrest you."

"Bribe?" Mr. Morelli's laugh rumbled like an engine

turning over. "You completely misunderstood my gesture, sir. I wish to make a donation to the Oklahoma Police Auxiliary." He wiggled his fistful of cash. "I'm sure those fine folks would be appreciative."

The officer's scowl didn't waver.

Mr. Morelli peeled off a few more bills.

A grin thawed the officer's face. "Well, shoot. I probably shouldn't detain you folks one second longer." He reached for the money and stuffed it into his creased shirt pocket. "The Oklahoma Police Auxiliary is most grateful, I assure you." His hand snapped a salute. "Keep an eye on your speedometer though, sport. This stretch of highway is heavily patrolled."

"Much obliged." Mr. Morelli returned the salute. Tires crunched gravel as he swung onto the highway.

"How dare you!" Mrs. Crowley's tone sent chills up Stryker's spine. "I don't believe what you just did. You bribed an officer of the law."

The air inside felt thick as mud. Stryker didn't remember Mrs. Crowley ever speaking in this tone before.

"Money talks." Mr. Morelli chuckled.

"Don't laugh, young man. I won't tolerate this blatant corruption of upstanding law enforcement personnel. You never showed him your driver's license. Such complete disrespect. You lied to an officer, and you made me a party to this... this..."

Mr. Morelli laughed louder.

"Stop laughing this instant!"

He laughed so hard the Studebaker zigzagged into the opposite lane.

With one hand, Mrs. Crowley braced herself on the dashboard. "Now you're going to kill us with your crazy speeding and recklessness. I insist that you pull over right now and let me drive my vehicle."

"Make you a deal. I'll stop laughing if you start saying my name right."

"Oh, all right." She let out a long breath. "Mr. Morelli."

With both hands on the steering wheel, he straightened the tires but didn't slow up to allow Mrs. Crowley to take over.

Several minutes passed while Mrs. Crowley fanned herself with her hanky and clutched her chest. Stryker dreaded the next round of confrontation which was sure to follow. She didn't move a muscle. When grown-ups got to fighting terrible things happened. Someone would end up hurt.

After sitting still for a long time, Stryker's legs began to ache. By then, Mr. Morelli and Mrs. Crowley had settled into a formidable quiet. Neither so much as glanced at the other. Stryker scooted to another part of the seat so Mrs. Crowley's silhouette was in her line of sight. Behind her glasses, her eyes dropped shut and her head rested on the back of the seat. She might be sleeping.

Or else she was praying.

The fighting had fizzled and no one got hurt. Surprise. Fatigue more overwhelming than any tired she'd experienced in many days flushed over Stryker. Clutching her little monkey, she leaned back against the seat and let her eyelids close.

When she opened them, dusk had fallen. The Studebaker slowed and the scenery changed too. Now they drove on smooth city streets. Automobiles, buses, taxis, and unfamiliar buildings whizzed by. "Where are we?"

"Oklahoma City." Mrs. Crowley turned toward her. "Did you have a good little rest?" The anger had melted from her voice, replaced by her familiar warm tone.

"Where's the map?" Mr. Morelli mumbled.

"Why? Are you lost?"

He didn't answer Mrs. Crowley right away, leaning forward on the steering wheel. "I don't think this is Route 66."

"What?" Fear tinged the old woman's voice. "When did you notice?"

"A few miles past the detour."

"Why didn't you stop and ask for directions then?"

Mr. Morelli tossed her a glare.

Her hand covered her mouth a moment before she spoke. "I knew I should drive. Pull over this instant and get directions."

Stryker stared out the side window at boarded-up buildings and shabby vagrants lingering in doorways and on the sidewalks. "I thought Oklahoma City was a nice place." Neither commented.

The squalor reminded her of the rough part of St. Louis where she hung out with the kids. "Are we lost?"

Mrs. Crowley studied the map, crinkling the paper as she folded different sections. "How did you get off Route 66? It's clearly marked all the way."

"We passed Washington Boulevard a few seconds ago." Mr. Morelli snapped at Mrs. Crowley as if she shared the blame for getting lost.

Mrs. Crowley slapped the map. "I have no idea where Washington Boulevard might be. Stop and ask for directions."

Mr. Morelli delivered a withering look.

"Stop right there—that filling station."

The station where Mrs. Crowley pointed appeared deserted. Its chipped enamel sign dangled from one iron ring. Rusty gas pumps stood like sentinels at a graveyard entrance. Near a dilapidated office building and garage, a 1939 Dodge sedan had been stripped of its tires. The raised hood revealed an empty cavity where the engine should have been. Stryker searched hard for some hint of a living soul. "I don't see anyone here."

Mr. Morelli had already parked. "There's light coming from the back room. Get out and ask the way out of this wretched city." He peered out the side window, thumping the steering wheel with his thumb.

Mrs. Crowley jerked her head toward him, eyebrows raised. "This does *not* appear to be a proper neighborhood for an old woman or a child. I suggest you drag your pitiful self in there and make inquiries. After all, you are responsible for our sorry predicament."

He heaved a longwinded sigh but opened the door without objecting, placing both feet on the pavement. For a few seconds he sat still, staring up and down the street. When he looked at Mrs. Crowley, his expression appeared friendly.

"On second thought, maybe it's best to stay together in this kind of neighborhood."

Her lips parted.

Mr. Morellli's words came out fast. "We've been driving a long time. Need to stretch the old gams. Come on. Everybody out."

Cold air assailed them as they piled out. Stryker stretched her arms above her head and yawned. "That does feel better." With a shiver, she reached back inside to tug her hat over her head and gather up Sophia before slamming the door.

Mr. Morelli opened the trunk to extract his overcoat, taking longer than seemed necessary. Noises made her wonder what he was doing. Counting his money?

"Humph," Mrs. Crowley said. "Always thinking of yourself." She tugged out Stryker's new sweater and helped the girl into it before grabbing her purse with one hand and Stryker's arm with the other. Stryker dragged Sophia by one of her long arms as they followed Mr. Morelli inside the filling station.

"Pick the monkey up, dear," said Mrs. Crowley. "This floor is greasy."

The sticky floor of the garage made walking slow. Probably hadn't been cleaned in a while. Oily automobile parts, trash, and torn books littered every available surface. Passage through the piles dislodged fine dust. Stryker hugged Sophia to her chest, squeezing hard.

Mr. Morelli continued toward a lighted room at the rear with Stryker and Mrs. Crowley following close behind.

Seated on a weathered desk, a clerk with a stubbly beard and dirty visor bent over disassembled pieces of a grimy distributor. Gunmetal eyes flicked an irritated acknowledgement of their presence. "Yeah?" His voice sounded as prickly as his hairy face looked.

With both arms, Mrs. Crowley tucked Stryker mother-hen close.

"Excuse us for intruding." Mr. Morelli cleared his throat. "We need directions to Route 66."

The fella picked half a cigar out of an overloaded ashtray. He hung the cigar out one side of his mouth and squinted, taking time to puff before speaking. "Y'all lost?"

"We know we're on Washington Boulevard. Where do we pick up the highway?"

His grin revealed spaces where teeth had gone missing. "Ain't lost, though, eh? You be pretty far off the highway for folks who ain't lost."

Mr. Morelli offered a small wad of bills. "Will this help you remember how to get to the highway?"

He arched his bushy eyebrows. "Say, now. That does jog the memory. What direction you folks headed?"

"West." Mrs. Crowley crossed her arms.

With a wink, the geezer pocketed the cash. Using his blackened fingers, he dug through the junk on his desk until he located a torn piece of blank paper. He scribbled on it, pausing once to blink at the ceiling. When he finished, he shoved the page toward Mr. Morelli. "That'll get you where you want to go."

"Thank you." Mrs. Crowley's smile looked phony.

Mr. Morelli had already hurried through the door with the directions.

But when Stryker and Mrs. Crowley caught up, they found him pacing up and down, gesturing and cursing like one of Mama's old Italian friends.

In the semi-darkness, Stryker followed his irate gaze. Lit by a lone streetlamp, the precise place he had parked was easy to find. But now the ragged circle of light displayed nothing but cracked asphalt.

The Studebaker was gone.

14

GEORGE

A monstrous sob wrenched free from George's gut as he fell to his knees. His nest egg, his future. Gone. Stolen. His insides roiled, alternating between seething rage and complete disbelief. How could this happen?

Who would have dared? Eyes barely able to focus searched darkened streets on all sides. No brown sedans disappearing into the night. Nothing. How had they gotten away so fast? Almost like someone was waiting.

Staggering to his feet, he stumbled back to the dimly-lit office, struggling for control. Just when he thought he had everything covered his entire plan had collapsed. Behind him, the tap of footsteps registered in some small corner of his mind, but he paid no attention to the old woman and child behind him.

"You." Heart pounding, George jabbed a finger directly in the man's face. "Someone took our blasted Studebaker while we were in here talking. You knew that would happen, didn't you? Do you get some kinda kickback on stolen cars?"

The attendant tottered to a stand. "'Fraid I got no idea

what you're babbling about, mister." He curled his lip, exposing the gaps in his teeth. "You got another problem now, 'sides being lost?"

With both hands, George shoved the old geezer back in his chair and yelled. "Get our Studebaker back here." His pointer finger jabbed the old man's chest. "Now."

"You're growling into the wrong cage, fella." He scooted back toward the wall. "Don't know diddly squat 'bout no missing vehicle. Been working here for hours all alone."

Mrs. Crowley stepped forward. "You don't understand how serious this is. We have a sick child to take to Los Angeles. We need our car." She dabbed tears with her handkerchief. "All our possessions are in the trunk. Please, help us."

"Sorry, lady. Like I said, I don't know nothing."

The veins in George's neck throbbed. Two more seconds and he would explode. His fists clenched and unclenched as he reviewed options. He could not report the vehicle missing to the police. He had no way to search the streets in this strange city. What could he do? "Okay. You got us right where you want us, pal." He drew out his wad of bills. "What's it going to take to get our car back?"

"Get it back?" The man cackled. "Do I look like a magician?" His eyebrows wrinkled together. "Did you leave the key in the ignition?"

George searched his pockets. No key. He squinted at Mrs. Crowley. "Do you have the key?"

"You were driving." Mrs. Crowley looked as if she might strangle him.

He never left keys in the ignition, especially not in a neighborhood like this. But he couldn't dwell on that now. Address the immediate situation. "I need a name. Who might poach our automobile?"

Another short laugh. "I keep mine locked in the garage while I'm working. This ain't no place to leave a car unattended."

Stomach churning, George held up his money. "Fine. *Your* car. We'll buy it."

The geezer shook his head. "Sorry, buddy. Mine ain't for sale."

"We need to look for ours. How much to rent your car for the night?"

Mrs. Crowley paced back and forth in the small space, wringing her hands. "We need our clothes. Blankets, pillows. Your box, your luggage."

Did she think he could possibly forget that? "I'm doing the best I can." He stepped closer. "Come on, pal. How much?"

Eyes narrowed. "Nope."

In some corner of the room, Stryker coughed.

"I strongly suggest we call the police." Mrs. Crowley kept pounding away.

The intense disgust obvious in her voice registered with George, but he rebuffed her with a snort. "What can the police do? Car's gone." He couldn't allow her to involve the authorities.

"I *insist* we call the police." Mrs. Crowley laced her arms across her bosom.

George must act quickly before she did. He fixed a stare on the old man. "I'll pay top dollar. Name the amount."

"Told you, it ain't for sale."

Everyone had a price. George started peeling off hundred dollar bills. "Five hundred?"

"Where is the phone? I'll call the police myself." Mrs. Crowley bustled around the small office, hunting under piles.

The old man paid no attention to the money. "What're you, deaf? Car ain't for sale."

Mrs. Crowley lifted an old black phone, examining the frayed end of the detached cord. "This thing is not connected. How can you possibly conduct business here?"

George kept unfolding bills. "Seven hundred?"

"A business has to have a phone." She dropped a cardboard box full of parts on the floor. The metallic sound captured everyone's attention. "Is there a pay phone outside?"

"Not in this part of town, lady."

"Nine hundred dollars? As long as it runs."

The codger shook his head but slower this time.

Mrs. Crowley brushed off her hands before placing them

on her hips. "Really, Mr. Morelli. You haven't even seen his vehicle. How do you know it's worth nine hundred dollars?"

George peeled off a couple more bills. "A thousand?"

"What kind of car do you have?" Stryker asked.

He scratched his stubbly chin. "A Packard."

Stryker's eyes glistened. "What year?"

"Guess it must be a '44. Maybe a '45."

A nod.

"Two-door or four-door?"

"Four."

"Well, then. A thousand dollars is at least three times what your car is worth. Maybe more, depending on the mileage." Stryker said with the swaggering braggadocio of a used car salesman. "Sounds like Mr. Morelli's making you a deal you shouldn't pass up."

Brows raised, he addressed Stryker for the first time. "You know this how, little miss?"

"How far to the nearest pay phone?" Crowley again.

George lifted the cash higher. "Believe me, this girl knows cars. Best listen to her."

Another guffaw slipped between the grizzled lips, obscuring Mrs. Crowley's incessant objections.

He eyed the money in George's fist with one eye closed for what seemed like a long time, making George wait for his answer. Then his lips parted. "Twelve hundred."

"Blasted thing better run." Grinding his back teeth, George peeled off two more hundred-dollar bills. "Let's take a gander at this piece of junk."

Pocketing the cash with a wink, the old man withdrew a set of keys from one of the metal desk drawers and picked off one greasy key. Without another word, he led them out of the office. After unlocking the garage door, he flicked on the hanging overhead lights and gestured toward their new purchase.

George sucked in air, feeling as groggy as if he'd over indulged in Johnnie Walker. Parked inside the garage, a rusty brown Packard rested on nearly bald tires. With so many dents on the fenders, the vehicle must have lost the race at the demolition derby.

"Thanks, folks." The old hawker grinned. "Pleasure doing business with you."

Standing stiff as concrete, Mrs. Crowley's hand covered her mouth.

Stryker slowly circled the old beater. "It's a '42. Considering the age and shape it's in, you overpaid a bit." Not until she stopped at the front did it register in George's brain that the left side had been replaced with a different color fender, also rusty and dented.

Every fiber of his being shouted, "No!" George Kendrick Stanton could not ride in such a dilapidated, shabby, rickety automobile. Not to mention the dubious dependability factor. How far would this relic take them before breaking down?

Immediately after rolling up the garage door, the shrewd seller retreated. The click of a locked door sealed the deal. George pounded on the door to no avail. Options evaporating like his nest egg, he turned to the car. Would the old clunker even start? He opened the driver's-side door, holding his breath as the stench of accumulated garbage wafted out. They'd have to drive with the windows rolled down.

George scooped an armload of trash off the front seat. It clattered to the garage floor. He tried not to look at the torn upholstery and stained floor mats. "As long as the stupid thing runs," he muttered under his breath. When he turned the key in the ignition, the engine labored to a start, sputtering as if awakened from Rip Van Winkle's sleep.

Once it got going, however, the engine continued chugging.

Mrs. Crowley cleared a spot on the passenger's side and settled on the seat, purse on her lap, with arms and ankles crossed. "Of course, you realize we're leaving all of our belongings in the Studebaker. What are we going to do without clothes and blankets?" She pinched her lips together.

Stryker climbed into the back seat and slammed the door.

"Can't be helped. You gotta get Stryker to California. We are in a strange city and we don't know where the car might be. We can't wait around for the police on the off chance they might locate the Studebaker. Could take weeks. What if they never find it?" Not to mention the fact that George could not be involved in any kind of investigation.

"I suppose that's possible," Mrs. Crowley said without conviction.

One good thing—no one could trace the registration on this pile of junk back to him. That meant the feds wouldn't know what car he was driving from now on.

George avoided eye contact with either of them as he backed out and headed toward the street. He couldn't deal with what the loss of his money meant. Didn't want to think of it right now. Good thing he'd tucked a few thousand dollars in his pocket and filled his flask from the Johnnie Walker bottle Mrs. Crowley rescued from the Continental when he got his overcoat out of the trunk. Although the other bottles were gone, having a flask full of whiskey gave him comfort, however temporary. Right then his body ached for a drink. He reached in his pocket, extracting both the flask and the directions to Route 66.

"I need something for pain," George said as he uncorked the flask and gulped a swig.

Mrs. Crowley looked away.

Silence loomed large while the old Packard backtracked through downtown Oklahoma City until George located the detour sign.

"The highway is clearly marked," Mrs. Crowley pointed out. "How on earth did you miss that sign before? It's big enough for me to see without my glasses."

George did not respond. Choosing careful good-humored words seemed an effort unworthy of exertion. If she wanted to nag, he would treat her to the same silent treatment he gave his mother.

Once they returned to Route 66 George's energy revived. They stopped for gas and grabbed a sandwich and soda once they'd put the lights of Oklahoma City behind them. For the next hundred miles, Stryker slumbered off and on in the back seat. Under cloak of darkness, George pushed the accelerator to its limit, speeding through five counties without so much as a sideways glance.

Several minutes after they entered Washita County, Mrs. Crowley nodded off. Light snoring assured George she was asleep at last. He'd had enough of her fretting over what they'd lost in the Studebaker and nagging about calling the police. How much longer would she sing her sad song? As if she was the only one who'd lost anything. She'd sing a different tune if she knew how much money had evaporated.

This thought aggravated the pain of the gaping wound in his soul.

He swigged more whiskey. The quiet gave George time to ponder. He opened the road map in front of him, steering with one hand. Between quick road checks, he studied possible courses. Many miles still separated him from the Mexican border, but this was only the second day of his escape. He might head south from here, but he'd planned to stay with Mrs. Crowley until Texas. *If* the stupid Packard ran that far. Then he'd buy another car and continue to Mexico.

Every thought of the envelope containing his nest egg—an entire fortune gone—made his stomach lurch. He ground his teeth, jaw tight. Son of a . . . what a low blow. He gulped more whiskey.

Nothing could be done now. He would have to make the few thousand he had left last as long as possible.

Stryker was right. He paid too much for the lousy car.

Acknowledging the insult, the Packard backfired. He jerked to look in the rearview mirror, seeking the source of the noise. Why'd he bother? Not much traffic this time of night. The headlights illuminated several feet in front but nothing else. They were traveling through a desolate area past Weatherford but hadn't yet reached Clinton. Would Oklahoma never end? Would this night ever end?

The Packard crunched over something on the highway.

Mrs. Crowley bolted upright. "What in the world is wrong with this car?"

"Nothing. A bump in the road."

She straightened her hat. "You purchased a lemon, you know." Her gaze flicked out the window. "Soon we will be stranded beside the highway in the middle of the night." She must be focused on him now. "Stryker is very sick. I do not think you appreciate the seriousness—"

"We're doing fine in this old rattletrap," he interrupted. "Don't go all huffy. We're making good time. In fact, we aren't far from the Texas border."

"How far?"

"Just passed a sign saying we're in Washita County. That's nearly at the border." He handed her the map. "Look for yourself."

Mrs. Crowley angled the map so the dash lights illuminated an inch or so. "I can't see a thing in this darkness. Turn on the overhead light."

George shot her a smirk.

"Oh. Right. For a minute I thought we were still in my Studebaker." She folded the map. "Well, we need to bed down. Driving through the night is out of the question. Find a motel, Mr. Morelli. And soon."

What made her think she could issue orders? He paid dearly for this junk heap. She was at his mercy now. If he wanted to drive all night, he would. He lit a cigarette and blew smoke out the wing window.

Mrs. Crowley bent toward him to check the dashboard. "Besides your incessant speeding, we're running hot. The engine needs to cool down."

George hadn't noticed the temperature needle inching upward. He had no idea how long he'd driven in such a condition. Maybe she was right. They should stop somewhere and rest.

In Elk City—the next town they came upon—*No Vacancy* blinked under all the motel signs along the highway.

"I can't believe this whole town has nowhere to stay." Mrs. Crowley shook her head.

George turned away so she couldn't see him smile. None of the motels they passed met his standards.

A sign announcing Sayre flashed by. In a few more miles, George spotted the Sunset Motel, a long line of attached units with a café on site. Looked maintenance-delayed. He did not slow down.

Mrs. Crowley's reproach sounded. "What are you doing? Did you see the motel with the Vacancy sign lit? Turn around. I insist."

"Hang on, lady." Was she capable of the corporal punishment her tone intimated? He didn't intend to find out. "I'll stop pretty soon. Been seeing signs advertising the Stardust for a hundred miles. 'Sayre's Newest and Finest Motor Hotel.' Sounds promising, doesn't it?"

Mrs. Crowley issued a loud harrumph.

They passed several motels before the Stardust sign appeared on the far side of town. When he surveyed the big modern sign and all-night café, George let out the breath he'd been holding. Not first class, as the Tulsa hotel had been, but it would do. He parked and entered the office with Mrs. Crowley and a sleepy Stryker in tow.

"Sure, we got two rooms for tonight," the somber desk clerk said.

A gust of chilly wind blew the front door open with a bang. The clerk hurried to close it. "It's colder than a coal miner's—"

"Been a long day," George said. "What about those rooms?"

Eyebrows arched, the clerk set to work checking the threesome in for the night.

George paid the trifling sum the clerk quoted for the rooms, less than a third what he paid per room at The Mayo. He might need to consider prices with his wad lighter and the rest of his stash gone. His chest clenched. How'd he get in such a mess after all his careful planning?

The clerk kept talking while he finished the transaction. "Which direction you folks headed?"

"West," said Mrs. Crowley.

The clerk hesitated, holding the room keys suspended in midair. He gave them a good once-over. "Hope you know what you're doing."

"Why?" George asked, catching anxiety in the clerk's eyes.

"Weatherman predicts severe thunderstorms coming from the West. This is tornado season, doncha know? Didn't you hear about the bad outbreak at the end of May? A couple weeks ago. Bunch of people got killed. Lotta damage. You folks might consider staying put until the storm blows over."

The clerk dropped the key in Mrs. Crowley's palm, but she didn't look at it. "Severe thunderstorms? In that old car?" She blinked several times. Behind her glasses, her eyelids brimmed with tears. "What if the windshield wipers don't work?"

Shooting pain invaded George's head. He pressed his temples with his fingertips. His left eye twitched madly. When the clerk mentioned tornados, George vaguely remembered hearing news of a spate of deadly weather not so long ago. Never gave the story any thought at the time. Who knew he'd be coming through here soon? But storm or not, pressing on was imperative. "Be ready to roll at eight. No matter what."

15

STRYKER

Clouds darker than a bad guy's heart greeted them the next morning as they emerged from the motel on their way to the café. Stryker and Mrs. Crowley had been up and dressed before seven, beating Mr. Morelli to the diner.

In the restaurant, a radio broadcasted the location and severity of the storm. After Mr. Morelli arrived at seven thirty, he smoked a few cigarettes while he wolfed down coffee and gobbled toast.

He kept asking questions as if speaking to the radio. "Should we alter our route? Does that mean we should go north or south? How bad will it be?"

Mrs. Crowley's forehead wrinkled. "Have you consulted the map?"

Mr. Morelli jerked toward her when she spoke. "Did you bring the map inside?"

"No."

"Then how could I look at the map?" He sounded grumpier than usual. "I was awake all night listening to the wind howl. Never heard anything like it." His nervous eyes followed Stryker's every move. "Can't you eat faster, kid?" He swore. "You always eat so slow."

Mouth full of eggs, Stryker swallowed the barely-chewed food. The big hunk made her throat hurt like it got stuck.

Mrs. Crowley wrapped the last two pieces of Stryker's toast in a napkin and stuffed them in her purse. "For later." She smiled too hard to be reassuring.

Stryker didn't understand all the fuss over a little storm. On the streets, the kids knew what to do when the weather turned bad. They hid until the storm passed. Scurrying after Mr. Morelli, Stryker tried to keep pace through the parking lot.

A brilliant lightning bolt zigzagged out of jet-black clouds. Thunder rolled soon after. Gusts of rain blew sideways, slapping Stryker's bare legs. She tugged her knit hat farther down on her forehead.

"I had an umbrella in my Studebaker." Mrs. Crowley held on to her hat with one hand while shielding her glasses with her purse.

"How do you think I feel?" Mr. Morelli yelled. "I used to have an expensive fedora." He ran a hand through his sopping wet hair.

"It's my turn to drive, young man." In her rush, Mrs. Crowley slipped in a mud puddle, breaking her fall on a parked sedan. She shook muck off one foot and hastened on. "Are you listening?"

Mr. Morelli beat her to the Packard and unlocked the driver's-side door. "You can't drive in a storm."

"I most certainly can." She faced him, panting. "I've had . . . years of practice driving in St. Louis. In fact, I've been driving longer than you've been alive." She wiped moisture off her glasses. "Let's not argue in the rain."

He threw up his hands then dropped the key in her palm and raced to the other side, overcoat flapping behind him.

Stryker threw herself into the back seat, wringing water from her dress and slipping out of her soggy shoes. The cold pierced through her body like an icicle. Her teeth chattered. What she wouldn't give to wrap up in the warm blanket they left in the Studebaker.

Shoving the key in the ignition and turning it produced an unusual clamor—clunking, thumping, and a series of thin shrieks, which might be one of the belts slipping. Despite stubborn objections, the engine sputtered to life after a few seconds, whining and vibrating.

Mr. Morelli glared. "Would you just let me drive?"

"Do the wipers work?" Mrs. Crowley searched the dash. "There must be a knob or lever to turn them on."

Stryker peered over the seat. "Try the stick on the right side of the steering wheel."

Mrs. Crowley obliged. The metal arm gouged a half-circle scratch across the front window with a thin strip of black rubber trailing behind.

"Turn them off," Stryker said quickly.

Mr. Morelli cursed.

"Puh-lease." Mrs. Crowley snapped him a look proclaiming her desire to slap him silly. "Control your tongue."

Rain battered the windshield, and occasional gusts of hail pounded the roof as if demanding to be let inside.

Mrs. Crowley hunched to peer through sheets of water, continuing her tongue-lashing. "You were the one who missed the detour. You parked in front of that garage and insisted we go inside. You left the key in my car, Mr. Morelli. You are responsible for our current quandary."

Probably best not to mention that Mrs. Crowley had insisted they stop at that particular filling station.

The gears grated as Mrs. Crowley shifted into reverse. "Kindly be on the lookout for somewhere to purchase windshield wiper blades. We need them immediately."

Grinding the gear into first, she slowly steered out of the parking lot and onto Route 66 East.

Mr. Morelli didn't watch for a place to buy windshield wipers. Instead, he smoked while fiddling with radio knobs. "At least we have a radio this time," he muttered.

Static crackled and hissed, making an occasional short squawk as he searched through channels. Then a voice broke through. " . . . producing damaging winds in Beckham County. Winds up to seventy miles an hour have knocked down electric poles. Several hundred people in the towns of Mayfield, Erick, and the outlying areas are without electricity. A few sightings of wall clouds and funnel clouds have been reported but remain unconfirmed. State police issued a highway warning—" Another blanket of static smothered the voice.

"We're in Beckham County." Mrs. Crowley leaned toward the radio. "Did they say exactly where those funnel clouds were sighted?"

Not bothering to answer, he continued twisting the radio dial one direction, then another, finding nothing more than static. After a while, he gave up.

Mrs. Crowley executed a sharp turn into a filling station. Off balance, Stryker fell into the car door, bumping her head. She sat up and rubbed the sore spot as Mrs. Crowley parked under a canopy.

"Go. Buy windshield wipers." Mrs. Crowley didn't say please.

Mr. Morelli drilled Mrs. Crowley with scorn before flipping up the collar of his overcoat. He opened the door long enough to jump out. Then he slammed it behind him and jogged toward the garage.

In a few minutes he returned with an attendant in a yellow slicker. The attendant ripped off the torn wiper blades and slid new ones in place. Job completed in minutes, the man waved before trotting back to the building.

Mr. Morelli massaged his temples. "Okay. Try them out."

She clicked the wiper lever and the windshield wipers swung to work, cleaning off a river of dirty water. As soon as they drove out from under cover of the filling station, however, the windshield wipers couldn't keep up with the torrential rainfall.

"And there you go." Mr. Morelli waved a hand in dismissal. "Glad we bought new blades."

Another bolt of lightning sliced the sky with a thunderclap following seconds behind. The storm was on top of them now. The rigid set of Mrs. Crowley's head showed how uncomfortable she was driving in the storm.

Stryker slipped to the edge of the seat, folding her arms

atop the backrest. "What's a tornado look like? Have you ever seen one?"

"No, dear, I haven't, thank goodness. But I read a newspaper article about the damage these latest ones caused—miles of devastation across several states. Some people lost everything. So very sad."

Head in his hands, Mr. Morelli groaned. "I can run faster than you're driving. We're barely crawling."

Mrs. Crowley tsk-tsked. "Would you like to run? I'd be happy to let you out." She exhaled a long sigh without taking her eyes off the road. "I can barely see the highway with this rain pouring down. It wouldn't be prudent to drive faster."

Eye twitching, he leaned forward to twist knobs. Warm air blasted through the vents. "Well, what do you know? Something works. At least we won't freeze to death."

Stryker couldn't resist. "The Clipper was a fine automobile when it first came out in 1941. Packard added lots of innovations like radios, heaters, whitewall tires with hubcaps and trim rings. Even with all the wear, you can still tell how fancy the dashboard used to be. See those chrome bands?"

"You sound like an advertisement." Mr. Morelli rubbed his forehead. "Ain't we lucky we got such a grand car." He lit another cigarette. Smoke billowed into the interior.

Stryker coughed.

Mr. Morelli flipped the wing window open to let the smoke out, but some lingered inside. Their clothes must stink by now.

One advantage to having no hair—it would never smell like smoke.

The three fell silent as the car inched through the relentless weather. Traffic on Route 66 had dwindled to a car every mile or so. Most people must be staying inside. Lightning hammered the sky with frightening frequency. Occasional hail balls pinged on the metal while the deluge persisted. Wind stronger than any storm Stryker had lived through pressed against the Packard as if determined to slow their progress.

All of a sudden, Mr. Morelli whistled. "What's that?" He rubbed vapor off the side window. "See the black cloud?"

Mrs. Crowley slowed, craning her neck. Stryker pressed her face against the window.

One of the storm clouds had developed a pointy end. Dragged toward the horizon by an invisible magnet, the end dropped lower until it resembled a tube reaching from sky to ground. The top widened as if sucking in nearby clouds.

The sight mesmerized Stryker. "It looks like . . ." Her voice dropped to a whisper.

"A funnel," Mr. Morelli said.

Lightning danced in the sky as Mrs. Crowley veered onto the muddy shoulder. For a few seconds, they stared. Rolling thunder echoed.

"It's less than half a mile away." Mr. Morelli's voice sounded odd—stripped of its usual high-and-mighty tone.

"What should we do?" The fear in Mrs. Crowley's voice couldn't be masked.

"Never been in this situation before. We don't have tornados in Chic—uh, at home."

Someone needed to take over if these two nuts were going to sit and chat like everything was hunky dory. Stryker scooted to the edge of the seat. "Find somewhere low to take cover."

Identical blank expressions blinked at her.

"Get back on the highway," Stryker said to Mrs. Crowley, voice ascending in volume as she issued orders. "Find a house or barn or somewhere to hide. A little valley would do. We need to be as low as possible when the tornado hits."

Mrs. Crowley shifted into first gear and veered back onto the pavement. The transmission rumbled then made a grinding noise before second gear took hold. They lurched forward, with Stryker and Mr. Morelli scouring the horizon.

The funnel cloud loomed behind. Every time Stryker glanced back, the cloud seemed closer. Was it gaining on them? How fast could a tornado travel?

Around a bend in the road, Stryker spied a driveway leading into a little valley. A half mile down the gravel road, an old shack hid behind a picket fence. Sheets of rain blurred the scene, but she could also make out several outbuildings. "There." Stryker pointed. "That farm."

The Packard swung onto the driveway, pebbles spitting on the fenders as the tires sped toward the picket fence. When Mrs. Crowley stopped they all jumped out, dashing for the front porch through wind, hail, and rain. Three sets of feet tapped up the creaky steps. Mr. Morelli whacked the screen door with his fist.

Stryker glanced over one shoulder. The awesome funnel cloud had grown in size, a huge black cobra spinning closer. Dark spots whirled around the sides. The tornado must be gathering garbage as it invaded each new field. A roar louder than an oncoming train accompanied the twister.

Mr. Morelli pounded on the door.

No one answered.

He threw back the screen door and tugged on the door-knob, but it didn't turn. The oncoming racket forced him to shout. "I don't know if I can break down the door."

Mrs. Crowley held her hat on with both hands. She shouted back. "Don't try. Perhaps they're already hiding in the cellar." Wind whipped her words out of her mouth as soon as she let them loose.

"What?" Mr. Morelli bent closer.

"The cellar." She pointed to the right.

Stryker and Mrs. Crowley followed him as he dashed down the steps and around a corner. No cellar. He tugged his over-coat tighter and continued to the back, rain plastering his curls to his head. Near the back door, they discovered a mound topped by a closed entrance, which appeared to lead into the waterlogged earth.

Mrs. Crowley yelled, "Cellar."

Mr. Morelli braced his feet and tugged on the doorknob.

At first the door didn't budge. Tugging harder, Mr. Morelli slipped in the mud but got right back on his feet, rubbing his leg. Stryker wrapped her arms as far as they would go around his middle. At her touch, Mr. Morelli glanced sideways, eye-brows arched, before shouting, "Okay. On the count of three, pull as hard as you can."

Stryker nodded and wiggled her saturated shoes deeper into the mud.

"One. Two. Three."

At the exact moment Stryker started to pull, the door flew open. They fell backward, landing in the sludge with a splash of flying mud.

On the top step of the open doorway stood an elfin creature with a shock of battleship gray hair sticking straight up all over his head like steel wool. Thick glasses couldn't hide his rheumy eyes. His bushy eyebrows arched. Clearly, he had not laid out the welcome mat. Stryker's heart flip-flopped.

In his arms, he held a shotgun pointed directly at Mr. Morelli's chest.

16

STRYKER

Rain pelted Stryker's face as she sprawled in the mud. Mr. Morelli stood next to her, staring at the wild man with the shotgun. This guy clearly didn't want visitors. Water poured down Mr. Morelli's head, flattening his curls and dripping off his face, but he didn't blink. For what seemed an eternity, nobody moved. All around, flying branches, broken wood shingles, and trash darkened the sky.

Mrs. Crowley broke the standoff, shouting, "The tornado will be here in minutes. Please, we need to get into your cellar." She took a step toward the door. "Now."

A jagged lightning bolt sizzled into the earth on the far side of the outbuildings, followed almost immediately by bone-jarring thunder. The short man's head jerked toward the sound.

Wind howled and whipped the skirt of Stryker's dress around her legs. She pushed it down with one hand and held her knit hat with the other.

Still Mr. Shotgun hesitated. What was he waiting for? Didn't he understand what Mrs. Crowley said? Finally, he let the gun drop to his side. "Why not? I ain't had lunch yet."

Did he say what it sounded like? Hadn't had lunch? That made no sense. Was he crazy?

The next instant, Mr. Morelli yanked her up to a stand. Curling an arm around her back, he hauled her into the cellar behind Mrs. Crowley and the old geezer. While Stryker tramped down the stone stairs, flinging mud with each step, Mr. Morelli hefted the door shut. With all the noise outside, she couldn't hear the door slam.

No one spoke while the tornado raged outside. The deafening freight-train noise passed overhead, although how close the twister actually came Stryker couldn't be sure. Perhaps it took away the house. The bellowing rattled her bones, made her teeth chatter. Stryker clung to Mrs. Crowley, burying her face. Comforting arms pressed her close.

When at last the noise passed, they all began speaking at once.

The raising of the shotgun stopped the chatter. "Whatta ya doin' here?"

Mr. Morelli stepped forward. His bandage had been lost in the storm, and the scar looked purplish and swollen.

"Looks like you been in a fight." One watery eye squinted as if taking aim down the barrel.

Mr. Morelli held up both hands. "Easy, mister. We mean you no harm. Needed to find a place to hide while the tornado went by. We have no intention of intruding on your privacy."

"Thank you for letting us in." Mrs. Crowley presented her kind smile. "I don't think we could have outrun that twister."

From his inner pocket, Mr. Morelli drew out a fat wad of money. "We're happy to pay you. What'll it cost for us to hold out here until the storm is over?"

Weepy eye still sighting down the gun barrel, he ignored Mr. Morelli's offer. "You have a run in with Clyde? He do that to your face?" He cocked his head, rolled his eyes, then popped his neck straight and raised the shotgun a notch.

"Clyde?" Mrs. Crowley turned to Mr. Morelli.

"I'm afraid you have us confused with someone else." Mr. Morelli shook his head. "We're just traveling through." He wiggled his money. "Like I said, we'll pay you for the shelter."

He snorted. "What do I need money for?" The gun lowered a couple of inches. "Maybe you oughta stay put. Least 'til I check with Clyde."

"That won't be necessary," Mrs. Crowley said quickly.

Mr. Morelli said, "We'll stay until the storms pass. After that, we must be on our way."

The shotgun pressed into Mr. Morelli's ribs. "What's yer hurry? Don't get visitors around these parts too often. What say we sit and talk a spell?" Using his shotgun as a pointer, he indicated a seating area of armchairs at the far end of the cramped space. "Ladies first."

The chairs looked like they came from the dump. Mrs. Crowley started for the chairs anyway, pulling Stryker with her. On the way, Stryker examined her surroundings. A row of shelves filled with grubby canning jars lined one wall. The contents looked murky and slimy. Stuffed gunnysacks were piled along another wall. The dirt floor must have been swept level. She could see the boom marks. Two kerosene lanterns cast circles of light in the cool darkness. Along with the odor of burning oil, the air smelled musty and damp. Long shadows on the walls lent the room a ghostly atmosphere.

Sitting rather stiffly, Mrs. Crowley dipped her head. Stryker settled on the arm of the chair where Mrs. Crowley indicated. The cool air made her shiver. She hugged her arms close over her chest. What a scary place for a chat.

Mr. Morelli lifted his hands in the air like he was under arrest.

Mr. Shotgun followed, aiming from one to the other without lowering the gun. "So Clyde thought he could outfox me."

"Look." Mr. Morelli gave a little laugh. "We don't know this Clyde you're talking about."

"If you don't know Clyde, who beat you up?"

"Not in a fight." Mr. Morelli shook his head. "Had an accident."

A thunderclap underscored the statement.

The man cocked his head and rolled his eyes. Bones in his neck popped like cracking knuckles. He turned back to stare at them, eyes watchful. That was the second time he did that weird thing. What was wrong with this guy?

Mrs. Crowley dusted off her skirt before speaking. "Perhaps introductions are in order. I am Mabel Crowley and this is Mr. Morelli. We're traveling to California to take Stryker for medical treatment."

"Medical treatment? Medical treatment?" The way Mr. Shotgun repeated the words reminded Stryker of one of Mama's friends who kept a parrot on his shoulder.

Silent communication passed between Mrs. Crowley and Mr. Morelli, but Stryker didn't know what it meant.

"Yes," Mrs. Crowley said. "Medical treatment."

He pointed the gun at Stryker. "You sick then?"

Stryker nodded.

"What's wrong with you?"

After a short pause, Mr. Morelli answered. "She's got leukemia. Her doctors in St. Louis can't help her, but some guy out in California is working on a cure."

The man's head and eye rolling commenced again. Then he focused on Mr. Morelli. "Long ways. California. Long ways."

"Well, Mr . . ." Mrs. Crowley's words trailed off and she sat in expectant silence. When he did not speak, she straightened in the chair. "What was your name again?"

"Name?" he asked. "Are you from the government?"

"No. No." Mrs. Crowley held up one hand. "I'm sure you can imagine how anxious we are to be on our way. Do you have a radio? Perhaps you wouldn't mind checking to see what direction the storm is moving."

"Radio's broke." He shook his head hard and swiveled to stare at Stryker. "Sick, are you? You could use some fattening up." He pinched Stryker's arm in a wicked-witch sort of way. "The magic bullet, that's what *you* need, little missy." He held out his open palm. "Keys."

Mr. Morelli frowned. "Why—"

"Give." Behind the thick glasses, his large unblinking eyes seemed ready to pop out of his head.

Mama had told Stryker about spells. Was he putting a hex on them?

To Stryker's horror, Mrs. Crowley's trembling fist opened as if pried apart by invisible fingers. In her palm, rested the car key.

Mr. Shotgun snatched the key away and grabbed Stryker's arm. Before anyone else moved, he jumped up with greater speed than Stryker would have imagined possible, pulling her toward the cellar steps.

With a gasp, Mrs. Crowley covered her heart with one quivering hand.

Mr. Morelli rose to a half-stand.

"Stay put," he snarled. "Or I'll shoot you."

He shoved Stryker up the stairs. She tripped, scraping her knee on the sharp stone edge. The sting made her wince. Her groping fingers touched something sticky oozing from the wound. He yanked her to a stand then pushed her forward from the back. She didn't cry out, although she wanted to.

Stumbling several more times, she made her way to the top of the steps where the old man grunted as he shoved open the door. She protested, but by then they were standing on the muddy earth outside.

The storm gloom made Stryker blink. Where did the sunshine go? She scanned the obvious path where the tornado had passed. A driving rain continued but the funnel had disappeared. Black clouds hung thick. The shack stood intact, though it appeared more battered than before, as if the storm peeled off a layer of paint. Several of the outbuildings behind the house had been reduced to heaps of timber and rubble. Gone was the picket fence, ripped out of the dirt. The trail continued out of sight, earth churned as if a giant plow went through. Not a plant or tree remained on the path.

Remarkably, the heavy old Packard stood exactly where they had parked.

The slamming cellar door drew Stryker's attention to the old man's activities. Out of his pocket, he pulled a large metal ring with dangling keys, which jangled together like tiny toll bells as his short fingers picked through. When he found the one he wanted, he inserted it in the lock and twisted until it clicked.

Stryker frowned. Why did he lock the cellar door? How would Mr. Morelli and Mrs. Crowley get out? Behind the door, footsteps pounded. Probably Mr. Morelli running up the stairs, but he was too late.

Nothing about this situation made a lick of sense. Stryker should run away. But where? She scanned the horizon. No other houses were close. No towns. Nothing but flat farmland. The old guy had leaned the shotgun against the side of the house while he locked the door. She could grab it, but guns were heavy. What would she do with it?

As if he heard her thoughts, Mr. Shotgun whirled and grabbed his gun, motioning her to move. Another flurry of rain and wind swirled around them as they scrambled through the mud around the side of the house and trudged onto the front porch. He unlocked the door and hastened inside tugging Stryker behind him.

She had a bad feeling about this house. She shouldn't go inside. What if she ran to the car and locked the doors until she figured out what to do about her traveling companions?

One good look at the shotgun convinced her running wouldn't be a good choice.

Once inside the house, he fumbled for the light switch. When he flipped it, nothing happened. No lights. A low growl escaped his lips. Muttering to himself, he found a candle. Striking a match, he lit the wick, but the small flame created little light in the thick darkness.

Bending quite close, he turned watery eyes on Stryker. "I know what you need." He cocked his head in his strange bird-like way adding a quick eye roll before shuffling from the room with his shotgun slung over one shoulder.

Stryker pivoted in slow, stiff motion. Every available space in the shadowy room held piles of something—books, boxes, papers, magazines, newspapers. Underneath the stacks here and there, she caught glimpses of shabby furniture. Under a newspaper, she found a black telephone. Stryker hauled up the receiver. "Hello? Hello? Operator?"

No dial tone. What had she expected? Of course the storm had knocked out phone service too.

Blankets or torn sheets tacked over the windows darkened the interior. Stryker shivered. "Someone walked over my grave." Mama used to say. What made Stryker think of that now?

Too soon, her host bustled back into the room carrying a faded blanket. Dust flew into the air when he shook it open. Stryker sneezed.

He hung the blanket on her shoulders like a cape. "Gotta move it before Clyde gets here." Out of one drenched overall pocket he retrieved Mrs. Crowley's key. With a chuckle, he tossed it in the air and caught it.

Murmuring, he spun and scuttled outside.

The screen door clapped shut behind him and Stryker flinched.

Despite being worn and dusty, the blanket warmed her. She wrapped it closer. Her wet clothes dripped and her toes had nearly frozen. A layer of mud covered her shoes. If she kicked them off and then needed to run, she wouldn't get far barefooted. So she sank to the floor, draping the blanket over her like a tent. With one cold hand, she rubbed her legs before tucking her feet underneath.

Would she ever get warm? Why did she leave Sophia in the Packard? How comforting it would be to hug her little monkey close. Then she wouldn't be here all alone.

The rain had started again. She imagined hearing Mr. Morelli pounding the cellar door, but it was probably only the raging storm. What to do? Mr. Shotgun had the key. She'd have to figure how to get his key ring. If she waited until he went to sleep, she might have a chance. Scary as it sounded, for now she'd have to go along with whatever he intended to do.

Which would be—what? What tonic was he getting?

She didn't have long to wonder. Like a cockroach, he scurried back. In one hand he carried a brown bottle, which reminded Stryker of her mother's whiskey flask. Once a label had identified the contents. Now the yellow paper curled at the edges, printed words faded to pale gray. Even if she knew how to read, so few letters were left she probably couldn't tell what had originally been in the bottle anyway.

He balanced a blackened spoon between dirt-stained fingers. Laughing like a stray puppy yapping, he squatted beside Stryker. "This'll fix you right up."

He unscrewed the bottle top and slid the lid onto a nearby table. With great care, he poured thick black liquid into the spoon. The pungent stench of rotten garbage filled the air.

"What is that?" Stryker shuddered involuntarily.

He puckered his lips as he moved the spoon closer to her face.

She shook her head. "It smells nasty."

"Magic bullet. Good for you."

Icy fingers of fear tightened around Stryker's throat. "I don't want any."

His hand jerked as she spoke, drizzling the filthy liquid onto the blanket. His expression darkened. "Open your blasted mouth."

Stryker pressed her lips tightly shut, squirming out of reach.

"My ma's special recipe. Good for what ails you." With his free hand, he grabbed her face. His grubby fingers gripped her jaw like a vice, drawing her mouth toward the spoon now only partially filled with vile tonic. "Come on. Open."

Unable to shake her head while the rough hand squeezed tight, she concentrated on keeping her lips together. Through clenched teeth, she yelled the best *no* she was able. Not much better than a loud grunt, but he must have understood.

The bulgy eyes narrowed, and his face contorted as he threw Stryker to the floor. She twisted, trying to wiggle free of his grip, but he was too strong.

Straddling her between his knees so she couldn't move, he pinned her thin body to the floor, clamping both wrists over her head with one burly hand. A horrible grimace deformed his face. He flung the spoon across the floor. It clattered to a stop near the opposite wall.

Cursing God's name, the old man reached for the bottle. "Open. Your. Mouth."

17

GEORGE

George kept pummeling the cellar door even after he'd broken the skin on his knuckles. His fist stamped blood every time it smacked the door—over and over. How dare this stupid hayseed lock him in the cellar. Sweat trickled down his brow. Through parted lips, he gulped air into his aching lungs.

No one came to help. Who did he think would come anyway? Off the highway in this rural location, nobody was likely to drop by and hear his pounding. Get a grip. Being closed in this small space had taken him right back to childhood—to his nanny's cruel punishments. While he pounded, the wicked woman's laughter echoed in his mind. Panic hadn't helped then, and it wouldn't help now.

He gulped a long swig of whiskey from his flask and closed his eyes for a moment while the liquid trickled down his throat. Wonderful thing, Johnnie Walker. Exactly the ticket to take the edge off.

Circles of light from the kerosene lanterns cast long flickering shadows up the steps to the locked cellar door. Below him Mrs. Crowley murmured prayers.

A lot of good praying would do. What kind of God would let a crazy guy abduct a sick girl and lock him in this cellar with a mumbling woman? He struck the door. Not a loving God, that's for sure.

He still didn't understand why the old geezer couldn't be bought. Everyone had a price. Should have upped the offer.

Mrs. Crowley's petitions droned on. Mopping his brow with his sleeve, George studied her. Eyes closed tight, she had removed her glasses and held them between steepled hands. She swayed in the small seating area, lips moving. Who was she kidding? Her pleas wouldn't go any higher than the ceiling.

George rested on the top step. Leaning one weary arm on his knee, he swiped a dribble of sweat off his cheek. "Do you think anyone will hear you? You're barely whispering."

She opened her eyes. "God hears."

He snickered. "You don't truly believe that."

"Yes. I do." She replaced her glasses on her face and pushed the frame up the bridge of her nose with one finger.

"Even if he could hear you, what do you expect him to do? Break through the door and rescue you? Like the cavalry?"

Her mouth curved slightly upward at the corners. "Actually, I was praying for *you*, Mr. Morelli."

Didn't expect that. "Me?"

"Exactly. I asked God to strengthen your arms and your mind. To show you how to get us out of this cellar. Why don't you stop a moment and think?"

George slumped, muscles throbbing from exertion. He leaned both arms on his knees. Sure. Why not? Think the door open. He shook his head. Abracadabra and the doors magically pop open? These holier-than-thou types were bizarre. Kooks. As if all he needed to do was think.

"I'm not a handyman, you know. Never worked with machinery and tools. I hire people to do those things. Sorry. I'm afraid you got stuck in a cellar with someone who knows no more about how to get out than you do."

Smile widening, Mrs. Crowley lowered herself into one of the chairs. "If thou faint in the day of adversity, thy strength is small."

"What?"

"It's from the Bible. Proverbs 24:10. You're a healthy young man. I asked God to supply added strength for you. Even in this cellar, God is in control." She folded her hands in her lap. "I'm sure the solution will come to you."

George blew out a long sigh and squinted at his Rolex. In the flickering light, he barely made out the time. Almost five-thirty. Dusk. Had they been in this cellar that long?

God is in control. Rubbish. "I control my *own* destiny." George didn't realize he'd spoken out loud until Mrs. Crowley answered.

"Oh, my dear boy. You are so wrong." She tilted her head. "Did you plan to have an accident in your fancy car?"

"No."

"Were you in control of who came to help you that day?"

"Well, no, but—"

"Was traveling with Stryker and me part of *your* plan? Did you make someone steal my Studebaker? Or bring the tornado and lead us to this particular house?" She slowly shook her head. "Your destiny has always been out of your control."

For a moment he'd been mesmerized by her monotone litany of rhetorical questions. When she stopped speaking, he hooted in disgust. "Give it up, will you? Bad things happen sometimes. The best plans can be thwarted by unforeseen complications. Preaching to me won't get this door opened."

George ran a hand through his damp hair, flinching when his fingernail gouged the wound on his forehead where the bandage used to be. Reflex jerked his hand away as if he'd been stung. His body still ached from the accident. Sore muscles reminded him to take it easy. He had no business pounding on doors. Wasn't helping anyway.

Sure could use a cigarette, but in this small space he figured Mrs. Crowley wouldn't approve, and he didn't want to listen to her grousing. He patted the inside pocket of his overcoat. Knowing the cigarette pack was safe and dry gave him comfort. Not as much as smoking would, but it helped all the same.

To mimic smoking, he filled his lungs with air then

exhaled, letting the breath out slowly, willing his body to relax. With concentrated effort, he pressed his tense shoulders down. The old lady might have something there after all. He circled his head on his neck and let his eyelids drop closed. Think. How could he get this door open?

Tools. He needed a crowbar for leverage. Could he find something useful in this cellar?

Descending the stairs, he picked up one of the lanterns by the bail on top. He shone the light up one wall and down the next. At the shelves of canned goods, he halted with the lamp at shoulder height.

Behind the shelves something glowed. Not exactly light, but less darkness than the rest of the walls. A reflection?

"Help me move this shelf." He didn't turn to see whether Mrs. Crowley was watching, but noises indicated she had moved toward him.

"What?"

"Something is behind here."

She didn't comment but started pulling jars off. Soon they had stacked all the jars on the floor. George lifted the lantern. "I think it's a window. Not a big window, but maybe I can squeeze out."

They tugged the heavy shelves aside to reveal a small ventilation window under the ceiling beams. Dust and grime obscured the view, but standing on tiptoe George ran a hand over the surface to clean away enough grime so he could see the ground outside.

"Now's when we need Stryker." Mrs. Crowley huffed, clutching her chest. "She'd be the perfect size to climb out that window."

"Got to open it first."

With his feet steadied on a wooden crate, George reached the latch at the top and twisted. The little window dropped open with a creak. He detached the chain holding it, and the pane banged against the cellar wall.

Icy wind dumped rain through the opening.

"Ta-dah." He glanced at Mrs. Crowley. "An escape route. Now I have to figure out how to climb up this high."

"Hmm." Mrs. Crowley tapped her mouth with her fingers. "How about one of the padded chairs?"

George grabbed the arm of the nearest one and shoved it under the window in the space she had cleared. When he stood on the back of the chair, his head bumped the ceiling, but he hunched over to peer out the window.

Rain soaked the wall, the chair, and George. Before long he realized he wasn't flexible enough to push his leg out the window.

"How about this wooden box?" Mrs. Crowley lifted the crate a couple of inches off the floor before it slipped out of her fingers. "Too heavy for me. Can you balance it on the back of the chair if I hold it steady?"

Teetering on the box elevated him enough so he could shove his leg through the tiny opening. What a sight he must be. Drenched by the rain, he straddled the narrow egress, one leg in and one leg out. The stretch was painful. Storm or not, he couldn't wait to get the rest of his body outside.

With Mrs. Crowley pushing, George contorted his body in ways he never thought possible. His pants ripped, but after much grunting and cursing he crawled through. Good thing he wasn't any heavier. Another ten pounds and he'd have been stuck.

Mrs. Crowley would never fit through the hole even if she somehow climbed high enough. For a moment, he considered leaving her. He glanced at the place where they'd left the Packard. It wasn't there. He threw up his hands.

Maybe the tornado took it.

No matter. The old geezer had the key anyway and he had no idea how to hotwire a car. Frustration spread through his body like wildfire. Was he being watched? He checked the house. No faces staring out the windows.

How did he get involved in this mess? He should leave them and go his way, but how would he get on the road? Whether he liked it or not, he should get Crowley out. Then they could figure out what to do next.

With the right tool, he might be able to remove the pins holding the cellar door hinges in place. He scanned the tornado-desecrated farm. A few yards from the window, he found the remains of a vegetable garden. The plants were long gone, but a few metal stakes remained. He trudged through the mud. Gripping with both hands, he tugged out a rod and returned to the little window.

Climbing back inside was far easier, except when he fell to the floor. He winced as his ribs took the jolt. The bottoms of his feet stung when he landed.

"Got a little idea," he said to Mrs. Crowley as he stumbled up the cellar steps. He tapped the rusted metal hinge lightly with the stake. After several minutes, he loosened the pin sufficiently and wedged his makeshift tool into the hinge. First he wiggled out one pin, then the other. Letting the heavy door fall took more strength than he realized he possessed.

He grunted from the exertion. A short laugh escaped his lips. She'd asked God to give him strength. Maybe God answered the old lady's prayers.

Mrs. Crowley grinned and clapped her hands. "Well done, Mr. Morelli."

"All due respect." George bent his head against the fierce wind. "We're far from out of danger."

"First things first." She motioned him to follow and led the way through the muck and rain. After plodding all the way around the house, they discovered little. Dark drapes covered all the windows.

To escape the driving rain, they huddled against the porch wall. Hours had passed and night had surely settled, but the stars remained hidden by storm clouds. Bending his back to the howling wind, George spoke directly into Mrs. Crowley's ear. "The Packard's gone. He must have taken Stryker away."

"Not in this storm. More likely, they're inside the house."

"Let's go in and find out."

Mrs. Crowley agreed and kept pace with him to the door. Much to his surprise, it was unlocked. How curious to lock them in the cellar but leave the front door opened. Must have been preoccupied with his evil plans for poor Stryker.

Inky darkness squeezed them like a vice. Mrs. Crowley clutched George's shoulder with one hand, keeping up with his slow steps. In the first room, he stood for several seconds waiting for his eyes to adjust. When at last he made out outlines of furniture, he hunted for signs of Stryker or the old guy. Nothing stood out, so he held his breath and listened. With the storm still roaring outside, he couldn't hear anything that sounded human.

George inched along a wall until he reached what must be a hallway where he stopped and listened once more. He detected a mannish snore from the right. Crossing to the other side of the hall he turned left, creeping his hands along the wall with Mrs. Crowley right behind.

George turned the knob on the first door they came to and pushed it open an inch or so.

With a pang of relief, he recognized the whistling sound of Stryker sleeping.

"That's her," Mrs. Crowley whispered.

Pushing the door all the way open, George tiptoed into the room, arms in front checking for obstacles. He bumped into a bed and patted along the frame until he found Stryker nearly smothered under layers of blankets.

The springs creaked when George sat on the bed, but Stryker did not wake. He shook her by one shoulder.

"Stryker," Mrs. Crowley said. "Wake up, dear."

The regular rhythm of Stryker's breathing continued without interruption.

"Pick her up." Mrs. Crowley's lips touched George's ear.

George stopped to listen. Had the old man awakened? Reassured, he gently drew back the covers and picked up the sleeping child. She did not awaken but stirred enough to snuggle against him and circle her arms around his neck.

Mrs. Crowley grabbed a handful of blankets and tucked one around the sleeping girl. Then gripping his shoulder, Mrs. Crowley followed George's bumbling progress out of the room, down the hall, and across to the front door. With the bumping into walls, it was amazing the old man didn't wake.

On the porch, George leaned against the wall. His breathing had become labored and the muscles in his arms ached. He couldn't help chuckling to himself. How did he get caught up in this insane drama? Definitely wasn't part of his plan. And they weren't out of danger yet. With George's luck, the old geezer would come out shooting any minute.

Stryker's soft cheek pressed his. A flutter of unfamiliar feelings stirred inside his stomach. Was he going soft? He clenched his jaw.

George carefully placed the child on a beat-up wicker settee.

"Now what?" George had run out of ideas. They got Stryker out of the house, but with the storm raging they still had no way to escape this farm. Any minute, the madman with a shotgun might blast them all to—

"We need a key and a car." Mrs. Crowley whispered. "He must have a vehicle of some kind, or else he hid the Packard in one of those outbuildings."

"Right." Impossible. "Any ideas?"

She prayed aloud. "Lord, we need to get out of here. Show us what to do."

Clearly delusional. Did she expect God to send a lightning bolt to point them to the key?

Stryker roused slightly. "He moved the Packard." Her voice sounded wispy and thin as smoke.

George bent toward her. "Where?"

She gave a small shrug, wagging her head back and forth before drifting back to sleep.

"Where's the key?" George jiggled her shoulder. "Do you know where he put the key?"

Stryker opened her eyelids a slit. "Table. Near the door." Her lids fluttered before dropping closed again.

Sure enough, when George returned to the front room and ran his hand over a table beside the door, he discovered a key. Now to find the Packard.

"You stay here where it's dry. I'll search the barn in back of the house." He nodded toward the ramshackle building behind the garden. "If I find the car, I'll push it into the driveway. When you hear me coming, get over there with Stryker. On the double."

Running through the pelting rain, George pondered how

Mrs. Crowley would manage to lift Stryker. No doubt she'd be praying. Maybe God would help her. This thought gave him a moment of amusement as he struggled against the wind to slide the barn door open.

Inside he found the Packard, cold and dry. Wonder of wonders.

He heaved open the front door, shoved the gear shift into neutral, and pushed the front bumper. A slight slope out of the barn made this task far easier than he had anticipated, but next came the challenge of turning around. Flashes of distant lightning provided illumination. He twisted the steering wheel first one way and then the other while he pushed. With the last of his strength, he managed to head the big machine toward the driveway.

Exhaustion nearly overwhelmed George. Slipping in the mud, he propped himself against a fender. He forced himself upright. Chest heaving, he entertained a selfish thought—start the stupid car and drive away as fast as possible.

In his pocket, his cold fingers closed around the key.

Leave Crowley and the kid to fend for themselves? Why not? They weren't his responsibility. His money had paid for this old jalopy.

Stooped against the wind, George's overcoat pressed his shoulders like a hundred-pound weight as he sloshed to the front of the Packard. Every instinct goaded him to grab this opportunity.

Time to consider his own needs for a change. No one else would. With one continuous movement, he vaulted into the front seat, shoved the key into the ignition, and turned over the engine.

18

MABEL

The sputtering Packard signaled their shrinking window for escape. Surely such racket would wake their host. Mabel breathed a prayer. *Dear Lord, give me strength.*

She scooped Stryker into her arms along with the blanket and clomped down the steps into the storm. Wind whipped a corner of the cover loose. It snapped her leg like a stinging insect. The tempest tore her favorite hat right off her head, hat pins and all, and she could not run after it. Tiny fists of rain beat against her flesh, and still she hobbled through the mud. In a lightning flash, she identified the edge of the driveway. Good thing. Her arms had nearly used every last ounce of strength her old muscles could muster.

A grating whine followed Mr. Morelli's repeated attempts to start the motor. The engine revved with power. Gears grinding, the heavy vehicle lumbered toward Mabel at a higher rate of speed than she thought prudent.

He isn't going to stop.

Adrenaline pumped her heart faster and faster. Lungs heaving moist air struggled as if they might burst. With one final burst of energy, she willed her feet forward, a few tottering steps until she planted her feet in the center of the driveway facing the oncoming car.

Back at the shack, the front door banged. The old man hurled a curse, anger seething in his voice. "Whattaya think you're doin'?"

She didn't check, but somehow she knew he was aiming the shotgun.

"Get back here. You got no right to take my girl away."

The gale whirled his words around Mabel. Her wooden legs refused to move.

"Come back. I ain't fixed her yet."

The shrill squeal of brakes broke the spell. The Packard's front bumper jerked to a stop mere inches from Mabel's knees. She half dragged her heavy bundle to the rear door on the driver's side.

Shotgun pellets exploded into the storm.

Mabel stuffed Stryker in the back seat and climbed in after her. Couldn't risk going around to the front. Mr. Morelli might take the opportunity to flee. Or she might get shot.

The Packard engine roared into another gear as the shotgun fired again. Shot pinged the rear fender but didn't slow the racing sedan. Mabel turned to see him load another shell in the chamber and raise the gun.

How soon would they be out of range?

At the entrance to Route 66, Mr. Morelli depressed the brake. "Come on," he yelled over the storm. "Get in front."

She was taking a chance in complying but dashed into the rain anyway. "Thanks." She slammed the door and slid into the passenger seat. "Stryker needs to lie down back there."

Mr. Morelli flipped on windshield wipers and headlights.

Mabel's heart throbbed abnormally fast, accompanied by a stabbing pain in her chest. She dropped her head back on the seat and closed her eyes. "You weren't going to stop."

He didn't respond.

She turned toward him.

Face drawn into a scowl, he squinted into the thunderstorm, one hand gripping the steering wheel with a tight fist.

With the other, he bumped out a cigarette and crammed it between his lips. "I know you don't like me smoking, but after what I've been through I need a cigarette."

Mabel watched while he dug out his lighter. A flick, a whoosh of flame, and then he sucked in a long drag. He flipped open the wing window to suck the smoke out.

"You weren't going to stop for us," Mabel repeated, trying to keep accusation out of her voice. "Why?"

Mr. Morelli shrugged one shoulder. "Thing is, I did stop."

"You act like someone on the run."

Without glancing her way, he pulled on the cigarette. "Are you?"

Smoke trailed away in a thin stream. "Am I what?"

"Running away?"

Lines in his face she never noticed before seemed to harden. His hand tightened on the wheel. "Don't concern yourself, Mrs. Crowley."

Cigarette squeezed between his lips, he reached for the heater and twisted the dial to high.

While her thoughts churned, Mabel removed her glasses to clean off the moisture and replaced them. The whole interior reeked of smoke. Mabel tasted it in her mouth. Stryker must be inhaling her share too. That couldn't be good for a sick person, but Mr. Morelli didn't care. He didn't deny being on the run. Had they hooked up with a fugitive? *Oh, dear Lord.* Were they safe? God gave her a job to do. How could she do it with this awful person along? She glanced over the seat at Stryker's sleeping form.

Huddled into a tight ball, the child had not moved for a long time except for an occasional shiver. Her breath sounded ragged. Being soaked and going without proper food and water wouldn't improve her health. How could Mabel get this dear girl the help she needed with this spiteful man to contend with? Add to his bad temper the probability he was a wanted criminal. Was she aiding and abetting? She didn't know anything about legal matters, having never been on the wrong side of the law at any time in her long life.

For several hours they barreled through the rain in silence.

Stryker didn't move, but she mumbled a few times. Something about Sophia. Was she speaking to the monkey? Her whisper sounded odd. Had she been drugged? Mr. Morelli planned to leave them stranded without money or a car. She'd lost her favorite hat, and her stockings were mud-spattered and streaked with runs. Her shoes were ruined too. How could she afford to buy all the things they needed—clothes, shampoo, shoes, medical supplies?

If only she knew how to turn off her worrying and get some sleep. Every muscle in her body felt sore. She knew she should trust God. He had never let her down yet. But what about those chest pains? If she died, what would happen to Stryker?

Whatever made her think she could survive this long trip? Of course, when she had made the decision she never imagined she'd have to contend with tornados, crazy people, stolen cars, and criminals all in three days' time.

The Packard whizzed over the North Fork of the Red River and through Erick. Mabel would be relieved to get out of Oklahoma. She looked at the gas gauge. "We're getting low on fuel."

Mr. Morelli didn't respond.

She saw a sign advertising an open-all-night Texaco station and pointed. He steered under the canopy and parked. Without saying where he was going, he slammed his door and sauntered off across the street. The attendant bustled out to clean the mud-caked windshield, check the oil, and fill the nearly empty tank.

Mabel urgently needed to use the restroom, but did she dare leave Stryker alone? The clean-cut attendant appeared to be trustworthy so she asked him to keep his eye on Stryker. The child might be frightened if she woke up to find both of them gone.

Mabel bit her lip, wishing she didn't have to leave her charge alone. Surely two vehicles wouldn't be stolen on the same trip. She dashed around the side of the building to use the facilities.

Back in record time, Mabel slipped off Stryker's soaked

shoes and socks. Warm air from the heater had already dried the extra blanket. Mabel peeled the soggy cover off Stryker. What a sight the child was—messy and rumpled, her arms and legs speckled with mud. Mabel wiped off all the dirt she could. Despite the jostling the girl slept on, but her skin felt clammy and cold.

Tucking the dry blanket close around Stryker, Mabel prayed it would be enough to take the chill off the girl's trembling body. Thankful to find the little stuffed monkey, Mabel placed it in Stryker's arms and cleaned out more of the trash left in the car.

Mr. Morelli returned carrying two paper cups and offered her one. "Coffee. Thought you might need some."

"Thanks." She accepted the cup and sipped the steaming liquid. "That was thoughtful." She wouldn't expect this kindness from someone so recently willing to abandon her and a sick child. Was coffee his way of making amends?

The attendant brought the oil dipstick to Mr. Morelli. "You need a couple quarts of oil."

Mr. Morelli okayed the purchase, grumbling about old junk heaps that guzzled oil like horses drink water. He drew out his roll of bills and counted his money. His expression seemed to darken as he paid the attendant.

Sometime after passing through Texola and the Texas border, Mabel dozed off. When she awakened, the rain had stopped and the first rays of sunlight appeared in the East. Mr. Morelli had parked on the side of the road and gotten out of the Packard, perhaps to relieve himself.

While he navigated back onto the highway, she studied him. How did he manage to drive through the night with no sleep? He must be desperate to get away. But from whom? Or what? "You must be exhausted. Are you ready to let me drive?"

He flicked his latest cigarette butt out the window and blew out a long breath. "Yeah. Quite an ordeal."

"Where are we?"

"Somewhere near Shamrock, Texas."

Mabel was about to ask when he planned to buy another vehicle and be on his way south when something outside exploded. It sounded like a bomb. She twisted her neck to see out the back window. Black chunks littered the road behind them. The Packard lurched to one side then thumped and rumbled, slowing speed.

Mr. Morelli's hand covered the red scar on his forehead. "Must've blown a tire."

She tuned out his colorful commentary of the situation as he maneuvered the Packard to the side of the highway, mashed the brake, and turned off the ignition. He climbed out and ambled back where he stood with his hands on his hips.

Mabel joined him.

The rear left tire—as well as the inner tube inside it—had shredded. Only a few strips of rubber remained attached to the rim. Perhaps one of the shotgun blasts had punctured the inner tube and air had been slowly leaking out ever since.

With a tilt of his head, Mr. Morelli glanced at Mabel. "What do you figure the chances are this crate will have a spare?"

What a pessimist. "Only one way to find out."

They walked to the trunk.

"What do you know?"

What appeared to be a new tire was nestled inside. He tugged it out, bouncing it on the gravel. Underneath lay a bundle of metal pieces.

"We've caught a bit of luck." Mr. Morelli leaned the tire against one fender. "Just one small problem."

"And that would be?"

"I don't know how to do this."

Surely she heard wrong. "You don't know how to change a flat?"

He shook his head. "Got people for that."

In the dawning light Mabel searched the horizon for a filling station, but all she saw was wide-open Texas landscape. Her shoulders slumped. She appraised Mr. Morelli over the top of her glasses. He was more namby-pamby than she had ever imagined.

Trouble was Stryker was too small and Mabel knew she didn't have strength to change the tire herself. That narrowed the choices down to one candidate—Mr. Morelli. "I watched Paul change a few tires. There's nothing to it. I'll talk you through the process."

Mr. Morelli's irritated visage left little doubt about his reluctance. Maybe he didn't want to get his hands greasy. He removed his cigarette pack from his overcoat before tugging the coat off and throwing it into the trunk. Then he extracted the last cigarette, balled the package, and tossed the wad to the side of the road. Was he stalling?

Mabel raised her eyebrows and crossed her arms, but he paid her no mind. With the click of his lighter, he lit the last cigarette then took several seconds to suck smoke into his lungs. He released the drag. Slowly. "Okay. Talk me through it."

Mabel untied the bundle. "This is a bumper jack. First, you put the flat piece on the ground. The other parts fit together." She offered the jack.

Taking a couple more puffs, he placed the pieces on the ground and squatted to peer underneath. "How does it work?"

Mabel bent as low as she could to check it out.

A door clicked shut and Stryker tiptoed over the gravel to join them. The greenish circles under her eyes had darkened. Her bare feet appeared skeletal and ghostly white. Blinking in the early morning sunlight, she stretched her scrawny arms over her head. "What happened?"

Mabel circled her shoulders with a hug. "You had a long sleep. Must've been extra tired after all that mess." She ran a hand over Stryker's bald head, wondering where the knit cap had gone.

Stryker produced a weak smile. "We got a flat tire."

"Our latest challenge." Despite what must have been an attempt at levity, Mr. Morelli's expression remained grim.

"Did you set the emergency brake?" Stryker asked.

Mabel and Mr. Morelli exchanged an amused glance.

"Good idea, dear." Mabel hurried to comply.

When she rejoined them, Stryker had placed the black square on the ground under the bumper and wedged the long straight part of the jack into the bottom piece. "To keep it stable."

Next she picked up the tire iron. "Take off the hubcap and loosen the lug nuts with this." She extended the tool to Mr. Morelli.

He picked up the iron as if the thing might bite and gingerly approached the tire.

"Use one end to pry off the hubcap and the other for the lug nuts." Stryker looked like she wanted to laugh.

With quite a bit of grunting, he got the hubcap off and removed the lug nuts. Sweat beaded on his brow. A few drops broke free to drip down his cheek. When he wiped them away he left a grease streak on his face.

Patiently, Stryker showed him how to wiggle the tire iron into the jack and lift the frame by pumping. After he got the rubber an inch or so off the ground, she held up her hand like a stop sign. "Now pull off what's left of the tire."

Even this task proved taxing for Mr. Morelli. He huffed and puffed before dropping the remains on the gravel.

One hand over her mouth, Mabel refrained from reminding him he would breathe easier if he quit filling his lungs with smoke.

Stryker pointed to the spare.

Sweat now pouring off his face like raindrops, he hefted the tire up and pushed it in place on the lugs.

"Tighten her up," she said. "Dump the old rim back in the trunk. We should have another spare put on it." She circled the car. "The other three tires are pretty bald too."

When Mr. Morelli finished, he sat back on his haunches and wiped his brow on his sleeve. Grease stained his pants and his shirt. Crescents of sweat discolored the fabric under his arms. His cheek looked like he'd applied war paint. "Now I need a cigarette. A drink too—a good strong drink to celebrate."

Mabel stifled the urge to chide him for such foolishness. What did he have to celebrate? He'd used up over an hour to change the tire. As an old man, Paul could have done it in half the time. Who was this stranger who didn't know such rudimentary survival techniques as changing tires and who thought he could buy his way out of every situation? Thank goodness the crazy old man refused to be bribed. Mr. Morelli needed to learn that not everyone would snap to his bidding when he waved his cash around.

Back in the car while Mabel drove, she questioned Stryker about what had happened inside the house. Stryker recounted her ordeal and showed them the shocking bruises on her wrists where the old man clamped her hands together over her head. Chills raced down Mabel's spine. Whatever was he up to? Was he insane? Did he truly believe his medicine would make Stryker well? She only appeared sicker.

Another stitch of pain skewered her chest. Mabel winced but prayed it away. *Please God, keep me going until we get Stryker to the hospital.*

"Well," Mr. Morelli said. "We should write up our adventures and apply for a page in the Guinness Book of Records."

"The what?" Stryker asked.

"I read about it in the newspaper. Some new gimmick out of England. Supposed to be published this year. A couple of rich guys got together to brag about who was the greatest. They decided there should be a list of record-breaking accomplishments somewhere. Since they couldn't find one, they wrote their own. The book is coming out this year. I'm telling you, we'd be a shoe-in for the most problems on a four-day-trip."

Odd idea. Mabel probed his face with a quick glance. He had turned halfway to converse with Stryker who sat on the edge of the back seat with her crossed arms resting on the front seat. He seemed to have a heart for the girl, and she liked him too. Disagreeable as he was most of the time, he was seldom grouchy with Stryker.

About that time, they rolled into Shamrock.

Mr. Morelli read, "Tower Station and U-Drop Inn. The most up-to-date edifice of its kind on the U.S. highway between Oklahoma City and Amarillo." He pointed at a white art-deco style building. "Stop there. I gotta get cigarettes."

"Really." Mabel raised her eyebrows. "We've barely gotten started. I thought you were in a hurry."

"I need to go," Stryker said. "And I'm hungry too."

With a long exhale, Mabel veered into the parking lot, slowing to find a space.

She hadn't driven far before she realized the atmosphere had chilled. She flicked a sideways look.

Brow furrowed, Mr. Morelli stared wide-eyed at something behind them. His expression appeared frozen in place.

Her gaze popped to the rearview mirror.

A shiny black sedan followed so close it almost rammed the Packard's bumper.

19

STRYKER

Stryker did not understand why Mr. Morelli insisted on leaving the Tower Station in such a hot hurry. What treasures might such a fanciful building hold? Grown-ups so often changed their minds for no good reason. Without cigarettes, Mr. Morelli constantly complained about Mrs. Crowley's driving but offered no explanation why he wouldn't buy more. Hadn't he said he needed some?

Not finding another filling station nearby, Mrs. Crowley stopped beside the road in the desert to allow Stryker to relieve herself. Mr. Morelli nervously stood guard at the Packard. Maybe he expected a cop to come along and say they'd broken a law.

Back on the road, she did her best to lighten the mood. "Who can guess the make and model of the cars we pass?"

"You'll win." Mr. Morelli drummed his fingers on the dash.

Every so often he turned to peer out the back window. About the third time, he said, "Tell you what, kid. If you spot the big shiny black sedan let me know, okay?"

"The Buick Roadmaster from the Tower Station?"

He nodded. "That's the one."

"Why?"

"Never mind why. Just tell me. Got it?"

Did he think it was the same black car from the filling station back in Lebanon where he left his Continental? 'Cause it wasn't. They were both black Roadmaster sedans for sure, but the other one was a '53 and the Tower one was definitely a '54. If he knew what to look for, he would have noticed the difference in the trim. Easy. She might point this out later when he wasn't so grumpy. She scooted back in the seat, tugged the blanket around her shoulders, and hugged Sophia to her chest.

Mrs. Crowley didn't talk much and kept staring straight ahead as she drove. After a while, rain started again and she shifted down to second gear.

Sure enough, Mr. Grouchy had something to say about that. "Don't slow down. You've got new windshield wipers. Turn them on high."

Mrs. Crowley flipped the wiper lever, but the wipers didn't speed up enough to clear the water off any quicker. "The rain is coming down too hard for those little blades to be much help."

Mr. Morelli flopped to a new position in the front seat. "Drive faster. There's hardly a vehicle on the road."

"If you let me drive without constantly pestering me, we'll be fine. I know how to drive in the rain, Mr. Morelli." Mrs. Crowley pointed to a big sign. "Over a hundred miles before Amarillo. In this rain, that will probably take more than two hours. We need to stop and eat somewhere along the way."

Mr. Morelli smacked the window with the side of his head, which must have hurt since he had a wound there.

Several miles rolled by in uncomfortable silence. Snuggled in her cozy blanket cocoon, Stryker stretched out on the seat. She didn't need to watch the scenery. Texas looked the same as Oklahoma. When would Mr. Morelli buy another car and shoot off to his brother's? He hadn't mentioned his plans for a while. Her heavy eyelids dropped shut.

Once when she opened her eyes a slit, Mr. Morelli's head had slumped. Probably taking a nap.

Stryker woke with a start when the Packard lurched to a stop. Mrs. Crowley muttered something that sounded like, "Oh, no."

Standing to peer out the rain-streaked windshield, Stryker saw a river racing through a small ravine where pavement should have been. On the other side of the gully, Route 66 continued. "What happened to the road?"

"Looks like the water eroded the highway," Mrs. Crowley answered.

A highway patrolman in a yellow slicker climbed out of his 1955 black-and-white Chevy to tap on the side window. Mrs. Crowley rolled it down a few inches. "Sorry, ma'am. The road's washed out. Flash floods are common around these parts. You'll have to turn around."

Mr. Morelli groaned. Guess the sudden stop woke him too.

The cop squinted through the open part of the window. "Got a sick passenger there, ma'am?"

Mrs. Crowley shot a glance at Mr. Morelli. Still facing out his window, he covered his face with his hand. "Tell him we must get to Tucumcari tonight."

Stryker frowned. Why didn't Mr. Morelli speak for himself?

"Ma'am?" The officer seemed unable to understand Mr. Morelli's mumbling.

"He needs to get to Tucumcari tonight. Is there an alternate route?"

The trooper wrinkled his forehead. "You're a long way from Tucumcari, I'm afraid, and this rain's not letting up anytime soon. My best advice is to head for the nearest motel and camp out until the storm blows over."

"We want to go west, not east." Mr. Morelli sounded like a whiny baby. "There must be another way to get back on Route 66."

"Oh, for pity's sake." Mrs. Crowley huffed. "Is there a way around this section of highway?"

The cop tipped his hat forward, cascading water into the window. "If you return to McLean, you could take 273 North. It will eventually link up to 60. Head toward Amarillo, and you can connect to Route 66 there."

Mrs. Crowley brushed rain off her sleeve while repeating the directions.

"Don't know how long it'll take or if those roads will be passable when you get there."

"Thank you, officer." She rolled the window back up.

Mr. Morelli motioned for Mrs. Crowley to turn around. Why was he so impatient?

Soon the Packard headed east on Route 66. After awhile Mrs. Crowley wiped a circle on the steamed window and strained to read road signs. How would she find the turnoff through the downpour?

Mr. Morelli straightened to see out the windshield. "Twenty-five miles since we started east. Where is McLean?"

"Why don't you check the map?" Stryker asked.

Mrs. Crowley looked into the rearview mirror. Behind Mrs. Crowley's glasses, her eyes sparkled and the skin around them crinkled. Stryker was delighted she had amused her friend.

Spreading the map between his lap and the dash, Mr. Morelli continued muttering. "How can I possibly tell where we are? What's the last sign you saw?"

"About ten minutes ago one posted Shamrock as twenty-five miles away."

"What?" He slapped the map with his hand. "You missed Highway 273. See the sign ahead? Can you read that one?"

Mrs. Crowley slowed, craning her neck.

"Don't slow down." He cursed under his breath. "We're crawling as it is." Mr. Morelli leaned forward. "Heald. Okay, turn."

"Are you certain? This is not the way the officer indicated."

"Yes, yes." He nearly shouted. "Turn."

With a heavy sigh, Mrs. Crowley steered the Packard onto the road toward Heald.

"Somehow you missed the turn. We're putting extra miles and extra hours on this old clunker." He hunched over the map. "This road should be a straight shot to Kellerville. When we get there, we'll go west to the 273. Then we can get on the 60, like the officer said." He refolded the map, dropping his shoulders while he released a long breath. "I knew I should drive."

The rest of the afternoon passed in much the same manner. Unplanned stops became necessary when disagreements over where to turn erupted. At those times, Stryker had to stare out the window to keep from laughing. The two sounded like Mama's married friends who argued all the time. The ones she called the Bickersons.

Twice Mrs. Crowley stopped to ask for directions. They all got out and tended to other needs then too. At the second stop Mr. Morelli bought sodas and a little bottle of whiskey for himself. Then he fussed and swore because it wasn't smooth enough. Not like he was used to. Stryker didn't know whiskey came in different kinds. She never heard Mama talk about anything but rotgut whiskey.

By the time they meandered onto Highway 60 toward Amarillo, the dark clouds had drifted aside to let spots of blue sky show through. Stryker's stomach gurgled with hunger. "Will we stop to eat soon?"

"It's still early, and we didn't get far today," Mr. Morelli said.

"We're spending the night in Amarillo," Mrs. Crowley shifted to look at Stryker. "We'll get food when we stop."

He cursed.

"Mr. Morelli, please. I have been patient with your ill humor today, but we ladies simply will not tolerate this vulgar language."

Stryker had heard much worse from Mama and her friends. Being included when Mrs. Crowley spoke of ladies was pleasant though.

Mr. Morelli stared out the side window. "You can stay in Amarillo if you want. I'm buying a new car. Something without rust. Maybe a Cadillac." He turned to Stryker. "What do you think about that?"

"What model?"

"How about an Eldorado?"

"Rocketship tailfins with sabre-spoke wheels." Stryker nodded. "Gotta be a convertible."

"Of course. In red."

Stryker pictured a cherry-apple red Cadillac with whitewall tires and smiled. Too bad she wouldn't get to ride in it.

Miles of windswept grasses whizzed by as they drove on and on and on—flat land in shades of green. They rolled into Amarillo, Texas in the late afternoon. The town sprawled over a mostly level plain with a big mountain towering over it as if keeping watch.

"Took us all day to get to the middle of the Texas panhandle," Mr. Morelli muttered.

"Yet here we are," Mrs. Crowley said. "So where should we spend the night? Have you been watching the signs? Anything suit your highfaluting taste?"

"Drop me off at a Cadillac dealership."

Over the top of her glasses, Mrs. Crowley blinked at him. "You're not serious. It's almost five o'clock, and this child needs to eat. I'm exhausted. I will not drive all over town hunting for a Cadillac dealership at this time of night."

"But I need to—"

"Not tonight."

Mr. Morelli crossed his arms.

Silence dropped over them for a few minutes until Mr. Morelli began reading signs aloud as they passed. "The Big Texan."

"Amarillo Cowboy."

"Bar-None Ranch Steakhouse. Do you notice a theme in this hick town?" He smirked. "And not one place fit for a city slicker."

About then, Mrs. Crowley pointed to a large neon sign. "Oh, look. The Triangle Motel. The vacancy sign is on. This one is perfect."

Stryker agreed. The neat cream-colored brick building with pretty blue wooden awnings was charming. So like the rest of Amarillo.

Mr. Morelli glared. "Another dump."

"A tourist court. Lovely." Mrs. Crowley depressed the brake, parking directly in front of the office. "The Stockyard Café is right across the street. What more could you ask?"

At the front desk, Mr. Morelli drew out money to pay for two rooms. The wad seemed smaller. Could he be running out of cash? Grinding his jaw, he twisted his lips tight and drew his brows together in a mass of wrinkles. Then he mumbled that he couldn't eat now and told them to go without him. Grabbing his key, he slumped off to his room.

Mrs. Crowley and Stryker hustled across the street to the café. Stryker's bald head always made people stare. She kept her chin high and wished she hadn't lost her new knit hat.

Stomach growling, Stryker ordered a hamburger, french fries, and a vanilla milk shake—her most favorite meal. But when the food came, fatigue overwhelmed her so she could barely chew. Mrs. Crowley encouraged her to finish. Stryker took one last bite, but the food wouldn't go down when she swallowed. Her stomach rumbled like thunder and the diner smells made her gag. She had to spit out the food in her mouth. A couple of tears squeezed out the corners of her eyes.

After Mrs. Crowley paid the bill, she took Stryker's hand and escorted her back to the motel where she insisted a hot bath would make them both feel better. Stryker soaked in the sudsy warm water while Mrs. Crowley washed out their muddy clothes and hung them to dry on the shower rod.

When Mrs. Crowley tucked the covers up around Stryker's neck, she gave a faint gasp and clutched her chest.

"Does your heart hurt?" Stryker asked.

Mrs. Crowley ran a wrinkled hand over Stryker's brow. "Only a little. I'm sure it's nothing." Mrs. Crowley sat on the edge of the bed, still pressing her hand on her chest. She took a couple of deep breaths before her eyes met Stryker's. "As soon as we get out of Texas we'll be about halfway to Los Angeles. That's exciting, isn't it?"

"I guess." *Exciting* wasn't a word Stryker would use. More miles on the road, more bickering. Then, when she arrived in California, she'd be poked by more doctors. She didn't have energy to do much except sleep. Seemed like she was sleeping a lot.

Mrs. Crowley tucked Sophia in next to Stryker. "We surely have packed a great many experiences into these four short days."

"Then we have four more days to go?"

"What's that? Four days? I expect so. Maybe three, depending on future adventures." Mrs. Crowley blessed her with a tired smile. "Hopefully the problems are over now, and we'll drive on through." She glanced down at her white slip. "Tomorrow we must find somewhere to buy a few clothes. We need underwear so we don't have to wash every night. And nightclothes. Your little shoes will never be the same."

"Another hat too?"

Mrs. Crowley beamed. "New hats for us both certainly seem in order. God has protected us through these trials. We have much to be thankful for. Shall we say our prayers?"

After Mrs. Crowley prayed, her lips brushed Stryker's cheek. "Good night, dear. Sleep well."

For a long time Stryker lay awake, blinking at the dark ceiling. Sometimes she liked Mr. Morelli. He knew a lot about cars, although he lied a lot, like about where he was going and what he would do when he got there and about buying another automobile and heading south. He wasn't in any hurry to get to his brother's house. What scared him about the black Buick? Why wouldn't he speak directly to the cop? Now he's sick and can't eat. After he picks up more cigarettes, he'll feel better. Mama said some people need cigarettes.

In the other bed, Mrs. Crowley moaned and thrashed from side to side for a long time. The sounds frightened Stryker because they were noises Mama made. Stryker hugged Sophia closer.

Maybe the pain in Mrs. Crowley's chest was something after all.

20

GEORGE

Exhausted though he was, George couldn't sleep more than a few hours. Nicotine withdrawal cramped his insides and set his nerves on edge. He needed a cigarette badly, but the bigger problem was his dwindling funds. Who was he kidding about buying a Cadillac? He had counted his cash twice. Not enough to buy a new car. Might have to settle for an old clunker like the Packard. Puerto Vallarta, Mexico was days away. Would he have enough money to start a business in Gringo Gulch as an investor for wealthy Americans who vacationed there? He moaned, once again grieving the loss of his nest egg.

Why hadn't he searched for the Studebaker in Oklahoma City? The Crowley woman had pressured him. Made him hurry. He hadn't had time to think matters through. But he shouldn't have given up so quickly, allowed his money to be stolen without a fight.

Perhaps he should continue on to California before heading south. He'd say he ran out of cash. Not a lie. By rights Mrs. Crowley should pay for the motel and gas up the junk heap instead of mooching off his generosity. Then maybe he could leave her in California and take the Packard to Mexico. The thought of arriving at his new home in a rusty beater wrinkled his nose. Somehow he must find more cash.

Still in his stained, wrinkled clothes, he trudged across Amarillo Boulevard to buy a couple Lucky Strike packs at the all-night Stockyard Café.

The door banged behind him while he gave the restaurant a quick scan. What a surprise to be the lone customer at one-thirty in the morning. Welcome to Hicksville.

George found the dispenser and bought a couple packs of cigarettes. Then he slid into a booth and unwrapped one pack. His hands trembled as he withdrew his lighter from his pocket. He needed this baby.

A lanky waitress with a short, pixie cut sauntered over to him. "Ouch." She pointed to his forehead as she popped chewing gum. "Betcha had a nasty accident. What happened?"

"None of your business."

"A little hungry are we?" She picked an order pad out of a pocket in her frilly apron and extracted the pencil from behind her ear. "What'll it be tonight?"

Her familiarity made him queasy. "Black coffee." He stubbed out the first cigarette and lit a second. "With a steak." He snarled the words, hoping to discourage conversation.

The waitress dashed off and returned in minutes to fill his mug with hot coffee. "What brings you to Amarillo, sugar?" Her lazy drawl made her unwelcome curiosity all the more irritating.

"Just passing through."

"Yeah? Where from?" With the eraser end of her pencil, she scratched her head through a hairnet tied in back.

George stared at the table, drumming his fingers. Why did these homely broads always want to talk? He blew smoke at her, hoping she would take the hint.

She waved the smoke away. "Not trying to be nosy, honeybunch, but we don't get many good-lookin' guys in the middle of the night." Was that big, red grin painted on her face?

"Didn't come for chit-chat."

She arched her black penciled eyebrows. "Sorrrrrry." With a flounce, she spun on one heel. Her crepe-soled shoes squeaked across the linoleum floor, calling attention to an unappreciated view of her wiggling behind.

George groaned. Did he look like an easy mark?

While he waited for his order, he smoked a couple more cigarettes. He had practically given up on his food when the waitress reappeared carrying two plates.

"'Bout time. Have to shoot the cow?"

"Funny." She set the plates in front of George. "You ain't from Texas, are you?"

"Texas?" The repulsive notion curled his lip. Without meeting her gaze, he picked up the knife and sawed into the steak. "No."

"I'm real good at guessin' accents. Say a couple more words."

George chewed and swallowed. "I don't care whether or not you can guess where I came from." He forked another chunk and lifted it to his mouth.

"Chicago?"

George stopped chewing. "Beat it."

"Am I right?" She bent toward him, coming within an inch of his face. "Come on, sweetie." Her voice went sultry. "Just say I'm right."

Banging his knife on the table, George cursed. "Get outta my face."

She tore the bill off her order pad and tossed it on the table before stomping away.

How did she guess he was from Chicago? A coincidence? Day five was upon him. The investigation into the missing funds and his disappearance must be well underway. His picture might be all over every major newspaper. He turned up his collar. Did the waitress recognize him from some blurry photo? Would he make the TV news way out here? He peered out the window, searching for a black Buick.

For a second his imagination wandered to what Mother must be saying. He forked another chunk of steak. And Gloria. How ironic he had lost the cash so soon. With the evidence gone, they'd never pin embezzlement on him. One good thing had come out of this mess.

George gobbled the rest of his food. Gut filled, he swigged one final gulp of coffee and threw down a couple of bills.

That would leave a three-cent tip for the snoop.

Back in the motel room, George forced his eyes shut. Every time he drifted off, fleets of black Buick Roadmasters appeared, revving their engines to a roar before speeding through the walls to run him down. Insides churning, he jerked awake.

Blast that T-bone steak.

He turned on the lamp. Leaning back on his elbows, he surveyed his surroundings. Get real. He was completely safe here. No one would ever search for George Stanton in a rundown motel in Texas.

Not his style.

Hours later, streaks of morning light spilled through the crack between the curtains. George squinted at his watch. Six fifty-five. Time to get moving. He threw back the rumpled bed-clothes and stood to stretch. Mouth parched and foul smelling, he slogged to the bathroom to perform rudimentary ablutions. Toothpaste would've helped. George stared at the tub. The towels, though not as thick and luxurious as he typically used, appeared serviceable. He could take a shower, but the thought of putting dirty clothes on a clean body quashed the idea. Shopping for some clothes was urgent. He'd stop at the first decent store he spied.

More awake after he splashed cold water on his face, he sauntered to Crowley's room and pounded on the door.

A bleary-eyed Stryker appeared in the open crack.

"Ready?" He tapped his wristwatch. "Got miles to cover today."

Mrs. Crowley stuck her head out the opening. "Do you mind? I had a hard time sleeping, and we aren't dressed yet." Not waiting for a response, she slammed the door.

George drained his flask and smoked two cigarettes one after the other before the door opened and the pair marched out wearing clean but wrinkled clothing.

"Hmm." He made a show of appraising their appearance. "We need to shop today."

"At least we're clean. You, on the other hand . . ." Mrs. Crowley crossed her arms.

"Yeah, yeah." George had avoided looking in the mirror. He stroked his growing beard. He had never in his life experienced this commonness. Like a day laborer, dirty and smudged. Wearing the same underwear and socks he'd left Tulsa in. Not to mention the body odor.

"It's too early for shops to be open," Mrs. Crowley said. "Breakfast first?"

George couldn't risk running into the prying waitress again. "Not here. We'll head down the road a bit." He held out his hand. "My turn to drive."

Mrs. Crowley pinched her lips together, but despite the obvious displeasure her expression conveyed, she handed him the key without comment. It wasn't much, but it was a slight favor. Didn't feel like dealing with her disapproval.

On the outskirts of Vega, Texas, George spotted a billboard advertising The Hickory Café, For Those Who Are Fussy About Their Food. "Sounds like my kind of place," George said. "We'll stop and decide for ourselves."

The restaurant occupied one corner of Main Street and Route 66 in downtown Vega. George wrinkled his nose at the faded red clapboard building. The café clearly lacked the upscale qualities George preferred. Dusty pickup trucks with rifles in the back windows made up more than half the vehicles in the dirt parking lot. On the plus side, a department store across the street promised all the items they needed to buy. After heaving a heavy sigh, he steered the Packard into the Hickory Café lot.

"Breakfast, anyone?" For the sake of the kid, George vowed to lighten the mood, although the sight of her made his insides clench. Stryker appeared gaunter and paler each day, and her energy was clearly fading.

A short waitress whose Texas-shaped name badge identified her as Betty showed them to a table while the radio blared country music. Some hillbilly named Ray Price sang goofy words about stars getting in your eyes and the moon breaking your heart. George made a face as he removed his overcoat and slid into the seat. "That's a real toe-tapper, that is."

Stryker cocked her head. "Do you like country music, Mr. Morelli?"

"I'd rather listen to Frank Sinatra."

"Sorry," Betty said. "Pearl's in charge of the radio. Most folks 'round here like their country music loud."

George took out his cigarettes. "Got any Johnnie Walker Gold?"

"Say, what?"

"Scotch. Whiskey."

Betty shook her head. "We got cold beer."

"Never mind." George opened the menu. "Just bring a pot of coffee when you come back, and turn down that infernal music so we don't have to yell at each other."

Over the top of his menu, George monitored the exchange between Betty and presumably Pearl. The two obviously discussed more than turning down the music. Betty pointed a chubby finger at George, shooting him several sideways glances.

At one point, Pearl opened a newspaper on the counter. Heads together, they huddled over it. A short time later, Betty lifted the newspaper and shamelessly ogled George over the top. Had she identified him from something in the paper?

George turned up his shirt collar. He needed more than four days of beard stubble for a disguise.

In minutes, Betty brought their food, balancing the plates on her arms like a circus performer. All business, she recited the orders as she placed the food on the table. When she set the plate in front of George, she hesitated. "Y'all heading east or west today?"

George arranged his napkin. "Why do you ask?"

She shrugged. "Just wonderin'. Looks like you been traveling a while. Got much farther to go?"

"That'll be all," George said, grinding his jaw.

Mrs. Crowley looked up as Betty walked away. "Thank you."

Were all waitresses nosy? He must see the newspaper. Was his face on the front page?

"Really, Mr. Morelli." Mrs. Crowley's mouth turned down at the corners. "You don't have to be rude."

Why did this old woman constantly try to control him? Stronger people than Mrs. Mabel Crowley had tried to dominate him and failed.

He wolfed down his eggs, hash browns, and toast and gulped coffee in record time. "Gotta make a pit stop." He swiped his mouth with his napkin and threw it on the table. On the way to the restroom, he slowed when he passed the counter.

A folded copy of the *Oklahoma City Sun* prominently featured a photo of a man on the front page. The lower half of the face and the headline were hidden on the other side of the fold. The part George saw showed a fedora shading a man's eyes. The eyes could be his. His stomach lurched. Unfolding the paper would draw attention. After a moment of indecision, he squared his shoulders and continued to the restroom.

On his way back, a farmer seated at the counter had picked up the paper.

Time for Plan B.

Stryker leaned toward him. "Could I have a quarter to get a gumball?"

"Sure, why not." He fished out a quarter and flipped it on the table. "Finish eating then meet me at the department store." He pointed across the street. "You can pick up the check this time. My funds are running low."

"You don't have money for breakfast, but you can afford clothes?"

"Well, that's the thing." George might as well tell the truth. "Most of my cash was in the Studebaker. Paying for motel rooms, food, buying a car and keeping it filled with gas, I'm not sure I'll have enough to buy clothes."

She raised her eyebrows.

"Why don't you two shop a bit too? If you have the money."

George didn't wait for her response but dashed out and

crossed the street. First he hunted for newspapers but didn't find the *Oklahoma City Sun* in any of the stands. Not surprising. No reason to have an Oklahoma paper in Texas. What was he worried about anyway? Lots of men wore fedoras. The picture coulda been anybody.

The department store carried a wide variety of cowboy apparel. Swallowing hard over a lump of distaste, George sorted through boots, shirts, and Levis. Pitiful, the way these yokels dressed, but he must blend in, look like all the other yahoos in these parts. No more suits and city hats. No shiny, soft leather Italian shoes and silk socks. Think cowboy.

While he hunted for a disguise that might leave some of his pride intact, Mrs. Crowley and Stryker entered and waved. He nodded as they headed off to the children's section.

George selected a blue denim work shirt and jeans and tried them on in the dressing room. The image scowling back from the mirror looked nothing like George Stanton. Wouldn't Mother be horrified? The jagged red scar healing across his forehead lent a kind of tough-guy charm, as did his growing crop of dark facial hair. He'd need a barber to trim the beard soon. All in all, it was quite a transformation and not all bad. Once he got settled in Mexico, he'd shop for better clothes, but he might keep the beard.

With a nod of approval at his reflection, he added a couple more shirts and another pair of jeans before moving on to purchase a pair of boots along with several pairs of socks and underwear. Last of all he bought a cowboy hat, a belt complete with silver buckle, a pair of Ray-Ban sunglasses along with various items for grooming. The clerk folded his filthy, wrinkled clothes and shoes into shopping bags, which he carried across the street to dump into the trunk of the Packard before returning to wait for the ladies.

Mrs. Crowley and Stryker finalized their purchases. Three bags of merchandise lined the counter next to the cash register. Mrs. Crowley dug money out of her purse to pay for their clothes.

Stryker appeared girly in a pink blouse and denim full skirt, black-and-white saddle oxfords and socks with lace around the top. A beige cloth hat covered her head, making her pale blue eyes look bigger. Mrs. Crowley was suitably attired in a new green hat and matching wool dress. She had not purchased new shoes, but at least she had on stockings without holes.

Back on the road, George sensed Mrs. Crowley staring at him while he drove. "Quite a change, Mr. Morelli. What made you decide to dress like a Texan?"

"When in Rome . . . you know."

Stryker leaned over the seat. "I like it. You look like a movie cowboy."

He favored her with a lopsided grin and lapsed into a drawl. "Well now, little lady, that's exactly what I was going for—a movie cowboy. Reminds you of Gary Cooper, doesn't it?"

Mrs. Crowley chuckled. "I was thinking more of Lash LaRue."

"Lash LaRue?" scoffed George. "You gotta be kidding."

"You have his dark good looks." She tilted her head. "But I never saw a cowboy wear sunglasses in the movies. What made you choose those?"

Again with the third degree. "The clerk sold me on them. Said they're made of a special new material designed to cut down highway glare."

"Uh-huh." Mrs. Crowley nodded, still studying him. "Your beard is getting quite thick too. Makes me wonder. Are you afraid you'll be recognized, Mr. Morelli?"

Would she never shut up?

She would not. "Yesterday you said you were going to buy a vehicle and head south to visit your brother. Then you drove right through Amarillo. Now we're almost out of Texas. What's going on?"

George's neck heated as anger surged through his body, but he refused to give this infuriating woman the satisfaction of knowing she got to him. He willed his jaw to relax and forced a smile. "Glad you brought that subject up. Been thinking I should accompany you to California in case you have another flat tire or something. With a clunker as old as this one, trouble is a real possibility."

"What about your brother? I thought he needed your help?"

"My brother?" Think fast. "I telephoned him last night from the motel and let him know I'd be detained. He said he's got neighbors to help him move, so I don't have to hurry."

"Really?" Mrs. Crowley's eyebrows arched. "And what about your job?"

Stryker nodded. "You had to hurry back to work because some big deals were cooking. That's what you said."

"Right. Well, I should call work today and let them know what's going on. I'll have to use vacation time, but I'm sure it won't be a problem."

Mrs. Crowley cocked her head. "Are you married, Mr. Morelli?"

"Married to my work. Been successful too."

"Exactly what kind of work do you do?"

He shot her a quick frown. "You got a lotta questions today, ma'am. And here I was proposing to give up some of my valuable time to get you and Stryker to California safely. I thought you'd be happy, but what do I get for my generosity? Suspicion." He shook a playful finger at Mrs. Crowley. "Just doesn't pay to do the right thing, does it?"

Mrs. Crowley appeared as cowed as he intended. "I guess I owe you an apology, Mr. Morelli. I'm terribly sorry. I completely misjudged you. I hope you will forgive me."

George lifted a victorious gaze to the rearview mirror.

In the back seat, Stryker had pinched her mouth shut like old ladies do. She crossed her arms and rolled her head back and forth on the seat.

George understood the message clearly.

Stryker didn't believe a word he said.

21

MABEL

Mabel couldn't keep her mind off Mr. Morelli's strange behavior. Puzzling, that's what it was. He lingered over the newspaper in the diner longer than one would think normal. Did he have more than a casual interest in the latest news? What made him turn his face away from the policeman as if his photo might be on the FBI's most wanted list? Now he'd changed his clothes. Facial hair, cowboy outfit, sunglasses—not a style she'd expect a businessman to choose. More like a disguise.

Why alter his appearance? He intended to accompany them to California. Why? One conclusion made sense. Mr. Morelli was running away from something or someone and using them for cover. He must have done something illegal. Was she harboring a murderer? *Dear God, what shall I do?*

She glanced in the back seat. Stryker had fallen asleep. Poor child. The slightest exertion seemed to exhaust her. Her precarious condition became more obvious each day. Despite her cute new outfit, Stryker appeared haggard and sallow. The angry red blotches on her arms and legs now resembled a bad case of measles. Under her eyes, bruise-like crescents darkened.

Clearly, this girl needed immediate medical care. How could she get Stryker away from Mr. Morelli and checked into UCLA Hospital? She must allow no more of his nonsense.

Pressure to get Stryker to California weighed heavily on Mabel. A new stabbing pain left her breathless for a moment. Another significant concern she could ill afford with Stryker's life in the balance.

Dear Lord, please keep my heart pumping.

In the early afternoon, the blazing sun created a fireball through the windshield, making visibility tricky. The Packard flew across the Texas border into New Mexico rattling at close to eighty. The speed limit was higher in New Mexico, but he was still going too fast. The entire chassis shook. Even Mabel's teeth jangled. Alarmed by the speed, she silently prayed for state troopers to stop the car. Surely they would rescue Stryker from this menace.

Alas, she sighted not a single patrol car.

Signs advertising tourist attractions in Tucumcari appeared every half mile or so as they neared the city limits. Tee Pee Curios had apparently heavily invested in signage. "Moccasins, rugs, handmade Indian jewelry." Mabel read aloud—anything to keep her mind off their predicament. No matter how she trembled inside, she must not alert Mr. Morelli to the fact that she had guessed his deception. "Apparently we have arrived in Indian territory."

Mr. Morelli snorted. "What gave it away? The squalor? The adobe hovels? The arid desert landscape?"

"I think the area's quite charming," Mabel said as they passed another large yellow billboard painted with a silhouette of a black jackrabbit. "I've never experienced this culture before, but I've read about it in books. New Mexico is a fascinating place—Carlsbad Caverns, Indian ruins. Too bad we don't have time to stop and sample—"

While she spoke, Mabel tossed a quick glance at Stryker but then did a double take.

Blood dripping from Stryker's nose had created an irregular crimson circle on the blanket under her chin.

"Stop the car!"

"What's wrong?"

"Stryker's bleeding."

Slowing the speeding Packard took longer than Mabel thought necessary, but at last the behemoth decelerated enough to allow Mr. Morelli to swerve onto the shoulder. In a swirl of dust, brakes squealed and gravel spun small rocks on the rear and sides. The Packard jerked to a stop.

Mabel struggled out and threw open the back door. "Stryker, dear. Wake up." Gently lifting Stryker's head, Mabel wedged her knee underneath.

Stryker's lids batted over her sleepy eyes. "What?"

Mabel tugged a handkerchief out of her sleeve and applied pressure to the bloody nose. "Tilt your neck back."

Stryker allowed her head to drop back.

"That's the way."

Wide eyes questioned.

Mabel smiled reassurance. "I need to pinch your nose."

"Pinch my doze?" With Mabel's fingers holding the hanky on Stryker's nose, her words sounded like someone speaking through a head cold. "Why?"

"You have a bloody nose. Don't worry. We'll get it stopped." The hanky was already saturated with sticky blood. Where was this coming from? "Get me something else to soak up this blood, Mr. Morelli."

Front window rolled down, he leaned his chin on his bent arm to smoke a cigarette. "Like what?" Did he intend to sit there like a lump?

Mrs. Crowley gritted her teeth. "Find some dirty clothes in the trunk."

Mr. Morelli sighed before opening his door and tossing his cigarette on the ground. He took his sweet time mashing it out before slogging to the back. Bangs and clanks emanated from the rear, but Mabel couldn't tell what he did from the time he opened the trunk until he closed it. Plainly, he wasn't in any sort of rush.

At length, he ambled back carrying an armload of wrinkled clothes—all belonging to Mabel or Stryker, she noticed. His skin appeared paler than normal. What was wrong with him? He threw the pile at Mabel, barely skimming a glance at Stryker. Was he truly so indifferent to this girl's plight?

The bleeding continued.

"Can you tilt your head back farther?" As tenderly as possible, Mabel took Stryker's head between both hands and tipped the delicate chin higher.

"That's the girl." Mabel made herself smile although she didn't feel happy inside.

"Am I going to die?" Stryker's gaze darted between the crimson-stained shirt and Mabel.

Dear Lord, please make this bleeding stop. "Oh, goodness no." Mabel tsk-tsked. "Nosebleeds are messy is all."

She pressed a new wad of fabric on the small nose. Stryker had already lost a lot of blood. What if Mabel couldn't stanch the flow? She looked out the window. Tucumcari should be close. Perhaps a hospital lay ahead.

Several shirts were soaked in the next few minutes until at last Mabel gingerly eased the saturated material off Stryker's nose. No more blood flowed out. Maybe a hospital wouldn't be necessary after all.

Tossing the shirt on the floor with the other stained items, she called out. "Mr. Morelli."

No answer.

"Help me, please."

He didn't come. Mabel could feel her forehead wrinkle. *Merciful heavens.* If he refused to help, she must tend to Stryker herself. Heart pumping rapidly, she raised the trembling girl to an upright position. Still no more blood. Mabel released a long sigh. "Thank you, God."

At last Mr. Morelli appeared at the door, skin pasty. "She's a mess." Disgust distorted his face.

Ruby-red blood streaked Stryker's new shirt. Smudges spotted her face.

What had he expected? Mabel pressed her lips together. Now was no time for reprimands. "Doctor Marston warned me she might have nosebleeds. Let's pray she doesn't have another one before we get to California."

Something akin to concern passed across Mr. Morelli's

face before his expression hardened. If he actually cared, why not offer to help?

Underneath the blotches, Stryker's skin had gone ashen. "My head hurts." Stryker pressed one hand to her temple.

Tears bubbled into Mabel's eyes. She swiped them away with one hand and swallowed hard. She must stay strong. She could fall apart later. "We need to wash her face."

"What about getting her to a doctor?"

Mabel gave him the most withering look she could muster. A person who couldn't be bothered to assist couldn't expect to call the shots. She took her time answering, tucking a few stray hairs into her bun. If he insisted Stryker see a doctor, an opportunity to get away might present itself. Could they afford the lost time? Mabel glanced at Stryker, who shook like a leaf in an autumn storm. "I don't think a strange doctor would be helpful right now."

Mr. Morelli's frown shifted from Stryker to the heap on the floor.

Mabel followed his gaze. "Had to soak up a lot of blood. If we leave the clothes and blanket like this we'll never get the stains out later. Especially in this heat." What was she saying? The bloodstains should not be her primary concern. In Mabel's mind, she heard her mother's voice argue the importance of washing out blood before it set. Childhood training died hard.

Stryker regarded the clutter with horror-filled eyes. "I'm sorry."

"Hush, now. No need to apologize." Mabel patted Stryker's shoulder.

He continued to stare at the pile. "Shouldn't we throw them away?"

"We'll need these." Mabel folded her hands. "We'd have to buy more and we don't have extra money."

"What else can we do?" Mr. Morelli gestured, with palms up.

Indeed, options were limited. Mabel couldn't imagine throwing away clothes because they were soiled. She hadn't been raised to be extravagant and wasteful. Yet Stryker's future lay in her hands. How could they get these clothes cleaned quickly? "Laundromats have more than one washing machine and dryer." It wouldn't take more than an hour or so to wash the items out. Stopping might also provide an opportunity to slip away.

Mr. Morelli's expression indicated that his areas of expertise did not include washing machines. "Where do you propose to find a Laundromat?"

"We'll ask someone." She motioned for him to get in and drive.

He muttered all the way to the driver's side.

Smiling, Mabel patted Stryker's knee. "Feeling okay?"

Stryker gave a wobbly nod.

Entering Tucumcari, Mabel read the names of businesses aloud while searching for somewhere to wash clothes. Or perhaps a police station.

"Need gas," Mr. Morelli said after a few blocks. Without further discussion, he wheeled the Packard into a Phillips 66 station and parked beside the red pumps.

The attendant bustled out. "Fill her up, sir?"

"Right." Mr. Morelli turned to Mabel. "You pay for this one."

"I thought you offered to pay for all the fuel?"

"That was before Oklahoma City. Even if this old jalopy makes it to California—which it may not—for sure it'll never make the trip back. We're gonna need another car or maybe two if we go our separate directions. I gotta save my money."

Mentally Mabel calculated the money left after shopping. They were more than halfway to California. If she managed to dodge Mr. Morelli, she would need funds to complete the trip. "Tell you what. We'll take turns. I'll pay for gas today."

The attendant hooked on the gas nozzle and hurried to the front to wash the windows. Mabel opened her door. "Young man, where is the nearest Laundromat?"

"Laundromat," he repeated. "Oh, sure. There's one around the corner from the Blue Swallow Motel on Tucumcari Boulevard. That's the main street running through town. Can't miss the motel. Got a fancy neon sign with a big blue bird."

"Hear that?" Mabel turned to Mr. Morelli. "Right on the way too."

Mr. Morelli spoke to the attendant about buying another spare tire. A new tire was expensive, so they settled on a patched one. Tire changing took longer than Mabel anticipated. Now they didn't have time for the Laundromat. She was about to say they should skip doing the wash, but the Washee-Washee turned out to be easy to find, exactly where the attendant directed. Better wash those stains out.

Before Mabel concocted a story about why she needed the keys, Mr. Morelli pocketed them and wandered toward the Tee Pee Curio which was kitty-corner from the Blue Swallow.

How would she get those keys? With a heavy sigh, Mabel wrapped the bloody clothing in the blanket. Stryker needed cleaning too. Mabel stripped off the girl's bloody shirt. They had bought another shirt, so she buttoned that one on the girl. Adding the pink shirt to the bundle, she entered the Washee-Washee with Stryker trailing behind.

Mabel selected three Westinghouse front-loading washers and bought a box of Tide from a woman who worked on the premises. She wet half a cup of detergent and rubbed the mixture vigorously into the stains, the way her mother taught her. Then she loaded each washer and selected cold water.

Two of the three washing machines were partially full. Good stewardship demanded better use of her money. She returned to the Packard and gathered Mr. Morelli's dirty clothing.

As she passed a row of newspaper dispensers lining the wall outside the Laundromat, she scoured the headlines. None contained the name Morelli—if that was his name—or a picture that looked similar to the fugitive in their car. The Quay County papers featured mostly photos of East Texas tornado damage.

Even as she stuffed the washers with Mr. Morelli's clothing, she chided herself for giving in to this ingrained sense of duty that seemed to control her every move.

Wide-eyed, Stryker stood transfixed. "This is how you clean clothes?"

"This is how it's done in a Laundromat. I have a washer at my house but no dryer. I hang the clean clothes on the line to dry. Never used a washing machine before, dear?"

Stryker shook her head.

"Well, let's get your face cleaned and then you can watch."

During the hour and a half consumed by washing, drying, and folding the clothes, Stryker alternated between sitting and wandering around the Laundromat, staring at the machines. She checked inside a dryer with an out-of-order sign. "What does this say?"

Mabel explained.

Stryker gave a slow nod then ended up on the long bench in the front picture window.

Mabel kept an eye on her. The child should not be exposed to Mr. Morelli's bad language and the risk of danger he might pose. What to do?

Stryker ran her hand over her bald head and put her cap back on. "That 1942 Packard is leaking oil." She said aloud to no one in particular. "If I got the car up on a rack, I could check the gaskets. One of them has probably gone bad." With the back of her hand, she touched her nose as if it might be leaking too. "Cars and dryers can be fixed." She sighed and leaned her head against the window.

Brushing a tear from the corner of her eye, Mabel continued folding the clothes. The washing provided much-needed busy work.

After she deposited the laundry in the back seat of the Packard, she laced her fingers through Stryker's. Together they walked to the Tee Pee Indian shop. Mr. Morelli hunched on a wooden bench outside. Elbows resting on his knees, he puffed on a cigarette.

"Anything interesting inside?" Mabel asked.

"Buncha junk." He blew out a long trail of smoke. "Nothing with any value."

Stryker yawned and sidled next to Mr. Morelli, leaning against his shoulder. "That old Packard is tore up on the outside, but the engine is pretty sound except for leaking oil. It heats up when you run it too long, but it'll make it to California and back if you baby it a little."

"That so, kid?" Mr. Morelli straightened and stretched his arm along the bench behind the girl.

Skin splotchy and stretched tight, Stryker seemed wrung dry like the clothes in the washer. Perhaps she lost too much blood. Poor girl appeared exhausted. Maybe anemic. Why had she taken to Mr. Morelli? Couldn't she tell he was bad? What if Stryker got attached to him, and then he turned out to be a murderer? Stryker didn't need another abandonment. Not in her frail condition.

Come on, Mabel. Think fast. Perhaps with the right distraction, she could finagle possession of the car keys. "We didn't get far today, but in light of Stryker's condition, I think we should camp out here tonight. We'll start fresh in the morning after a good night's rest. If you give me the keys, I'll go over to the Blue Swallow and get us checked in for the night. You can join us at your leisure."

With Mr. Morelli's eyes hidden behind the sunglasses she couldn't read his expression, but his mouth looked hard. "Thought you were in a big fat hurry."

"Well, yes. I am. We need to get Stryker to Los Angeles as soon as possible, but I'm afraid to push her too hard. What do you say, dear? Do you want to keep going or stop for the night?"

Stryker snuggled into Mr. Morelli's side.

His hand cupped off the seat, just shy of touching Stryker's arm.

Mabel felt a flush of panic. "Someone in the Laundromat said the rooms at the Blue Swallow are comfortable." Would God strike her dead for these lies?

Stryker looked as if her eyelids had become heavy. "I'm kinda tired. Think I need a little nap."

Mabel surveyed her surroundings. Would someone come to her aid if she screamed? An *Albuquerque Tribune* newspaper dispenser sat beside the Tee Pee Curios door. A big city paper. Mabel dug change out of her purse and approached.

Mr. Morelli stiffened. "What're you doing?"

Her hand froze, about to drop a coin into the slot. "Getting a newspaper."

"No." His tone demanded compliance.

"I haven't seen the news since—"

"I said *no* newspaper." He pushed Stryker off of him, rose, and stepped toward Mabel. "Get back in the car."

Countenance ferocious, Mr. Morelli towered over her. An unspoken threat of violence passed between them. She didn't dare challenge him. The strong set of his jaw, feet spread, fists clenched—this person did not make idle threats.

Fear's shadow fell across her heart and left her speechless.

Stryker picked up the Lucky Strike pack fallen on the filthy gum-covered pavement and handed it to Mr. Morelli. "You might want these." She smiled.

He did not return the favor.

Mabel bristled. A great longing for attention radiated from Stryker's eyes. Was he too busy being a bully to notice how little this child required?

Mabel narrowed her eyes. Ordering them around. Such presumption. How dare he. God had given Mabel Crowley work to do. She would escort Stryker to California with joy and Mr. Morelli better not get in her way, regardless of what crime he had committed.

Mabel grabbed Stryker's hand. They tramped back to the Packard ahead of Mr. Morelli. As Mabel walked, she plotted. She would get help. If it meant she had to turn this fugitive in, she must work up the gumption to do so.

Somehow she must get Stryker away from Mr. Morelli.

22

STRYKER

Stryker watched the scenery race by while the Packard sped through Tucumcari and into the New Mexico desert. They passed yet another big yellow billboard painted with a black jackrabbit. That made three they'd seen that day. Mrs. Crowley said it was an advertisement for a store in Winslow, Arizona. How many more miles now?

Soon they were rolling through the desert. Stryker curled up on the back seat and let her thoughts drift. Why didn't Mr. Morelli want Mrs. Crowley to read the newspaper? He scared Stryker, but sometimes his eyes looked kind and she sensed his heart could be trusted like Mama's friend, Uncle Harold. When Mama and Stryker lived in Uncle Harold's apartment, he taught Stryker all about automobiles. Uncle Harold drove a terrific shiny black 1952 Cadillac Fleetwood with a gray leather interior. Soft as baby skin, Uncle Harold would tell anyone who admired his car.

Stryker turned over and pulled up her knees. With Sophia snug between her arms where no one could take her, she tried to relax on the sloping seat. Hard to imagine herself a princess in the back seat of this old clunker, but, oh, riding in that beautiful Caddy . . .

Uncle Harold was a great guy, except when he and Mama went to drinking. Then his caring eyes blurred and the goodness disappeared, a sure sign to run and hide until they slept the meanness off. Later, Uncle Harold would say sorry for scaring Stryker and offer her another ride in his wonderful automobile.

One day Mama packed up their few belongings and they left Uncle Harold's apartment. Stryker never saw him again, no matter how many times she begged.

Stryker peeked out one eye. Mrs. Crowley might be dead except for the small movement of her cheek when her jaw clenched and relaxed. Probably mad or maybe scared. Hard to tell, because she couldn't see Mrs. Crowley's eyes. Mr. Morelli's shoulders lifted and fell. Short breaths. In, out. In, out. He hadn't said sorry for being mean to Mrs. Crowley.

Was Mr. Morelli a good man or a bad man? He sure was handsome in his cowboy hat. Mama said Stryker's father came from Texas. Did he wear a cowboy hat too? Would he be handsome like Mr. Morelli? She didn't remember her father, but she hoped he had a good heart.

What kind of heart did Mr. Morelli have? She couldn't call him honest. In fact he lied a lot, but every so often he had that warmhearted Uncle Harold quality.

Not now though.

Mr. Morelli huffed and puffed. Mrs. Crowley clenched and unclenched. Like an ever-expanding balloon. Stryker dreaded the inevitable explosion.

Sitting up, she turned her attention from the adults to the unusual scenery outside. Peculiar round shrubs and twisted, stubby pines rather than green trees and flowers dotted miles of dry, mostly flat land colored in shades of brown and gray. Strange, curved-roof Indian houses whizzed by. Red rocks and odd shapes appeared and faded from view—all quite different from anything Stryker ever saw in St. Louis. She breathed easier as the sun set, stretching long rays of orange and purple across the darkening sky.

A devastating fatigue overwhelmed her body. She had never suffered such tiredness before. Tugging the blanket snug, she lay down and closed her eyes. Within a minute, her head began to throb. She twisted her neck to one side to apply pressure to her temple, but that position made her back ache. Heaving a long sigh, she flopped to her stomach. Now everything hurt.

Stryker rearranged the blanket. Stretching out her legs, she folded the blanket over them to cover her feet.

Mrs. Crowley turned her head. "What's the matter?"

"I'm trying to get comfortable."

"Are you tired, dear?"

"Uh-huh." She yawned. Tired seemed too small a word, but Stryker couldn't think of a better one. "Only I can't sleep 'cause my head hurts."

"You need a nice soft pillow, but we left our pillows in the Studebaker." She leaned slightly forward, peering at Mr. Morelli above her glasses. "How far do you intend to drive tonight?"

Mr. Morelli jerked his head toward her as if she'd broken his trance. "What?"

"It's nearly dark. How much farther are you driving before we turn in? Stryker can't get comfortable."

Their voices made Stryker's head pound.

"How far?" He pushed his cowboy hat off his forehead. "Another couple of hours, I think. I want to go as far as possible tonight."

"Well, the least you could do is stop for something to eat and let the poor girl walk around a bit."

"Sure, sure." He blinked at Stryker in the rearview mirror. "Santa Rosa's coming up soon. We'll stop and grab a bite to eat. Okay?"

Stryker nodded her aching head. She closed her eyes, trying to manage a wave of nausea.

After ignoring a long line of travel courts, motels, and restaurants on the outskirts, they entered downtown Santa Rosa. Mrs. Crowley delivered a steady commentary about the suitability of each restaurant. Then they would pass it. Stryker had almost given up hope Mr. Morelli would keep his word when he parked the Packard in front of a painted brick building.

Mrs. Crowley ogled the sign. "What makes Lettie's Café any better than the half dozen restaurants we flew by with your nose in the air?"

Mr. Morelli had his door open and his cowboy boots on the pavement. Stryker unwound from her warm wrap, slipped her new saddle oxfords over her socks, and followed Mrs. Crowley and Mr. Morelli into the restaurant.

Light in the room seemed overly bright. Stryker blinked. An older lady in a baby blue uniform escorted them to a table. Mr. Morelli made a point of requesting one near the window.

The waitress distributed menus. So many choices, pages of pictures displaying different kinds of food. She hadn't gotten through half when the woman stopped at the table to ask what they wanted to eat.

Mr. Morelli ordered. "I'll have the pot roast special and a salad. With a cup of coffee." He slapped his menu shut and handed it to the waitress, tugged the ashtray closer, and bumped a cigarette out of his Lucky Strike pack.

"Do you know what you want to eat, dear?" Mrs. Crowley asked.

Stryker shook her head. Not one thing appealed to her.

"She'll start with soup."

Stryker glanced from one woman to the other.

The waitress tapped her pencil on her order pad. "Is she sick?"

Stryker's gaze bounced back to Mrs. Crowley.

"I'm sure chicken soup will help. If she tolerates that, we'll order something else."

Why did grown-ups always talk about her as if she wasn't in the room?

The waitress scribbled on her pad.

"Is the trout fresh?" Mrs. Crowley's gaze didn't lift off the menu.

"We serve nothing but fresh and made from scratch at Lettie's." The waitress pointed to a painted sign and beamed.

Smiling in return, Mrs. Crowley requested trout and the waitress pranced off.

"Homemade chicken soup is exactly what you need." Mrs. Crowley patted Stryker's knee. "After you get some in your stomach, you'll be fit as a fiddle."

Mr. Morelli seemed preoccupied studying the handful of people in the café. After a few minutes, he turned to Stryker. "Have you spotted the black Buick again?"

"They were two different Roadmasters, you know."

"I don't follow."

Stryker glanced out the window. "First we saw a 1953 at the garage where we left your car. But the other was a '54, the one at the Tower."

He frowned. "You positive?"

Stryker nodded. "Absolutely. The trim is different."

His body seemed to melt into the bench, accompanied by a long sigh.

Mrs. Crowley babbled on and on about the food, the café, and the waitresses, commenting on each plate delivered to other tables.

The soup arrived. Stryker leaned over the big red bowl and drew in a long breath of steam rising off the surface. Delicious.

Mrs. Crowley cleared her throat the way she did when she wanted Stryker's attention. She watched Mrs. Crowley unfold her napkin and place it in her lap. A tip of her head indicated Stryker should follow suit. Mrs. Crowley bowed her head and said a little prayer. When Stryker opened her eyes, Mr. Morelli was busy cutting his pot roast.

Stryker picked up the large spoon. The soup was too hot. She blew on it. Queasiness swirled her insides. She laid the spoon on the table.

Mrs. Crowley's forkful of trout and vegetables halted halfway to her mouth. "What is it?"

"I don't feel so good." Stryker pressed her fingertips into her temple and closed her eyes.

Mr. Morelli slapped his fork on the table. "What now?"

"Eat slowly. Your stomach is empty," Mrs. Crowley said. "Swallow a little and then wait to see if you feel better."

That made sense. Stryker picked up the spoon and sank it into the soup. When the spoon filled with broth, noodles and a carrot slice, she lifted it to her lips. Her stomach gurgled. She opened her mouth and tipped the contents inside.

The soup burned but tasted divine. "This is good." One gulp at a time she ate, stopping to chew the chicken. After each swallow she rested a moment. Food soothed the gnawing hunger and calmed the queasiness.

Mr. Morelli watched her. "Try a little of this pot roast. It's very tender and the gravy is terrific."

His eyes said he cared, but his dinner did not look appealing. "Maybe just a bite."

With a lopsided smile, he cut off a chunk of meat from the side he hadn't been eating and transferred it to the small plate that held his bread. Then he scooped potatoes, carrots, and a spoonful of gravy over the top.

"Thank you." Stryker considered the roast. The sick sensation returned. She picked up her fork to stab the meat and gagged.

"Cut a small bite, dear. That's too big for your little mouth." Mrs. Crowley leaned over and sliced the meat into cubes.

Stryker's skin felt sticky and cold, but she took a deep breath and shoved meat into her mouth. Delicious flavor melted over her tongue. "Yum." After a few chews, she swallowed and waited. She ate the rest before tackling her soup. The gravy was as terrific as he promised.

Along with the little sample of Mr. Morelli's pot roast, Stryker managed to get down half her soup and a few soda crackers. Mrs. Crowley fretted about how much more a growing child should eat. On the way to the Packard, she touched Stryker's forehead and fussed over it being warm.

"We have no pillows, so Stryker needs to sit in front. Then she can lie on my lap." Mrs. Crowley announced.

"All of us in front?" Mr. Morelli frowned. "Not much room for that."

"She'll bend her legs. It'll be fine."

A black Buick Roadmaster veered into the parking lot as they drove out.

"Quick. Check out that one." Mr. Morelli slowed, watching the rearview mirror.

Stryker peered out the back. "That's a '54."

His expression reflected panic. "Like the one at the Tower?"

"Right. Only dirtier."

"Didn't see whether it was the same one though." She snuggled back into Mrs. Crowley's lap. Funny, they didn't ask how she knew.

Before many miles had rolled under the tires, Stryker realized she had made a giant mistake. Being squashed between two grown-ups made her dinner want out.

"I need to get in back," she whispered.

"Why?" Mr. Morelli's eyebrows arched villainously. "You just got up here a minute or so ago."

"I'll climb over." Without waiting for further discussion, Stryker hiked one leg to the top of the seat.

Without ample room between the adults, Stryker's elbows, knees, and feet poked them as she scrambled over. Mr. Morelli swore and yelled. "Stop it!"

The Packard veered out of the lane. Mr. Morelli jerked the steering wheel to the left. The chicken soup felt the jolt all the way from the bottom of her stomach. The clammy coldness returned.

She could not stop herself.

Dinner erupted from her lips like a volcano. Chicken broth, chunks of chicken, pot roast, and vegetables gushed out, landing mostly on the front of Mr. Morelli's shirt. The pungent odor of vomit overpowered all other smells in the stinky interior.

Mr. Morelli yelped, gripping the steering wheel with tight fingers. His head swiveled away from the chewed food on his shirt. The Packard swerved sideways, narrowly missing a ditch. He swore a chorus of curses.

In the back seat, the yelling paralyzed Stryker, although her stomach suddenly felt better. Lowering her eyes, she peeked through the lashes at Mrs. Crowley. The woman had flattened one gloved hand over her mouth, but behind her glasses, the skin around her eyes crinkled. She was laughing.

"Do something," Mr. Morelli yelled at Mrs. Crowley.

She moved her hand away slightly to speak. "What would you suggest?"

Screeching brakes were followed closely by a jolt that dumped Stryker on the floor. The next instant, Mr. Morelli lunged out of the parked car and pitched his cowboy hat onto the ground. Shouting curses, he tugged off his new blue shirt as if it was on fire. With a mighty hurl, he flung the sopping wet clothing over the top of the car.

He marched to the rear and opened the trunk. Must be hunting for his old shirt, freshly laundered and folded at the Washee-Washee.

Mrs. Crowley did her best to tidy up the upholstery. She opened the door to retrieve the blue shirt. Having both doors open allowed a slight breeze to air out the strong odor.

"I'll be happy to drive for a few hours," Mrs. Crowley said when Mr. Morelli returned.

"No."

"You need a break."

"I'm fine."

He didn't sound fine.

Mrs. Crowley let him drive. After a few minutes back on the road, Stryker slid to the edge of the seat. "I'm sorry, Mr. Morelli. I didn't mean to throw up all over you."

He harrumphed.

"It was a accident."

Still no answer.

"If I have to do it again, I promise to aim the other way."

Mrs. Crowley turned her face toward the window.

Mr. Morelli flicked a moody gaze into the rearview mirror. In the dashboard lights, Stryker saw scarcely more than his eyes. The skin at the corners of his eyes wrinkled. Next thing she knew, he started to laugh. Not a mere chuckle but a full, rolling belly laugh.

Stryker joined in.

Mrs. Crowley shook her head, staring at them as if they'd lost their minds. Then her laughter blended with theirs. They howled until tears rolled down their cheeks. Mr. Morelli exaggerated the gagging sounds and gestured wildly, making them laugh till they gasped for air.

"Next time it's Mrs. Crowley's turn." He sputtered dramatically, sending them into another round of hilarity.

Sometime later, Stryker fell asleep. When she woke, Mr. Morelli had parked in front of a long, low building. Mrs. Crowley's head, resting on the seat, had rolled to the right. She must be sleeping.

"Where are we now?" Stryker asked, stretching one arm.

"We're in Moriarty. This skeevy joint is called The Cactus Motel." Mr. Morelli finished a yawn before whispering, "Can't drive any farther tonight. We're nearly to Albuquerque anyway. We all need a few hours of sleep." He turned to look out his side window. "What do you say?"

From what Stryker saw in the headlights, the flat-roofed building would meet Mrs. Crowley's standards. "Okay by me."

Stryker watched Mr. Morelli's stiff totter. His legs must be sore. When she saw him coming back, he smiled and motioned thumbs up. She woke Mrs. Crowley.

Mr. Morelli handed a room key to Mrs. Crowley and opened the car door for Stryker. He helped them carry their belongings. "I booked one room this time. We need to be careful with expenses."

Mrs. Crowley's expression communicated horror. "One room? Where do you propose to sleep?"

"The clerk suggested a privacy screen. Never heard of that before, but it seems he is in possession of such a handy item. You and Stryker will have to share a bed. Given the savings, we should at least give it a try."

Tired as Stryker felt, being together comforted her. By the time they entered the large room the screen had already been placed, providing a private cubicle for Mr. Morelli near the door.

"I'm going outside for a cigarette while you two get ready for bed." Mr. Morelli started for the door.

After Mrs. Crowley and Stryker bathed, he came back for his turn washing.

When he closed the bathroom door, Mrs. Crowley

grabbed her chest and sucked in a deep breath. Hunching, she crept into Mr. Morelli's area. "Quick, child. Where are the keys to the Packard?"

Why did she want the keys? Where was she going? Although Stryker didn't understand, she helped hunt. The keys were not to be found. About the time they gave up, the bathroom door snapped open and Mr. Morelli emerged.

"That was surely the fastest bath in history," Mrs. Crowley said. "How did you manage to get clean?"

Without answering, he trudged behind his screen.

Mrs. Crowley's hands were shaking when she knelt with Stryker to say prayers. What was wrong with her?

For a long time after Mrs. Crowley turned out the light, Stryker puzzled over Mr. Morelli. She couldn't hear regular breathing. He'd said he was tired. Why didn't he sleep? A couple of times before she drifted off, he got up and peered out the curtains. Was he searching for black Buicks?

What about Mrs. Crowley? She wasn't sleeping either. The bed creaked when she tossed from one side to the other. Sometimes she moaned or sighed.

What kept them awake? Something was terribly wrong. Stryker felt it.

23

MABEL

Seated at the restaurant next morning, Mabel monitored Stryker's slow progress with her meal. The child coughed and waved her hand at the smoke curling in her direction. Mabel moved the ashtray to the edge of the table. That man's filthy habits would kill the poor girl before they ever made it to California. Today she must ditch Mr. Morelli. Stryker's health must be her primary focus.

Not without the keys though. Mabel took a deep breath. Let the battle begin. She concentrated on buttering her toast. "I'm going to drive today."

Mr. Morelli's mug thunked on the table, sloshing coffee over the sides.

Mabel forced herself to look at him.

His forehead puckered, and the dark pupils contracted. "Your driving makes me crazy. We want to get there before Christmas, don't we?"

She heaved a mighty sigh. Arguing wouldn't be good for Stryker. They would do this his way. Again.

The tense silence continued on the drive through the

rugged Tijeras Canyon between the Sandia and Manzano mountain ranges. Glancing back, Mabel gave thanks for the temporary return of Stryker's appetite. Wrapped in her blanket shield, Stryker had fallen asleep hugging Sophia tight to her chest. Hopefully, the banana, half bowl of oatmeal, and buttered piece of toast would stay in her stomach today.

Mr. Morelli had stolen a nearly-new pillow from the motel. Mabel had verbalized her dismay at finding it on the back seat and insisted he return it. Stryker's eyes glistened, accepting it with awe like a gift from Santa. Before Mabel could protest any further, the child had tried out both sides. When Mabel saw how much Stryker appreciated the softness for her aching head, Mabel gave up the fight. But really. Stealing a pillow from a poor motel seemed rather pathetic.

The Good Book said, "To obey is better than sacrifice."

She raised her face heavenward. *God, I've disobeyed your commandment. Please forgive me for not being bold enough to stand for what I know is right.* Already, she had lied. Now she was an accomplice to stealing. How many more temptations would she yield to before her work was completed?

The Packard backfired and she flinched. A black puff trailed behind them and the engine sounded like something important was missing. Would the car make it to California? Each breath Stryker took might be her last. Could the child survive this strenuous trip? Mabel placed her hand on her chest as another pain stabbed her heart.

Would *she*?

She sensed every tick of the clock as if waiting for a bomb to explode. The detonator was currently driving ten miles over the speed limit.

Mr. Morelli—or whoever he was—might be wanted for a serious crime. Somehow she must break free of him. God could do the impossible. She would trust Him, although she saw no sign of Him working yet.

She settled back and crossed her arms. "How far to Albuquerque?" The New Mexico city was forty-five miles away. She'd seen the sign, but any kind of conversation had to be better than counting black jackrabbits on the gaudy yellow billboards advertising the Winslow trading post every ten miles.

"Should be able to see it soon after we get through this pass." He used his cigarette for a pointer.

She peeked at the gas gauge. A quarter tank. She would have gotten fuel at this point. Why wait until they ran dry in the desert with no filling stations in sight? "And when do you plan to stop for gas?"

Instead of answering, he drew another drag on his cigarette.

Stryker coughed and Mabel waved away smoke. "Please open the wing window."

Mr. Morelli flipped the latch and pushed the triangular window out. Immediately, a draft sucked most of the offensive fumes outside. "Better?"

His tone sounded sarcastic. Maybe conversation wasn't such a good idea. She clicked on the radio. Static. She twisted the dial one direction and then another. Nothing but static.

"Wait until we get out of these mountains." Mr. Morelli stared straight ahead, one elbow leaning against the window ledge.

Mabel took one more stab. "Where did you grow up?"

He glanced her way and blew out smoke. "Why do you ask?"

She waved away vapors. *Because I'd like to solve the Vincent Morelli mystery before we go another mile further.* "Making small talk. Chatting will pass the time."

"Okay. You first. Where did you grow up?"

"Kankakee, Illinois. I had three sisters and two brothers, but only one sister is left. Haven't seen her in years. Us kids spent many carefree days swimming and picnicking on the Kankakee River until World War I came along. All the eligible bachelors went off to fight, the good ones anyway. Didn't think I'd ever find someone to marry. But after the war ended I met my husband Paul." She would forever be indebted to her best friend Babs for forcing that blind date to the church ice cream social. "What a handsome man in his uniform. We got married and moved to St. Louis." She gazed at him. "How about you?"

"Where does your sister live?"

"California."

Mr. Morelli eyed Mabel. "Yeah? Where about?"

"San Bernardino. Route 66 goes right through there. It's not far from Los Angeles."

"You gonna visit her after you take Stryker to L.A.?"

She hadn't seen Laura in over thirty years. They maintained a tenuous connection through occasional letters, but nothing more. Ever the rebellious child, her youngest sister Laura had trekked to Hollywood many years ago with impossible aspirations to become a motion picture star. After snagging a couple of bit parts, she married another failed actor and settled in San Bernardino. No one in the family approved. "I don't know." Mabel's hand moved to cover her heart, and then she glanced at the sleeping child. Stryker's cap had slipped off, exposing her hairless head. How could she think past getting Stryker to the clinic? "Maybe."

Mr. Morelli shifted gears, and the Packard began the descent from the mountains. A few more miles on a windy road and then they rounded the final curve. A wide valley spread before them. Silhouetted against the distant horizon, a good-sized city came into view.

"Albuquerque." Mr. Morelli said.

"You grew up in Albuquerque?"

"No." He indicated the city with a tip of the head. "I think that must be Albuquerque there."

"Oh." Mabel took in the sprawling metropolis. "But where did you grow up?"

Mr. Morelli reached for the radio dial. "Let's see if we can pick up something now that we're through the mountains."

After a few static stops, he found a country music station. A man was singing "I Don't Hurt Anymore" with a real country twang. Mr. Morelli shook his head and muttered. "Guess we can't expect real music in this neck of the woods."

"Sorry," Mabel said with a slight chuckle. "Among certain sets, Hank Snow is quite popular."

"That a fact?"

"He is." She studied him for a moment. "Ever hear of Tennessee Ernie Ford?"

Mr. Morelli wrinkled his nose. "Sounds like a real yokel."

"You might be surprised. He has a lovely bass voice."

The song ended. Next up, Eddy Arnold crooned "My Everything." They listened for a mile or so before Mr. Morelli commented. "The words are always so sappy."

Mabel almost smiled. "Perhaps you've never been in love, Mr. Morelli. Didn't you ever meet a woman who made you say sappy things?"

He shook out the last cigarette and balled up the pack. Poking it between his lips, he tugged out his lighter. The flame whooshed. He puffed a few times. Eddy Arnold warbled the final word of his song, and Hank Thompson came on singing "Honky Tonk Girl."

Mr. Morelli had not answered her question. Mabel watched the highway fly past, supposing he'd finished with small talk. Several miles rolled by before he focused on Mabel again. "Can't say I ever met anyone who made me say stupid stuff like 'You're my winter, summer, spring, my everything.' That's what you call love?"

"Sometimes people in love say things to each other that sound silly to others." Paul's sweet words echoed in her mind. "Real love makes you willing to let all your defenses down."

Mr. Morelli snorted. "Then I don't ever want to be in love."

Involuntarily, Mabel's eyebrows hitched up. Perhaps Mr. Morelli had carefully insulated himself from love because someone who should have loved him had let him down.

How encouraging that he'd opened a hole in his defensive wall, however tiny. Would he answer any more questions? "Did you grow up in St. Louis?"

"No," came the quick response. "Lake Forest. Our house overlooked Lake Michigan."

Mabel stared. That might be true. Could she get any more out of him? "What about brothers and sisters?"

"Nope."

Probably not a good idea to mention his "brother" in Texas. "What did your father do to afford lake view property?"

A veil lowered over Mr. Morelli's face like the final curtain in a play. "We're coming into Albuquerque. Be on the lookout for a filling station."

Typical of most towns along Route 66, motels and motor lodges, restaurants, cafés, and tourist shops lined the main street heading into town. They passed El Sombrero Restaurant without commenting on the unique hat-shaped building. A couple of blocks in, Mr. Morelli veered into a Texaco station with a small market next door. The attendant breezed out, and Mr. Morelli directed him regarding the automobile.

"I gotta get cigarettes." Mr. Morelli extracted the keys from the ignition and scrambled from the car. Before he shut the door, he rolled down the window a couple of inches. "It's hot. You might need some air." He looked back at Stryker. "Do you want anything? My turn to buy."

Mabel shook her head.

He headed toward the restrooms. Now was her chance. Her heart beat rapidly. She scanned the front of the building for a newspaper dispenser but didn't see one. Should she risk searching inside? She couldn't leave Stryker. Should she call the police? What would she say? My traveling companion doesn't want me reading newspapers? He lied about having a brother? Mabel's shoulders slumped.

Yea, though I walk through the valley of the shadow of death, I will fear no evil: for thou art with me. The words of the twenty-third Psalm always comforted her.

Her wandering gaze lit on the radio. How fast could she find the news? With trembling fingers she twisted the dial, stopping when she heard a male voice. But he was discussing an upcoming election. She turned the opposite direction, past several country-western stations until she located another speaking voice.

A weatherman forecasted a dry spell. She didn't want a weather report.

Mr. Morelli ambled around the building. Mabel quickly settled back against the seat. Perspiration soaked the back of her dress. He stopped to converse with the attendant before scanning the parking area. The attendant lifted the Packard's hood.

Mr. Morelli tipped his hat in Mabel's direction and zig-zagged through the parking lot into the market, presumably for cigarettes.

Moisture gathered on Mabel's forehead.

Time was running out.

The attendant rapped on her window. Caught with her hand on the dial, Mabel started.

"Tell the driver the tire pressure's okay, but you might want to keep an eye on the left rear." The attendant lifted the oil stick. "You're a few quarts low. Should I add oil?"

"Please do."

Heart thumping, she visually followed the attendant's return to work before she rotated the dial one more click. ". . . prominent Chicago accounting firm. A national manhunt is underway for George Kendrick Stanton, a suspect in the crime. Mr. Stanton stands six feet tall and weighs one hundred eighty-five pounds. He has curly, dark brown hair and brown eyes. He left Chicago driving a 1955 black Lincoln Continental."

Mabel gasped. The physical description matched Mr. Morelli down to the make and model of car he wrecked. She missed the description of the crime. Why were they hunting for him?

The attendant carried a couple cans of oil to the front.

The newsman's voice droned on. "Police recovered the Lincoln Continental from a garage in Lebanon, Missouri where it was apparently abandoned following a severe accident in which Mr. Stanton suffered a head injury. He visited a doctor in Lebanon and was last seen leaving the garage in a brown 1948 Studebaker."

Mabel's hand trembled when she clapped it over her mouth. Someone saw the Studebaker. Did they write down her license number? Was she wanted too? Her eyes darted across the filling station to the market. Were they being followed? Suppose the black Buick Mr. Morelli was always worrying about was the police.

". . . direction unknown. This morning the FBI issued an all-points bulletin."

The FBI? The crime was serious.

"Anyone with any information—"

The hood slammed shut. Mabel winced.

In one hand, the attendant carried cash.

Mabel's head jerked the opposite direction.

Mr. Morelli scowled through the driver's window.

How much did he hear?

He yanked open the door and flung himself onto the seat, hurling a bottle of whiskey and several cigarette packs between them.

Mabel recoiled, shrinking against the door.

Veins in his neck throbbed. He shot her a disgusted glare, and his hands clenched the steering wheel.

Without a word, he slammed his door and punched off the radio. Mabel jumped. Warning bumps prickled her skin. How much actual danger did Mr. Morelli pose? She had seen no sign of a weapon. Yet.

Dear Lord, protect us.

She locked her arms over her chest and rocked back and forth. Should she grab the child and run screaming into the building? Did she have the strength to drag Stryker out of the back seat?

She wasn't fast enough.

Mr. Morelli—whom she now knew to be wanted criminal George Stanton from Chicago—shoved the key into the ignition. The engine roared. Tires screeched as the vehicle raced out of the filling station.

His nostrils flared. His mouth was a rigid slash across his face.

Dense silence descended like a hangman's noose.

24

GEORGE

George gripped the steering wheel until his hands cramped. Better than strangling that meddling woman sitting beside him with her arms smugly folded across her chest. Flooring the gas pedal, he blasted out of the Texaco station reaching for lightning speed. *Must get out of Albuquerque.* The tires screamed around a corner. Pulse racing, his insides roiled. The pounding in his ears deafened all other sound. With a hard twist of the steering wheel, he jerked the heavy automobile back onto Route 66.

Mrs. Crowley had deliberately turned on the news. What did she hear? He had covered his tracks well. Investigators could not have pieced together the truth already and broadcasted it to the media. How would Mrs. Crowley connect any news flash to him? She didn't even know his name.

Eyes fixed on the road, he slowed through the downtown area. He tried to regulate his rapid breathing and sound nonchalant. "What was on the news?"

No answer.

George glanced at the passenger side.

Mrs. Crowley stared straight ahead. Color had drained from her face.

He swore under his breath, attempting to quash his welling desire to smash her self-righteous face in. "You were listening to the radio. What did they say?"

She drew in a deep breath. Words trickled out in a shaky stream. "George Kendrick Stanton is wanted by the FBI for questioning about a crime in Chicago."

More curses exploded in his brain. His jaw ached. He unclenched his teeth and spoke slowly and deliberately. "Why would you be interested in something so far away?"

Mrs. Crowley appraised him. "The description . . ." Her chin trembled. "It's you, isn't it? You are . . ." Her voice dropped to a whisper. "George Stanton." She covered her mouth with one hand.

George depressed the gas and passed a station wagon zooming ahead, increasing pressure on the pedal.

She fussed with her sleeve. "I have no clean hanky."

As if anyone cared. "What do you intend to do?"

She pressed her quivering lips together. With her gloved hand, she dabbed away a few tears. Her eyes sparked when she turned to stare at him. "I don't suppose you're talking about my hanky. The question is what do *you* intend to do?"

George lit a cigarette. He must not allow her to contact the authorities. Would he have to take them hostage now? Violence did not appeal to him. So messy. Especially with Stryker getting sicker. Besides the fact that his pistol had vanished with the Studebaker in Oklahoma City.

He puffed away at the cigarette until it burned to about half. "I don't know *what* to do now."

"Then it's true? You are George Stanton?"

He eased off the gas, dropping the speed to ten miles over the limit. "Yes."

"You're running away from something in Chicago." She sniffed. "What happened?"

He flipped the cigarette butt out the wing window and checked the rearview mirror. Stryker wasn't sitting up, so she must still be sleeping. "Worked for a big accounting firm for over ten years. Kept getting passed over for promotions. Someone higher up had it in for me. A petty personality issue. Jealousy, probably. I had a terrific life in Chicago. Then I discovered I'd been framed for stealing a large sum of money from several client accounts." He checked to see if Mrs. Crowley was buying his explanation but couldn't tell from her expression.

"Missing funds." She made a single nod. "Go on."

"One night, a couple of federal agents showed up at the office and asked questions. When I realized they were trying to pin embezzlement on me, I panicked and ran." He shrugged. "I wrecked my new Lincoln in Missouri, and the rest you know."

Her probing gaze felt like a searchlight burning into his brain.

"There's no more to it?" She blinked several times. "What about the wad of money you had on you when we first met you?"

"My own personal nest egg."

She raised her eyebrows. "You had that much money?"

"Been saving for years."

"No one got murdered?"

Apparently she didn't know much about the crime. His shoulders relaxed. If she bought his story, she might yet prove an asset in his escape. "No one."

"Then why a national manhunt? Why is the federal government involved?"

Preparing an answer, he inhaled deeply through his nose. "Money went missing from several big accounts—a governmental agency, pension funds from a few large corporations, and a couple of high-dollar investment groups. We're talking large-scale fraud."

"But you aren't involved in the crime?"

With her natural ability to dig, this woman should work for the FBI. He looked away when he answered, "No."

"What about the black car you keep seeing? Who do you think that is?"

George shook his head. "Might be one of the guys who

came to my office. I don't know. Thought I recognized one of them at the garage where they towed my Lincoln, but I can't be sure."

"So there's no brother in Texas?"

"No."

She seemed to consider what he said. "Then where are you going?"

Explaining to Mrs. Crowley was proving far easier than he had anticipated. He swung a worried look at her. "Should I tell you? What if you're questioned after we get Stryker to L.A.? The less you know of my whereabouts, the better."

She stared out her side window.

George read signs without comprehending—the KiMo Theatre, Franciscan Hotel, Sleepy Hollow Court, the Dog House. What was going on with Crowley?

Finally she spoke. "Your story sounds convincing, but you aren't. You've lied during this whole trip. Why should I trust you now?"

"That's a tough one." George's mouth curved up at the corners. "I have no proof of my innocence, which is why I had to run. Stryker trusts me though. You've seen that."

Mrs. Crowley tilted her head. "I'd like to believe you are a victim in this horrible situation." She spoke softly. "You remind me vaguely of my son. Richard would be about your age, if he'd lived."

Her son? She'd never mentioned a son before. Perhaps he could use the resemblance to his advantage. "What happened to your boy?"

"Richard died at Normandy on D-Day. Tuesday, June sixth, 1944. He was with the 29th Infantry." Her voice hitched.

"Must've been awful for you."

Mrs. Crowley's shoulders drooped. "They buried him in France. I've never seen his grave." She hung her head. "One day you send your only child off to war and the next . . ."

George couldn't think of a comforting word to offer at this point. He opened the Johnnie Walker bottle and guzzled a couple of gulps, waiting for her to raise her head. The whiskey burned going down. Not Gold Label, but he was glad to have it.

Next Mrs. Crowley would start ragging on him about drinking while he drove. Could he bear another round of her grousing? Maybe he should split now, buy another car and go on alone. Then he wouldn't waste any more of his cash on motels, food, and gas. He needed every bit to make a fresh start. Big problem—with his identity out in the open, how would he control Crowley? Could he trust her if she pledged not to talk?

However, if she noticed his drinking she said not a word about it. After a long pause, she looked at George. "You must promise me something."

"What?"

"I want your solemn vow you won't lie to me anymore. That's the deal. If you continue to lie, I'll take the Packard and Stryker."

No problem. He'd made plenty of promises he never intended to keep. Like with Gloria and Mother. "I promise." He lifted one hand as if swearing before a judge. "I will not tell you any more lies."

Mrs. Crowley's stiff features relaxed. "Very well." She peeked over the seat at Stryker. "The most important thing is to get treatment for this child as quickly as possible. You may come with us, but you must not slow us down. If you break this promise, I will immediately take her and go on alone. Agreed?"

"Agreed." He offered his hand and they consummated the deal with a shake.

Several miles west of Albuquerque, the Packard climbed Nine Mile Hill. The winding road through the Laguna Pueblo lands twisted through fascinating rock formations and huge boulders that must have been blasted out to make way for the highway. Miles of red sandstone glimmered in the sun.

A few hours later when they neared Gallup, Stryker woke and tapped her window. "Are those red-and-white signs like the other ones?"

Mrs. Crowley nodded. "The same as in Texas, advertisements for Burma-Shave."

"Read them please," Stryker begged.

The Packard whizzed past the evenly-spaced signboards, and Mrs. Crowley read each one. "Beneath this stone," said one sign.

"Lies Elmer Gush," said the next.

Stryker rolled down her window and hung out her head.

"Tickled to death," Mrs. Crowley read.

"By his shaving brush."

Holding her hat on, Stryker giggled.

"Burma-Shave."

Stryker drew her head inside and clapped her hands. "That's great. What if we make up our own?"

"We could," Mrs. Crowley said. "What should ours be about?"

"Let's make up one about our trip. What do you say, Mr. Morelli?"

What did Crowley's frown mean? She didn't want to make up a jingle about the trip or she wanted him to confess his true identity? He blinked at Stryker's upturned face in the rearview mirror, innocent, expectant. His chest clenched. What did he care what this child thought? She was nothing to him.

A lie. He cursed quietly. Why had he let those pale blue eyes burrow through the well-fortified defenses around his heart? He couldn't afford to get attached to this waif.

But he was.

He couldn't force himself to speak.

"Actually, Mr. Morelli wants to tell you something, Stryker."

Leave me alone, woman.

Stryker tilted her head. "What?"

"Well." He cleared his throat. How to explain? "The thing is, Vincent Morelli is not my real name. Mrs. Crowley thinks you should know."

"Oh." Stryker waited. "What's your name then?"

"George." He caught her gaze in the mirror. "George Stanton."

She nodded slowly. "George Stanton suits you better."

He exhaled a long breath. Was he off the hook with Stryker?

A colorful Kachina statue at the entrance to Gallup proclaimed the city as the American Indian Capital. George read the sign for Stryker as they drove slowly past and continued through town.

After that, several miles of desert flashed by until they approached the Arizona border.

"Oh, lookie." Stryker pointed.

Fake animals had been posed on the ledge of a tall bluff overlooking the Fort Chief Yellowhorse Trading Post.

"What does the sign say?"

Mrs. Crowley read hand-painted words displayed on a substantial billboard outside the trading post. "No Scalpum Paleface, Just Scalpum Wallet."

Desert humor. "Hmm," said George.

Mrs. Crowley smiled back at Stryker. "Arizona. Then California. We're making progress at last."

Despite the funny saying, Stryker's solemn face stared out the window. Now she connected with George's gaze in the rearview mirror. "Why?"

"Why what?" he answered. "Why don't we stop? Because that's silly stuff."

"No." She scooted to the edge of the seat with her face close to his ear. "Why did you tell me your name was Vincent Morelli?"

George exchanged a pleading look with Mrs. Crowley. Then he shifted his gaze away, but her sharp stare continued to pierce his reticence.

"I . . . had a small problem in Chicago and had to leave. People might be searching for me. I didn't know if I could trust you two." He linked eyes with Stryker's. "But now I know I can."

"I knew you were lying."

"Yes."

"But you aren't now?"

He focused on the road. The kid was ten times worse than Crowley. "No."

"And you think whoever is in the Buick Roadmaster is after you?"

"Maybe."

Stryker's silence left him wondering what she must be thinking. "I've seen the Roadmaster a couple more times."

He fixed her in the mirror. "You have?"

She nodded. "It's following us."

Mrs. Crowley jerked her head toward Stryker. "How do you know it's the same one?"

"The Roadmaster at the Tower is almost new, but it has a long scratch on the left front bumper."

"Amazing," George said. "I didn't notice that."

Stryker hung her head. "I scratched the bumper."

"What?" George and Mrs. Crowley asked together.

"Remember the day we ate at the café and then went shopping?"

George remembered. "In Texas."

"I asked you for a quarter to get a gumball."

"Right."

Now it was Stryker's turn to nod. "Well, I saw the Buick outside the restaurant, and I wanted to be sure it was the same one in case I ever saw it again. So I took the quarter and scratched the fender."

"Well, I never," said Mrs. Crowley. "What a clever idea. Although, of course it's wrong to damage other people's property. That's vandalism."

"Why didn't you say anything about seeing it?" George asked.

"Lots of Roadmasters on the highway." Stryker shrugged. "But now I'm sure. The same 1954 Buick is definitely following us."

George took his foot off the gas and let the car drop back. Racing around the curve they'd passed seconds earlier, an ominous black Roadmaster hugged the road in an evil embrace. George depressed the brake, squinting into the mirror, trying without success to identify the lone occupant.

Distance between the two cars narrowed until George saw clearly.

The driver wore what appeared to be a gray hat with a distinctive U-shaped indentation in the crown.

25

STRYKER

Stryker kept an eye out the back window on the tiny speck that used to be a black Buick. Mr. Stanton's boot must have flattened the gas pedal. The Packard shimmied. She angled her head to watch the speedometer needle. Sixty-five. Seventy.

Tires squealed as the car veered right onto a country road. *Whack!* Stryker's body slammed against the door. Her head bounced off. "Ouch."

Mrs. Crowley's fingers clutched the back of the seat. "What are you doing?"

Not paying any attention, Mr. Stanton continued barreling down the highway. Just before it was too late, he jerked the steering wheel and took an exit to the right.

Stryker flung out her arm to brace herself.

Without warning they screeched to an abrupt stop. Stryker ended up on the floor on top of Sophia, and Mrs. Crowley was practically sitting in Mr. Stanton's lap.

He made a U-turn and parked behind a tall stack of reddish rocks that partially hid the car from view. He turned to face Mrs. Crowley. "Let's see if that Buick follows us."

"Really. Like a kid playing chase." Mrs. Crowley adjusted her hat as she scooted as far away from Mr. Stanton as possible. "You could've told us to hold on."

Stryker opened the back door and dangled her feet in the bright afternoon sunshine. "How long're we gonna stay here?"

"Not long," Mr. Stanton said.

"Can I get out?"

"Yes." Mrs. Crowley smiled.

"No." Mr. Stanton turned toward Stryker. "Stay in the car in case we need to make a fast getaway."

"But my legs want to stretch."

He hiked his shoulders and lowered them as he sighed. "Don't go far."

"Yippee!" She tumbled out. Never thought she'd want to get out of a car before, but today she did. Her legs wobbled when she stood. Odd. Must be the hours of sitting or the saddle oxfords. She stared at her new shoes. Not broke in yet.

On slightly shaky legs, she hiked to the rocks to explore. Wadding her skirt in her left hand, she hauled herself up the side of one boulder, then another. The rocks were hot to the touch, and she couldn't leave her hand on them long. At the top she bent over, panting until she could stand up again.

A perfect lookout point. From this height, she could see the long stretch of road leading back to Route 66 and even farther. She doubled over trying to get enough air and realized she'd forgotten to bring the monkey. She looked back at the Packard. She could keep an eye on it from here. Sophia should be okay. She straightened and stared toward the highway.

"Nobody's coming yet," she yelled, teetering slightly. Surely Mr. Stanton knew he had left the Buick in his dust. Why did he think it might follow them here?

She tried to sit, but the rocky surface was blistering. A gust of wind blew Stryker's skirt. She held down the front with one hand. The lovely breeze made her want to run and play, but she only had enough energy to squat.

What were her friends in St. Louis doing? Late afternoons they usually gathered together to share loot from the alleys and the handouts of strangers. Stryker tilted her face to the sun and closed her eyelids. Echoes of the children's laughter floated through her mind. Did they miss her?

"Come down, Stryker," Mrs. Crowley called.

Stryker squinted below. Near the roadside, Mrs. Crowley shaded her glasses with one hand. "Careful now. You mustn't fall."

Would she ever see her friends again? Cushioning her legs with her skirt, Stryker slid along the face of the biggest boulder and jumped to the ground. At the hard impact, her feet stung like they'd been slapped hard. She inhaled sharply. "Yikes."

Mr. Stanton hurried to her, hand out. "Are you okay?"

Tears threatened to spill, but she wouldn't cry. "I'm fine. You know why?"

"Why?"

"'Cause I'm tough." She balled her fists like a fighter.

His face went kind of mushy. For a second, she thought he might hug her.

"Right." He spun away quickly and returned to the car. "Let's go. The Buick must've passed by now."

Back on the highway, they kept a lookout for the black car. Mr. Stanton drove close to the speed limit. Mrs. Crowley explained the Petrified Forest as they passed the turnoff. Stryker longed to see such an amazing sight but didn't ask to stop. Another colorful sunset spread across the sky while they continued through the desert.

In the darkness, Stryker drifted between wakefulness and sleep. Occasionally adult conversation reached her, but she had no energy to listen.

After hours of driving, Mr. Stanton parked. Stryker roused to sit on the edge of the seat. In the headlights, she made out a small motel in need of paint. Part of the neon sign had gone dark. "Where are we?"

"The Chief Motel. Holbrook, Arizona." Mr. Stanton's voice sounded hushed. "This dump has gotta be an all-time low."

Mrs. Crowley turned tired eyes on Stryker. "Our choices for sleeping accommodations seem rather limited in this town."

How would Mrs. Crowley smooth things over with Mr.

Stanton this time? Stryker stretched her shoulder blades together. "I'm sure it'll be fine."

Mrs. Crowley's smile looked tired. "Gather your things, dear."

The cramped room smelled musty like the ground under the abandoned house where Stryker sometimes slept with her street friends during bad storms. The swamp cooler rattled and rumbled when cold air blew out. Sleeping in the same room was fine with her, although she wondered why Mr. Stanton didn't sleep in his own cheap room.

After prayers and lights out, Stryker lay awake listening to their breathing and staring at the low ceiling. A couple of spider webs hugged the corners. Her fingers clutched Sophia tighter. What if the spiders crawled out and wandered around in the dark? How big were desert spiders?

Mr. Stanton tossed, headboard thumping the wall. Occasionally he muttered to himself. After a long time, he got up and tiptoed outside.

Stryker must have drifted off to sleep because she jerked awake when the cooling machine clanked to a start. Cold air roared out like a lion. Mrs. Crowley didn't move. She had rolled on one side with her face toward the wall. Her light snore was comforting. Stryker closed her eyes and relaxed.

The cooler made a loud thud and bang. She tensed. A burning smell filled the room and the blower quit. Blinking into the darkness, Stryker waited for the machine to start, but it didn't.

Without the cool air blowing, the room warmed.

Mr. Stanton trailed cigarette smoke into the room when he returned. He tugged the curtain back an inch or so. Light from a flickering street light trickled inside. Mr. Stanton bent to pick up Sophia from the floor and tucked her back into Stryker's arms. Then he squatted to tinker with the machine, but it wouldn't start. Muttering to himself, he adjusted knobs but nothing happened, so he climbed in bed with a big sigh.

Stryker clutched Sophia close as he groaned. Maybe his mattress was lumpy too.

When she woke next, rays of morning sun streamed

through the crack between the curtains. Mr. Stanton was not in bed. Neither was Mrs. Crowley. Running water meant one of them was in the bathroom. A faint odor of cigarette smoke drifted through cracks around the door leading outside. Must be Mrs. Crowley in the bathroom.

After a few minutes, the woman emerged. "Good morning, sunshine. Did you sleep well?"

Stryker yawned. "The cooler made a lot of noise and then quit."

"Yes," Mrs. Crowley said, securing her green hat with hatpins. "The temperature's warmer than usual for this time of year but not unbearable. Good thing we're traveling in early summer. I hear it gets quite hot here in July and August."

Mr. Stanton insisted on driving. For once, Mrs. Crowley didn't seem to mind. After a quick stop for breakfast, they began racking up miles. Before long, they passed a motel with wigwams for rooms.

"Oh, lookie." Stryker pressed her nose against the window. "Can we stay there tonight?"

Mrs. Crowley bent to peer out the driver's side. "They are interesting, but unfortunately we need to get to California and it's still morning. Sorry, dear."

"Maybe when you come back through," Mr. Stanton offered.

They exchanged one of those unreadable grown-up looks before Mrs. Crowley turned her gaze away.

Soon the desert sun had moved straight overhead. Mr. Stanton wiped sweat off his neck. "Boy, it's cooking in here."

"The heater worked. Maybe we've got an air conditioner," Stryker said.

But when Mrs. Crowley twisted all the dials, nothing but heated air poured into the car.

"Turn the knob off," Stryker said. Probably needed coolant.

Mr. Stanton let out a low curse and Mrs. Crowley didn't scold him. Maybe she was thinking the same word.

Just west of Holbrook, Mr. Stanton braked to a stop behind a long line of motorists.

Stryker stared toward a building close to the road. A bead of sweat trickled off the side of Mr. Stanton's head. His eyes darted between the mirrors.

Stryker slid to the edge of the seat. "Why are we stopping?"

"The sign says Arizona Agriculture and Horticulture Inspection Station," Mrs. Crowley answered.

"Should I try to go around?" Mr. Stanton muttered.

"I don't see how you can." Mrs. Crowley bent to peer out. "There's no road around the outside. You'd draw attention to yourself." They kept their voices low.

Ahead, the small white building had an open-ended carport stretched over the highway. Vehicles waited for a few moments before slowly driving forward. When the Packard moved nearer, Stryker saw a man waving people past him. How could that be dangerous?

She spoke near Mr. Stanton's ear. "Why do you want to go around?"

Mr. Stanton continued scanning from one side to the other. "They might stop us."

"Why?"

Another look passed from Mr. Stanton to Mrs. Crowley, but neither answered.

Stryker crossed her arms and let out a long breath. Did they think she was a baby?

Autos kept stopping and then moving forward. Now five were left between the Packard and the carport. Stryker noticed several parked cars beside the building, one a 1954 black Buick Roadmaster. The driver's seat was empty. With the other vehicles in the way, she couldn't tell if the side had a scratch, but she should mention it.

As she opened her mouth, Mrs. Crowley spoke. "I won't lie for you, but perhaps I ought to drive. We can't afford to be detained."

He nodded. Swinging the door open, he hurried around the back to the passenger side. Mrs. Crowley slid across the seat and dragged the door closed. Mr. Stanton slumped, crossed his arms, and angled his cowboy hat low over his face so nothing but his beard showed.

Stryker wanted to know why they might be detained, but they probably wouldn't answer.

Mrs. Crowley steered the Packard forward one car length. When she stopped, she reached for the radio dial. A lady sang, "Once I had a secret love . . ." Mrs. Crowley hummed along.

Only two more vehicles separated them from the inspection station. Stryker swallowed saliva and stiffened her back, waiting. The vehicle directly in front drove off.

Next was their turn.

The Packard inched to a stop beside a man in a brown uniform. "Morning, ma'am." He took out a big white handkerchief and swiped his brow. "Unusually warm for this time of year."

"Certainly is hot." Mrs. Crowley's voice came across cheerfully. "I thought it was always this way in Arizona."

"Not usually in early June. We're having a heat wave. How far have you folks come?"

"We're driving through from the Midwest."

He nodded. "Transporting any produce or vegetation?" His tone sounded flat.

Mrs. Crowley shook her head. "No food or plants either."

The man leaned closer to see Mr. Stanton and then Stryker. "Have a good trip." He motioned for them to pass.

The Packard surged ahead. Mr. Stanton straightened to check behind. Lips parted, a slow smile spread across his face. Soon they left the inspection station in the distance.

"There you are, Mr. Stanton," Mrs. Crowley said. "Nothing to worry about."

Did the ag station man think they were a family like the policeman in Oklahoma did? Stryker hoped so. She loved the idea that Mrs. Crowley might be her grandma and Mr. Stanton was her father. *Dad.* She rolled the word on her tongue. It felt great. Maybe she'd try it out on him sometime to see what he thought.

For a while, Mrs. Crowley continued to drive while Mr. Stanton relaxed. Between her own naps, Stryker kept a lookout for the black Buick. The morning rolled into afternoon without another sighting.

Outside Winslow they stopped to eat and fuel up, and Stryker tried to run, but her legs didn't cooperate. A stumble brought Mr. Stanton racing to her side, offering his hand to steady her.

She rubbed her knee, aware that her cheeks were heating. "Thanks." How embarrassing. She'd been running since before she could remember.

When they returned to the Packard, Mr. Stanton climbed in the driver's seat. Mrs. Crowley didn't comment. Maybe she felt tired after driving in the sun. The temperature continued to rise as the day wore on. Stryker remembered the coolant for the air conditioner, but it was too late to mention it. Without cool air, they drove with the windows rolled down.

In Winslow, they passed the final and biggest black jackrabbit painted on a giant yellow billboard. Mrs. Crowley read the words for Stryker. "Here it is."

"Can we stop? Please?" Stryker could hardly contain her excitement. "Let's see what all the fuss has been about."

"It's an advertising trick to get people to come in the store," Mrs. Crowley said.

"They might have real petrified wood." Stryker wanted to touch a piece.

Mrs. Crowley stared over her glasses. "The store is full of tourist things we don't need."

"And can't afford," Mr. Stanton said.

Stryker's stomach clenched. She slid back on the seat and hugged her knees to her chest. Turquoise jewelry and Indian souvenirs. They'd passed those jackrabbit signs through several states. She wanted to see inside, that's all. She didn't have to buy anything.

Mr. Stanton slowed when they spied a gigantic curvy cowgirl on a sign outside another store. "Wayne L. Troutner's for Men," he read. "Now *there's* a place I'd like to stop." He let out a long sigh, which sounded phony. In the rearview mirror, he caught Stryker's gaze. "Can't do that either. No time for sightseeing."

The scenery changed as the Packard approached the mountains. Spotty forests of Christmas trees flashed past. The

air cooled a few degrees. In the front seat, Mrs. Crowley
nodded off, hat pressed against the window.

Stryker bunched her pillow and placed her head on it.
Lying down felt so much more comfortable. She slept too,
but not for long. Her bones ached. Must be all the driving.
She flipped the pillow over to the cooler side. That helped,
but about the time she drifted off, the vehicle slowed. Mr.
Stanton swore under his breath.

The Packard stopped at the end of a long line.

"Another inspection station?"

"Not this time," Mr. Stanton's low tone had an edgy
quality.

Stryker opened her window and stuck her head out. At the
front of the line, a row of state trooper cars blocked the westbound
lane. An officer stood at one side, bending to peer into each
vehicle. Like the inspector, he straightened after a few seconds
and waved the travelers on their way. She'd never figure out
adults.

She pulled her head back inside. "What is it?"

"Looks like a road block." His words squeezed out between
clenched teeth. Mr. Stanton's gaze flicked to Mrs. Crowley who
appeared to be sleeping with her head against the window. Then
he watched Stryker's reflection in the mirror for a moment.

"Hang on," he said and executed a tight turn onto the shoulder.
Headed in the opposite direction, he accelerated to the
speed of an advancing tornado.

Out the back window, the line of cars disappeared. "Where're
we going now?"

"A short detour." His sunglasses met her eyes.. "Don't
worry. It'll be okay." He braked beside a tall stone marker to
make an abrupt turn. One road split into two. The Packard
veered left. Another sign whizzed past. Not a Route 66 sign
like they'd seen along most of the trip.

The power surge threw Stryker backward onto the seat.
Wind poured in the open windows. Stryker held her hat on her
head with one hand and gripped Sophia with the other. The
sun shone from a different part of the sky than before. They
were not going west anymore.

Stryker looked out the back. The black Buick wasn't behind them. So why did they change direction?

Her shoulders tightened. They weren't going to California. With clammy hands, she hugged her monkey to her chest to calm her trembling insides.

At times like these, Mrs. Crowley prayed. Would God hear Stryker's prayers too?

Against the fierce dry wind, she batted her eyes closed.

"God," she whispered. "I'm scared. Please keep us safe. And help Mr. Stanton find the right way to go."

26

MABEL

Mabel blinked awake from her late afternoon nap as a highway sign flew by. Not the familiar black-and-white Route 66 sign. "What?" She twisted to see behind her. "Highway 89?" Couldn't be. She dug the map out of the side well, spread it open, and located Route 66. The two highways didn't even run the same direction. He had taken another road while she slept.

She dropped the map. "What have you done? We shouldn't be on 89."

Staring straight ahead, George puffed on a cigarette. Wind sucking through his open window snatched the smoke away before it spread through the interior but also made hearing difficult. He turned toward her. "What are you talking about?"

Mabel leaned closer. "We're not on Route 66."

He shook his head and yelled. "Had to make a detour."

"Are we going west?" she yelled back.

George pointed to his ear.

Mabel picked up the map, searching for Highway 89

again. When she found it, she gasped. "South." A flash of heat covered her face. "We're headed south, aren't we?"

He stared ahead. "You were sleeping. Detour. Roadwork ahead."

"Well, turn around."

"What?" He cupped his hand over his ear.

Mabel yelled. "I said turn around. Go back. We must stay on Route 66."

George scowled, shaking his head. "Can't. It's all torn up ahead." He focused on the highway. "I asked the officer how far we'd have to go until we hooked up with 66. He said right before Prescott we should take 89 north and angle back."

Pain shot through Mabel's core. How well she understood his refusal to look at her. He was lying. She pressed a hand on her chest and checked Stryker. Tucked into a ball, the child faced the back. The rise and fall of the tiny body suggested deep sleep.

Mabel willed the stab in her chest to fade. *Have mercy upon me, O Lord; for I am weak. O, Lord heal me.* Perhaps the prayer from Psalm 6:2 would be answered. She must not give in to this weak heart. "You promised to tell the truth."

"Okay." He flicked the cigarette butt out the window with his thumb and middle finger. Gripping the steering wheel with both hands, he straightened in the seat. "I took a detour."

She wanted to scream. Was he incapable of telling the truth? Well, he wouldn't get away with this constant deception.

George rolled up his window. "Came up on a police roadblock. Didn't know what to do. Can't risk being questioned. So I turned around and went a different way." He glanced at her. "That's the whole story. We'll get back on 66 in an hour or so. Are we square?"

His hangdog expression showed how much it mattered whether Mabel accepted his explanation. She blew out air. "That's better. I mean I'd rather you spoke the truth as you promised, not better that we're taking longer." She peeked at Stryker. "I'm don't know how much time we have."

George nodded without comment, but his face looked tight.

Mabel settled back and forced her shoulders to relax. With no choice in the matter, she might as well enjoy the ride.

Driving through the Coconino National Forest provided sweeping vistas of mostly green in contrast to the shades of gray and brown they had been traveling through for the past several days. What a refreshing change. Clattering and sputtering, the Packard labored over a range of mountains, speed slackening by the minute. About the time she wondered if the car would make it to the top, George downshifted. The engine shuddered before the racket faded to a steady hum.

Mabel lifted her eyebrows. She never knew there were mountains this high in Arizona. Always thought deserts were flat.

The highway next wound through scenic Oak Creek Canyon. Shaded by gnarled oaks, a sparkling stream meandered beside the road. Once they left the deep gorge, amazing sandstone formations glowed orange and red in the sun. Passing through picturesque Sedona, the engine clunked and wheezed. Mabel checked the dashboard then pointed to the temperature gauge. "It's running hot."

Frowning, George flicked a glance at the dash. "I'm watching it." He didn't appear overly concerned.

Please God, keep this engine working.

On the crest of a mountain, a sign claimed an elevation of five thousand feet above sea level. Shortly, they arrived in the town of Jerome with its quaint nineteenth-century brick buildings. Breathtaking views of the Verde Valley reached north and west. Mabel almost wanted to wake Stryker so she could experience such magnificence.

George maneuvered into a Texaco station and shut off the engine. Wearing a crisp white uniform and a smile, the attendant bustled to the driver's-side window. George opened the door and planted both feet on the concrete. Then he reached in and took out the keys. "Fill her up, young man. The engine's hot. Careful when you check the radiator."

To Mabel George said, "I'll be right back and let you take your turn in the facilities. Wake Stryker if you think that's a good idea. Don't know when our next stop will be." He shut

THE ROAD TO TERMINUS

the door and sauntered off, tossing the keys in the air and catching them with one hand.

Mabel tsked. "He doesn't trust me any more than I trust him."

While the attendant busied around the vehicle, Mabel dug out the map. She placed one finger on Jerome. State Highway 64 connected Jerome to Route 66 in an almost straight line. If they stayed on their current course, they'd have to drive all the way to Prescott before they could turn north. Miles out of the way. She folded the map and left it on the seat.

When Mabel woke Stryker to take her to the restroom, the girl suggested coolant for the air conditioner.

The attendant complied. After George came back, they turned on the engine. Cold air did not flow out.

Smile fading, the attendant tinkered for a few minutes without success. "Needs parts and a good cleaning. You got a lot of corrosion." He pointed to something.

George nodded.

To Mabel it meant nothing. Probably George didn't understand either.

"We don't want to spend extra time and money on parts today." George said.

Mabel agreed.

"Another thing that doesn't work." George slid behind the wheel. "This stupid gauge must be broken too." He thumped the gas indicator with his finger. "We filled the tank, but it still registers empty."

Stryker popped up. "Told you this old Packard wasn't worth what you paid."

Mabel lifted a silent prayer.

George started the engine.

"Before you take off, I want to be sure we take the fastest route." Mabel unfolded the map. "Look at this."

George frowned. Stryker perched on the edge of the seat.

Mabel pushed the map toward him. "If we take 64 out of Jerome, we can start north immediately. We'll be back to Route 66 much faster than if we stay on 89."

George tapped the map. "Not many towns for miles along

that road. What if we have car trouble? You know the Packard's been acting up."

Out of the corner of her eye, Mabel saw Stryker look from one to the other and back. No matter how frustrated Mabel felt, she didn't want to upset the child, but really. The man was so annoying. She spoke through gritted teeth. "Lots of open space the other way too. Also several needless hours of driving."

"Sorry. We're staying on 89. It's a better traveled highway, which makes it more likely someone will stop to help us if we have trouble."

A snappy retort formed in her mind, but for Stryker's sake she kept it to herself.

He jammed the gear in reverse. The transmission produced a loud grinding noise.

Mabel turned away.

Pulling out of the filling station, George said, "I'll get you back on track as fast as I can."

Mabel didn't dare doze, although Stryker curled up in minutes. George might try to slip past the turnoff for Highway 89 North. The late afternoon sun streamed through the windows, warm and lazy-making. Mabel's eyelids drooped until all she could see were the hands in her lap. To stay awake, she crossed and uncrossed her arms and legs. She rolled down her window then closed it. She mumbled hymns. Slightly more than an hour passed before she spotted the first signs for Prescott and the northbound highway.

"There," Mabel pointed. "Don't miss the turn."

George shot her a cutting look. Maybe he wasn't used to being reminded. Too bad. They couldn't risk missing this road.

"Let's take a look at the map," George said.

She spread it open. He gave the map a once-over then stared back at the road. She started to fold it up. "Wait." His eyes swept over their route. "We've got two or three more hours before we get to any place large enough to have decent motels. Maybe we should stay overnight in Prescott."

Mabel couldn't believe her ears. "No. We cannot afford to stop here. We're too far from California."

George shrugged. "Okay. Long as you understand not stopping might mean a long drive in the dark tonight."

"Can't be helped." Mabel's blood pressure must be rising as the latest pain now stabbed her chest. "Need I remind you, if we'd stayed on Route 66 we'd be at the California border by now? Especially with you driving." Pressing one hand against her bosom didn't bring relief. The pain worsened. She panted in and out through her mouth a few times. That didn't help either, so she dropped her head back on the seat.

Pain. Such pain. *Please, God.*

George didn't seem to notice.

Slowly the episode subsided. Mabel drew a long breath and closed her eyes. What if she didn't live to get Stryker to treatment? A tear squeezed out the corner of one eye. God would surely keep her healthy enough to finish her task. The possibility of not getting there was almost more than she could bear. She brushed away the tear.

Highway 89 North continued into a vast desert valley dotted with cactus. Very exotic. The temperature continued to rise and didn't abate much as dusk settled. The engine chugged, missing now and then.

George mumbled. "Think we actually found the middle of nowhere." His gaze swept the horizon. "Not a single crumb of civilization as far as I can see."

Mabel checked the temperature gauge. "The Packard is hot."

He followed her focus. "That didn't take long."

The needle didn't stop at *Hot*, but kept moving until it hit the side. "That's about as red-hot as—"

Mabel's sentence trailed off as the engine sputtered. Sounding like a person choking for air, it gasped a few times and then stopped. In tense silence, George coasted to the side of the road.

Mabel stared at George.

George stared back at Mabel. "Now what?"

She wanted to slap him. "Well, *do* something."

"What?"

"For pity's sake." She spoke through clenched teeth. "Get it started."

"I don't work on cars, remember?" He threw up his hands.

"Oh, right. You have people for that."

The loud voices or the cessation of motion—or both—woke Stryker. She sat and yawned. "What's going on?"

Mabel struggled to conceal the angry words ready to spew from her mouth. "The car broke down. Mr. Stanton can't get it going."

Stryker hunched over the seat where she could see the dashboard. "It's overheated. Turn off the ignition. We'll have to wait for the engine to cool off."

"You sure?" George asked.

Busy putting on her shoes, Stryker nodded. "Pretty sure. See the steam coming out the front? Need to raise the hood to cool off the engine."

"How can the engine cool off in this heat?"

"Trust me," Stryker said with a short laugh. "That machine is way hotter than this air."

George got out with Stryker. She instructed him how to lift the hood and stabilize it with a bar. Mabel followed. Steam off the radiator rocketed skyward like pictures she'd seen of the Old Faithful geyser about to erupt. The engine sizzled and popped, radiating enough heat to keep Mabel's house warm all winter.

"Well," Mabel tried to put on a cheerful face. "Let's take this opportunity to stretch our legs, explore this wonderful desert. We may never have this chance again."

George scowled.

Stryker tilted her head to one side, leaning against the fender. "My legs are a bit wobbly."

What was I thinking? Stryker cannot explore anything. Hollow eyes and shallow breathing ought not to be ignored. The child put up a brave front, but no one could deny she was getting worse. "Please forgive me, dear. You're right. Your legs are far too shaky for walking." Mabel's breath hitched.

George turned away and blew his nose.

A wan smile played on Stryker's lips. "I'm not as helpless as that, but I don't think I'm up to a hike." She hobbled back and slid into the seat.

"Please tuck me in," Stryker said.

231

"You want the blanket in this heat?" Mabel asked.

"It makes me feel better."

So Mabel wrapped her into a cocoon, folding the edges around her legs. "Let's talk then."

Stryker's head on the pillow appeared so small, but her smile was big. "I'd rather sing. Do you know 'You Are My Sunshine'?"

Mabel's quivering voice blended with Stryker's. The third time around George chimed in with his bass, eyes moist. Stryker stopped singing and folded her hands over her chest, listening. "Again," she whispered when they finished.

So they sang. Stryker directed them in song after song, her face glowing like an angel. They sang until they had exhausted all the songs they knew and their voices began to become scratchy. George had a surprising repertoire. The sun dropped below the horizon and darkness tucked the desert in for the night before they thought of checking the engine to see whether it had cooled.

When George turned the key in the ignition, the engine chugged to life. Rolling down the road, Mabel thanked God for safety and for getting the engine started. They may be tired, thirsty, hungry, and many miles from the California border, but in her heart Mabel knew they were never out of God's providence. She whispered words from Philippians 4:19, "But my God shall supply all your need according to his riches in glory by Christ Jesus."

George ignored her.

A highway sign announced Chino Valley. Mabel would happily forgo the scramble to the state line in favor of a meal and a good night's sleep. After all, Stryker needed nourishment to keep her strength. They should carry drinking water on such hot days. Paul always advised keeping a jug in the trunk. Why didn't she remember that in St. Louis before they left?

George slowed coming into town. "Dinner?"

Mabel nodded. "Great idea."

They drove down Main Street without finding a single restaurant with an inside light.

George's dry laugh sounded as if he needed water. "Looks

like they roll up the sidewalks at dusk." His dark countenance dared Mabel to disagree. "Guess we have to keep going."

In another hour, they came to the turnoff for Route 66. The tiny town of Ash Fork was likewise dark. No rooms available in the town's lone motel or for the next hundred and sixty-two miles. The pitch-dark desert rolled under the wheels without anyone spying a light. At 11:37 by the dashboard clock, they dragged into Seligman, Arizona but couldn't find a motel room there either.

Mabel exhaled. "I'm beginning to think motel people switch all the vacancy signs to *No Vacancy* when they go to bed."

"It's over a hundred miles to the next town." George yawned. "I don't think I can drive that far tonight."

Mabel licked her dry lips. "I'm sure I wouldn't last long either. I'm hungry, thirsty, and tired, but what can we do?"

"We could find someone hospitable enough to let us stay the night. Or we could sleep in the car."

"Oh, mercy." Either choice presented horrific possibilities.

27

GEORGE

George's shoulders ached as he motored through the western fringes of Seligman, Arizona in the dark. The longer he drove, the farther apart motels seemed to be spaced. Each marquee's glaring No Vacancy sign urged them to drive on.

About two miles from town, George spied a sign for the Hyde Park Tourist Camp and Shell station. "Park your hide at Hyde Park," he read. His stomach gurgled loudly enough to be heard in the back seat. "My hide could use a rest."

Darkness shrouded the camp, but in the glow of the head-lights he located the entrance and parked on the concrete at the Shell station.

"Not a sign of life, and the marquee is flashing No Vacancy." Mrs. Crowley's sigh sounded as exhausted as George felt.

"Right." He opened the door but left the lights on and the engine running. "But like you said, maybe the managers want to sleep so they turn off the Vacancy sign."

Careful not to slam the door with Stryker asleep in back,

he pushed it shut until the latch clicked. Then he marched through the crunchy gravel toward the motel office. Midway, he realized he'd forgotten to grab the keys. Could he trust Crowley? He smirked. Where would she go tonight?

The headlights illuminated a small sign near the door. *Ring bell after hours.* He didn't notice hours listed anywhere, but a dark office probably meant a sleeping clerk. George gave the button two quick pushes and one long.

No one came. He pounded out his frustration on the chipping paint.

Pain radiated through George's back from sitting. He rolled his head, listening to his neck pop before letting out a long breath. Then he pressed the bell one final time.

Inside, shuffling approached the door. The lock snapped. Another lock sounded like it slid off. A third lock scraped. The door creaked open a few inches.

A haggard, middle-aged woman stood barefoot in the wedge of open door. Attired in a ratty, plaid flannel robe bunched at the middle by a tie, she wore a faded bandana over her hair. Eyes puffy, her expression screamed *don't bother me.* "We ain't got no vacancies tonight. Cancha read the sign?"

"I saw it." What happened to the customer-is-always-right attitude? Hopefully the smile plastered on his face wouldn't betray his irritation. "But we've driven a long way today and are tired. I thought you might have one room. There are three of us—two adults and a child. We're not particular about the accommodations, but we need three clean beds." What was he saying? What if Mother heard him now? Begging for a room at this filthy motel. If he weren't so tired he would've laughed.

The woman's eyes snapped. "You think we turn on our No Vacancy sign when we have a room?" Her laugh reminded him of sandpaper on rough wood. One corner of her mouth twisted into a sneer. The door started to close.

"Please," George said as loudly as possible without yelling.

Movement ceased and the sagging eyes peeked out around the door.

"We'll take anything. Put a couple of rollaway beds in the lobby. We have a sick child with us. She needs to stretch out."

The woman yawned, allowing her mouth to flap open to the hinges without bothering to cover the toothless, gaping cavern with her hand. "Can't help you."

She had no idea who she was dealing with. Wearily, George tugged out his wad of cash. "What do you get for a room? I'll double the amount." He started peeling off money. "Tell me how much you need."

Forehead wrinkling, she cocked her head as if mesmerized by the whisper of fanning bills. "How much you got there?"

George stared. Was she kidding? She couldn't possibly want it all. "Look. During peak season in these parts, motel rooms go for about ten bucks a night. Might get as high as twenty if the joint is nice. Right?"

She gave a slow nod.

"We are a party of three, like I said. How about I give you fifty dollars?" He shelled out fifty and shook it toward her. "That's a great profit for one measly old room." He waved the money in her face so she could smell it. "What do you say?"

She released the door and crossed her arms. "Two hundred and you got a deal."

"Two hundred?" And the FBI accused George of being a thief. He should turn this woman in to them. Disgusting. He did an about-face into the headlights and closed his eyes. This shrewd, old broad had him right where she wanted him. He needed a few hours' sleep. So did Stryker and Crowley. She beat him at his own game. He dropped his shoulders.

Slowly, as if heading to his execution, George circled back. "You got a deal."

She opened the door wide and flipped on a light.

Heart dragging the floor, he entered to complete the arrangements.

Directions to the "room" he rented started with getting back on the road and heading a mile west. While he drove, he explained what had happened.

"I don't understand," Mrs. Crowley said. "We got a cottage, but it isn't on the motel property?"

"Right. Used to be a miner's cabin. She said it has enough

beds for all of us. They bought it a few years ago and rent it out now and then, mostly during hunting and fishing season."

"Fishing season in the desert?" Mrs. Crowley frowned. "Doesn't sound logical. Where would a person fish? Are there lakes or rivers nearby?"

Mental head thump. "Got me there, didn't she?" George squeezed out a brusque laugh. "I suppose she might mean up at the Grand Canyon. That isn't far away, is it? But what're they gonna hunt, jackrabbits?" He shook his head. "I bought the whole story to get a room for the night."

Driving up the road to the cottage, George silently cursed this woman for cheating him. And then he saw it—a pile of timber leaning to one side. Not enough shingles remained on the roof to keep out rain.

Stepping into the desert night, George faced the cottage with his hands at his sides as if preparing for a gunfight. He'd like to shoot the greedy motel woman. The sound of pumping blood thrashed in his ears. Why didn't he see this scam coming? He ground his jaw until it hurt. Someone tell him this was a bad dream. He did not shell out two hundred dollars for this piece of—

"Is this where we're sleeping tonight?" Stryker's sleepy voice interrupted his thoughts.

Mrs. Crowley's tender tone was soothing. "We're here. Gather your things and let's get you inside. I hope it's cooler than outside."

But it was hotter. The room seemed a breeding place for heat. And it was dark. George moved the car snug to the door where the headlights shone inside. In the half-light they discovered beds—mere frames with tattered woolen army blankets covering the springs.

Mrs. Crowley located a candle and matches and soon had a portable circle of light to explore the rest of the spartan accommodations. George gathered Stryker's two blankets and pillow from the back seat before switching off the headlights.

Blowing air through his mouth, he shut the front door and turned to assess their latest misfortune.

The room was merely that—one room.

"No bathroom," Mrs. Crowley blinked at George over the flickering flame. "Let's hope there's an outhouse."

Six single beds lined the back and side walls. No windows. No kitchen. Not even a sink. George let out a low whistle. "Unbelievable. How do we do it? Every night we find a worse place than the night before."

"I don't feel so good." Stryker dropped onto the first bed. Shoulders hunched, she rocked back and forth holding her stomach.

"Probably starving. We have no food." Mrs. Crowley shone light on the girl. A thick red trickle ran out her nose and down her chin, dripping onto the front of her blouse.

Mrs. Crowley gasped.

Handing the candle to George, she knelt beside the bed. Tipping the girl's head back, she pressed a handkerchief against Stryker's nose. "Quick, Mr. Stanton. Find something else to soak up this blood."

George gagged. Not another nosebleed. The sticky, red ooze made him queasy. He'd never been able to stand the sight of it, his or anyone else's. He averted his eyes. Grateful for a job, he carried the candle all over the room. At long last, he stumbled on a roll of toilet paper, which he handed to Mrs. Crowley.

She squinted up at him. "Is that all there is? This won't last long."

A second search unearthed a couple of stiff, scratchy towels.

"Oh, dear." Mrs. Crowley shook out a puff of dust. "I hope we're not risking infection."

Helplessness overwhelmed him. He scanned the small room. The accommodation had beds, but how would they sleep on rusty springs? He had paid dearly for the chance to try. Had he completely lost his touch? His cash was running low. What would he do in Mexico?

Candlelight bounced off his blue diamond ring and tossed a kaleidoscope of colors on the wall. The gem would be worth a fortune in Mexico, but he would never part with it. This heirloom comprised the last trace of George's prior lifestyle. That and his expensive gold watch were all he had left. Even if forced to live under an assumed name in Puerto Vallarta, he would always be George Kendrick Stanton in his heart. In this insanity, he dare not lose his identity. He must hold his head high and remember his heritage, especially when he felt completely worthless.

Like now.

Before Stryker's blood had soaked the first towel, the flow ceased. Mrs. Crowley dropped the crimson-stained towel on the dirty floor and sank onto a bed next to Stryker's. Rocking back and forth from side to side, she crossed both hands over her chest and moaned.

Stryker lifted up on one elbow, appraising the woman. "Does your heart hurt again?"

Mrs. Crowley panted through her mouth a few times. "I'll be fine. Don't you worry about me."

The bottom dropped out of George's stomach.

Pale and gaunt, Mrs. Crowley did not appear well.

Both of them sick? No, no, no. He would not allow it. Dizziness made George's legs weak. With all his heart he wanted to bolt from the room and never look back. His muscles tensed. With all the fortitude he could muster, he held in the primal scream threatening to break free. He'd become a prisoner to two strangers. Why couldn't he get away from this peculiar bond?

About to hurl, George spun on one heel and sprinted for the Packard. Throwing open the driver's-side door, he groped for the Johnnie Walker. He ripped off the stopper and upended the bottle. Whiskey poured into his throat, and he gulped it like water.

He dropped onto the seat, half in and half out, both feet planted in the dust. Resting his arms on his knees, he waited for the liquor to dull his anxiety. How low he had sunk. Chased across country by some Texas detective wearing a gray Stetson. His nest egg evaporating in the desert heat. Now the growing possibility that he might become nursemaid to both Stryker and Crowley. How would he survive when the whole world had turned against him?

His father's voice mocked him. Who else but stupid Georgie Stanton would sit in an outdated jalopy that barely ran, wear cowboy boots and hillbilly clothes, and actually contemplate sleeping on a scratchy army blanket in a shack with no running water or electricity?

He'd finally become the complete loser his father always predicted.

His head spun and his stomach lurched. None of this was his fault.

Suppose Mrs. Crowley was right. Perhaps he didn't control his destiny. Was it possible that some unseen being pulled the strings of his life? He gulped another swig of whiskey.

And another.

Millions of tiny lights glittered in the desert sky. So many. He had never imagined such a mind-boggling number of stars existed. For a moment, the quiet beauty sucked his breath away. Mouth slack, he slowly scanned the heavens. The enormity and orderliness left him awestruck, made his head spin.

He lowered the whiskey bottle. Did he truly believe creation happened randomly as he'd always claimed? How did those stars appear in the sky without a plan? Yet no mortal had the ability to design such an enormous array of planets and suns and keep them in place. Someone bigger than the universe must have created all this. Someone smarter than anyone on Earth. Someone with no beginning and no end.

Impossible.

Or was it?

28

MABEL

In darkness thick enough to scoop up by hand, Mabel lay on her stomach, wide awake. Eight days of unimaginable obstacles had delayed their arrival in Los Angeles. They should have made the trip in half the time. Would have, if not for George and his foolishness. Mabel exhaled a long vexed breath and rearranged her legs on the prickly blanket. An old woman should never try to sleep in her clothing. Was it merely a week ago she let Stryker talk her into stopping at George's wreck?

Dear Lord, please forgive me for complicating the job You gave me to do.

She flopped onto her back, folded her hands over her middle, and whispered, "I will both lay me down in peace, and sleep: for thou, Lord, only makest me dwell in safety." She'd recited Psalm 4:8 from childhood whenever sleep eluded her. Even in this remote place it comforted.

Every time George tossed, the springs on his cot squawked like a flock of chickens. For the third time that long night, he crawled out of bed. On the way to the door, his foot banged something, and he whispered a curse. The door clicked shut. Seconds later, smoke trickled through cracks in the shanty walls.

Stryker's moaning and jaw grinding amplified. Such restless sleep couldn't continue without draining her energy. Even hugging Sophia didn't seem to comfort her. How much was she suffering? If only Mabel knew how to help the poor girl. Painkillers might ease the discomfort. Why didn't she ask Doctor Marston about giving her aspirin? Maybe there would have been something to help her sleep better too.

At some point Mabel must have drifted to sleep, because all of a sudden she started awake. Heart pounding, she blinked, trying to focus in the disorienting blackness. What woke her? She fluttered fingers above her head to make sure a sheet didn't cover her face.

When Mabel stood, her foot connected with something and sent it spinning. She reached down and picked up the empty Johnnie Walker bottle. Apparently, sometime in the night George had drained all the whiskey. Did he need to chase away demons? Perhaps alcohol helped him sleep.

She felt her way to the door and opened it. Streaks of light appeared in the eastern sky minutes before the sun rose. One hand on her mouth, she stood transfixed by the simplicity and beauty of God's creation.

Mabel turned back in the room to find the two sleeping peacefully. After such a fitful night, she didn't want to wake them. She found a rickety chair outside and used the time for much needed prayer and reflection.

About eight o'clock, they packed up to get back on the road.

"I've a mind to set fire to this disgraceful shack." Standing at the car, George glared at their night's shelter. He flicked his lighter with his thumb. A flame shot out.

"What a ghastly idea." Mabel pressed her hand on her chest. "Whatever makes you say things like that? How would arson help anything?"

"Consider it a public service." His expression darkened. "No one else would get hoodwinked like we did. I'd say that makes it a great idea."

"No," Mabel said with as much force as she could manage. She would not be a party to the senseless destruction of someone else's property. What kind of person would come up with such depraved ideas?

He stood a moment longer before shoving the lighter into his pocket. With one finger, he slid his sunglasses over his nose and settled in the driver's seat.

As they drove back onto Route 66, the sun already beat down on the roof. Mabel's mouth felt as dry as Melba toast. Stryker's lips had crusted over. They needed water. With her now bloodstained hanky, Mabel mopped perspiration from her brow. No water meant no rinsing out dirty clothing.

Mabel licked her lips. "First thing we need to do is stop for food and water."

"Uh-huh." George's gaze never left the highway. "See anyplace to stop so far?"

Desert stretched on every side. He was right. Where could they find water out here?

George pressed the side of his head. Maybe she wasn't the only one with a headache.

A rectangular mileage sign announced three miles to Kingman.

The engine hiccupped a couple of times and then shut off.

"What?" George pumped the pedal as the car coasted. Nothing happened. He tapped the gas gauge with one finger. "It says we're out of gas but this stupid thing is broken, like I said. I put gas in the tank late last night. We can't be out of gas already."

Mabel stiffened.

George steered to the shoulder. The Packard slowly rolled to a stop. Once movement ceased, Mabel scanned the dashboard. "Not too hot this time."

A drowsy voice from the back seat said, "Turn the engine on."

When he twisted the key, a grinding sound preceded a tired chug before the engine shut down again.

"Sounds like we're out of gas." Stryker sat, rubbing her eyes. "Don't keep trying to turn the engine over. You might drain the battery."

With an animal-like growl, George dropped his head onto the steering wheel. "What next?"

"We're a little less than three miles to Kingman." Mabel tried to sound positive. "You could walk it. Most towns have filling stations on the outskirts. You might not have to go all the way to Kingman to find one."

Lifting his head as if it weighed a ton, George glared. "You want I should walk three miles to a filling station?"

"Well, that makes the most sense, doesn't it?" Mabel did not understand the problem.

"No, ma'am." He waggled his head. "I don't do that."

"Oh, for pity's sake. Why not?"

Stryker stretched her arms above her head. "We should all go. The interior will get too hot even with the windows open."

Together, George and Mabel gaped at Stryker.

"Why?" Mabel couldn't imagine anything more implausible than walking along scalding asphalt in this blazing heat. "The sun will be on us when we walk the same as if we stay in the car."

Stryker peered out the window. "There's a light breeze outside. We'll be okay. Trust me, this car is gonna get much hotter than the outside temperature."

George's frown spread to his whole face. "Only if we leave the windows closed."

"I'm too old, and I'm wearing the wrong shoes," Mabel said. "Stryker can't walk. Someone would have to carry her. We'll slow you down. You're the logical person to go for help, young man."

George didn't give up easily. "I say we flag down a passing motorist to drive us to the next filling station."

That sounded easy enough, so they waited. And waited.

The interior heated noticeably.

Mabel waved her handkerchief in front of her face, wishing for a real fan. Perspiration dripped down her neck and back. Behind and beyond, the highway spread as far as the horizon. Heat radiating off the black pavement made the ribbon of road appear wavy. If she stared too long, she might fall under some mesmerizing spell.

A moving spot ahead indicated a vehicle coming from the West. Mabel straightened in her seat, watching it approach. "Should we stop it?"

"It's going the wrong way. We don't want to backtrack."

Mabel clapped a mental hand over her mouth to keep from screaming. *Sure, detours, no problem, but Heaven help us if we backtrack.* She tsked.

George snorted. "We're closer to Kingman than the last town we passed. Makes more sense to keep moving forward."

For once, Mabel agreed with his logic. "While we wait, perhaps we should consider how we're going to make a car stop for us." Her experiences didn't supply her with this ability.

"I'll do it." Stryker grinned. "Who wouldn't stop for a bald-headed kid?"

"True." Mabel caught her wink and played along. "But you shouldn't be outside in the heat. I'll be the one to wave." She demonstrated with her hanky. "Yoo Hoo! Old ladies elicit sympathy too. I'd be much more likely to get help than Mr. Stanton."

George arched his eyebrows high above his sunglasses. "A stranger would be most apt to stop for a handsome guy." He struck a pose that made Stryker laugh.

How clever. Why hadn't Mabel ever tried that on George before? When you want him to do something, intimate you can do a better job. Mabel said, "Oh, all right. You flag down a ride."

When George looked out the window, Mabel winked back at Stryker. For a child, she certainly possessed many useful skills.

The eastbound truck zoomed past. Within a minute, a car appeared from the opposite direction. As it advanced, Mabel nodded to George. "Okay, handsome, you're on."

George stepped onto the highway and walked into the middle of the westbound lane, waving his arms over his head.

"Do you need my handkerchief?" Mabel called after him.

He kept walking, but his shoulders stiffened.

Hand over her mouth, Mabel held her breath.

The light blue sedan approached, slowed, and stopped.

Head and arms hanging out the window, Stryker said, "He did it."

Mabel blew out the breath she'd been holding.

George swaggered to the driver's side and bent at the window. A couple of times he gestured toward the Packard. More talking followed. George reached into his pocket and withdrew his folded money.

Oh, great. Another bribe. So much for his handsome guy theory.

He will run out of money at the rate he throws it around. Mabel shook her head as the driver maneuvered the blue car to a stop on the shoulder ahead. A farmer-type in dungarees and a faded plaid shirt waved at her while hobbling toward the front of the Packard.

She smiled back.

George opened the hood.

"I wanna see too." Stryker jumped from the back seat before Mabel could object. For several minutes, Mabel waited, hands folded on her lap. What were they studying? Did this stranger know more than Stryker?

The hood slammed shut.

The farmer and George shook hands.

Grinning, George hurried to the driver's-side door. "What luck. This fellow's a mechanic."

Not luck, of course, but Mabel didn't contradict him. *Thank you, God.*

Tugging on her hat, Stryker wadded her blankets in her arms and grabbed her pillow and monkey from the back seat. "I think he's wrong about the engine, but we're all going."

"Wrong? Why?"

George leaned farther in to pull out the keys. "Says the Packard not only ran out of gas, but all the oil has leaked out. The block is cracked. This heap of junk would never make it to California. Not without a new engine. It's a wonder we got as far as Arizona. This friendly guy will take us into Kingman to a car dealership where we can buy another one."

"Leave the vehicle by the side of the road? Again, Mr.

Stanton?" Mabel could not simply abandon it for others to deal with. It wasn't right. So irresponsible.

The wretched man wouldn't listen. "Get your things, and don't worry. I promise you this is the fastest way to L.A."

Before they got around to proper introductions, the blue car slowed in front of a ramshackle Phillips station. "Here's the road where I turn toward home," their chauffeur said with a wide grin. "Old Pete'll be more than happy to help you folks."

George stared out the side window. "We haven't reached the Kingman city limits yet, and there are no vehicles for sale at this station. You agreed to take us to a dealership, remember?"

The driver's grin looked lopsided. "Don't you worry none. Pete'll fix you up in a jiffy. You can trust him one hundred percent."

Stryker and Mabel slid out of the back, and George climbed out of the front seat, muttering. Soon as the doors closed, the blue sedan rumbled down a dirt road to the left of the station, dust billowing in its wake.

Hands in his pockets, George narrowed his eyes. "Another scumbag taking advantage of our misfortune. Can't trust a living soul these days."

Mabel waved away flying dirt. "Why do you say that?"

"I gave him a hundred dollars." He faced her. "We could've walked to this place, and we're still not in Kingman."

Mabel pressed her lips together. A hundred dollars? Why didn't George wait to pay after they got into Kingman? Her husband always advised her to approve the work before she settled the bill. "No getting your money back now. You'll never catch him on foot. Chalk it up to lesson learned, and let's see what old Pete has to say."

Stryker laced her fingers through Mabel's, and they walked toward the filling station.

Mere seconds later, a short, dirty tramp in threadbare clothing shuffled out of the building behind the station. A scruffy white beard masked his face. Wrinkles lined his leathery skin. Pete was either old or he'd been outside way too much.

"Who be you?" The man's unusually loud voice might indicate a hearing problem.

George plastered a smile on and advanced with an extended hand. "You must be Pete. A fellow in a blue car dropped us off. Didn't get his name. We had engine trouble, and he said you'd be the person to help us."

"That so?" Pete squeezed one eye shut. "What kinda help you reckon old Pete might give you?"

"Well, we . . ." George glanced at Mabel. "Mrs. Crowley and Stryker and I are traveling to California. We're pretty thirsty and hungry. Our vehicle broke down, and we need a new one."

"You want food and water?" Feet apart, he locked his arms over his chest.

Mabel stepped forward, enunciating her words clearly. "Our most urgent problem is that we've had nothing to eat or drink all day."

"But we also need another car." George interjected.

"Food and water I got." Pete squinted. "For a fee."

With a heavy sigh, George reached into his pocket and tugged out his money. "You have a car to sell too?"

"A car, you say?" Pete shook his head. "Not one that runs." His dull eyes lit up at the sight of the cash. "Got a bicycle though."

"A bicycle?" George threw up his hands. "There are three of us. What will we do with a bicycle?"

"How should I know?" Pete scratched his chin. "But it can be yours for a mere hundred dollars. I'll throw in the other stuff as part of the deal."

"We don't want your lousy bicycle," George yelled, gesturing with his arms. "How much for food and water?"

Pete stroked his beard. "Fifty for the three of you."

"Ridiculous." Red in the face, George huffed as if about to breathe out fire. "How do you people get away with such gouging?" Glancing at Stryker, he dropped his shoulders and counted out the money.

Mabel closed her eyes. How could anyone be this foolish? Did he know nothing about the ways of the world?

Pete demonstrated his method for drawing water. At the

side of the station, a well pumped groundwater into a cement holding tank. Attached to the tank, a cracked rubber hose made the water accessible.

Before Mabel could stop her, Stryker twisted the spigot and held the hose over her head. Murky water poured out, thoroughly drenching the girl, clothing and all.

When Mabel stammered an objection, Stryker shrugged. "But it feels good."

Mabel wiped streaks of mud off Stryker's face. "I suppose the sun will dry you soon."

After running the water a few seconds, the murkiness cleared enough to make the water drinkable, and they took turns quenching their thirst.

Pete stored food in a small room, which also served as his bedroom. The air inside the room felt dense with grease and grime. The kitchen area consisted of crates tipped on end, covered with cardboard boxes from a wholesale distributor. For the fifty-dollar fee, he offered them each a bruised apple, melted candy bars, and a peanut butter sandwich on stale bread prepared in Pete's filthy kitchenette.

George declined the food with a shake of the head. "Can't make myself eat something from this dirty place." He shivered in the stifling heat. "Must be cockroaches in here the size of cats. Repulsive."

He might be right, but Stryker needed nourishment. The child was getting so weak she could only stand for a few minutes. She ate a couple bites of her apple, a nibble of the sandwich, and broke off a small chunk of a candy bar. Not much nutrition, but something in her stomach at least.

While she ate, Mabel surveyed the room. Where did he keep his phone? Not seeing one, she asked, "We need to call a taxi. Where's your phone?"

Pete gave her the once-over. "All them new-fangled contraptions cost money."

Mabel exhaled. "I take it you don't have one."

George rolled his eyes.

"What you gonna do with that car what don't run?" Pete asked.

Why did he want to know that? What good was a broken-down automobile?

George shrugged. "How far to the next filling station?"

Pete cocked his head. "A mile or so."

"The distance to Kingman." George dropped his chin to his chest. A moment later, he glanced up. "Look, Pete. I have a proposition for you."

"Yeah?"

"You ride your bicycle to the next station and call a taxi to come get us. I'll pay you a hundred dollars."

Pete's mouth curved at the corners into what must have passed for a smile in his odd world. "If you throw in the keys to your car, I'll do it. I need the cash up front, so I know you ain't gonna stiff me."

George furrowed his brow. "You won't come back."

"'Course I will." A weird chuckle popped out of Pete's lips. "I live here." He thrust out his hand, wiggling grungy fingers. "Keys plus a hundred simoleons, you said."

What did he plan to do with a rusty, broken-down car? Mabel would have given him half the money and kept the keys. She couldn't believe her eyes when George flipped the keys to Pete and counted out the full hundred. Apparently, he hadn't learned his lesson. She blew out frustrated air. Plain foolish.

The tramp pocketed the cash, plopped a tattered, wide-brim straw hat on his head, hopped on the bicycle, and pedaled out of sight along the highway. A sinking feeling settled into Mabel's stomach.

No matter how long they waited, Pete would *not* return.

A taxi wouldn't be coming to get them either.

29

GEORGE

Chain-smoking his last pack of cigarettes, George paced in front of the abandoned Phillips station. He peeked at his Rolex. Almost five o'clock and no taxi.

As if that weren't infuriating enough, he had endured hours of Mrs. Crowley's I-told-you-sos. Would he ever be rid of this tiresome woman? Several times during the interminably hot day, George plotted ways to shed her. If only he could sneak away. Of course, he couldn't. The old biddy would blab to the cops.

George reached into his pocket and withdrew his remaining cash. Shuffling through it, he counted silently. Eight hundred sixty-three dollars. His heart flip-flopped and his fingers hunted through other pockets, finding no more. That's *all* he had left of his original nest egg? Sight of such a paltry sum cramped his stomach.

Hundreds of thousands of dollars, gone like smoke in the wind. Nausea churned his empty stomach. What would he do in Mexico? How would he buy another vehicle?

He spun on his heel and strode into the office where

Crowley and Stryker had taken refuge from the relentless sun. "Let's guess where old Pete hides his cash."

"What?" Mrs. Crowley sounded incredulous.

George had already commenced searching cupboards and rifling through boxes of supplies. Stryker stood watching. "Are you going to steal his money?"

"Just taking a refund of the hundred I gave him. He's not keeping up his end of the bargain. Besides, he's going to make money on the Packard when he scraps it."

Stryker tugged at her ear. "Is this right to do?"

"Of course not," Mrs. Crowley said. "Thou shalt not steal. It's one of the Ten Commandments."

George didn't need to defend his actions. Pete owed him. A deal should be honored.

After a few minutes, Mrs. Crowley spoke. "Come on, Stryker. We'll go out to the road. Maybe we can flag down another car."

Good riddance. If he found Pete's stash, he didn't want Mrs. Goody Two Shoes hovering over his shoulder clobbering him with Bible verses.

George rummaged through every box and cupboard, scattering the contents on the floor. No need to put it back. Time was not on his side. Sweat beaded on his forehead and formed rings under his arms. Hidden at the bottom of a worn shoebox, at length he unearthed a stack of bills. He counted out five hundred, thirty dollars in fives, tens, and ones. He smirked smugly as he stuffed it all in his pocket and hurried to the road.

"How much cash do you have?" he asked Mrs. Crowley.

She turned, eyebrows raised. "I beg your pardon."

"Cash," he repeated, not trying to veil the indignity in his tone. "You brought along money for the trip. How much do you have?"

"Well, I declare." She blinked rapidly. "That's akin to asking my age. Why on earth would you question a lady about something personal like that?"

"Take a look, will you?" He pointed at her purse. "I don't have enough money to buy another vehicle. You're gonna have to pitch in."

She narrowed her eyes. "Wait a minute, young man. This whole trip you have mismanaged your money, and now you want me to—"

"Bail me out? I'm not asking that. You want to get Stryker to L.A." He cracked his knuckles. "I lost my car, but I bought another one. You lost a car too. The next purchase is on you. So come on, how much?"

Indecision played across Mrs. Crowley's face like an orchestra tuning up. After a moment, she reached in her purse. Unzipping the inner pocket, she tugged out a drawstring bag and removed folded bills. Turning slightly away, she concealed her actions behind one shoulder. Whispers indicated counting. When she finished, she tucked the money back in the bag before facing George. "I have about a thousand dollars."

"Good," George said. "You have enough to buy a new car."

"Surely we don't need a *new* one." Mrs. Crowley glared.

"I mean new to us."

She nodded. "Right."

Even if she paid, he'd still come up short when he arrived in Mexico. He would have had a good cushion but for that stupid wrong turn. He'd need another ride. Or else he'd have to buy a plane ticket to Puerto Vallarta. With careful planning he might make his eight hundred plus Pete's money last until he got to Gringo Gulch, but he certainly didn't have enough to set up the investment business he envisioned. At the minimum, he needed several thousand. If only he could find a room full of suckers ready to play poker. George always won at poker.

A dusty white pickup rolled into sight, heading west. George sauntered into the middle of the lane and waved his hands, same as before. Brakes squealed, and the truck jolted to a stop.

George stepped back, wiped his brow with one hand, and pasted on a smile. "Hey, fella. Our Packard quit and left us stranded down the road a ways." He spoke while walking to the open driver's-side window. "Can we hitch a ride into town?"

A lanky youth in a Forty Niner's ball cap peered at George

over aviator sunglasses. "You want a ride into Kingman to get a tow truck?"

"Our vehicle isn't worth fixing. Need to buy another one." Would George need to pull out the dwindling cash? "What's the first dealership you come to?"

The kid scratched his cheek. "That would be Stone's. It's right off Route 66. 'Bout four miles from here. It's after five though. Don't know how late they stay open."

"We'll take our chances. Can you give us a ride?"

"Uh." He stroked his chin. "Happen to be going into town myself. Three more people might fit if we get real cozy."

Afraid to allow him time to change his mind, George summoned Mrs. Crowley and Stryker. They toted their belongings—two blankets, one pillow, Sophia, George's overcoat, a couple department store bags of clothing and toiletries—to the truck where George piled everything in the back. The three climbed into the cab with Stryker balanced on George's lap.

Crowded but relieved, they headed west onto the highway bound for Kingman.

"So you're a Forty Niner's fan, eh kid?" George asked.

"Yup." The truck rumbled along the highway.

"I'm a die-hard Bears fan, myself. Your rookies don't stand a chance against seasoned players like the Bears."

"That right?" The kid flashed a grin. "We'll see."

Nobody beat the Bears.

The short drive offered hardly any time for football debate. Soon the teenager swung the pickup into the parking lot of Harry Stone's Ford, Mercury, and Dodge. When they climbed out and retrieved their property from the truck bed, Mrs. Crowley thanked the youth profusely and pressed folded money into his hand. Grinning, the driver saluted. The truck screeched onto the street, leaving them standing on the pavement.

Eyes glistening, Stryker turned to survey rows of shiny new and used vehicles. "Oh. Look at this one." She made a beeline for a spiffy red-and-beige Ford Crestline Victoria. The kid sure had good taste in cars.

George frowned as he followed. A red car would draw all

kinds of attention. They needed something more discreet. "1953." He read on the sticker. "This one's almost new. And how about that price—$1499." He whistled. "We can't afford this baby."

Mrs. Crowley stood guarding their possessions but nodded in agreement for once. "Far too expensive, dear." She called. "I'm sure we can find a more suitable one."

A rotund salesman bustled out of the office wearing a button-front shirt gaping open over his stomach. "Hi there, folks. I was closing shop, but looks like you're interested in this beauty here." He patted the Crestline's fender. "Excellent choice. This is a fine automobile."

"Sure it is." George attempted to hide his distaste for pushy salesmen. "Thing is, it's way overpriced, and we don't want a red one."

"You said you wanted a red Cadillac." Innocent eyes connected with George's. Stryker cocked her head and flapped her skimpy eyelashes.

Darn this child. She never forgets a single thing. "Maybe I mentioned that once, but when it comes right down to actually buying one, I wouldn't get a red one. Much too showy."

"Fine, fine." The salesman grinned. "Let me introduce myself. I'm Fred Stone. And you are?"

George ignored Fred's outstretched hand. He had no intention of getting chummy with a salesman. "We junked our car and got a ride here." Might as well explain enough so the fellow wouldn't jump to wrong conclusions about the state of their desperation. "We want something to finish our trip in, nothing fancy. If you don't have anything we like, we'll call a taxi for the nearest motel and car shop tomorrow." Had he said too much? Didn't want the guy prying into every detail of their lives. Confound it. Coming here was a bad idea. Too much paper trail. Should *borrow* one instead.

Fred's salesman smile froze. "Fine, fine. Would you folks like to put your things inside while we look?"

"They'll be fine right here." The lot was small and there were no other people in sight. Stryker picked up Sophia.

"What kinda budget you folks working with?"

No wasting time with Fred. George waited for Mrs. Crowley to answer but got a blank stare instead. Used vehicles in Arizona should be cheap. "I'm thinking four or five hundred dollars," George said, crossing his arms. "What can you show us in that range?"

"Fine, fine. Four or five hundred." Fred fumbled with his tie, tightening and straightening the knot. "Let me think. Inventory in that price range is limited. But I might have one or two possibilities." He grinned and spread his arm to indicate the direction. "This way, folks."

Stryker kept pace with Fred. Mrs. Crowley lagged behind with George.

"Can we afford five hundred dollars?" She whispered.

"We're almost to California now." George whispered back.

"But I have to get home too."

George bent close to her ear. "You gotta buy it, you understand. I can't sign paperwork in my name. Too easy to trace."

"You could use Vincent Morelli."

Was she kidding? He glanced sideways. She wasn't grinning. "What I'm saying is we're using your money, *and* you have to sign the papers."

Mrs. Crowley didn't argue.

Speaking softly while they walked, they rounded the building where Stryker and Fred had disappeared and found the two in conversation over a dull brown Hudson coupe. Rather shabby looking but definitely more discreet than the red Ford.

Stryker's forehead puckered. "I don't know. It's a '49 with over 90,000 miles on it. Plus it needs new tires." She kicked the nearly bald front tire. "We already had to change a flat. Don't think this will do."

George peeked at the interior. The upholstery was worn thin and ripped in places. Part of the ceiling lining sagged. The inside smelled worse than the Packard.

"How about air conditioning?" George searched the dashboard.

Fred tugged out a large white handkerchief and mopped sweat off his brow. "Afraid not, folks. The engine hums like a sewing machine, but this basic number is low on extras. As such, I can let you have her for a mere six hundred fifty dollars. You don't want to pass up this deal. Won't come across another one for many miles. Shall we go inside where it's cooler and write it up?"

Hard sell type. Typical car salesman. An involuntary sigh forced it's way through George's mouth. "What else do you have?"

"You sure you want to let this one go?" Fred's gaze swept over each of them. "Fine, fine. Let me think." He held up one finger. "You are in luck. Got another hot prospect for you."

He squeezed between two automobiles—no easy task— and waddled toward a gray two-door with Stryker trailing right behind. His hand lightly brushed across the hood. "Here's a wonderful 1951 Chevrolet Styleline Deluxe Bel Air. Two-tone with a sleek, white roof. A real beauty. Formerly owned by a local couple who never went anywhere. Thirty-five thousand easy miles on her. Chrome everywhere, even on the clock. See that radio? Everything works. Tires in fine condition. Take a look, folks. This car is for you."

"How much?" Mrs. Crowley asked from too far away to look inside.

"I'm almost embarrassed to say, with such a fine automobile. A mere eight hundred dollars for this baby." Fred mopped his brow.

Spouting such malarkey must be hot work. George shook his head but bent to assess the inside anyway. The upholstery in the back seat appeared new. That would be good for Stryker. A deep indentation on the seat behind the steering wheel indicated an overweight former owner. No dents in the fenders. Tires looked okay. "I don't know. It's a two-door, Mrs. Crowley. Stryker will have trouble getting in and out of the back."

"And no air conditioning. Although it does have a radio." Mrs. Crowley stood on the opposite side shading her glasses.

"Does the radio work?" Stryker asked.

"Everything works fine on this car." Fred dabbed his forehead.

"How does anyone exist in this heat without air conditioning?" Mrs. Crowley asked.

Fred had an answer for everything. "Easy enough to add air."

"That would be an additional expense," George said.

"Can I look at the engine?" Stryker handed Sophia to Mrs. Crowley.

Fred's expression said he didn't hear that correctly. "She wants to—"

George gestured for the man to get on with it.

With raised eyebrows, Fred popped the hood.

"Needs a new air filter. Don't think anyone's changed the oil recently either." Stryker went to the other side, stood on tiptoes, and bent in toward the engine. "Start it up, please."

Fred smirked, but George nodded. With a shrug, Fred produced a key and revved the gas pedal a few times. To George, it sounded solid. What would Stryker say?

"Spark plugs sound okay. Belts seem tight enough." She peered underneath. "No oil leaking."

Fred turned off the ignition and slammed down the hood. "Yes, sir. This is a fine automobile. Shall we write her up?"

Mrs. Crowley's brows closed in the middle. "Eight hundred is entirely too much to pay for a used two-door with no air conditioning." She pressed her lips together. "I don't think this one is right either."

Stryker tilted her head from one side to the other. "It's nice." She tapped her chin with two fingers. "But you're right. Eight hundred is too much money, considering the needed maintenance and all. Plus no air conditioning, as you say."

Were they haggling? Perhaps he'd underestimated Mrs. Crowley's business savvy. George rubbed the back of his neck. "Yeah, I guess you're right."

Fred threw up both hands like a stop sign. "Now hold on there, folks. I'm sure we can come to an agreement. How about if I make it seven seventy-five?" He grinned all over, as if he'd offered them the deal of a lifetime. "And I'll even throw in a free air filter."

Stryker shook her head.

Mrs. Crowley clamped her arms across her chest.

George gave the Chevy another once over. "I don't think so."

Out came the big handkerchief again. "What would you give me to drive away in this fine automobile tonight?"

Without hesitation Mrs. Crowley answered, "Six fifty. Plus the free air filter."

George's jaw dropped open. She knew how to dicker. Who would have expected that?

Fred's eyes glazed over. "Well, now. I don't know." He choked out a chuckle. "That's quite a deep cut. We have to make a living here. Would you consider seven twenty-five?"

"No," Mrs. Crowley said. "Six fifty, cash. That's my offer. What a pity you're unable to accommodate us." She gave a quick smile. "We mustn't take up any more of your valuable time." She stepped around the back where George and Stryker waited. Stryker pirouetted like a ballerina and retrieved Sophia from Mrs. Crowley. Linking arms, the two walked slowly back. Heads together, they nodded and pointed at other vehicles like a couple of sightseers.

The corners of Fred's eyes sloped down like a sad pup. "You understand, don't you? I can't let you have this fine automobile for six fifty. Make me a reasonable offer."

"Six fifty is as reasonable as we get." George followed the ladies without looking back.

He had almost gotten to the corner when Fred called. "Wait."

Red-faced, the stout salesman scurried to catch up. "I'm feeling generous tonight. Today only you can buy the Chevy for six fifty." His breath huffed in and out. "But don't spread the word. I got a reputation in this town."

Fred scarcely glanced at Mrs. Crowley's driver's license—not long enough to read it. Probably could have signed the registration as Vincent Morelli and claimed he lost his driver's license without being questioned further.

Better still, George could've pinched the Chevy. That way no paperwork would exist and they'd still have their money. Although being wanted for auto theft by Arizona state troopers would add to George's already overwhelming problems.

After Mrs. Crowley signed the papers and paid for the car, George threw the blankets and pillow in the back seat, popped the trunk, and deposited the rest of their meager possessions inside.

He slammed the trunk and turned.

His heart skipped a beat.

Beside the dealership office, someone had parked a black Buick Roadmaster. The interior appeared empty. Heart thumping in his throat, George approached the driver's side with slow deliberate steps, noting a long scratch along the fender. Like a quarter might make.

On the front seat, a gray Stetson lay tipped upside down.

30

GEORGE

Hurtling out of Kingman, George spotted a pawn shop with an Open sign displayed at the entrance. He checked his watch. 6:50. How many people would be shopping this late? A short stop might be okay if he was careful. He veered into the lot and parked behind a panel truck, which hid the gray Chevy from the road. "You two wait in the car."

He grabbed the keys, hopped out, and dashed into the shop.

If either of his traveling companions commented, he didn't hear it.

A bell chimed when he opened the door. George flinched then hesitated long enough to take stock of his surroundings.

Dust covered the secondhand junk—radios, helmets, old cameras, flashlights, hand tools, violins, and clocks of every size—that crammed every inch of the compact store.

Flat glass cases side by side served as a counter with all manner of rings, watches, coins, and knives big and small stuffed inside. George approached a man wearing a visor, the lone occupant of the shop. A jeweler's loupe protruded from one of his eyes.

He didn't look up from the ring. "Can I help you?"

"I want to sell my watch." George unfastened the smooth, gold band and ran it through his fingers. It must be worth thousands of dollars. His heart seized. How he hated to part with this beauty.

The clerk removed the loupe and glanced at the Rolex. "Is it hot?"

George snorted. "Of course not. Had a run of rough luck; otherwise, I'd never part with it."

Eyebrows raised, the fellow nodded. "Sure." He replaced the instrument on his eye and wiggled his fingers. "Let's see it." His tone sounded as bored as he looked.

Perhaps this was not a good idea. This jerk would lowball him, one more person taking advantage of his misfortune. Maybe he should sell it in Mexico.

The pawnbroker's fingers continued to wiggle.

With a deep sigh, George surrendered the watch.

He turned the timepiece front to back and inspected the gold band. "Give you a grand."

"A thousand?" Did he hear right? "You gotta be joking. Feel the weight? That's a solid gold band on a gold case."

"I see what it is." The clerk handed the Rolex back. "You came to me, buster."

"I need at least four." Might as well aim high.

The pawnbroker lifted his eyes. "I look like a bank or something?"

"Thirty-five hundred."

"You sure it ain't hot?"

"A gift from my father."

The pawnbroker scratched his head above the visor. "Twenty-five hundred. Tops. And that's 'cause I ain't made any other purchases today."

This exquisite, high-end piece would bring three or four on the black market. Had probably cost his father twice as much. One problem—no time to find another buyer right now. Glancing out the window he saw Mrs. Crowley lean over the front seat shaking her ever-ready hanky. Kid probably had another bloody nose. He swallowed a lump in his throat. "Okay. I'll take it."

To complete the transaction, he gave his name as James Grant from Kansas City and made up an address. Said his ID had been stolen with his money, and the pawnbroker didn't question his story.

Pocketing the twenty-five hundred gave George a surge of power, almost as good as the happy pills. A fair beginning, this would allow him enough reserve to begin a new life. He must take care with expenditures, but this small cushion put him in a better position. No sentimental brooding over the fact that his Rolex was lost to him forever. He still had his diamond ring. It would have to be enough.

"Was this stop necessary?" Mrs. Crowley asked when he slid into the Chevy and drove toward the parking lot exit.

Distracted by a Kingman city police car cruising past the shop, he didn't favor her with an answer. Sweat beaded on his forehead. What was he worried about? No reason local cops should be after him. He was getting jumpy and paranoid.

Mrs. Crowley babbled on, but he focused on the road. Driving the opposite direction, he wound around a couple of blocks before hooking up with Route 66.

Climbing into the Black Mountains outside of Kingman, George downshifted through miles of hairpin curves. Primitive stone-and-turnbuckle guardrails separated the Chevy from a deep canyon. He kept a tight grip on the steering wheel, maneuvering along the narrow, windy road.

Mrs. Crowley slid to the middle for the umpteenth time. "Be careful, young man. It's quite a drop to the bottom." She grabbed the armrest and pulled herself back to her side, murmuring to herself.

Was she praying?

George tuned out her worrying.

Streaks of orange and gold ruffled the desert sky as the Chevy crested the mountains. Nestled on a plateau, the Summit Station and Ice Cream Parlor seemed an inviting place to stretch their legs. Conveniently, the compound included a filling station and market.

George parked the Chevy and let Stryker out of the back. "Are you hungry, little one?"

"Starving." She tugged on her hat. "Can I get a hamburger and fries? That's my favorite."

"I remember," George said. "Maybe you want a vanilla shake too."

Mrs. Crowley took the girl's hand and guided her to the order window.

George scanned the highway. No sign of cops or black Buicks, but he tipped the cowboy hat lower over his face anyway. Why was he feeling so nervous?

In the market, he purchased four packs of cigarettes and a fifth of Johnnie Walker. At the last minute, he added a handful of chocolate bars, a three-gallon bottle of water, and a canteen to his purchases. Should have been carrying water long before this. Stryker's lips were cracked and dry. Noticing Chap-Stick beside the register, he picked up a tube.

George hefted his purchases back to the car. He filled the canteen with water and stowed it in the front seat before joining Stryker and Crowley at an outside picnic table.

Stryker had eaten one bite of burger. Shivering, she slouched over her food. "I don't feel so good."

"It's been a long day. You need nourishment. Come on, dear, try a few bites." Mrs. Crowley coaxed and pleaded but to no avail. Stryker gulped a few swallows of milkshake but had no appetite for the rest. She produced an anemic smile, but her weary eyes told the real story.

Letting out a long heavy breath, George turned away.

Mrs. Crowley wrapped the uneaten food in a napkin and tucked it in her purse. Back at the car, she settled Stryker and Sophia on her pillow with one blanket swaddled around her. George handed her the ChapStick.

"Thank you." Stryker ran a finger down the side of the tube.

Mrs. Crowley showed her how to apply the ointment.

Darkness dropped over the desert like a black wool mantle as they descended the western side of the mountains. "How do you turn on the light?" Mrs. Crowley pushed every button until she found one that produced a dot of light inside. She spread the map underneath, turning the paper this way and that before refolding it. "Can't see a thing."

"What were you looking for?" George asked.

"How far to the state border?"

"Probably less than an hour."

Stryker yawned. "I can't wait to get to California. I want to see movie stars and palm trees. And the ocean. I want to splash in the water. Wake me if I go to sleep, okay?" Her voice sounded like she was already drifting off.

"At least this part of the desert cools down at night," Mrs. Crowley said. "That's one good thing, don't you think?"

He tossed her a blank stare to acknowledge he heard her, although her words barely penetrated his mind. Grieving the loss of his gold watch, he didn't have much to say. His watch stood for status and value in society. A link to his father. Who would have thought a watch would be so important? Without it he felt naked and vulnerable.

Mrs. Crowley continued. "This is far more comfortable than the Packard." She stretched her neck to check on Stryker in the back. "She seems to be sleeping better. Buying this Chevy was the right thing to do."

"Uh-huh."

"I'm trying to say thanks."

George squinted at her. "Your negotiating skill surprised me. Where'd you learn to bargain?"

Mrs. Crowley's laugh sounded tired. "Paul was an expert shopper. He'd convince a person to sell something at half the asking price, but he was so gentle they'd go away thinking they got the best end of the deal."

"Sounds like an upstanding fellow."

"I was blessed to know him." She dabbed a tear off her cheek.

George stared straight ahead. "But he died, and so did your only son."

"Yes."

"How come you're not angry with God? You still pray to Him, read His book. So much loss and you still think God is good?"

"God's character is good. I trust whatever He allows in my life."

George shook his head. "That's what I don't get. Maybe there is a God, but if He is so good as you say, why does He let such terrible things happen?"

"These things only seem tragic to us because we don't understand how He's going to use them."

The mighty manipulator in the sky. How could she buy such claptrap? "So we're puppets?"

Mrs. Crowley chuckled. "Not at all. There's a verse that speaks to that issue. Second Corinthians 4:18. 'While we look not at the things which are seen, but at the things which are not seen: for the things which are seen are temporal; but the things which are not seen are eternal.' Soon this earthly life will be over. Our reaction to challenges and tragedies prepares us for eternity."

Again with the Bible verses? George snorted. "Heaven or hell? You don't believe *that*, do you?"

"The Bible says it's true."

"How do you know the Bible is true? What if it's a collection of fables and traditions and nothing more?"

"I assume you've never opened a Bible. It is the word of God, filled with wisdom, encouragement, and comfort. Besides all the historical evidence that the Bible stories are true, the words are relevant for each life." She leaned closer. "When I read them, it's like they were written for me alone." She hesitated.

George stared straight ahead, wishing he hadn't asked.

Apparently, the pause meant she was just gathering steam. "Do you realize the Bible was written by a number of authors over a period of some one thousand five hundred years, yet it tells one story? What other book in all the history of the world can make such claims?"

How could a modern woman be so easily deceived? How could the Bible contain God's words? George rolled his eyes. Rubbish. She kept talking, but he tuned her out. Opening the Johnnie Walker, he gulped a swig. The blathering trailed off after a while. Her reliance on the Bible made no sense whatsoever. Eternity? A fantasy. Today was all anyone could count on. Take what you can get and move on. Every man for himself.

That's what he did when he collected—not stole—his nest egg in Chicago. McBride, Reynolds, and O'Neill owed him after all he'd done over the years. Now he'd lost almost all of his money and been forced to sell his Rolex. Not what he planned, but he would revise the plan. Mother, Father, Gloria and the bratty kids never understood him, never made him happy like he had every right to be. Didn't the Constitution guarantee the right to happiness?

The western side of the Black Mountains had several treacherous switchbacks. George gladly obeyed the speed limit, keeping an eye out for patrol cars with flashing red lights. Under cover of night, he drove through Oatman and continued south. It wouldn't be long until they crossed the Colorado River and then the border.

By the time they reached California, Stryker and Crowley were both sleeping. He gulped another swig of whiskey. Maybe he should wake Stryker as she asked, but she needed to sleep after such a long day.

George finished the Johnnie Walker before midnight. Eyes blurring with need of sleep, he swerved onto the shoulder before jerking awake. Crowley turned her head and made a sound but kept on sleeping. Good thing he didn't wake them.

The second time the car swerved, he caught himself just as the Chevy began to drift. No getting around it. He needed a few minutes of shut-eye. Steering toward a level spot, he parked off road. Slumping, he let his eyelids drop shut.

Sounds intensified in the dark.

The desert wind howled. Coyotes yapped. Tumbleweeds skittered across the hood and thumped into the fender. Stryker's breathing sounded strangely irregular. Was she taking a turn for the worse? Tomorrow they must press on to L.A., no matter what.

The possibility of a future without money constricted his chest like a hundred-pound weight. He'd been forced to let go of nearly everything he held dear—the power of being a bigwig in a prestigious Chicago firm, his social standing as a Stanton, the steady income that was never enough, all the trappings of the American dream, the beautiful wife all his friends envied, and the requisite son and daughter.

Being tailed certainly hadn't been part of his plan. What if someone followed him to Mexico? Would he spend the rest of his life watching for the FBI, local police, the gambling boss, or whoever drove the black Buick?

Already he'd gotten too involved with Crowley and the kid. He didn't like kids. How did he get so attached to Stryker?

Something special about this kid. She needed him. No one ever needed him before. Certainly not his own children.

But he must take care of himself—head out to Mexico as soon as possible.

Stryker coughed.

If they didn't hurry to L.A., it might be too late. Right after he took her to the hospital, he'd leave. Tomorrow he'd buy another car and head south.

Surely God would not allow Stryker to die.

31

STRYKER

Stryker blinked in the sunlight. Why were their voices so loud? She struggled to get up and stare out the side window. If this was California, shouldn't it look different? The same old brown desert flew past in the early morning light. Where were the movie stars and palm trees? Where was the beach? Forehead pressed on the glass, she listened to the bickering.

"Every cell in my body aches." Mrs. Crowley sounded angry. "Were you drinking again?"

Stryker looked down at the empty Johnnie Walker bottle on the floor of the back seat.

Mr. Stanton raised his voice over Mrs. Crowley's. "I suppose you'd rather I keep driving and fall asleep at the wheel. Coulda dumped us into a ditch at the side of the road. Would that be better for you?"

"Heaven knows you've had experience dumping cars into ditches. Maybe no one ever told you before, but you have a serious drinking problem, young man." She shook her finger but stopped mid-waggle when she saw Stryker. "Oh, dear. Didn't mean to wake you."

How was a person supposed to sleep through all that

noise? "What's going on?" Stryker stretched her arms over her head and winced at a pain in her armpit. She ran her finger over a new lump under her left arm.

"We slept in the car. All night." Mrs. Crowley sniffed. "Now my muscles are so stiff I can hardly move. How are you doing this morning?"

Stryker held up her blanket. "I'm wet and I hurt all over."

The two in the front seat exchanged a grown-up look.

Mrs. Crowley inspected her. "Your shirt is soaked. Must've been perspiring."

That didn't make any sense. She was shivering. "But I'm cold."

"Throw that damp blanket on the floor and wrap yourself in the other one." Mrs. Crowley gestured as she spoke.

Pulling the dry blanket over her shoulders like a shawl, Stryker spoke close to Mr. Stanton's ear. "Is this California?"

"Yeah."

"It looks like more desert."

He shrugged. "We're coming into a town pretty soon."

"What town?"

"Needles."

Weird. Maybe they named the town for the cactus. Sure were plenty, and they looked prickly. Stryker's head swirled. She snuggled back on the upholstery and tugged the blanket over her chin. Impossible to find a comfortable position. "I feel sick today."

Mrs. Crowley handed the canteen over the seat. "Try some water."

Stryker slid to the edge of the seat. Mrs. Crowley tipped up the canteen and Stryker managed to swallow a sip. "That's all." Her hand shook as she pushed it away.

"You need to drink more than that, sweetheart. You'll get dehydrated."

"Don't want more." Tears formed on her lids. Why was she crying? Sadness flooded over her, pressing so hard on her chest she had to force herself to breathe. She sniffed back tears. "I'm tired of riding. Can't we stop?" Her words came out whinier than she intended.

Mrs. Crowley reached over the seat to place her hand on Stryker's forehead.

"She's hot to the touch, and her skin seems paler." Mrs. Crowley spoke in a hushed tone. "Should we stop?"

"Stop, go. Make up your mind." Mr. Stanton shook his head. "I'm having a hard time keeping up."

"I think she has a fever."

"Want me to find a hospital?"

Stryker shook her head. She hated when they talked about her as if she couldn't hear. With a groan, she pressed her face against the cool window. "I wanna stop right there." She pointed at the first thing in sight.

A gleaming white building rose out of the desert. High atop the roof, a cross lifted its arms to the sky.

Mrs. Crowley followed her pointing finger. "That's a church, dear."

"Stop there." Here came the tears. "Please. You haven't let me stop anywhere this whole trip. I wanna see inside that church." All of a sudden, nothing seemed more important than getting out of the car.

In the rearview mirror, Mr. Stanton's brow wrinkled between his sunglasses and cowboy hat. He veered into the flat dirt parking lot and stopped.

Now Stryker wished they'd bought a four-door. She wanted to throw wide her door and hang her legs in the sun. Instead she had to wait until one of the adults let her out. To get ready, she tugged on her hat, pulled on her shoes, and tied the laces. "What a beautiful place. I love churches. Did you know that?" The thrilling notion that she'd be outside soon improved her spirits. She mashed her nose against the window, studying the building. It looked like it sprang up out of the brown dirt—a gleaming white flower in the desert. The sides and top of the cross ended with curly tails. "What kind of church is this? How did it get here?"

No one paid attention to her questions. Mrs. Crowley and Mr. Stanton murmured softly to each other, got out, and rummaged through the trunk.

When they finally freed her from the back seat, Stryker's

legs wobbled so much she nearly fell. In the nick of time, she braced herself on the fender. Mr. Stanton reached toward her and held her elbow.

"You'll catch cold wearing a wet shirt." Mrs. Crowley held up dry clothes. "Mustn't risk infections."

Standing beside the Chevy, Mrs. Crowley tugged off the wet top and buttoned on a dry one. Stryker protested, but the fabric muffled her words. She blew out a long sigh. How would Mrs. Crowley like to get naked in a parking lot in front of the whole world?

Dressed again, Stryker looped one arm through Mr. Stanton's. "Okay. Let's go." But she didn't have enough strength to walk. When she stumbled, Mr. Stanton scooped her up in his arms and carried her.

Stryker pressed her face into Mr. Stanton's chest and breathed. He smelled reassuringly familiar. Being held securely in his strong arms made her feel treasured in a way she never felt before. If only he was her father.

He set her down in front of the double wooden doors. With all her remaining strength, she yanked the door pull, but it didn't open. Big drops ran down her cheeks. She swiped them away with the back of one hand and wailed, "Nobody's here."

Mrs. Crowley patted Stryker's back. "It's quite early, dear."

At mention of the time, Mr. Stanton glanced at his wrist the way men do, pushing back his shirtsleeve with one finger to take a peek at his watch.

His wrist was bare.

Stryker covered her gasp with one hand. "Where's your watch?"

"Uh." He shoved his hands into the pockets of his jeans. "Took it off yesterday. Felt kind of heavy in this heat." He shuffled and looked away. "Put it in the pocket of my overcoat."

Stryker narrowed her eyes. She didn't believe him. In Kingman when he wouldn't let them come inside, he must've sold his expensive gold watch. Once Mama had to sell Grandma's fancy brooch at the pawn shop. Mama cried but said she must do it. Did Mr. Stanton cry? Was money that tight?

Mr. Stanton's brown eyes darted in the opposite direction. "Someone's coming. Maybe he can open the door for you."

Stryker turned. Sure enough, still a block away, a rider on a bicycle approached, head bent against the sun. Hard to tell how old he was. His hair was snowy white, but judging from how fast he rode, he must be fit. He wore a dark ball cap, riding shorts, and tennis shoes like a kid.

The rider greeted them with a big toothy grin. In front of the church, brakes squealed. He jumped off, flipped out the kickstand, and balanced the bike. "Hi there, folks. I'm Father Tim. How may I serve you?"

"I'm Mabel Crowley." She stepped forward and extended her hand.

Father Tim grasped it between both of his. "What a pleasure."

"This is George." She gestured toward Mr. Stanton. "We're taking Stryker to L.A. for medical treatment."

Nodding, Father Tim shook hands with Mr. Stanton and bent to Stryker's level. His clear eyes were an amazing green like new leaves in spring.

Mrs. Crowley continued. "She admired your lovely church and wanted to see inside. Would that be all right? We've been many days on the road. A short break would be most welcome."

Still gazing at Stryker, Father Tim beamed. "I'd be delighted to show you our church." From around his neck, he withdrew a long chain with a big black key at the end. He inserted the key into the door lock and twisted until it clicked. He pushed the heavy door open. "Please come in."

The sweet air inside welcomed Stryker with a cool embrace. She stopped after one step, sucking in a long breath. "I love it here." She cocked her head, listening to echoes of her words.

"What a charming old church," Mrs. Crowley whispered.

Mr. Stanton fidgeted, as if he didn't know what to do

with his hands. He shifted from one foot to the other then removed his cowboy hat and gripped it behind his back.

Father Tim walked ahead. Soon lights sparkled from chandeliers dangling off high rafters. Along the sides, white lamps threw a golden glow on the ceiling. Multi-colored windows shaped like Mrs. Crowley's praying hands glittered. A shaft of sunlight highlighted a tall bench with candles and a fancy book. The whole effect gave Stryker a sense of calmness and rest, despite her pain.

Grogginess spun Stryker's vision. "I feel kind of . . ." Her voice trailed off as her stomach contents gushed up to her throat. She gagged, but nothing came out. Weak knees gave way. Going down, she grabbed the nearest wooden bench and the light went black.

Jostling roused her. She opened her eyelids a slit. Mr. Stanton carried her down a long hall. She peered up at dark wooden beams in the ceiling. Steps echoed a rapid beat. Clapping her eyelids shut, she nuzzled into his chest.

"She's awake." His voice was gentle.

Somewhere behind, Mrs. Crowley and another person murmured, but Stryker couldn't follow their conversation. Closing her eyelids seemed to lessen the throbbing.

Next thing she knew, a door creaked open. Stryker squinted into a small dimly-lit room with nothing more than a narrow bed, dresser, and chair. Mr. Stanton laid her on the sheets and arranged the covers around her neck.

Stryker sank into the softness. Heaven, after riding in the back seat so many days. A fluffy pillow too. Warm blankets smelled like the fresh laundry at the Washee-Washee. She breathed deeply. Her chest hurt and she coughed. Where was Sophia?

Mrs. Crowley brought a warm, damp washcloth. "Stryker dear, let me clean you up a bit. Riding in that car all night, you need to wash your face at least. Might help your fever go down too."

Embarrassed, she looked around to see who was watching. Father Tim stood at the door, hands folded. Mr. Stanton knelt beside the bed, one hand on the blanket covering her leg. The corners of his lips quivered ever so slightly. He placed Sophia on the pillow near Stryker's head and caressed her cheek with his fingers before joining Father Tim outside the door.

Stryker cringed while Mrs. Crowley washed her face, chest, arms and legs. Too shameful. She endured this washing only because she knew Mrs. Crowley would feel much better having a clean girl sleep in such a beautiful bed.

When Mrs. Crowley finished, Father Tim took the towels, washcloths, and basin of water away. Magically, warm chicken broth appeared. She swallowed about half before she could not handle another spoonful.

Mr. Stanton hovered over the bed for a few seconds like he wanted to say something. Stryker waited, her gaze glued to his face. Then he hung his head and turned away.

Cowboy boots clipped a rhythm on the tiles, growing fainter.

Thinking she was alone, she nestled into the bed, praying to God for relief from pain.

Father Tim spoke. "Do you want to talk before you sleep?"

Her eyes snapped open. The priest stood beside her bed, hands clasped at his waist. He had changed clothes. Now he wore a black shirt with a white collar circling his neck. Without the ball cap, his hair surrounded his head like a puffy halo. Like the carved angels at Trinity church. His green eyes reminded her of Mama's friend, Uncle Harold, only kinder.

"Thank you."

"For what?"

"This is the best bed I've ever been in. Even better than the fancy hotel in Tulsa." She relaxed her shoulders, letting her head sink farther into the pillow. "Riding in the car bumps me. My body doesn't hurt so much when I'm still."

Father Tim moved the chair close to the bed and sat. "Are you in a lot of pain?"

"Uh-huh."

"Does that scare you?"

She shook her head then flinched. With two fingers, she pressed against her temples and coughed again.

"I'm sorry you have so much pain."

His soft, even voice made her feel better. He folded his hands in his lap. His hands looked kind too.

"Who's your stuffed friend?"

Stryker's fingers closed around the worn monkey. "Sophia." From somewhere deep inside a sob burst out. "I named her after Mama."

"Oh." His lips curved. "What a lovely name."

Tears overflowed. So frustrating. She didn't want to cry. "Mama left." She brushed away moisture, but more took its place. "With a man from Blackwater."

She saw her sadness in Father Tim. "Is she coming back to get you soon?"

"No." Stupid tears. Stryker blotted them with the sheet. "Is Blackwater far away?"

He shook his head. "I don't know."

"It must be very far and that's why she can't come back."

"How difficult for you."

Stryker turned her head so she could look at Father Tim full on. "I was mad for a long time. Not anymore." She sniffled. "Mrs. Crowley says God wants us to forgive people who are bad to us."

"That's a hard thing to forgive." Father Tim leaned closer and laid a hand on top of hers. "God is very pleased with you."

She shrugged one shoulder and winced. "I guess. I never would've met Mrs. Crowley and Mr. Stanton if Mama stayed."

"What about your father? Where is he?"

"My father?" People didn't usually ask that. "I don't remember him." She tried not to yawn.

He smiled. Not his toothy grin, something more tender. "Before I go, I'd like to pray for you. Okay?"

Stryker bobbed her head.

Father Tim sandwiched one of her hands between his and bowed his head. His words soared around her, blending with her spirit, lifting to the heavens. "In the name of the Father, the Son, and the Holy Ghost. Amen." He touched his forehead, then the left and right sides of his chest.

She whispered. "Thank you."

He folded his hands in his lap. "Is Stryker your real name?"

Mama's repeated instructions assaulted her like an army with sharp weapons. Keep your mouth shut. Never speak the names. Telling would mean trouble for Mama. Panic clutched her heart. "I can't tell you. Mama said."

"I see."

His gentleness soothed her fear. Talking to a priest was kind of like talking to God, wasn't it?

Father Tim stirred as if he prepared to go. "I must let you sleep. Mr. Stanton and Mrs. Crowley are resting. They'll come back soon." He stood. "Can you reach the bell on the table beside your bed?"

Tugging her hand from under the warm covers, she demonstrated ability to do so.

"If you need anything ring it, okay?" His hand rested lightly on top of her bald head for a moment. What did he think of a bald girl? Where was her beige hat?

At the door, he stopped a moment.

She could tell him. Might as well come all the way clean. "Grace."

Father Tim turned, hand on the knob. "What?"

"My name is Lily Grace, but most times Mama called me Grace. Then she changed it to Stryker and told me never to say my old name again."

"Grace means good will, God's undeserved favor." He grinned. "The perfect name for you. What about your last name?"

"Lambros."

"Mama's name is Lambros too?"

Stryker gave a single nod.

With a parting grin that lingered like warm rays of the setting sun, Father Tim closed the door behind him.

Slowly, Stryker exhaled. A heavy load lifted off her back. Nothing bad happened when she spoke her name. Was it possible she wouldn't be punished like Mama said?

"God," Stryker whispered. "Forgive me for disobeying Mama. Thank you for letting us stay here for a rest. Please keep us safe. Especially Mrs. Crowley and Mr. Stanton."

Fatigue weighted her eyelids. Sleep would come soon. Along with the tiredness, a terrible weakness had invaded her body. She could barely walk anymore. New pain in her chest made breathing hard.

She needed a nap, maybe a long one. And after that would she have strength to continue to Los Angeles?

32

MABEL

Waking in the tranquil surroundings of the small rectory room, Mabel couldn't remember anything beyond removing her hat and glasses then slipping out of her shoes before sinking onto the bed.

Fingers laced over her middle, her gaze swept across solid wooden beams. Severe fatigue burdened every part of her body. She blew out a long sigh. "I know you gave this task to me, Lord, but perhaps you should've chosen a younger woman."

Time to check on Stryker. Mabel groaned as she pushed to a sitting position on the side of the bed. The poor child had collapsed so near to getting treatment. Would she be able to travel after she rested?

She replaced her glasses and tugged shoes over her stockings. After brushing wrinkles out of her dress and tucking in a few stray hair strands, she tiptoed across the hushed hall to Stryker's room.

How small and ill she looked. Did such a tiny girl have strength to fight this illness? Her bald head centered on the pillow and eyes closed, Stryker breathed shallowly at regular intervals. The sweet child needed sleep.

Mabel brushed a tear away. *Please dear Father, give her strength to continue.* She wanted to pat Stryker's head but remained in the doorway lest her touch wake the child.

Satisfied she could do nothing more, Mabel pulled the door almost shut. She glanced right and left. Which way to the sanctuary?

Soft lights glowed in the long windowless hallway. Turning left, she took a few tentative steps, stopping to think and listen before she continued. At the end of the hall, she turned the corner to another corridor. This she remembered. A short distance to the right she found the open double doors leading back into the church. When she arrived, she found the doorway open.

Father Tim knelt at the altar, face tilted toward the ceiling. Mabel sank into one of the front pews.

Thick adobe walls maintained an even temperature in the sanctuary. The coolness and muted lighting created a reverent atmosphere—soothing and unhurried, fitting for a house of the Lord. How different was the grandiose Trinity Church in St. Louis with its stiff tradition and pompous ambience. Both were magnificent, historic buildings. Was it the calm presence of Father Tim that made the difference?

Mabel studied the simple, carved crucifix on the wall behind the altar—the cross of Christ. God entrusted Jesus with a seemingly impossible task—to leave Heaven and come to Earth, live sinlessly and die a horrible death, taking on Himself the sins of all mankind. In every detail, He accomplished His father's work with perfection. Had she done as well with the job entrusted to her?

She had dragged the poor child across country but certainly not with a perfect attitude. Memories of complaining and whining about George made her hang her head. How displeasing her sniveling must be to God.

Was it possible the Lord sent George on this trip too?

Father Tim stood and presented Mabel with his sunny grin. "You're awake." He slid onto the pew next to her. "Are you rested?"

"I didn't realize I was so tired. How long did I sleep?"

He checked his pocket watch. "Mrs. Santiago will have dinner ready soon."

"Mercy. You mean I slept away a whole day?"

"You must've needed rest." He draped one arm along the back of the pew between them. "Do you want to tell me more about your journey?"

"I was thinking about that very thing. I'm sure God gave me this job to do—taking care of Stryker." A glance into his attentive face encouraged her. "I told you about her condition."

"Yes."

"God provided everything I would need to finish this work, yet like the children of Israel in the wilderness grumbled, I complained about George—his speeding, his terribly bossy attitude, his irresponsibility, the way he throws his money around. I truly wanted to get rid of him. I didn't ask what God wanted me to do with him. I thought of him as trouble. Never once until this minute did I consider that perhaps God brought us all together as part of His plan."

Father Tim smiled. "Often God uses disagreeable people to teach us about ourselves."

Teach me what? She'd have to ponder that later. His solicitous expression coaxed her to reveal more than she'd told anyone before. "For many years, I felt unnecessary. I didn't truly understand why God took my husband and our son and left me behind. I read my Bible and prayed on schedule. In desperation, I did what old widow ladies do. I joined the Women's Aid Society. I packed barrels for missionaries. I took casseroles to shut-ins. Still, I had no purpose. No joy."

"Then God brought Stryker to you."

"Yes." The thought birthed a smile. "A precious, sick child. Next thing I know, I'm planning a drive to California. Mind you, I never drove as far as Chicago by myself before. For someone like me it was a monumental task, but in my heart I knew I'd been called and God would provide. Then George came along and ruined everything."

At mention of George, she glanced up. "Where is he?" Surely he wouldn't stay in his room all day.

Father Tim straightened. "Said he couldn't get comfortable and that he'd be gone a few hours."

Oh, great. He probably already drank himself into oblivion. How fit would he be for travel after that? Mabel would have to drive the rest of the way. "Did he take the Chevy?"

"I offered my bicycle, but he said it was too hot for exercise."

Would he leave them stranded in the desert? A surge of anger flooded over Mabel. "George is a fugitive. The FBI is after him. He says he didn't do what they accuse him of, but he lies."

Father Tim held up one hand. "Best not tell me any more. I'm bound by confidentiality, but the less I know of the actual facts the better. In case the authorities ever question me, you understand. Besides, his part of the story is not yours to tell."

A diminutive woman with a pleasant round face bustled into the sanctuary. "*Su comida, Padre.*"

"Good." Father Tim gave his knees a quick pat before standing. "Rosalinda Santiago, please allow me to present Mabel Crowley, our guest tonight."

Giving a curt nod, Rosalinda lowered her gaze. "*Muy bien.*" Without making eye contact, she gestured for Mabel to follow while she led the way back to the rectory.

A long wooden table with benches on each side commanded the dining room. Two simple place settings with plain pewter candlesticks between them indicated Mabel's seat across from Father Tim. A large glass vase stuffed with pinkish-violet lilac sprays added charm to the austere furnishings.

The fresh flowers swirled the room with fragrance, mixing with the delicious aroma of pork and beans. Next to the vase, steam rose from a platter of fresh cornbread. A bowl of jewel-toned fruit salad completed the meal.

"Oh, my." Mabel gave a single clap. "Who would have expected lilacs in the desert?" As she settled on the bench, she inhaled deeply. "Smells divine."

"Flowers are Rosalinda's passion." Father Tim grinned. "This woman can make anything bloom in the desert. Perhaps she'll show you her patio garden. She grows herbs, vegetables, fruit trees, and many types of flowers."

Beaming, Rosalinda ladled the beans into bowls and set them in front of Mabel and Father Tim.

A tall farmhand peeked in the door. His skin reflected years of work in the sun.

"Ah, there you are, Pablo." Father Tim motioned him in. "This is Mabel Crowley. She's visiting us tonight."

Pablo dipped his head. "Pleasure to meet you, señora." Holding his straw hat to his chest, he remained in the doorway.

Rosalinda finished serving the food and sidled next to Pablo. They bowed before exiting together.

Mabel turned to Father Tim. "Don't they eat here with you?"

"Most days, but tonight Rosalinda thought you might want private conversation."

"How thoughtful." Mabel eyed the doorway. "I do hate to put them out, though. This is their home, right?"

"Yes." He steepled his fingers. "Shall we offer thanks?"

She closed her eyes and listened to his simple-but-profound offering of gratitude for God's bounty. Did she thank her Provider often enough for all He had done?

When she opened her eyes, she found Father Tim studying her. "You mentioned the children of Israel grumbling in the wilderness."

"I did." Mabel picked up her spoon, stirring the hot beans to cool them.

"God never left them, although they were quick to complain and disobey."

"Well, He made them wander for forty years." She lifted a spoonful of beans to her mouth. Delicious. After so many meals in restaurants, she'd forgotten how good homemade could be.

Father Tim buttered half a piece of cornbread. "But notice He never abandoned them. He led them all the way to the Promised Land by a cloud during the day and a pillar of fire at night. Even when we disobey, God never turns his back on His children."

The adventures of the last ten days flipped through her mind like a slideshow. God provided another car when someone stole her Studebaker. He kept them safe in the tornado, protecting Stryker from harm at the hands of a lunatic. Through torrential rain, flooded roads, nosebleeds, heart pains, unplanned detours, night driving, and all kinds of car trouble, God had brought them safely to California. She made sure to tell George God is in control. Did she believe what she said? If so, why wasn't she rejoicing?

"God creates a special nest for each of His children. In that place He can grow us and care for us. He controls the boundaries and keeps predators at bay, but often we focus on the gnats buzzing around our heads rather than on God's awesome provision." He took another bite. "May I tell you a story?"

"Please do." Mabel slathered butter on her cornbread and sunk her teeth into the scrumptious food.

"I arrived at St. Anne's twenty-two years ago. A thriving school met here. Many priests were on staff. I came to teach and to study God's word. It was also my duty to perform the holy sacraments, speak the Sunday mass, and shepherd the local flock of parishioners."

Gazing thoughtfully at the priest, Mabel sipped ice water.

"For the first ten years, the school grew in numbers. We enjoyed God's blessings in every part of this parish. People gave me credit for the success. The bishop sent me to teach others how to achieve what we had accomplished here. Magazine articles were written about me. I listened to the flattery and began to think of myself more highly than I ought. I imagined I'd soon be moving to a big city where my fame would grow. Soon I began performing my duties halfheartedly, without asking for God's help."

Mabel could hardly believe her ears. Was Father Tim confessing his sin of pride?

He dropped his gaze. "I'm not proud to admit these things."

Mabel swallowed. "What happened?"

"The biggest employer in Needles, a mining company,

went out of business. Many parishioners lost their jobs. Without income, they moved away. Not enough students stayed to keep the school running, and it closed too. One by one, the other priests were reassigned. The bishop suggested I retire. I gather he blamed me for not keeping the flock together. Everything in my world that could fall apart did." He leaned one elbow on the table. For a moment he rested his mouth on his fist. When he looked up again, his eyes were moist. "Worst of all, I stopped studying God's Word and spending time in prayer. I thought God had abandoned me."

"But you stayed."

"Shortly after the bishop's visit, Pablo brought a dying Rosalinda to me. He begged me to prepare her for death." Father Tim pressed his lips tight, shaking his head. "I was convinced God would not listen to my prayers, but the man insisted. He can be quite persuasive. I was a complete hypocrite, but I administered Last Rites to Rosalinda."

Father Tim laced his fingers together. "When I finished, God's small voice asked, 'What about *your* pride?' I dropped to my knees, pleading for forgiveness. More than anything else, I wanted to walk with God."

"And God healed Rosalinda?"

His eyes glistened when he met Mabel's gaze. "Oh, give thanks unto the Lord, for he is good: for his mercy endureth forever."

Gratitude filled Mabel's heart. "Psalm 107." She patted her face with her cloth napkin. "What a precious story."

"All we do is meant to glorify God and enable us to enjoy Him. God must be the focus or we will never fulfill the purpose for which we were created."

Mabel had slogged through endless years of church work out of duty or to fill the long days with usefulness. No wonder her work never satisfied her soul. By taking Paul and Richard to Heaven, God had given her a unique opportunity to spend more time glorifying and enjoying Him each day, and she'd squandered the time in self-pity.

Father Tim radiated joy. "My lighter load provides additional time for me to soak in God's presence. He speaks to me daily from His Holy Word. He provides for all my needs. God fills my time with small ministries. I am privileged to see Him working in the people still living in this town. This blesses my soul."

God touched Mabel's heart. What about her complaining, her bad attitude toward George, her lack of faith in God's ability to complete the task He had given her? Over the lump in her throat she prayed silently, asking for forgiveness.

Quick steps clipped over the tile hall before Rosalinda burst into the room. "*Perdóname, Padre.*" One of her hands clutched her throat. "*La muchacha.* Very bad." Her voice sounded strained. "Quick. Please come."

33

GEORGE

Woozy, George staggered out of the Scrawny Crow Bar. He squinted at the brightness of the pink and blue banded sunrise. A wave of nausea washed over him. Hunching, he covered his mouth and waited, but the impulse to vomit passed. He straightened to a stand and swiped his lips with the back of his hand.

Last night the parking lot had been half full. Now only three cars remained. Even with bleary vision, he had no trouble locating the Chevy.

Head hanging, he trudged toward the car. When he got there he steadied himself against the fender. His head throbbed. Keys? With tremulous fingers, he dug through pockets in his jeans and came up empty. No keys. Nothing? Muscles tensed.

Where was his wad of cash?

His gaze jerked toward the sleazy bar he left mere moments before. Pain skewered his brain. He raked through his curls with his fingers. The scar from the accident still felt tender to the touch, more so with his head hurting. Queasiness churned his insides and his skin went clammy. He grabbed his stomach and crumpled onto the hood.

The fateful poker game sequence in the back room of the bar replayed in his brain. Game after game, lasting long after the bar closed. Raucous laughter echoed. Cheap whiskey flowed like the Chicago River. Winning at first then losing. Hours passed in the smoke-filled room, still losing. The visibility faded.

Poker was his game. He knew the tricks. His plan had been to double, or perhaps triple, his cash. He couldn't have lost all his money. No. He always won. Forehead still pressed on the hood, he squeezed his eyes tight trying to remember. Blank. Someone must have fixed the cards and drugged him.

He patted his shirt pocket for a Lucky Strike pack and came up with his lighter. No money, no cigarettes, no whiskey. Could life get any worse?

George flung open the car door and slumped in the seat. Well, he hadn't locked the car and no one stole it this time. That was *something*. Where did he think he was going? Impossible to start the car without keys. Cursing, he pounded the dash with both fists. His throbbing forehead thumped onto the steering wheel.

"Hey buddy," an unfamiliar voice penetrated his fog.

Someone shook his shoulder.

"Wake up."

George lifted his head. Couldn't focus. He winced and turned away from the sunshine. So bright. He bent his arm to block some of the glare. "Who . . . ?"

A fuzzy figure leaned close. "Your keys. You dropped them." Metal jingled.

"Oh."

"You don't look so good, pal. Are you all right?"

"Fine." George licked his dry lips. "Just dandy." His fingers closed around the hard objects—he needed these keys.

"Your hat fell off too." A cowboy hat moved into sight.

George dumped it on the seat.

"Maybe you should let me drive you home."

Home? George scanned the undulating horizontal view through the windshield. Where was home?

Stryker. Mabel. Where were they? The church. He had come down the street to the bar. Memories dribbled into his stupefied brain. When? Must have been last night.

Shaky fingers fumbled the key into the ignition. The engine revved to a raucous roar. Lights at the back of his eyes exploded like fireworks. The sound hurt his head.

The stranger held the door open. "You sure you can drive, fella?"

George groped for the door handle and pulled.

The slam smarted like a slap to the face.

Squinting, he bent forward to peer out. Where was the road?

The car lurched and bumped over rocks at the edge of the street. George fought to drive straight. Should get the stupid tires aligned.

Sighting the white church, George stomped on the brake. "Ow." The pain to his ribs where his chest contacted the steering wheel rivaled that of his accident. Holding himself together with one arm, he gingerly put the gear in park and tumbled out.

Opening the double doors to the church, the tranquil sanctuary atmosphere zapped all his remaining bravado. George fell to his knees, sobbing.

What did the future hold without money?

Hurried steps clipped over stone tiles. Father Tim's strong hands lifted George, supporting him as he stumbled. The priest gently lowered him onto a back pew.

Sorrow such as George had never felt before swept over him head to foot. "It's all gone, padre. Every last dollar. What am I going to do?"

Father Tim settled beside him. "What is on your heart, my son? Tell me."

George blew out air. "I saved a fortune in Chicago, planning to use it for a fresh start. What wasn't stolen along with Crowley's car in Oklahoma City I used on our trip to get Stryker to the hospital. When that ran out, I sold my gold watch. Now it's . . ." His voice hitched. "All gone."

Father Tim folded his hands in his lap. "You joined that poker game in the back room at the Scrawny Crow Bar."

"Why didn't you warn me they were cheats?"

"Ah, yes." A slight smile played on Father Tim's face. "They're a devious lot."

Was he mocking? "Someone must've drugged me."

No reply.

George dropped his face into his palms and wailed. "My future is ruined."

Father Tim's fingers pressed George's shoulder. "Would you like me to pray with you?"

"What?" Would God give him back his money? "What's the use in praying? Do you understand what I'm saying? I've been duped. Nothing's left."

Green eyes penetrated George's sorrow, like a searchlight into his heart. When Father Tim spoke again, his voice was calm and soothing. "My son, you believe you have suffered a great loss. At this moment, you cannot see the good in what happened."

"Good?" George's voice squeaked. "What do you mean?"

"God sent you on this journey with Stryker and Mrs. Crowley."

George swore under his breath. "Crowley's been preaching that same old garbage about God and His plan clear across country. I choose my own future." For emphasis, George beat his chest with his flattened palm and then grimaced as a shard of pain shot through his rib cage. "I'm in charge of my life."

"You crowned yourself god instead of allowing the one true God to rule. The struggle you face is as old as the ages. We humans desire to control our own destinies, but the truth remains constant. There is only one God."

George turned his face away. "That changes nothing. My money's still gone."

Father Tim's voice warmed. "One day, my son, you will discover how your own selfishness brought you to this place of despair. When your eyes are opened, you will see how much your bad choices have cost." He faced George. "If you ask God to forgive you, He will lead you to a new path."

Bad choices? So he knew. George glared at Father Tim. That's what all this mumbo-jumbo was about. His voice hardened. "Crowley told you who I am. Have you called the authorities?"

Clasping his hands in his lap, Father Tim eased back in the pew. "Reporting to the authorities is not mine to do. I am happy to hear your confession, if you wish to make it."

Confession? Was he nuts? If George thought he'd done something bad, he certainly wouldn't tell a stranger. "Time to head outta here."

First he must return to the bar and demand his money from those card hustlers. He had nowhere to go if he didn't get his stash back. "Is the kid better?"

"Stryker had a restless night—a nosebleed, chills, and fever. Couldn't hold down any food. She didn't get back to sleep until after midnight. I suggested calling a doctor, but Mabel said no. She's determined to get the child to Los Angeles today. It's a long drive and Stryker is quite ill, as you must know. Mabel asked me to administer Last Rites." He paused as if George would respond.

What could he say? Last Rites sounded final. Not something George wanted to think about.

Father Tim folded his arms over his chest. "You might want to give Mabel a break. She must be exhausted."

"Right." George stood and followed the priest down the long corridor. At Stryker's door, Father Tim rapped lightly before turning the knob.

Mrs. Crowley slouched in the chair beside the bed, face drawn like she hadn't slept for days. At their entrance, she glanced up and placed a finger to her lips. "She's sleeping."

The child appeared to have shrunk overnight. Blue veins bulged in her closed eyelids. Dark crescents underneath her eyes gave her face the haunted look of a Holocaust survivor. A smattering of red spots dotted her cheeks and arms. Her breathing huffed out unevenly.

Moisture collected on George's face, but he wiped it away before it could run. "She doesn't look good."

Father Tim dipped his head toward the bed like he

expected George to move closer. Panic gripped him. *You can do this, George.* Straightening his shoulders, he shuffled to the side of the bed.

Nothing he could say or do would help.

After what seemed forever, Mrs. Crowley touched his sleeve.

George cleared his throat. "You reckon she's strong enough to travel today?"

She removed her glasses and rubbed the lenses with a corner of Stryker's sheet, replacing them before she answered. "Do we dare drag her into that car again?"

Nerve endings sizzled beneath his skin emitting a peculiar humming in his brain like overheated electric wires. He must get out of there. "Look, I need to rest if I'm gonna drive to L.A. Be back in a couple hours."

He stumbled out and collapsed against the door for support. The rumbling between his ears amplified like a freight train. He needed a drink. Maybe more than one.

The door to Mrs. Crowley's room had been left ajar. The slit of opening highlighted Mrs. Crowley's purse perched on the chair beside the bed.

Surely she wouldn't miss a few dollars.

Determined strides carried him across the hall. In one heed-less swoop, he scooped up her purse and fished inside until his fingers closed around the drawstring pouch where she kept her money.

Crowley needs these funds to finish the trip.

The gnawing in his gut intensified to a growl. His heartbeat ratcheted up to abnormal speed.

Nothing else in the world mattered as much as getting a drink.

Setting his jaw, he slipped Mrs. Crowley's money into his shirt pocket, turned on his heel, and hurried to the Chevy. Wouldn't be long before his nerves would be as calm as an unplugged lie detector. He'd make those crooks return his cash too.

Even if he had to steal it.

No one cheated George Stanton and got away with it—especially not some stinking hayseeds in a bush-league town.

34

GEORGE

George exploded through the front door of the Scrawny Crow Bar. Feet planted apart, hands on hips, he struck a menacing pose in the doorway while his vision adjusted.

A jukebox blared another vapid country song. George inwardly rolled his eyes and tuned out the simple-minded words. Three customers hunched over drinks at the bar. Huddled in a booth, a couple bent their heads together as if whispering or plotting. A few customers sat at tables. Not a familiar face in sight including the bartender.

George's gaze shifted to the door near the restrooms at the far right where the card game had been held. Closed. Should he break it down in case the hustlers had already rounded up a new sucker? His fists itched for action.

Reality. George's skill set ran more along the line of defeating his foes mentally rather than physically. Perhaps he'd try the civil approach first. If that failed, he'd deal with the poker players later.

Squaring his shoulders, George stomped to the bar. "Hey, you, barkeep."

"What'll it be, mister?"

Answers first or booze? "Just gimme a whiskey." He laid a couple of dollars on the table. "Got any Johnnie Walker Gold Label?"

The bartender cocked his head. "Gold Label? Never heard of it."

"Figures." George slouched. "How 'bout some other decent aged whiskey?"

"Hang on." The man held up one digit. "You may be in luck, fella. Seem to remember we had a bottle of the old stuff somewhere." He reached high on the back bar to run his finger along the dusty labels on the row of bottles lining the top shelf. About midway, he tapped one and raised himself on tiptoes to drag the container down. "Yup. Chivas Regal. Twelve years old. Think it was a gift from some grateful patron years ago. Nobody with any sense drinks this stuff." He looked at George. "You like these seasoned spirits?"

"I'll give it a try and let you know. How much for the bottle?"

The quoted price ran somewhere near twice what good whiskey cost in Chicago. Making profit off the city slicker again. George narrowed his eyes, but his brain already anticipated the numbing effect of a couple belts. He needed the buzz. Maybe he should have settled for the cheap stuff. "You oughta be locked up for robbery." He tugged out more cash and flopped it on the bar. "Pour."

The bartender nodded, pulling a short glass off the rack. "Whiskey for the cowboys, water for the horses." He popped out the stopper.

Guess he thought he'd made a joke, because he chuckled while dribbling a swallow into the tumbler.

Mouth watering, George lifted the glass to the dim light, examining the legs as they flowed down the side. Nice and slow. He swirled the glass gently and tipped it toward his face. Taking a deep breath, he sniffed the delicious fumes. He sipped—a thick, creamy balance between sweet and bitter. He rolled it on his tongue and taste buds, savoring. Excellent. Closing his eyes, he downed the rest.

"Didn't know you planned to make love to it."

Ignoring the rude comment, George lifted the empty glass. "Hit me again."

Filling the glass about half full, the bartender scooped up the money and dumped it in the till.

George downed the rest of the contents, feeling the first flush. "Where's the guy from last night? Big fellow with a mustache."

The bartender looked up. "You mean Larry?"

"Don't know his name. He was here last night."

"Ain't here now. I'm Tom."

George lowered his voice. "You hear about the poker game last night, the one in the back room?"

Tom placed both hands on the bar and leaned toward George. "Not much."

Cheeks burning, George drew his lips tight. "The players, they regulars?"

"You the city fella?"

George poured more whiskey in the empty glass and chugged it down.

"Sorry." Tom let out a low snicker. "I missed that."

George jerked his chin up. *Nobody* laughed at him and got away with it. Pushing to a stand, he grabbed the front of Tom's shirt in a tight fist and yanked his simpering face closer. "They stole a bundle from me last night. That doesn't sit well. Where can I find these slick operators?"

The smirk vanished. Tom fixed his gaze on George's hand. "You don't really want trouble, do you?"

George heard the distinctive click of a trigger. Out of the corner of his eye he caught motion. One of the men at the bar pointed a snub-nose .38 at George's head.

Dropping Tom's shirt like a hot poker hand, George lifted his mitts in the air. "Don't want any trouble."

"Didn't think so." Tom dipped his head toward the gunslinger. "Maybe you haven't met our local police chief."

George swung his attention to a steely stare that drilled a hole through him.

What were the odds the chief of police would be sitting

next to him in this dump? More dumb luck. Must not draw attention to himself. Didn't want the man to start asking questions in an official capacity.

Right now, George sure could use a cigarette. He forced a smile at the stranger before turning back to his empty glass. Fingers trembling, he poured his Chivas Regal. Escaping into the unique solitude only available in a room of strangers, he lifted the glass to his lips.

An inner voice breathed *Here's to Stryker.*

He blinked into the golden-brown liquid.

Reflected in the whiskey daze, he saw and heard his little travel companion.

Stryker's bald head caressed by the soft pillow he borrowed from the motel, red freckles dotting her pale skin, bruises, nosebleeds, and throwing up all over the car. Stryker, who knew every make and model of automobile on the road by shape and trim. Stryker's giggly laugh. Singing with her "You Are My Sunshine." The child who plucked his Lucky Strike pack from the filthy pavement because he might need cigarettes. The sick girl who climbed the red rock outcropping, crouched at the top, and grinned down.

Carrying Stryker into the church and how she mashed her face in his chest. Her pale blue eyes locked on his—in an embrace of adoration.

The glass slipped from his fingers and smashed onto the bar. Expensive Chivas Regal sloshed out. A murmur went up around him. He stared at the puddle.

Stryker loved him. A pure unsullied love, like none he'd ever known before.

She knew him at his worst, had seen and heard the real, unvarnished George Stanton every mile of their trip across country. Yet she cared deeply for him. Not for anything he could give her or do for her—for himself alone.

Even more incredible than Stryker's love for him, a strong and powerful emotion for this child surged through him to his core. Dare he call this feeling love? He'd used her illness to his own advantage. What kind of love was that? Did he actually care whether she lived or died? If he wanted her to live, why hadn't he done everything in his power to get her to the hospital as soon as possible? Wasn't that her sole hope of survival?

Blinking away tears, George recognized with alarming certainty that no amount of money or whiskey or happy pills would ever fix what was broken in him.

Neither would a new identity in Mexico.

Could Father Tim be right? Did George's selfishness cause Stryker's pain? No. She was sick when he met her. He was not responsible for her illness, but perhaps he'd added to her pain. Did her life hang in the balance because he insisted everything be done his way? Was he trying to be god of his life when there is only one God?

His mind whirled like a tornado churning away the fog of confusion, leaving a path of clarity in its wake. Where did George get money for this whiskey? He stole it from Mabel. Sure, he stole from McBride, Reynolds, and O'Neill as well as from Pete at the Phillips station. But they deserved it, failing to fulfill their duties to him. Fair was fair.

Did Mabel Crowley deserve the same treatment? True, he'd used his own money to get them across country, even sold his gold watch. But Mabel's motives were good. She griped about his behavior and language, was a pain in the neck sometimes, but he had used Mabel as a cover for his escape. How had her actions earned what she got for her bother?

Muted voices around him ebbed and flowed as if the world suddenly shifted to slow motion. Words and actions blurred as George turned his attention to the interior of the Scrawny Crow Bar. For the first time, he noticed the dirty, stained carpet, the torn booth seats, scratched tables, and mismatched chairs. When did he quit caring about where he spent his time? Had he truly sunk to the low end of the food chain? He'd been willing to forgo everything he held dear for a lousy drink.

"You have a serious drinking problem." Mrs. Crowley's voice echoed in his mind.

A drinking problem? Lowlifes and scumbags had problems with liquor.

Not George Stanton.

Left eye twitching, he surveyed the people in the bar once more. Only losers habitually huddled in a bar early in the morning for another belt. Only people with alcohol problems couldn't start the day without a drink.

What did Crowley know? George could take it or leave it. He was definitely not like these washouts.

When he sucked in a deep breath a choking mixture of spilled liquor, stale tobacco, and rotting garbage invaded his body—that cloying, old neighborhood bar smell. The stench turned his stomach.

What was George Stanton doing in this dump at seven in the morning? After being up all night losing his money in a rigged poker game, did he go to the authorities to lodge a complaint like a good citizen? Flop into bed to sleep the drunken stupor off? Shrug into his responsibilities and drive Stryker to L.A.? Do anything that proved he was better than the other regulars at this bar?

No.

Truth crashed over him like a tsunami nearly knocking him to the floor.

What had he done with the money he stole from Crowley? He'd rushed to the bar first thing in the morning to liquor up.

Right along with the other boozers.

35

STRYKER

Mrs. Crowley's words soothed Stryker's nerves, but the longer her nose bled the more concerned Mrs. Crowley's face became—brow furrowed, lips trembling, smile forced into place.

Mrs. Santiago carried out bloody towels and changed sheets and blankets, helping Stryker into a clean flannel nightgown and underwear. Where did she find the right size? The woman's hands were loving and gentle. Stryker didn't understand the Spanish words Mrs. Santiago muttered over her as she worked, but certainly they flowed out of a good heart. Perhaps they were prayers. Did God send an angel to care for her? Mrs. Santiago made Stryker feel safe like the time Mama let Stryker sleep in her lap.

Father Tim checked in several times during the long night. His presence imparted strength and comfort. Stryker tried to return his smiles.

Sometime after she went to sleep, she swam part way out of grogginess to find the three of them kneeling next to the bed pleading with God for healing. He would hear Father Tim's prayers. Mrs. Crowley's too. The most wonderful calmness swept over Stryker. Everything would be all right. She wasn't afraid. Wrapped in sweet warmth, she snuggled back into sleep.

Later, when Father Tim splashed water on her head, she tried to speak but couldn't. Her whole body felt stiff as wood. He touched her head and said things she didn't understand. Was she bad? She wanted to ask him what sins or faults she had committed, but she wasn't able to open her eyes or move her body. Tired. Weak.

The bad night was passing . . .

Stryker's eyelids fluttered open. Such a tidy room, peaceful and quiet—glowing in soft light. Was she in Heaven? She raised her head. Shooting pain stabbed her neck. Her yelp shattered the reverie. Dropping her head on the pillow, she squeezed her eyes until the worst of the agony subsided.

The door opened slowly. She moved nothing but her eyes to watch Father Tim peeking around the door. "May I come in?"

She tried to nod but wasn't sure he understood so she licked her lips and whispered, "I'm glad to see you." Too hard to raise herself up on her arms. Would this weakness never go away?

"You must lie still, Lily Grace." Father Tim's voice melted her worry. "Conserve your strength." He drew up the chair and settled close.

Stryker hadn't heard anyone say her real name in a long time. It reminded her of Mama. That little longing for Mama whooshed into her heart again. Mama was strong. Mama knew the answers. Why did Mama leave?

Stryker tried to work up enough moisture to swallow, but her mouth felt dry as the desert sand. "I'm very sick, right?"

"Yes."

"Am I dying?"

He looked down at his folded hands. "God alone knows the answer to that question."

He hadn't said *No, of course you're not dying*. A fresh wave of exhaustion washed over her body. Her eyelids drooped. Sleep beckoned.

Mrs. Crowley told her about Jesus and what He did for the whole world. Stryker asked Him to forgive her sins and come into her heart. Jesus came in, because He promised He would. Mrs. Crowley said that when Stryker died she would go and live with God. She never needed to be afraid again. Surprisingly, she didn't fear death. Rather, a sense of relief held her in secure arms. Mrs. Crowley was right again.

Stryker batted her lids open to find Father Tim intently studying her face. "Thank you for praying for me." Her words trailed to a whisper. "In the night."

He nodded. "Mrs. Crowley was afraid. She wanted me to baptize you and perform Last Rites. Is that what you heard?"

"You sprinkled water on my head and then you spoke. Was that the Rites?"

His smile added light to the room. "You lost a lot of blood. Your cough is quite deep and your fever is high. That's why Mrs. Crowley wanted me to pray over you. She knows God lives in this place and that He hears and answers prayers." He bent toward her. "In fact, it appears He has given you another day."

Stryker tried to swallow again. Still not enough spit.

"Do you need water?" In Father Tim's expression she saw his concern.

"Uh-huh."

He reached for the bell. "Let's see how well this thing works, shall we?" The crisp jingle echoed off the rafters.

"If it is okay with you," Father Tim said, "I'd like to tell Mr. Stanton and Mrs. Crowley your name and about your mother. May I do that?"

Stryker nodded.

Rapid steps sounded in the hall. Wiping her hands on her apron, Mrs. Santiago stuck her head in the slit of opened door.

Father Tim made a show of checking his pocket watch. "That was a drill to see how quickly you would come. You performed quite well." He grinned at her. "Stryker needs water, please."

Mrs. Santiago wagged her finger at Father Tim with a

smile. She turned to leave and nearly collided with Mr. Stanton. The small woman mumbled apologies before scooting out.

Mr. Stanton propped himself against the doorjamb as if he might not be able to stand otherwise. His hair looked messy. The cowboy hat was missing. Sunglasses too. But her heart swelled with joy at sight of him. Mr. Stanton hadn't abandoned her like Mama did.

Part of his wrinkled shirttail hung outside his jeans and part was tucked behind the belt. The jagged scar on his forehead stood out bright pink against his tan skin. A ragged, brown beard hid the lower part of his face, but his dark eyes looked miserable. What happened to him?

"There you are." Stryker lifted one arm. "I was afraid you went off and left us here."

Something wet moistened his cheeks.

She did her best to smile. "Did you get some more cigarettes so you won't yell at Mrs. Crowley?"

Mr. Stanton blinked but didn't come closer.

"Where's your hat?" Stryker continued. "You look like a cowboy movie star when you wear that." Too many words. Exhausting. Strength in her arm failed. The arm dropped limply to her side. "I'm glad to see you." She whispered.

She heard a gut-wrenching cry but didn't know where it came from until Mr. Stanton flung himself on his knees beside her bed. Burying his face in the blanket, his shoulders shook.

Was he crying?

Stryker shot Father Tim a plea for help. Something terrible was wrong with Mr. Stanton.

Father Tim's lips curved slightly upward at the corners. "Don't be frightened. It will be okay."

Watching Mr. Stanton's body tremble, she felt his great sadness. Sobbing racked his body, wave after wave. She reached out to touch him, but her arm wasn't long enough. Helpless tears spilled from her own eyes.

Father Tim bent his head.

He must be praying for Mr. Stanton.

After several minutes, Mr. Stanton's shoulders stopped

shaking. He lifted his puffy-red face and grasped Stryker's hand in his own. "Please forgive me." His voice sounded gruff.

Stryker felt her forehead wrinkle. Forgive him for what? Had he lied to her again? Was he going to leave her? "Why?"

"I thought only of myself." He sniffed. "This whole trip. I knew you were sick, but I was busy planning how to stay out of trouble. You are suffering because of my bad choices. Look at you." His voice hitched. "Please don't die, little one. I'll do everything in my power to get you to the hospital." His brown eyes pleaded. "No matter what."

The hospital? Stryker had forgotten about that. Maybe she wouldn't die today and they'd finish the trip. "Am I strong enough?" She watched Father Tim's kind face. "What do you think?"

Father Tim crossed his arms and stroked his chin with one hand. "It's a six or seven hour drive to Los Angeles from here."

"I'll take care of her." Mr. Stanton stood. "Drive straight through. No more detours."

"If you leave now, you'll be driving all day. Are you certain you can do that without resting first? Would it be safe? Have you slept or eaten in the last twenty-four hours?"

Mrs. Santiago bustled in carrying a pitcher of water and a glass. The men stepped to one side. She poured the glass half full and plopped a straw inside. Cupping one hand under Stryker's head, she lifted it slightly until Stryker could drink.

Cool water flooded Stryker's mouth with refreshment. She swished it around her mouth and then gulped several swallows before feeling too tired to suck anymore. "Good." Breathing had become more like panting, shallow and fast. She needed to rest a little. "Enough for now."

Mrs. Santiago lowered Stryker's head. "I leave the water here." She placed the pitcher and glass on the bedside table and scurried out of the room.

"Thank you," Father Tim said as she left. He turned to Mr. Stanton and spoke so softly Stryker had to strain to hear. "How about that nap?"

"If you think it would be best."

"I do." Father Tim laid his hand on Mr. Stanton's shoulder.

"I understand your heart, but she's very weak and you're in no shape to drive. Neither is Mrs. Crowley."

Mr. Stanton looked around. "Where is Mrs. Crowley?"

"She stayed up all night with Stryker. This morning she was grasping at her chest like she had pain. She's exhausted and went back to her room to rest."

Mr. Stanton nodded. Then he fixed his eyes on Stryker. "Do you think she can make the trip?"

"Only God knows the answer, my son."

"Okay. I'll be back in a few hours then." Mr. Stanton brushed his lips across Stryker's cheek. His whiskers tickled her skin a little, but she loved the feeling. Real daddies must kiss like that. She covered her cheek with her hand.

The men left together.

Would she always feel Mr. Stanton's kiss?

Father Tim's words echoed in her heart. "Only God knows. Only God knows. Only God . . ."

Stryker blinked, lids getting heavier. "God," she whispered. "Please get me to the hospital. Mr. Stanton and Mrs. Crowley really need to finish this trip."

36

MABEL

Hours passed in the darkened rectory room. Mabel clamped her eyes shut. She recited scripture. She changed position. No matter what she did, sleep evaded her. After sleeping all day she certainly didn't need to sleep again even though she'd been awake so much of last night, but perhaps she could use a little quiet time, as Mrs. Santiago suggested. Thank goodness for that sweet woman and for Father Tim.

One more night.

Would staying make a difference between life and death for Stryker? Urgency compressed her chest until her heart hurt. She squinched her face up and held her breath trying to hear Stryker. Not a sound.

Mabel rolled out of bed and opened her door a crack. The cool quiet intensified every noise, but she still couldn't hear anything from the room across the hall.

On tiptoes she crossed the space between them, twisted the knob slowly, and pushed the door open. The child was sleeping peacefully. Not like the night before. *Thank you, God.*

Maybe they shouldn't leave. Wouldn't it be better for

Stryker to spend her last days in the comfort of the rectory with Father Tim? Mabel sucked in her breath. Mustn't think Stryker might die. *Dear Lord, please help me stay positive.* Besides, if they stayed, how would they ever know whether the treatment would've been beneficial or not?

Mabel wanted to touch Stryker but was afraid it might wake her. She watched the shallow breathing a bit longer. Stryker's temperature had not come down.

With a heavy sigh, she returned to her room and climbed in bed.

On her back, Mabel stared at the dark ceiling. *God, please help me know what to do. Are You going to make her well? Please, Lord.* A tear dribbled down her cheek.

Mabel sniffed and rolled to her side.

One more night.

Tomorrow they would get up early and pack the Chevy. If they left by eight, they could be in Los Angeles by early afternoon and get Stryker checked into the pediatric unit at UCLA Hospital. Where did she put Doctor Woodruff's phone number? Perhaps she should call his office first thing in the morning to alert him.

What would Stryker's treatment entail? Experimental, Doctor Marston said. Visions of mad scientists with test tubes and deformed lab rats circled Mabel's brain—too grotesque to ponder.

Something odd was going on with George. He was acting skittish and more irresponsible than ever. Wouldn't look her in the eye. Why had he been gone again? At least he agreed to get some rest. Still. Dare she allow him to make this last part of the trip? His drinking was clearly out of control. If he would cause more trouble for Stryker, Mabel must be strong and forbid him to come along.

She punched her pillow before easing onto her sore back and folding her hands over her middle. His cocky attitude exasperated her so. "Why, God? Why is George with us? If this trip is about more than Stryker, please give me wisdom. Give me Your love for George. I certainly have trouble working up any of my own."

In the early morning light, Mabel's eyes popped open. Time to get moving.

As soon as she dressed, Mabel looked in on Stryker again, but she was still sleeping. Mabel arranged the covers under Stryker's chin and patted her little hand, but she didn't wake up. As Mabel came out of the room, she found George in the hall. Together they walked to the dining room.

Rosalinda Santiago had spread a fine breakfast on the table. Father Tim welcomed them and gestured where they should sit. Once they were settled on the benches, he offered thanks.

He looked up after the prayer and smiled his sunny grin. "The food looks wonderful, Rosalinda. Thank you for making this special feast for our friends on this important day."

The woman dropped her gaze. "*De nada.*"

Rosalinda had washed all their soiled clothing too. Everything looked like new. Mabel would very much like to know how Rosalinda managed to get all the blood stains out.

A night's rest and a clean body gave George a look of vitality. Perhaps he would be able to make the trip after all. He dug into the eggs, sausage, and biscuits on his plate. Rosalinda poured freshly-squeezed orange juice. He guzzled it down, raising the glass for seconds.

Rosalinda beamed.

"Before you go," Father Tim said, "I have news for you."

Still chewing, George looked up. Mabel held a jam-covered biscuit suspended between her plate and her mouth.

"Stryker shared her given name with me and the whereabouts of her mother."

George raised his eyebrows.

A chill shuddered down Mabel's back. She replaced the biscuit on her plate. *The irresponsible mother is alive?* Automatically, her lips pursed.

"I made several phone calls yesterday and located the woman. She lives in a Missouri town called Blackwater." Father Tim lifted a folded piece of paper. "The treatment you seek for Stryker is experimental in nature. You might be unable to get her into the program without parental consent.

If that happens, you will have the necessary information to supply the hospital."

Relief surged over Mabel like a wave. "How did you manage it?"

"Oh, I know a few tricks." When he smiled, his face lit up. "In seminary they teach us to bully people into confessions, you know."

George's voice sounded strangely gruff. "What's her real name?"

"Lily Grace Lambros."

George repeated the name softly. "It fits her."

"Yes, it does." Mabel had to agree. Lily Grace. Precious child. "What did the mother have to say for herself?" Mabel's ire flushed over her chest. "Did she give a reason for abandoning this child?" Mabel would like to give that woman a piece of her mind. What kind of mother would stay away when her child was so ill?

Father Tim glanced at his hands for a moment. When he looked up his eyes exuded sympathy. "She wanted to come, but she has been ill herself. She is unsure whether she can physically or financially afford such a trip. However, she is grateful you have taken good care of Stryker and promises to cooperate with treatment. That's the most important thing, don't you agree?"

So many unanswered questions about this woman. Mabel could not imagine leaving a sick child on the streets to fend for herself. Someone else to forgive. Mabel would have to ask God for a double portion of mercy.

After breakfast, Mabel used the rectory phone to notify Doctor Woodruff's office of Stryker's imminent arrival and to get directions.

Rosalinda supplied extra pillows, warm blankets, old towels in case of more nosebleeds, and a sumptuous lunch packed in a big basket. George carried the passenger of honor to the Chevy and settled her in the back seat. Propped on pillows so she could see out the window, Stryker looked almost comfortable.

Father Tim leaned in to lay his hand on Stryker's head and say a prayer.

When he straightened, Mabel gave him a big hug. "Surely you've earned many jewels in your heavenly crown these past days." She released him and wiped her eyes with her handkerchief. "I will pray for your ministry here. Thank you from the bottom of my heart."

"It was my great honor to serve you." Father Tim grasped one of Mabel's hands.

Then he turned to George. "God has His eye on you, my son. I will pray that your choices lead you to our heavenly Father."

They shook hands solemnly before Father Tim grabbed George in a bear hug. Over Father Tim's shoulder, George's eyes looked like melted chocolate. Mabel dabbed her tears again. It was the most obvious display of emotion Mabel had seen in George.

Leaving Needles, their conversation remained subdued and quiet. Before long, Stryker fell asleep. Miles of flat Mojave Desert stretched on all sides. Over the next couple of hours, an occasional cluster of buildings indicated a small town—Amboy, Ludlow, Daggett. They all looked the same. Thank goodness Stryker slept through the monotony.

"What are your plans, George?" How would she know what to expect if she didn't ask?

"Plans." He repeated the word without looking toward her. "Don't really know. Just wanna get Stryker to the hospital."

"You have no money."

"Right." George shot her a glare. "Thanks for pointing that out."

"Well, I hope you don't intend to come home with me."

"No." The word sounded hard as stone.

What would he do? "And I don't think you should rob a bank."

He didn't smile at her attempt at levity.

"Don't worry."

But she did worry. George had very few options as far as she could see. Maybe he thought he'd get a job in Los Angeles. Lots of people did that, she'd heard.

A short distance from Daggett, they motored onto the main street of Barstow.

At the Gilmore Gas Station, George parked beside a tall pump to fill the tank with fuel. After giving the attendant instructions, George wandered into the office and came back with a couple packs of cigarettes. Tone flat, he declared he hadn't had a smoke in more than a day. As if he expected Mabel to feel sorry for him.

Stryker woke briefly and drank sips of water from the freshly-filled canteen. George carried her to and from the restroom.

Almost an hour later, they passed through Victorville and then started down the Cajon Pass in the San Bernardino Mountains. Finally, they were leaving days of desert behind.

Acres of tidy orange orchards lined the hills and valleys around San Bernardino. What beauty. Again Mabel thought of her sister, Laura. No wonder she stayed in California.

Beautiful Spanish-style homes with red tile roofs bordered the palm tree-lined streets. Did Laura live in a house like that? How many years since she'd seen her little sister? Must be thirty-five, at least. Perhaps Mabel wouldn't even recognize her anymore. Laura's beautiful blonde hair might be gray now. Oh, how Mabel would love to hear that girl laugh again. She must stop here on her return trip.

Mabel glanced in the back. Would Stryker still be with her then? She breathed a prayer. *Please God. Make this child well.*

"Look." George lifted his foot off the gas pedal, and the Chevy slowed. He jerked his thumb out the side window. "Just like in Arizona."

A row of white teepees stood inside a circle of tall palms. The marquee advertised The Wigwam Motel. Charming and inviting.

"Stryker would love to stay in one of those." Mabel said, hand over her heart. "What sort of beds do you suppose they have?" She didn't want to sleep on the floor, but she'd be willing to give it a try for Stryker. Couldn't be much worse than some of the places they'd already stayed on this trip.

George smoked a few cigarettes, careful to open the wing

CATHERINE LEGGITT

window and let out the smoke. Soon he pointed to an orange juice stand shaped like a giant orange. Mabel smiled. This state seemed filled with fanciful things.

George turned on the radio and found rock-and-roll music. No more country. Judging by his quick smile, he seemed pleased. Mabel's fingers tapped a rhythm on the purse in her lap. She had the phone number of Stryker's mother. Maybe she should call that woman and ask why she wasn't on the way to California right now. No decent mother would allow her child to die surrounded by strangers.

Mabel's hand flew to hold in a gasp. *Forgive me, God. I will trust you to make Stryker well.* If that woman did come, she would take over Stryker's care. Did Mabel really want the mother to interfere? They'd come so far without her. Perhaps she should be grateful Sophia chose to stay away.

City after city melded together with only signs to delineate the boundaries. Rialto, Fontana, Rancho Cucamonga—Stryker would laugh at that one. Mabel repeated it to herself. It tickled the mouth as it rolled off her tongue.

About noon, Mabel woke Stryker to eat lunch. George turned into the Santa Anita racetrack and found a spot with a lovely view of the park-like track. Settled there, they rolled down the windows. Too bad they couldn't find a picnic table.

Only Stryker's lack of appetite tainted Mabel's enjoyment of the repast. The food was perfect. Stryker nibbled on a sandwich and ate a few bites of fruit but after that could not be coaxed into more than a couple sips of water. Hoping to take her mind off her malady, Mabel kept up a running travelogue of the sights they'd seen while Stryker slept.

"No movie stars?" Stryker asked.

"Not yet." George's eyes sparkled. "Maybe you should stay awake a while. If anyone can spot them, I bet it'll be you."

Back on the road, they passed a curious building in Pasadena shaped like a black boot. Mabel read the sign out loud. "Mother Goose Pantry. Well, of all things."

Stryker pressed her nose on the window and let out a sweet, girly giggle.

Traffic increased. Overpasses and tunnels multiplied in

number. Freeways intersected the highway in varying patterns and intervals. Instead of a two-lane road, Route 66 doubled to an impressive four.

Behind the wheel, George stiffened each time a new highway branched off. "Do I turn here?"

Mabel kept the map spread open on her lap so she could direct him. Somehow they managed to navigate the maze of Los Angeles freeways. Close to the terminus of Route 66, they turned into the stately grounds of UCLA, precisely as the polite receptionist in Doctor Woodruff's office had instructed. The new hospital looked near completion, with mounds of earth piled around it where sidewalks would soon meander through freshly-planted landscaping. George followed the detour arrows to a sign announcing Pediatric Specialties.

Winding through the parking lot, all of a sudden George sucked in air. His gaze locked on the rearview mirror and his jaw slackened.

Mabel jerked her head to peer out the back window.

Veering into the lot directly behind them was a black Buick Roadmaster. As it turned, Mabel saw the scratch on the side.

"Oh, dear Lord." Mabel felt her blood pressure rising.

The Chevy accelerated toward the entrance. "No one's going to stop us now."

George tightened his grip on the steering wheel until Mabel saw his knuckles whiten. He drove as close as he could to the building before jamming the gearshift into Park. The Chevy jolted to a stop. Jumping out, he folded back the seat and reached in for Stryker. She locked her arms around his neck. With a grunt, he snatched her out, blanket and all. "Where should I take her?"

"The front desk. Ask for Doctor Darrell Woodruff."

He took off at a fast clip.

Mabel didn't know what to do. Should she park the car properly? They couldn't leave it here. It would be ticketed or towed away. Should she follow George and Stryker? Her purse contained Father Tim's information about the mother. Perhaps she should do her best to discourage the man in the black car from following George.

What to do?

With Stryker held firmly in his arms, George hadn't stopped to look back.

First things first.

Although it went completely against her moral fiber, she left the Chevy illegally parked. She'd take her chances with the parking authorities.

Mabel straightened her hat, grabbed her purse, and hobbled after George and Stryker. Chest heaving air, she willed her feet forward. "Fear thou not; for I am with thee . . ." She murmured the soothing words of Isaiah 41:10. The rest of the verse spun through her mind as she hurried. *Be not dismayed; for I am thy God: I will strengthen thee; yea, I will help thee; yea, I will uphold thee with the right hand of my righteousness.*

At times like this, Mabel thanked God for bringing His words to her mind.

A car door slammed and footsteps clipped across the blacktop. She dared not look back.

George and Stryker had disappeared inside the building.

Mabel gulped air as she walked faster, wishing her shoes were made for hurrying.

A few more steps and Mabel made it to the doors. Panting hard, she stopped to catch her breath. One hand on the wall for support, she straightened to her full height and turned toward the parking lot.

A tall, burly fellow in a navy suit and distinctive gray hat lumbered toward her. Face all rigid angles, his brooding expression did not look friendly.

37

STRYKER

Stryker squinted at the white ceiling and bright lights as the gurney rumbled through hospital halls at a speed that tickled her tummy. She took a deep breath to let out a squeal. The sound caught in her throat as she tried to raise her hands. A burning sensation sizzled in her arm where the nurse had stuck in needles.

She hated being strapped in the little bed. She liked the doctor though. He had gentle eyes and a big smile, kind of like Father Tim. And he protected her when a mean-looking man with a gray hat had pushed his way into the office, yelling about his rights. The doctor made him wait outside.

The gurney jolted to a stop in front of an elevator. Mrs. Crowley finally caught up. In and out her friend breathed. Her face looked pale, but she was trying to smile. Unable to speak, she grabbed Stryker's hand. Being with Mrs. Crowley comforted Stryker without a word being said.

Shiny metal doors slid open and the gurney rolled out, gliding to a rest in a long room separated by curtains. Nurses slid Stryker onto an empty bed and hooked up machines with tubes. One of the women explained the call button near her hand, promising to come running the minute she was summoned.

Mrs. Crowley had to wait at the door.

Stryker's eyes grew heavy.

The nurses were still getting her set in the bed when Mr. Stanton joined Mrs. Crowley.

A warm peace settled through her body as she watched her family through the doorway.

Then Mr. Gray Hat yanked Mr. Stanton away by the shirt. Mrs. Crowley covered her mouth with her hand. Stryker couldn't make out what the men said to each other, but the raised voices and the scary looks on their faces left no doubt this was not a happy conversation.

When the nurses finished they left the room. Mr. Stanton tried to block the doorway. The man pushed him aside and stomped into the room. A dark cloud came with him. Stryker gasped. The hair on her arm prickled. Who was this person?

He marched to her bedside. Sinking into the chair beside the bed, he lowered his big face close to hers. "Lily Grace? Can you hear me?" He took her hand. His fingers were cold enough to freeze water, same as his eyes.

How did he know her name? She tried to pull away but didn't have strength.

"You don't remember me, do you?" His voice boomed like he wanted everyone in the hospital to understand his words. "I'm your father, Melvin Dumond."

Her *father?* A flush whooshed over her body. Words wouldn't form on her lips. She tried to make them, but moans came out instead. What was wrong with her? She coughed hard to clear her throat but still couldn't speak.

"I came a long way to find you, and it cost me plenty."

Mr. Stanton and Mrs. Crowley stood stiff like guards. Stryker's gaze shifted to her friends. *Please help me.* Would they protect her from this stranger? Mr. Stanton came to the bedside opposite Mr. Dumond looking ready to fight. Mrs. Crowley moved to the bottom of the bed, wringing her hands.

Stryker tried to smile.

"You drive a black sedan." Mr. Stanton's words came out husky. "A Roadmaster, right?"

Mr. Dumond fixed Mr. Stanton with unfriendly eyes. "Yeah."

What? The man in the 1954 black Buick? Stryker's heart pounded faster.

Mr. Stanton's face hardened. "How long you been following us?"

"Been looking for Lily Grace a long time. Sophia—the kid's mother—took my daughter away in the middle of the night five years ago. Had people searching all over St. Louis for her, and I followed up on every lead. Nothing panned out until one of my agents told me a girl about her age visited Doctor Marston's office. Took me three trips to the good doctor before I convinced him to tell me where she'd gone."

"The doctor didn't know her as Lily Grace." Mrs. Crowley's words growled out low and emotional.

"His nurse recognized the picture." Mr. Dumond examined the fingers on Stryker's hand. "This is my Lily Grace, all right. I'd know her anywhere."

"Even after five years?" Mrs. Crowley's frown wrinkled her whole face. "How?"

"I know the shape of her face, her hands. She has my mother's eyes."

Stryker's mind whirled. Was it true? How *could* this mean man be her father?

Mr. Stanton placed his hand on her arm. Her chest swelled. She didn't need a real father anymore.

"It must have been difficult to trail us across country." Mrs. Crowley narrowed her eyes. Obviously, she didn't believe this man. "We changed cars a couple times and made several unplanned detours."

The stranger's booming laugh rumbled like ear-splitting thunder. Not a happy sound. "Well, I must say, you didn't make following easy, but Doc Marston told me where you were headed."

"When did you catch up with us?" Mr. Stanton's words slashed the air.

"I got stopped in Texas where the road flooded out. Described you to a patrolman who said you turned around there driving a Packard less than an hour before. He gave me the same directions he gave you. I caught up with you in Amarillo."

"So you weren't at the filling station in Lebanon?"

"Lebanon?" Mr. Dumond shook his head.

Mr. Stanton glanced at Stryker. "But you did stop at the Tower Station in Texas?"

"Tower Station?" The stranger's brow furrowed.

"A white art-deco building in Shamrock."

"Oh, sure. I stopped there."

Stryker wanted to say, "Told you there were two black Buicks." The words wouldn't come out. Mr. Stanton's eyes met hers and he winked. He understood whether she spoke or not.

"Why go to all that trouble?" Mrs. Crowley asked. "What do you want with the child?"

"She's my daughter."

"Got any proof?" Mr. Stanton reminded Stryker of a lion waiting for the right moment to pounce.

"Matter of fact, I do." Mr. Dumond dropped Stryker's hand to reach inside his shirt pocket and pull out a folded paper. "This is her birth certificate." He handed it across the bed.

Mr. Stanton's fingers shook when he unfolded the page. He scanned all the way to the bottom. "You weren't married to Stryker's mother."

"Right." Mr. Dumond stiffened in the chair. "Got a problem with that?"

"Depends what you're planning to do." Mr. Stanton leaned closer. "See, I don't believe you. You want something."

"My wife never had kids." Mr. Dumond shrugged one shoulder. "The kid's my only heir."

Mr. Stanton's eye twitched and his fist clenched.

Stryker's head spun like a carousel. Fear filled her chest. Everyone in the room got kind of fuzzy. "Please," she pushed the words out with all the force she could muster. "Don't fight." She lifted her head off the pillow, but it flopped right down again. She coughed hard. Her chest hurt. "Please." Why didn't she have more strength?

The machine near Stryker's head repeated a short, high-pitched sound.

A nurse in a starched white uniform bustled in. "That's the IV. They're new and they malfunction quite often." She pressed something and the beeping stopped. Then she turned to the visitors. "Two of you will have to leave." She gestured toward the door. "Lily Grace is very sick and can't tolerate so many people at once. That's why we keep visitors to one at a time in ICU."

Nobody moved.

The nurse placed her hands on her hips. "Perhaps you don't realize what a fragile state this child is in right now."

Mrs. Crowley tsked. "I'll be in the hospital chapel, dear. If you want me, press that call button and ask the nurse to come get me." She patted the blanket over Stryker's feet and hobbled out.

Stryker watched her go. Unbidden tears flowed. *Don't leave me.* She wiped moisture away, but the tears wouldn't stop. What was wrong with her? She didn't want to cry. What did *fragile* mean?

"It's okay, little one. She'll be back." Mr. Stanton pulled out a tissue from the box beside the bed and pressed it on Stryker's cheek.

The nurse appraised the two men with narrowed eyes. Mr. Stanton and Mr. Dumond glared at each other across the bed. The stranger did not stand up.

"Only *one* visitor at a time," the nurse repeated in a stern voice.

"She's my daughter."

Mr. Stanton's shoulders slumped. He swallowed hard and looked down at Stryker. "Up to you. You don't have to talk to this fellow. Do you want him to stay?"

Panic zigzagged up Stryker's back. With Mama not here, she'd much rather have Mr. Stanton or Mrs. Crowley close. Without them, she felt alone in this big cold place.

She studied the stranger. Was Melvin Dumond her father

like he said? He didn't look familiar. Had she lived with him? Surely she'd remember someone with such cruel eyes.

Blinking at the ceiling, she thought back. They lived with Uncle Harold. Before that, they lived in the car or sometimes slept at the mission downtown. She remembered a grandmother who fought with Mama. Did they live with her? Maybe. And before that? She couldn't think. Her chin trembled when she forced herself to look at Mr. Dumond.

"I don't remember you," she whispered.

"What?" He bent near enough she could smell his stinky breath. "You visited me several times. Don't you remember? We used to play with that brown monkey. Do you still have her?"

Stryker gave a single nod.

Mr. Dumond's frosty stare swept the room. "Where is she? Did you bring her to the hospital?" He glanced at the nurse. "She kept that old thing with her all the time. Have you seen a raggedy, stuffed monkey?"

The nurse stood her ground. "Doesn't matter to me which of you goes, but one of you must leave now."

"Me and the mother didn't live together. Thing is, I'm married—*was* married . . ." Mr. Dumond's words trailed off.

The nurse pointed to the door. "You can trade off after a few hours."

"Time's up, pal." Mr. Stanton's voice had a tough edge Stryker hadn't heard before. "Stryker doesn't know you." He tightened both fists like he would fight if he had to.

Mr. Dumond dragged his body to a stand, still gripping Stryker's fingers. "Don't cry. I'm going for now, but I'll be back, Lily Grace."

He turned to the nurse. "I'd like to speak with the doctor as soon as possible."

Without seeing his face, Stryker knew Mr. Stanton didn't look pleased.

"Of course. I'm expecting Doctor Woodruff back any time now." The nurse motioned Mr. Dumond out of the room. "I'll let him know you wish to speak with him."

Walking in front of the nurse, Mr. Dumond stopped with

one hand on the doorframe. "Where's the monkey?" His eyes sparked at Stryker.

In a flash, the memory curtain opened and Stryker remembered those eyes. A long time ago. Something raw and bitter as a winter storm shuddered through her. He must not touch Sophia.

Mama said.

Mr. Stanton answered, "I'll let you know when you can come back."

Stryker never saw Mr. Stanton look so powerful. Inside, she smiled. Made her feel protected. If only Mr. Stanton was her father and not this awful man.

After Mr. Dumond stormed out of the room, Mr. Stanton moved the chair so he faced the door. "Good riddance, eh? I don't like the looks of that one."

"Where's Sophia?" Stryker whispered.

Mr. Stanton shook his head. "The car, I guess. Want me to get her?"

Relief washed over her. "Not now." Stryker's bones ached and her chest hurt when she coughed. Fatigue overwhelmed her. Breaths puffed out short and shallow.

None of that mattered. Sophia would be safe in the Chevy. The black Roadmaster wasn't someone coming after Mr. Stanton. They finally made it to the hospital. The long trip across the country had ended in victory. Their peculiar little family had arrived safely.

Tears pooled under her closed lids. *Thank you, God.*

Through the moisture, Stryker smiled. God answered her prayer. Mr. Stanton watched over her.

Now she could sleep.

38

GEORGE

George wanted to stay with Stryker all through that interminable night. Near her he felt useful. Even if he could do nothing else, he determined to defend her from the man claiming to be her father. The nurses tried to shoo him out when visiting hours ended, but he didn't go far and kept checking on her often when the nurses weren't looking.

Hooked up to machines, breathing irregularly, the child fought hard for her life. Helplessness rolled over him in waves. If only he knew how to make Stryker well. In the hours he sat next to her bed, he alternated between nail-biting silence and talking to her. They had given her medicine to make her sleep. Most of the time she gave no indication she heard him, but no matter. It comforted him to talk to her.

He chuckled when he admitted to himself how much he enjoyed talking to Stryker. She was special, an angel. When that thought crossed his mind, it amused him too.

Angels didn't exist.

Mrs. Crowley appeared at Stryker's door around midnight, and George marched out to the waiting room like the changing of the guard. He smoked a pack of cigarettes and paced. Although he had no appetite, he made himself walk downstairs for a cup of strong coffee in the hospital dining room. A change of scenery and plenty of time to ponder.

The black Buick he'd avoided all across country wasn't coming for him. What a relief. Riding up in the elevator, he sipped his black coffee. The robust brew tasted like it sat on the warming pad too long, but he drank it anyway, grateful for a free beverage.

Two gray Stetson Open Road hats. Two black Buick Roadmasters. George shook his head. Some kind of cosmic joke? Stryker had been right all along. He was paranoid to think he'd been followed. Why would anyone take the trouble to trail him? He'd only taken what was rightfully his.

A small voice suggested his sense of right and wrong might be skewed.

He crushed the paper coffee cup in his fist and tossed it toward the trash.

Hogwash.

George sat and massaged his forehead with his fingertips. What had made his conscience come alive and prod him? Questions echoed in his brain. What about the stealing? What about the drinking? The selfishness? The lies? Who was responsible for all that?

Too much thinking. He paced a few more minutes before setting off for the coffee shop again. He had just come upstairs half an hour before, but he needed to be doing something.

On his second trip downstairs, George retrieved the Chevy and drove it into an actual parking space. Back inside the hospital he stopped at the newspaper dispensers to examine the *Los Angeles Times* and the *Mirror-News* through the windows. Nothing about any kind of inquiry into fraud at McBride, Reynolds, and O'Neill. The story didn't make the top half of the front page anyway. After almost two weeks, the investigation must be old news.

He poked a nickel in the dispenser and yanked out a copy of the *Times*. Something to read while Crowley sat with

Stryker. Paper under his arm, he rode the elevator back to Stryker's floor and settled in a different chair in the empty waiting room.

Hours later, Dumond's distinctive Texas growl summoned George on a run. Face grim, the man had the audacity to demand the nurses locate Stryker's toy monkey. Why wasn't he asking about Stryker?

George blocked the doorway to Stryker's room with arms locked across his chest. That jerk would not disturb her again. Surrounded by a group of medical personnel, Dumond never so much as looked George's way.

As the disturbance escalated, George felt Mrs. Crowley behind him.

"It's the middle of the night. What does *he* want?" she asked.

George spoke without turning around. "From what I gather, someone from the hospital contacted Stryker's mother. She made it quite clear Mr. Dumond has no legal parental rights or any authority to make decisions regarding Stryker's care."

"Thank God," Crowley whispered. "Why doesn't he go away then?"

"Apparently he is prone to violence, according to one of the nurses. They're telling him to leave or they'll call security," George said. "The mother was clear that under no circumstances were they to release either Stryker or her toy to him."

"Her toy?"

Very curious. George couldn't keep the smirk off his face when two burly hospital security men hurried in and hauled the offensive man away.

With the immediate danger past, George relaxed. "Nothing to worry about. They handled the situation just fine. What puzzles me is why he's so interested in a stuffed monkey." He scratched his head. "With luck, we'll never know the answer."

A nurse arrived to tell Mrs. Crowley about an empty room. She offered to let Mrs. Crowley sleep there a few hours if she wished. Mrs. Crowley produced a wan smile and shuffled off. How nice to let the old woman rest a bit. She looked bushed.

They also allowed George to resume his vigil at Stryker's bedside.

Nurses scampered in and out every hour for the rest of the night, taking blood pressure and temperature, changing the bags of fluid dripping into Stryker's arm, resetting the blasted beeping machine. If George had wanted to sleep—which he didn't—he couldn't have with the constant flurry of activity and noise.

Still seated in Stryker's room when morning dawned, he stood and extended his arms over his head. A twinge of sadness cramped his gut. How many times had he watched the rearview mirror while Stryker stretched her little arms? Would he ever see her do that again?

He squeezed her thin hand. "We'll be out of here soon. Can't wait to try out the bed in the teepee motel." What was he saying? Did he harbor some silly fantasy he'd be returning with Crowley and Stryker? What about his escape? He didn't even want to think about it. Without any money, every part of his plan had become impossible. Heart heavy, he pushed thoughts of the future away.

Stryker moved her head on the pillow. Under her eyelids, her eyeballs wiggled to and fro before opening.

George bent close. "Morning, little one."

She mouthed *morning* without making a sound.

A nurse poked her head into the room. "Excellent. She's awake. Doctor Woodruff is on the floor. He'll be in shortly."

Stryker radiated heat. Inwardly, George cursed the raging fever.

As if she knew Stryker was awake, Mrs. Crowley hobbled into the room, looking quite disheveled. He tossed her a greeting and stood to give her the chair. He wanted to hear what the doctor would say, so he lingered in the doorway.

Mrs. Crowley sat stiffly, holding Stryker's hand.

Stryker's eyes suddenly looked stormy. "Where's Sophia?"

Mrs. Crowley answered. "She's in the Chevy, dear."

"Do you want me to get her?" He straightened to attention, body humming with need. Give him a job. Something to be helpful. Anything.

"No," Stryker whispered. "Just . . . take care of her." She stared at Mrs. Crowley. "I promised I would keep her with me.

Mama said . . . she's a valuable friend." Getting out a few words seemed to exhaust her and she slumped into the pillow.

"Don't worry, dear." Mrs. Crowley's glasses had fogged up. She removed them and wiped the lenses with her hanky just as Doctor Woodruff buzzed in, head bent over a clipboard of papers.

She didn't seem to notice his arrival. Pushing her glasses back on her nose, she pressed a light kiss on Stryker's cheek. "How are you doing this morning, sweet girl?"

"Glad you're here," Stryker whispered.

"Are you hungry yet?" Mrs. Crowley asked.

The doctor glanced up. "Hunger might be a bit much to expect, short of divine intervention."

"Well, that's exactly what I'm praying for." Mrs. Crowley folded her hands at her middle. "A miracle."

Doctor Woodruff approached the bed. "Hi, Lily Grace. Good to see you awake." Placing the chart on the bed, he removed the stethoscope from around his neck and stuck the ends in his ears. "Let's take a listen." He fitted the flat disk above her heart and concentrated. Staring at the ceiling, he listened to sounds in several areas of her lungs and asked her to cough. Her deep bark sounded painful.

Doctor Woodruff tugged the earpieces out of his ears. "How are you feeling?"

"Okay, I guess." Her voice was weak.

"How's the pain?"

She glanced at George before answering. "Hurts when I move or cough."

"Hurts real bad, or not as bad as before?"

"Real . . . bad."

Inside, George winced. He crossed his arms over his heart.

Doctor Woodruff patted Stryker's hand. "We'll try to help you out on the pain. Do you need anything else?"

"No. My family is here now. Couldn't they stay with me all the time?" The radiant smile she shared with George and Mrs. Crowley surpassed any picture of an angel George ever saw—sheer perfection, glowing and sweet. Ethereal, almost.

"We'll see about that too." Doctor Woodruff grabbed the

chart and scribbled a note on the top paper before ambling from the room.

George followed him to the nurses' station. "Doctor, I have a few questions."

Turning, the doctor stopped. "Sure. Mr. Stanton, is it?"

"Is she going to make it?"

"Uh . . ." The doctor drew in a long breath. "She's in critical condition right now with pneumonia in one lung and her lab tests aren't good. Unfortunately, the leukemia is progressing aggressively. We're doing what we can to ease her pain, but no question, she's a very sick girl."

"I thought you were going to give her some kind of treatment for the leukemia."

The doctor stuffed both hands in the pockets of his lab coat. "The tests Doctor Marston sent indicated we might have a small window for therapy, but it's possible we were prematurely optimistic. At this point, I'm not sure it would be beneficial."

"There's nothing you can do for her?"

"We're giving her pain meds intravenously. That's a new way to administer medicine. Goes right into the veins instead of being processed through the digestive system first. I ordered the respiratory team to try to loosen her chest, but I can't begin treating the leukemia until we get the pneumonia under control."

George's knees wobbled and he grabbed the edge of the counter at the nurses' station for support.

"Wish I had better news." Doctor Woodruff squeezed George's shoulder. "I'm sorry."

Vision blurred by gathering tears, George covered his mouth with one clenched fist. The impossibility of Stryker's precarious situation struck him hard in the gut like a sucker punch. He couldn't bear to watch Stryker suffer. Must get away—dull the pain.

He needed a drink.

Head down, he raced toward the stairs. By the time he flung himself out of the hospital entrance, he was panting. The heavy doors closed behind him, and he stopped just outside.

Total disorientation overwhelmed him. Which way to the nearest bar? He jerked his head to the right and left. Where did he leave the Chevy? He lit a cigarette and scanned the rows of cars. When he spotted it, he groped his pocket for the key and hurried through the parking lot.

With trembling hands, he had trouble unlocking the door, but at last he flung it wide, mashed out his cigarette, and collapsed inside.

Sophia lay on the front seat.

Rage exploded in George's heart. He grabbed the stupid monkey and shook it. "You're her best friend. Are you gonna let her die?" His tears obscured all reality. He blinked rapidly and lifted his eyes heavenward. "She doesn't deserve this, God. She trusts you. Why don't you heal her?"

As he banged the monkey head on the dash he heard tinny pings. Metal inside the monkey?

The hulking form of Stryker's biological father appeared in the open door. "Give me that thing," he snarled.

Through his grief, George couldn't see who spoke. "What?"

"The monkey." Dumond roared. "Hand it over." His fingers groped for Sophia, but George held tight to one leg.

"No!"

Dumond leaned into the car. "I'm not asking you again, pal."

The cold steel of a gun barrel kissed George's temple.

39

MABEL

While technicians administered oxygen therapy to Stryker, Mabel searched the lobby and the cafeteria for George without success. Short of breath, she stumbled outside the building. Her chest ached. Should she go to the emergency room herself?

Stryker, precious child. How could she be so sick that no leukemia treatment could be started? Had Mabel misunderstood her God-given mission?

Her head spinning, she steadied herself on the wall. Surely God had called her to bring this child to Los Angeles, and she had accomplished that. Mabel glanced at the big glass doors leading into the hospital. The pain intensified. Would she die or was there still more to do?

Mabel stood on the steps and let the tears fall. Her hanky was useless, soaked through and through. She grasped the railing for support.

Where in the world had George gone? How could he run away at this critical time? Stryker needed him. Mabel needed him too. As her crying dwindled to shoulder-hitching hiccups, she surveyed the parking lot. Where did he leave the car?

Several rows back, she spied Mr. Dumond's hulking figure. But what would he be doing there? She took a few unsteady steps. Oh, dear. Her hand covered her trembling lips. He wasn't alone. Fists flew amid a flurry of angry raised voices. Dumond threw a right jab. A thin man with dark curly hair ducked.

Mabel gasped. George? She staggered through a row of parked cars.

Each man gripped a leg of Stryker's monkey. What on earth?

"This monkey belongs to my daughter," Mr. Dumond yelled. "Let go."

Every bit as ferocious, George shouted back, "You let go."

Brawling over Stryker's toy? Merciful heavens. A couple of fools.

A small crowd of onlookers had gathered nearby, yelling taunts and encouragement as if enjoying a boxing match.

Mabel toddled toward the combatants. Hands righteously planted on her hips, she spoke as loudly as she could, "George Stanton. What are you doing?"

"Gun," George panted, struggling to stand after a punch threw him to his knees. "He tried to shoot me."

Mabel didn't know whether to laugh or scream.

"It's mine." Mr. Dumond yelled over the din.

George leapt to his feet. "Stryker told *us* to take care of Sophia."

Smack! George landed a wallop squarely on Mr. Dumond's jaw. The solid blow sent the burly fellow reeling backward, but he maintained his hold on the stuffed animal.

Two uniformed police officers sprinted into the fracas.

As the officers dragged the two apart, the monkey leg clutched by Mr. Dumond tore off with a loud *ripppp*. White stuffing popped out.

The crowd issued a collective *oooh*.

"Fight's over." One policeman gestured to the crowd. "Go on about your business, folks."

The onlookers disbursed, men and women throwing back disappointed glances.

The officer restraining George spoke. "Okay, fellows. You gonna settle down, or do we drag you off to the police station for disorderly conduct?"

George swiped blood off his cheek. "Arrest this man for attempted murder. He pointed a pistol at me."

"Where's the gun, sir?"

"I knocked it under that car, and he grabbed the monkey." George pointed to the nearest vehicle. "He intended to shoot me."

The officer crouched where George pointed, fingers groping underneath the sedan. After a moment, he dragged out a black revolver. "Ain't you fellas a bit long in the tooth to be fighting over a toy?"

"It belongs to my daughter," Mr. Dumond growled. "She's lying near death in your hospital." He nodded toward the building. "Name's Lily Grace Lambros. Got her birth certificate in my pocket. I insist you hand over her monkey."

George's lip quivered. "Not his."

"Grief makes people do weird things," one policeman said. "But this is the kookiest I've ever seen." He shook his head. "I say we haul them into the security office. Let someone else decide this one."

Both men protested loudly but were yanked back into the hospital anyway.

While George and Mr. Dumond were questioned, Mabel paced in the corridor turning every few steps to make a loop. The respiratory people must be finished by now. She really should head on up there. *Dear Lord, please heal Stryker.*

Exhausted after a couple of passes, she settled in a chair in the hall. Why would Stryker's father fight over custody of this toy? Stryker's mother told Stryker to keep it because it was worth a lot, but what value did a ragged, stuffed monkey have? Why would the toy be worth *anything* to Dumond? He didn't even care enough about his child to sit with her.

Perhaps Sophia Lambros wasn't talking about sentimental value. Mabel closed her eyes and rubbed her temples, forcing herself to breathe deeply.

In the quiet hall, the pain in her chest began to diminish.

She should sit a bit longer. Dropping her head back until it rested on the wall behind her chair, she forced her muscles to relax.

Sweet days with Stryker rolled across her memory—their meeting at church, their first meal, the bath, watching Stryker sleep. Shopping together. Getting ready for the trip. What high hopes she had for God to use this illness to bring glory to His name. But now? Mabel blew out a long sigh.

Washing Sophia that first night, Mabel remembered feeling stiff round objects that made the ears stand out from the side of the head—the single hard part on an otherwise soft stuffed toy. Something round. What made those ears rigid?

Mr. Dumond seemed determined to get this toy. He'd questioned Stryker and the nurses about the whereabouts of the monkey. Maybe his cross-country pursuit was never about Stryker. Mabel's eyes popped open. Was it possible that valuable objects had been hidden *inside* the toy?

She frowned. Like what?

The ears were about the size of quarters. Coins? What kind of coins would be worth five years of searching for Stryker all over St. Louis, then chasing her clear across country and threatening George with a gun?

Must be mighty expensive coins.

Preposterous. Mabel shook her head. Still, she couldn't come up with a more plausible explanation.

Mabel stood and smoothed her wrinkled skirt. Must look a mess after sleeping in her clothes. She tucked a couple of loose hair strands into her braided chignon and centered her hat. Then she stepped to the office door and rapped smartly.

"Enter." Someone yelled.

She opened the door to find Mr. Dumond and George slumped in chairs. Sophia lay on a desk, white stuffing protruding where the leg had been ripped away. The gun was close by. A portly gentleman wearing a security uniform sat behind the desk, hands folded.

"I had a thought," Mabel started.

The two officers stopped talking. Everyone in the room turned toward Mabel.

"And you are?" Boomed the authority behind the desk.

"Mabel Crowley. Mr. Stanton and I brought Lily Grace here from St. Louis."

"Let's hope you can shed some light on this fiasco, Mrs. Crowley. These two yahoos aren't making a lick of sense."

Mabel stepped closer. "I've been pondering Mr. Dumond's interest in the monkey. Apparently, it is more important to him than his only daughter's fight for life." Mabel fixed Mr. Dumond with her best accusatory expression. "Perhaps the monkey is valuable."

Mr. Dumond straightened in the chair. "Hold on there."

Mabel smiled inside, knowing she was on the right track. "If you examine the ears, I think you'll find they're stiffer than the rest of the toy."

The security chief picked up Sophia and squeezed one ear between his fingers. "Yeah. So?"

"I think something valuable is hidden inside those ears."

Mr. Dumond scowled.

One of the officers checked the other ear. "Like what?"

The chief security guard raised his eyebrows. "Are you suggesting I cut off one of the ears?"

"No." Mabel held out the paper with the information Father Tim had provided. "I suggest you contact this woman and ask her about the ears. She's probably the one who sewed them on."

"They're mine." Mr. Dumond howled. "She stole them from me."

A call to Stryker's mother confirmed Mabel's theory. Before she fled St. Louis, Sophia Lambros sewed two extremely rare 1913 Liberty head nickels into the monkey's ears. She claimed they were a gift from Mr. Dumond. According to Sophia, those coins might be worth several hundred thousand dollars. When she fled St. Louis because of Mr. Dumond's violent outbursts, she had hoped to secure Stryker's future with these coins. She said she didn't realize Stryker was so ill. She had planned to come back for Stryker as soon as she was able.

Hospital security wrote up a full report of the incident. Mabel pursed her lips when George gave his name as Vincent

Morelli with a St. Louis address, claiming his identification had been stolen. He seemed more haggard and worn than she'd ever seen him, so she didn't make an issue of his latest deception. Father Tim was right. This part of the story was not hers. God did not call her to be George's conscience.

The security guards decided to turn the monkey over to the police until rightful ownership of the coins could be determined. Mr. Dumond was clearly not happy about this. As George and Mabel left the office, his booming Texas drawl could be heard trailing behind them all the way to the elevator.

"I hope they award the coins to Stryker's mother," Mrs. Crowley said as the elevator neared Stryker's floor. Even as she heard herself speak, she was surprised to realize that God had already answered her prayer to forgive the woman.

"Imagine that. The whole time I worried about money that little monkey held coins valuable enough to set me up royally in Mexico." George chuckled softly. "I had that monkey right in my hands more than once." His clenched fists relaxed. "Talk about irony."

"Good thing you didn't know." Mabel peered over the top of her glasses. "You'd have stolen Sophia and ripped those ears right off the instant you found out. That would've devastated Stryker."

Staring at the floor, George waggled his head. His grin almost looked sincere. "I don't know how Sophia will prove the coins are hers, but I hope she does too. Better that than for that awful man to get his hands on them."

The elevator doors slid open.

"You go ahead," George said quietly. "Take your time. I'll be in the waiting room."

Mabel watched George drag his feet down the corridor, shoulders stooped. He must be bone-tired. If only she knew how to help him. *Lord, George needs Your comfort and rest right now. Give him strength to walk through whatever You have in store for our girl.*

She turned to enter Stryker's cool, semi-dark room where machines gurgled and beeped.

Stepping closer to the bed, Mabel placed her hand lightly on Stryker's forehead. Burning hot. "How long can she go on this way, Lord?" Mabel groaned as she lowered herself into the chair. The burden of the child's future felt ponderously heavy. When had Mabel grown so feeble?

The effort Stryker required to breathe was evident. Just like Paul before he died. First Richard, then her dear husband, now this sweet child. Why must Mabel always be left behind to pick up the broken pieces of her heart and go on?

She lifted her face heavenward. "I'm old and ready to go, but Stryker has many things left to accomplish. Let her live, Lord."

40

GEORGE

In the small waiting room, George jiggled his knees by bouncing on the balls of his feet. He crossed his legs and uncrossed them. Smoked cigarette after cigarette. Stood and stretched, then dropped back into the seat.

What was going on in Stryker's room?

His eye twitched annoyingly. He rubbed his face with his hands, fingers probing the persistent tenderness of the scar across his forehead. How long since the accident?

Only two short weeks since he'd met Stryker. Could it be? Seemed like she'd been part of his life forever.

Fatigue assaulted his muscles, but he must stay awake. Stryker might need him.

Mrs. Crowley hobbled into the waiting room. "Stryker is stirring." Her eyes were red and her mouth quivered. "You should go in."

If only he could assure her everything would be okay. But all he could do when she flopped into the chair next to him was squeeze her hand.

Then he raced into Stryker's cubicle and bent over her bald head. "Hey, little one."

Paper-thin lids fluttered like fragile butterflies. The pale blue eyes he longed to see stared into his. "What time is it?" Her words edged out, scratchy and weak.

"Nearly noon." George leaned closer. "How ya doing?"

The corners of Stryker's mouth turned up. "I'm fine." Her voice stronger. "You know why?"

"Why?" The word squeaked out like a teenager as he played along, remembering the last time she'd asked him the same question.

"'Cause I'm tough." She clenched her tiny white hand for a few seconds before dropping it limply onto the covers.

Sinking into the chair, George lifted Stryker's fist to his lips. He buried the little hand between his own and let his chin fall to his chest. Unashamedly, he watched his tears spill onto their fingers.

"Are you scared?" she whispered. "Pray to God."

He turned up his wet face to connect with her eyes.

"It helps a lot."

"I don't know how." Despite all efforts to be strong, he couldn't keep his lips from trembling.

"Mrs. Crowley showed me." The corners of her tentative smile wobbled too. "Want me to show you?"

He nodded.

Stryker scooted closer to George and blinked up at the ceiling. "God, my friend Mr. Stanton needs You. Show him who You are and how much you love him. He wants to ask You to live in his heart, and he needs to know You'll never leave him." Her words came out soft and gentle. She paused to breathe. "Help him not be afraid like You always help me."

Weeping, George beheld her dear little face. Tilted upward, her countenance had taken on a soft, unearthly glow.

Maybe she really was an angel.

"Oh, and please, God, help Mr. Stanton tell the truth from now on. Amen."

George buried his face in the covers.

Stryker gently laid one hand on his curls.

Warmth radiated through her fingers. He'd never been blessed before, but he knew that's what she was doing. Power infused her touch and penetrated deep inside him. In that instant, he knew God had answered Stryker's prayer. If he prayed, God would listen.

"God." The blankets muffled his words. "I want to stop doing things wrong and do them Your way." With all his heart he truly wanted to change. If only he knew how. He lifted his head. "Please help me understand what to do."

George swallowed over a lump in his throat. "And thank you for sending Lily Grace to show me the way."

The luminous quality of her face seemed to dim. Her eyelids sagged. Flapping in slow motion, her lids closed.

He stroked her blistering-hot hand.

Outside the room, hospital business continued as usual, but Stryker's little cubicle suddenly seemed to be a world all its own, surrounded by a shell of peace.

Her breathing gradually grew labored.

Minutes passed without improvement. Helplessness over-powered George, but it surprised him to realize he was no longer afraid.

He glanced toward the doorway. One-person rule or not, if the end was nearing, Mrs. Crowley should be here too.

As though she heard his thoughts, Mrs. Crowley appeared. Sorrow creased her tired face. They exchanged a look, but neither spoke. Mrs. Crowley eased near Stryker's bed, staring at the child as if trying to memorize every feature.

An odd rattle far down in Stryker's throat added to the ragged breathing.

George leaned over the bed. "Don't leave us, little one."

At the sound of his voice, her delicate vein-streaked lids opened. Her eyes clasped George in an embrace. Oceans of love washed between them. So much he almost fell back from the impact.

The hospital room tunneled around them. Noises muted. From either side of the bed, George and Mrs. Crowley hovered close.

"My . . . family . . ." Stryker's voice trailed off.

Her eyelids fell like the final curtain. George waited for her to open them again, but she did not. In his body, he felt the time ticking away.

A minute went by, then ten, twenty. Neither George nor Mrs. Crowley said a single word, both fixed on the small body lying in the big white bed.

George's feet hurt from standing in the same position too long. He shuffled, shifting his weight. He could get another chair from the hall, but he didn't want to leave her for even a second.

When the nurses changed shifts, someone bustled into the room to take vital signs. Although she frowned at Mrs. Crowley and George while she listened to Stryker's chest, she didn't suggest that one of them should go.

"She seems to be in a coma," the nurse said with a sigh, hanging the stethoscope on her arm.

"What?" asked Mrs. Crowley.

"I'm afraid her body is shutting down." The nurse offered a small smile as she dashed out.

All too soon, an anemic stream of air whooshed between Stryker's lips. She did not inhale again.

Grasping her hand, George willed her to take another breath.

Five seconds, ten seconds, twenty seconds.

Half a minute.

Stryker did not breathe again.

Beepers shrieked like air raid signals.

A nurse dashed in, took one look, and ran out again.

"No!"

Behind her glasses, Mrs. Crowley's eyes ripped into George like claws. "I told you we had to hurry."

Mind numb, George stared.

Mrs. Crowley mopped her cheeks with her limp handkerchief. "This is your fault." With a strangled cry, she clutched her chest and crumpled face-down onto the bed.

Strangers surged into the room. A nurse pried Stryker's small hand from his. Someone hoisted Mrs. Crowley into the chair. Soon uniformed staff packed the room—wires, instruments, and commands flying.

The infernal beeper.

Busy, busy.

Everyone except George had something to do.

His vision blurred. This was not happening.

Stryker could not be dead.

In a daze, George looked down to see his shoes running along the corridors. His footsteps tapped a regular rhythm on the floor—but where was he going? Forcing air into his lungs, he puffed and panted. Couldn't run much farther. Must stop.

Someone tell his feet.

They didn't slow down. His shoes pounded down the stairs.

He shoved open the front doors and burst outside, instantly blinded by the sunlight. Reeling, he filled his lungs with air as if he hadn't breathed since leaving Stryker's room. His head and chest ached. His entire body trembled.

Worst of all, his heart had exploded into jagged pieces.

Mrs. Crowley's words echoed in his brain. *This is your fault, your fault.* He let his head drop back and raised his arms toward the sky. "God help me." He fell to his knees.

The presence of God washed peace and comfort over the raw, gaping wound and woke his sleeping conscience. For the first time he understood the damage his duplicity had caused. Not only had Stryker suffered. He saw with shocking clarity how shirking his responsibility to Gloria and the children, to McBride, Reynolds, and O'Neill, and to Mabel had caused them pain. As Father Tim rightly said, George put his own selfish desires on the throne of his life where God should be.

The time to face the truth had come.

"Forgive me, God," his anguished soul cried. Once again, the manifestation of God overwhelmed him. He experienced being enclosed in strong arms. God filled the emptiness in his soul. He felt no craving for a drink or happy pills. He didn't need to run away. He didn't even desire a cigarette.

"Oh, George." Mrs. Crowley hobbled toward him. "I'm sorry. I shouldn't have said what I did. It wasn't your fault."

"But it was," George wailed. "I should have driven you straight here, no detours or stops for my benefit. If we'd come before she got pneumonia, they could've started leukemia treatment. I wasted several days. How can you ever forgive me?"

He fell into her open arms. Grief poured between them in torrents of tears. Sometimes speaking at the same time, sometimes crying together, they remained locked together while time ceased to be relevant.

With a loud sniffle, Mrs. Crowley finally released him. "We'll have to make arrangements."

George's three-carat diamond ring sparkled in the sunlight, the last remaining vestige of his former identity. Selling the ring would provide funds to bury Stryker with a proper headstone, perhaps somewhere overlooking the ocean she never got to splash in. Money to meet the expenses of Mabel's trip home. Might have enough money left over to hire an attorney if he needed one. He would throw himself on the mercy of the court, pleading guilty.

He held Mrs. Crowley at arm's length. "It would be an honor to take care of the final arrangements for our little one."

She tried to speak, but he laid his finger on her lips. He wasn't finished. "You were right about my alcohol problem. I see that now. For years I convinced myself I could take it or leave it. Sometimes I suspected I might not be able to quit for good, but I wouldn't allow myself to entertain that possibility. Liquor controlled me. I must stop drinking. From this moment on."

Mrs. Crowley smiled a shaky smile.

"I've told you a lot of lies too. Please forgive me. I say what I think people want to hear. Most of the time I know I'm lying just to get them off my back. From now on, I intend to live a life of truth. In fact, I want you to know everything." He led her to a bench in a small grassy area and settled next to her. "I did what the FBI accused me of—embezzled money from my firm." Saying the word *embezzled* for the first time in this context unlocked a door in his soul where he'd long imprisoned his God-given sense of right and wrong.

George told her the whole story, revolting start to disgusting finish—even about Gloria and the children, George Edward, and Judith. At the mention of their names he realized he'd always treated them as objects rather than family—acquisitions, like his Continental—to make his life look perfect on the outside. Would he get another chance? It surprised him to realize he wanted to learn to love them as he loved Stryker.

He admitted to stealing Mrs. Crowley's money after he lost his cash in the all-night poker game. When he finished confessing, a new freedom swelled in his chest. He felt so light he glanced at his feet to see if they were still planted on the ground.

"I appreciate your honesty, George," Mrs. Crowley said slowly, gazing into his eyes. "But I have no power to absolve you. If you confess to God and ask Him for forgiveness, He will free you. God provided redemption through Jesus. He's the only one who can take away the guilt of your sin."

"I want to do that," George said. "I hope you'll tell me more."

"I'm afraid your journey is only beginning. Many of your actions demand long-term consequences. A simple *I'm sorry, please forgive me* to those you've wronged will not rectify what you've done."

George nodded. "I know I have a lot of changing to do. It will take a long time to regain the trust of my family and the other people I've injured. Every day I'll have to fight the urge to drown my frustrations in alcohol. But with God's help, I will do it." He took Mrs. Crowley's hand, wishing she had been his mother. "I'd really appreciate it if you'd come with me when I sell my ring and then turn myself over to the authorities."

"Of course, I will." Mrs. Crowley squeezed his hand. A tiny smile crept onto her lips. "I'll stay as long as you need me."

George swiped a tear from his cheek.

That was so much more than he'd hoped for.

"Oh, George, George." Mrs. Crowley removed her fogged-up glasses. "What a long and difficult road you're traveling. You'll continue to have temptations. The possibility to make bad choices won't ever go away." She wiped the lenses with her hanky. "Even at my age, I struggle with the consequences of my sin." She slid the glasses back on her nose. "Every time we succumb, there's a price to pay."

"I see that now. There won't be any happily ever after for me on this earth. Each day will be a struggle to do the right thing. The biggest thing I have to fight is wanting my own way."

With her hanky, she dabbed her cheeks. "Many times during our short acquaintance, I despaired that you would ever come to this place. You can't possibly imagine how thrilled I am to see you running toward God. If you search for Him, I promise He will be found. Even if there's no happily ever after, there will be plenty of joy, satisfaction, and purpose to make up for the losses." She hugged George tightly then drew back. "Can you stand another Bible verse?"

"Sure." he grinned. "Fire away."

"While you told your story just now, I kept thinking of a special verse. Isaiah 11:6 speaks of the peaceable kingdom to be found in Christ. The verse ends with this phrase: . . . *and a little child shall lead them.*"

"Perfect." Hope for the future bloomed in his soul. Whatever daily—even hourly—horrors he must endure to make things right, he would never be alone again. To have Mrs. Crowley's support was wonderful, but not the most important thing. God would be with him forever. No matter what. He tipped back his head and surveyed the heavens.

The California sky had turned pale blue.

Just like Stryker's eyes.

Author's Note

The concept for this story grew in my imagination in a rather unique manner, which might be of interest to the reader. To begin with, one night in 2012 I dreamed about three strangers—a child, an older woman, and a fugitive—traveling in a car on a journey of discovery. When I woke this possibility intrigued me, so I wrote it down.

During this time, a family member was grappling with several issues. He acted out but refused to assume responsibility for the fallout of his exploits. This struggle seemed to drag on and on. Just when we thought he had conquered, he would fall into the pit again. I wondered how many times a person must hit bottom before he or she comes to the place where change is the only option left.

One day, my husband and I were discussing this quandary when we drove past a sign for Terminous, California. I felt a nudge. Terminus means the end of the road. The story idea had a name—*The Road to Terminus*.

So I knew I would be writing a road trip with three strangers traveling together. We've always been fascinated with Route 66. That seemed a great setting. During the process of plotting chapters, my husband located a 1955 *State Farm Road Atlas* showing the exact placement of Route 66, which he bought at an antique store years earlier. Setting the story in 1955 would eliminate the need to deal with modern technology. Cross-country flight without quick detection might not be so simple today since the widespread use of computers.

Then we visited my brother-in-law in the Mohave Desert. That weekend Victorville was hosting a Route 66 classic car show. I snapped a lot of pictures of pre-1955 autos and got the idea for Stryker and George connecting around the love of cars.

At the same event, I purchased several books about roadside attractions and spoke with experts on Route 66 folklore. Instant research. My daughter sent me a replica Route 66 sign to hang on my wall, and I was on the road, so to speak.

Although I never discovered the answer to my initial question about what it takes to get to the final bottom, pondering this question revealed information I value. First off, happily ever afters only exist in fairy tales and in our future in Heaven. Every day is a struggle against temptation.

For deep-set issues, human willpower or determination cannot transform the heart and mind. If it seems I interjected too much "religion" into this story, please consider this conclusion: Heart issues can only truly be changed by the power of God. Sometimes God changes people instantly, but sometimes this change occurs over a long period of time. The Bible promises that God will make His chosen ones into the image of Jesus. This transformative work is accomplished as we obey and walk in His way.

It occurs to me that Bill W. and Alcoholics Anonymous embrace this very concept. Success in AA involves reliance on a Higher Power. Those who depend on willpower, determination, discipline, or whatever other human powers there may be, sometimes turn from the addiction that initially drove them to AA, but the end result will be substitution of another addictive behavior. The tendency toward addiction will be lasting. For true freedom to occur, God must be the primary piece of the equation, one day at a time.

Always along my writing journey, I need concrete affirmations to keep me going. In His great mercy, God faithfully gives me exactly what I require at the precise time it's needed, and once again His provisions came right on time.

Although I don't know why He desired me to write this story, I have no doubt that writing *The Road to Terminus* was accomplished within God's will and with God's power.

May reading this book minister to the needs of your heart.

Catherine Leggitt
Lodi, CA ~ 2015

Discussion Questions

Includes spoilers!

1. George Stanton is trying to escape the consequences of his actions. What was his hidden flaw? What inner conflicts propelled him? How did this journey reveal his issues?

2. What was Mabel Crowley's obvious need? How did Stryker bring a sense of purpose to her life?

3. Did Stryker have needs? What was her greatest inner conflict?

4. When the Studebaker was stolen in Oklahoma City, George lost his "nest egg." What would you have done at that point if you were George?

5. The tornado forced them to seek shelter outside of Hext, Oklahoma. What would you have done in that situation? What do you think the crazy old man's problem was?

6. What about George's paranoia? Do you think the story of George's embezzlement actually made newspapers in the big cities? Did he have a legitimate concern about Mabel reading newspapers?

7. What would you have done differently on this trip if you were George?

8. What would you have done differently on this trip if you were Mabel?

9. Should Mabel have taken Stryker to a doctor before she got to Los Angeles? What happened because she didn't do that? Does this make Mabel partly responsible for Stryker's death?

10. How did the change in George occur? What catalyst made change inevitable? What if George had not changed? What might have happened?

11. Describe the role of Father Tim in the lives of Mabel, George, and Stryker. How did he come alongside each of them just as the Holy Spirit woos us to God?

12. Do you believe it is possible for people to truly change? Or do we only adapt in certain areas to make it easier to deal with the other people in our lives?

13. Does altruism—selfless concern for the well-being of others—truly exist? Or are all our actions done for selfish reasons? Is there always something "in it" for me?

14. Were you hoping for a "happy" ending? Did you want Stryker to live and for George to see the error of his ways and instantly change? Do you think it was necessary for Stryker to die?

15. Do you identify with one of the characters in *The Road to Terminus*? Which one and why?

About the Author

Catherine Leggitt is the author of the cozy mystery novels *Payne & Misery*, *The Dunn Deal*, and *Parrish the Thought*. She is also an inspirational speaker presently residing in northern California. During her first career, after raising children and before caring for her aging parents, Catherine worked as an elementary school teacher, where she developed her flair for playacting and storytelling. Struggling with retirement, Catherine needed a distraction. She found it at her keyboard. In addition to writing and speaking, Catherine is the mother of three brilliant children who have collectively produced six incredible grandchildren. An avid Bible student, she sings in the church choir. Catherine is passionate about reading.

Visit her website: www.catherineleggitt.com

Visit the Mountainview Books, LLC website for news on
all our books:

www.mountainviewbooks.com